THE *BISON* KING

Kenneth Miller

THE *BISON* KING
Convictions of the Courageous

TATE PUBLISHING & *Enterprises*

The Bison King

Copyright © 2009 by Kenneth Miller. All rights reserved.

No part of this publication may be reproduced, stored in a retrieval system or transmitted in any way by any means, electronic, mechanical, photocopy, recording or otherwise without the prior permission of the author except as provided by USA copyright law.

The opinions expressed by the author are not necessarily those of Tate Publishing, LLC.

Published by Tate Publishing & Enterprises, LLC
127 E. Trade Center Terrace | Mustang, Oklahoma 73064 USA
1.888.361.9473 | www.tatepublishing.com

Tate Publishing is committed to excellence in the publishing industry. The company reflects the philosophy established by the founders, based on Psalm 68:11,
"The Lord gave the word and great was the company of those who published it."

Book design copyright © 2009 by Tate Publishing, LLC. All rights reserved.
Cover design by Amber Lee
Interior design by Jeff Fisher

Published in the United

ISBN: 978-1-60799-54
3 2890 00082 6137
1. True Crime, General
09.03.20

SPECIAL THANKS

There are several people who have helped make this work possible. Thanking them here alone won't do, but at least I can start. First, I want to thank my wife Roxy, for helping me get started, and then for her unbelievable patience; spending so many of her evenings alone for the most part, while I worked in my office on this novel. I love you. Special thanks to Peggy Lyon for her perfect transcriptions of the digitally recorded interviews I conducted. Thanks to Rose Dressander and Bill Roller for their review of the manuscript, their comments and encouragement. Special thanks to Jim Fleming for his ideas and significant contributions in the form of emails and notes.

Special thanks again to my wife, for understanding how important this writing was to me.

CHAPTER 1

Bartow Kilgo and his fiancée Jennifer are playing cards with the Nowak's, Robert and Mary, in the living room of the Nowak home. Bart and Bob work together at Linfor Manufacturing and are good friends. They've all been joking, laughing and drinking, generally having a good time. This is a fairly regular activity for the couples; a nice way to spend a Friday evening after the long work week. The Nowak home is out in the country, two miles or so north of Montrose, on County Road 12. Montrose is a typical rural Minnesota village, maybe 750 residents, mostly of German descent; a little more than a wide spot really, on a rural two lane highway in the middle of the upper Midwest farming country.

It's 2:30 a.m. on the morning of August 11th, 1979. The Nowak kids are long asleep. The last hand of 'Euchre' ends and Bart says its time to head home. They clean up the table, finish their drinks, and the two couples head outside.

It's an exceptionally dark, overcast night; no moonlight penetrates the cloud cover. The air is unusually cool for an August evening in central Minnesota. The bugs have long since retired, and with the cool relief from the afternoon heat, it's nice outside. Quiet. Dead calm. As they all gather near Bart's car, the evening's silence is broken by indiscernible voices and noises (yelling and laughing) from up the road, and they stop saying goodbye to look and listen. They hear more voices talking, but they can't understand them, then the noise abates and the quiet returns. Jennifer makes a comment about somebody having a good time. They finish their goodbyes and Bart and Jennifer depart. As Bart drives north on County Road 12, they approach the area from which they heard all of the commotion. Up ahead, they see a car stopped on the road with its lights on. They approach from behind and Bart slows down some. "Somebody's having car trouble" he says. "Maybe we should stop and help."

"No, it's just a bunch of guys drunk, taking a leak," says Jennifer. "Let's just keep going; they're just drunk, peeing in the ditch."

As they pass around the car, they see that it's an older model Chevy Impala. They see two or three people at the right rear of the car and one person standing on the road in front of the car, illuminated by the cars' headlights. They don't recognize anyone and there doesn't appear to be any trouble. They continue on into the night, heading north on CR-12 a few miles, towards the town of Buffalo, then on to St. Michael and home. A short time later, back at the Nowak home, as Bob climbs into bed next to his wife, he hears tires squeal from up the road, and then the still summer silence returns.

Jane Filek, a florist by trade, is driving north on CR-12 after leaving Montrose. Her 80-year-old mother is in the passenger seat. It's 3:00 a.m. and they are headed home to Buffalo from their floral shop in Watertown, MN. Jane is driving her white Dodge work van after a very late night, making flower arrangements for a wedding the next day. Jane is concentrating on staying awake, watching the road; not much conversation, as they are both exhausted from the long day's work. Off on the left side of the road, they pass the Nowak home, now dark except for the yard light throwing mysterious shadows around the yard. They continue on towards town. Up ahead they see something in the headlights; its large, laying half on the road and half on the shoulder. It looks like something was dropped there; maybe out of the back of a truck. It could possibly be a piece of a tree, as people have been cutting and hauling large trees for firewood in that area for some time. She thinks she'd better stop and move it off the road, so no one will hit it. Jane keeps looking in her review mirror to make sure there is no traffic coming up behind her. She slows down and stops along side of it. Jane crawls out of the driver's seat and moves between the seats into the back of the van. She opens the side door of the van and steps down to look down on the crumbled body of young white male in his late teens or early twenties. She feels the air rush from her lungs but can only hear her pounding heartbeat, resonating in her head. She panics. She later testifies that "the way the body was laying there, there was no way he could have been alive." Jane jumps back into the van and slams the door. She scrambles into the drivers seat and takes off towards Buffalo, to the courthouse, as fast as she can. Her mother, half asleep moments ago and unaware of what Jane has just seen, keeps shouting at her. "Jane! Slow down, slow down, you are going to get a speeding ticket!" Jane is hoping for a policeman to stop her for speeding so she can tell him about the body. It's a little over 4 miles from where she saw the body on the road to the courthouse in Buffalo. Jane parks the van in front of the entrance and runs into the courthouse. She finds a man behind a thick glass window and tells him what she has seen. The dispatcher looks up at her and tells her he just got off the phone with a man who had reported a body lying on the road.

Earlier the night of August 10, 1979

Jeffrey Hammill is twenty-one years old. He is a good-looking kid: medium build, well dressed, with a nice smile and long brown hair. Jeff is enjoying a drink at the Rockford House. It's approximately 10:30 p.m. on the evening of August 10, 1979. He is sitting at the bar and talking to a nice looking girl seated next to him. He looks up and sees some guys he knows are big time trouble entering the nightclub. He's afraid these guys might be looking for him. They have threatened him in the past;

talking about getting their hands on him and beating him up, even killing him. Jeff is a ladies man of sorts, but he has a nasty reputation for stealing other guys' girlfriends and then dumping them. He quickly leaves the bar, sneaks out of the supper club and high tails it down the hill to the Country West Bar. Although he has a driver's license, he has no car and always hitch-hikes everywhere. He knows that some people from the place he works are planning to be there this evening, and he figures if he hangs out with them, these guys might leave him alone. He knows it's only a matter of time before these guys leave the Rockford House and move down the hill to the Country West Bar to look for him.

The Country West is a new night club located in Rockford. It's a popular hangout for the local country rock crowd; it's only a half a block or so from the Rockford House. There are few places around the county that offer good music in as large a venue. The more popular local bands and some Minneapolis/St. Paul bands play there on the weekends and draw large crowds of young people. It is a cool place to hang out and meet your friends. It has its share of trouble, but the crowds are friendly for the most part.

Twenty-five-year-old Ron Michaels is at the Country West to meet up with his friend, twenty-three-year-old Jeff Cardinal, and Jeff's date Debra Segler. Jeff and Ron met back in grade school, and although Jeff was a grade behind Ron, they grew up in the same small town of Montrose. They shared interests and had many friends in common.

Debra Segler, recently divorced, has her own place in Montrose, while Jeff lives with his folks. Ron is renting a place a mile or two south of Montrose where he lives alone. It is the finished basement of a house yet to be built. Money is tight for most everyone and people entertain themselves by playing sports, listening to music and going to parties. Jeff had invited Ron to meet him and his new girlfriend Debra at the Country West that night. They planned to party along with other friends at the club until nearly closing time. Debra's brother, Terry Olson and one of Terry's friends from work, Dale Todd, met up with the group earlier and they are partying along with them. Terry and Dale are good buddies and spend most of their free time together. In fact, Terry is staying with his sister, and had invited Dale to stay there for a couple weeks while Dale worked some things out with his parents.

Jeff Hammill arrives at the Country West Bar and works his way through the crowd to Terry and Dale. He is obviously agitated. Jeff just started working with Terry and Dale a few weeks earlier. Although they have just recently met Jeff, they like him well enough. Jeff tells them that he is in serious trouble. He has just left the Rockford House where some guys are looking for him. They want to beat him up and have previously threatened his life. Both Terry and Dale are decent size guys. Terry is more aggressive than Dale, prone to fight at the drop of a hat. Jeff asks them if he can hang out with them for the rest of the night. They agree and Jeff settles down some. He stays close to Terry and Dale, always keeping an eye open, until the bar closes at 1:00 am.

Jeff Cardinal knew Debra's brother Terry, and had met Dale a time or two. Ron knew neither of the men. Jeff Cardinal suggests they all go over to Debra's house in Montrose to continue the party. Debra agrees and others from the partying group at Country West are invited to join them as well. Among them are George Salonek and his wife Kathy, who had both been Ron's classmates at Buffalo High School. As people start leaving the bar and heading toward their cars, Terry and Dale ask Jeff Hammill if he wants to go with them to the party in Montrose. He thinks for a minute. He hasn't seen the group he had been avoiding since he got to the Country West. The Rockford House was closed by now too, and those guys most likely had already gone. He felt comfortable hitching a ride back home to Buffalo, some ten miles away, so he decides he will pass, but thanks them for the offer. He walks off downhill toward the highway, heading west toward Buffalo.

At approximately 1:20 am, everyone has gathered outside, and they are getting into their cars to head to Debra's house to continue the party. Terry and Dale get into Dales' car. Terry is driving as usual. Terry always drove. Terry had lost his license a while ago and Dale always 'let' him drive his car. Besides, Terry knew the area his sister lived in better than Dale. Terry told Dale the way it was going to be most of the time.

As everyone heads out for Montrose, Dale and Terry see Jeff Hammill hitch-hiking along the highway, just a few blocks down the hill from the Country West. The Crow River crosses under the highway at the bottom of the hill, just at the south end of Main Street in Rockford. The river runs parallel to, and one block east of, the towns' main street; the bridge is just east of where Main intersects the highway. The town has yet to install its first traffic light. Old fashioned streetlights hang high above the bridge on posts to light up the intersection at the west end of the bridge. Terry pulls the car over and asks Jeff again if he wants to go with them. He tells them he would like to but he would need a ride home after the party, as it would be late and hard to hitch a ride on the back roads. They agree to give him a ride home after the party and he gets in the back seat.

As they drive to Montrose, Terry and Dale smoke some grass and pass the joint back to Jeff on occasion. Jeff is much more relaxed now and looking forward to the party. About two blocks from his sisters' house, Terry drives over something in the road. One of the tires goes down quickly and since they are so close to Debra's house, he creeps along the street until they reach her driveway. All three of them get out of the car. They look at the flat tire and Dale goes into the back seat of the car to get a screwdriver. His 1971 Chevy Impala was far from new, and the trunk lock had been punched out. To open the trunk, he inserts the screwdriver where the lock used to be and trips the latch. The lid popped up and the trunk light came on. He grabs the spare tire and lifts it out, dropping it on the driveway. It is flat. There is a Mobil station down one block, across the street from Debra's. They decide to take the tire up there and see if the air station is working. As Terry and Dale head there with the tire, Jeff stays at the car.

When Terry and Dale reach the Mobil station, they discover that the air station isn't turned on. Terry looks around and sees another early 70's model Chevy Impala parked on the side of the building. They decide to take one of the wheels off of this car and use it on Dale's. They go back to Debra's house, return with Dale's car jack and remove a wheel. They return to Debra's house with the stolen tire and wheel.

Jeff is no longer by the car. Dale and Terry mount the wheel onto the car and then go inside the house.

Several people from the bar have made it to Debra's house and are inside talking and laughing. Some people are outside, milling around the back yard. The house is very small and fills up quickly. As is common with parties like this, people come and go freely, mostly unnoticed.

People move in and out of the house; small groups are standing around, or sitting at the table or on the couch. Jeff Hammill is inside talking to a girl; someone doesn't like it much and things begin to tense up. Apparently, Jeff's reputation precedes him. George Salonek and his wife Kathy are there. George lives just two blocks away and has walked over with Kathy, leaving their car at home after returning from the bar. George has been drinking heavily and is feeling his oats. He has been visiting with friends but has heard someone is hitting on his wife. George thinks it is Dale Todd and tries to pick a fight with him. Dale is sitting on the couch with Terry Olson. George intentionally spills his drink on Dale. Dale is pretty drunk and mildly protests. Terry Olson, however, is having none of this; he gets up and straightens George out. George is pissed. Terry is brewing now also.

Ron Michaels is nearby and sees what is going on. As is his

practice, he steps between the men and jokes with them, trying to settle things down. George sizes Terry up and decides he needs to leave, now. He finds Kathy and they leave the house and walk back home.

Jeff Hammill decides now that he wants a ride home and starts bugging Terry about it. Terry says they are too wasted to drive and Jeff can crash here and wait until morning, or walk home. Jeff gets pissed and leaves the party on foot, deciding to hitch-hike home.

Chief Deputy Jim Powers wakes up to the sound of a ringing phone. He looks at the alarm clock; its 4:05 a.m. The alarm shouldn't be going off. The phone rings again. His head clears and he realizes that it's the phone ringing. He fumbles for the receiver and answers the call. It's his boss. Powers is told there is a body out on the shoulder of County Road 12, south of Buffalo, and he needs to get to the scene. He gets out of bed, freshens up his face, gets dressed and leaves the house. The dawn is some time off yet and as he heads for his cruiser. He thinks to himself, *real nice way to start my forty-eighth birthday.*

Powers had started his law enforcement career in 1953. He worked as a police officer in Oakland, California, then in Las Vegas, Nevada until 1963. He then worked three and a half years as the Chief of Police in Monticello, Minnesota, just ten miles north of Buffalo. In 1966, he hired on with the Wright County Sheriffs' Department. Now thirteen years later, he has more than twenty-five years of law enforcement experience under his belt.

He was recruited into the field by older cops who knew he had spent about seven years boxing, both Golden Gloves and amateur, and had served in the Marine Corps. There wasn't any special training required for patrol officers back then; however, the ability to handle yourself in a bar fight was considered a great asset. The guys read books, bulletins, magazines and picked the brains of the experienced officers for information. The FBI put out a monthly bulletin and they read that. It was on-the-job training. Powers had received formal training in later years, graduating from the FBI academy in Quantico, Virginia in 1972.

Powers arrives at the scene around 4:35 a.m. Other police officers have already been dispatched to the scene. He recognizes all of the officers present; Deputy Mike Simmons, Sergeant Jim Lammers, Deputies Mike Even and Lenny Walker, and Powers' boss, Sheriff Daryl Wolff. Lying on the side of the road is the lifeless body of a young white male. The body is dressed all in black: black shoes, black trousers and a shiny black jacket zipped to the neck. His clothes are relatively neat and unrumpled, his shoes still on. He is lying face up; his head is on the pavement facing north and his shoulders, torso and legs are on the gravel shoulder of the road facing south. A large amount of blood had poured out from under his head, pooled there and continued onto the shoulder of the road. One of the officers checks the victims' pockets and possessions. He still has some money in his wallet. This is most likely not a robbery victim. From his driver's license, they determine that the victims' name is Jeffrey Hammill. Jim looks at the kids' head again. There is a large abrasion on the right side of his head that looks to have shaved the hair down to the scalp. He also sees a wound to the top of the head that looks like a machete had been used to cut a large flap on the scalp. One officer notes some minor bruises on the victims' hands.

All six of the men spend the next hour or so walking up and down the road, some one hundred yards in each direction from the body and on both sides of the road, looking for anything that would indicate what had happened here: Cigarette butts, cigarette packs, candy packages, footprints if they can be seen; any evidence that a vehicle might have swung onto the shoulder, tire tracks, anything that might have been a weapon. No one finds a thing. No broken glass, no tire impressions. Nothing.

Powers returns to the body and kneels down. He starts to think this does not appear to be a hit and run accident. There is no major trauma to the body, beyond the head, and the clothing is not all torn up. This kid was put down right here, right now. He didn't kick or wiggle or nothing. He was done when he hit the ground.

The Sheriff begins taking photographs of the body and the surrounding roadway. A hearse from Petersons' Mortuary in Buffalo arrives. A few minutes later, they load up the body and the officers depart, except for Jim Powers and his boss, Sheriff Wolff. They both are frustrated at the lack of evidence and continue to discuss this, until they finally decide to follow the body to the mortuary for further review of the wounds.

On the drive into Buffalo, Sheriff Wolff contacts two investigators: Brooks Martin and Denny Compton. He tells them to come in early; they are going to be assigned to this case. They all meet at the Peterson Mortuary in Buffalo. They go over the wounds and what little evidence they have. Powers looks closely at the wounds on Jeff Hammills' head. The boys' right ear lobe is torn clean through, as if an ear ring had been pulled right out of the lobe. There is a hole in the skull just below the right ear lobe as well. It appears to be the size of a man's thumb in diameter, and it looks like it broke the skull and the bones just inside. Powers thinks, *this must have been a tremendous blow! Hardly a wound you would find with an assault victim.* He reexamines the large flap of scalp torn loose on the top of the head. They look over his clothes in detail. Slip-on shoes, still on the feet. No dust on them to speak of. His clothes are very clean and not torn or crumpled. Another thing puzzles Jim too; no blood on the boy's face. None that amounts to anything, and no blood on his shoulders or clothing. Powers had seen a lot of assault victims. People hit with night sticks, pool cues, baseball bats, one with a flat iron and one with a frying pan. Most of the time, the people are not knocked out, seldom knocked down; they usually stagger, but there is always a ton of blood. It's all over everything and it splatters. This kid was hit so hard and so fast with such velocity he didn't start bleeding until he hit the ground. All of the blood found had exited from and was pooled directly under the boys' head; then drained off onto the shoulder of the road, soaking the gravel.

Powers and Compton decide to go back to the scene now that the sun is coming up. A short time later, the body of Jeffrey Hammill is transferred to a much larger facility for autopsy in St Cloud, MN, some thirty miles to the northwest.

Sheriff's deputies show up at the Country West Bar and the Rockford House Nightclub on Saturday August 11th and interview several people. Police go to several people's homes, or call them at their place of employment over the next few days, to take statements. This list of potential witnesses grows to twenty-seven as each person recalls who was present.

As the supervisor for this investigation, Powers is overseeing the other investigators activities and reviewing their reports. There is a description of a vehicle that a witness had claimed to have seen in the area where the body was found. It is described as a '67 or '69 Chevrolet. It is also stated by this witness that the vehicle had three red taillights on each side that were flat on the top and round on the bottom. No information is provided to indicate this vehicle was involved in the incident however. There is little information beyond what was gathered from the scene to push this investigation in any specific direction.

Powers begins to theorize what might have happened to Jeffrey Hammill that night. He believes it possible that Hammill could have been struck by something protruding from the back of a pickup or trailer. Something that struck the young man with such tremendous force, as to drive his head down into the payment directly where he stood. He realizes he is thinking two things at the same time. *Why are we looking at an assault? How can this be an assault? It doesn't really make sense.*

During the course of the next few days, Chief Deputy Jim Powers completes his initial report of the incident, and files it with Sherriff Darryl Wolff. Powers also reveals his theory to the Sheriff about something extended from a vehicle, striking the victim and causing the fatal injury. He details this theory somewhat in a follow up report he writes and files a few days later, concluding that Hammill may have been hit by part of a vehicle or something towed by a vehicle passing by in the dark, due to the lack of any signs of struggle, lack of blood spatter, lack of defensive wounds or facial injuries, the location and position of the body. Officers Compton and Martin continue to question potential witnesses, twenty-seven of whom had seen Jeffrey Hammill at the Country West Bar. However, without any additional evidence from the investigation coming in from the field, the Sheriff releases a report to the press indicating the possibility of the 'Powers Theory', and that the case is still under investigation. The coroners report also lists the incident as an 'unsolved, violent death'. Over the course of the next couple of years, investigators speak with nearly seventy-five people regarding the death of Jeffrey Hammill. Follow up police reports dated from 1981 and 1982 indicate that Jeffrey Hammill could have been murdered; one suggested his death was motivated by a $2,000 unpaid drug debt. The murder weapon was proposed to be a pipe and the incident made to look like a hit-and-run accident. This lead is never pursued, however, and the investigation stalls. The case lies dormant for the next two decades.

CHAPTER 2

November 4, 2005

Ron Michaels is now a fifty-one year old man, living in a quiet, older neighborhood in a small town, just a few miles north of Minneapolis. He lives there with his second wife, Jean. Ron had worked as a state accounting manager in the Department of Administration for the state of Minnesota.

Ron grew up strong, always in good shape, and participated in various organized sports as well as being an avid hunter and fisherman. As a youngster, Ron was the starting half back on the Buffalo 'Bison' High School football team. He was a ferocious wrestler as well. He was well liked and was one of the most popular kids in that class of 175 students. He was also popular with underclassman that participated in sports with him. After graduation, and for most of his adult life, Ron continued his sports activities, frequently playing softball, volleyball and basketball, many times with men half his age; and hunting and fishing, more than most. As his boys were born and raised, and even after his divorce from his sons' mother Sandy, he was sure to expose them to sports and supported them every chance he could. He coached many of their sports teams; took them bass fishing in the summer, and ice fishing for walleyes in the winter.

Ron married Jean in 1997. He and Jean were very happy and living a good life, active in their church, enjoying dining and dancing; nurturing their newly combined families (Jean had three children from her previous marriage). Things were going very well for them.

Then Ron contracted the stomach virus 'H-pylori'. It took him several months to recover from this. He then tore a bicep muscle playing volleyball and underwent two surgeries to repair the damage to his shoulder and muscle. He recovered, but was not quite the same. Ron had flu-like symptoms: aches, pain and fatigue. He started missing work and was always too tired to do anything. Ron's doctor thought he had sleep apnea. Tests were done and Ron was put on a sleep machine at night, which he wore faithfully. But Ron still had widespread pain. Just wearing his watch caused him pain; his shoes caused pain in his feet. Even the pressure of clothing touching his body caused discomfort. He tried wearing larger shoes and baggier clothing. Ron's doctor referred him to a neurologist who, after many tests, diagnosed him with fibromyalgia. Ron and Jean researched the disease and learned that Ron had *all* of the symptoms. They also learned that there was no cure. Their search continued, and eventually brought them to the Mayo Clinic for more tests. The doctors at the Mayo Clinic diagnosed an electrical imbalance in Ron's brain that was sending pain messages to all parts of his body, which sometimes happens after a major surgery or injury. They thought it might correct itself in five years but there were no guarantees. They returned to their primary care doctor with a list of medications from the Mayo Clinic. The medications didn't help. They tried more tests and another sleep study. Their doctor, frustrated, referred them to an infectious disease specialist who diagnosed Ron with fibromyalgia and C.F.S. (Chronic Fatigue Syndrome). After all of the tests and specialists, they were forced to accept this diagnosis.

Ron visited a clinic for fibromyalgia. They tried everything from biofeedback, pool therapy and dietary changes to occupational therapy. Ron received Botox shots for the pain. They helped somewhat. Ron even tried acupuncture, strange vitamins, Noni juice and nearly any alternative people would throw at him. But there was no cure.

Ron tried to work in spite of his health issues, but his employer was not accommodating. She didn't believe Ron was really ill. Ron eventually got even sicker. He took a medical leave of absence in January of 2003, and shortly after that, permanent disability. Memory loss, pain and fatigue prevented him from doing his job, or any other. He could barely function, even at home.

Ron no longer enjoys his favorite activities. He barely has the strength to walk the steep hill down to his mail box and back. He still suffers from sleep apnea and is easily exhausted from the least bit of exertion. He has his good days and his bad. On a good day, he can go watch his boys play basketball. However, he never escapes the constant pain. His prognosis is not promising, as there is no really effective treatment, and Ron has one of the most severe cases of fibromyalgia.

Ron is not discouraged by all of this however. He has a strong belief in God, and over his lifetime has grown in his faith to where he can accept his condition and not be bitter; knowing that he needn't suffer alone, his faith gives him comfort when his condition becomes difficult to bear. He also adores his loving wife, who faithfully stands with him and deals with the disappointments and restrictions the condition brings with it. Sometimes his friends have a harder time dealing with his illness, especially when it prevents Ron from participating in the things they enjoyed together in the past. Ron is always positive and lets them know he is patient, and trusts the Lord will help him through this. His faith is uplifting to others, even though he is the one suffering. He really doesn't want you to worry about him, as he knows that God is looking after him. That seems to give some comfort to his friends.

The Arrest

It is Friday, November 4, 2005, about 4:00pm. One of Ron's' friends, Matt, a prayer partner from church, is visiting Ron. They have a prayer meeting every other Friday. Matt is a pro-life activist of sorts, who protests regularly at the abortion clinic, recently opened on the other side of town. After the protests,

Matt comes over and he and Ron visit and pray about the clinic. This helps Matt maintain his conviction to battle with the clinic.

They have just finished up their meeting. Ron is walking his friend to the door and saying goodbye. The front door is open to allow the autumn breeze in. Suddenly from nowhere, police officers appear and grab Matt and put a gun to his chest. Ron is pushed back inside by officers with assault weapons and handguns pointed at him. He sees several red laser dots dancing on his chest. A handgun is put to his head and one to his back. He is taken into custody by the police. One of the officers roughly thrusts his hand into Ron's groin, nearly causing him to drop to his knees from the pain, as he frisks him. Matt is also manhandled and controlled by the police. Ron keeps asking the officers, "Why are you doing this? You don't have to do this. We have asked if you wanted to see me. I would have come in anytime you asked me to! You knew we were willing to come to the police station anytime you asked us to!"

Ron is told he is being charged with first degree murder in the death of Jeffrey Hammill on August 11, 1979. Ron is handcuffed and shackled, then led outside to a police car. Matt is released shortly thereafter. Most of the neighbors are now outside in their yards, watching the commotion. Ron can see several police cars parked down the street, out of sight of his home. Ron is placed in the back of the police car, transported across town to the parking lot at the Lino Lakes Prison, then transferred into a police van. He asks the officer in the police van if he can call his wife on his cell phone. The officer allows him to make the call. He gets through to Jean and tells her he has been arrested. Ron is then driven some thirty miles to the Wright County jail in Buffalo, Minnesota. Ron's home is left empty and unsecured, with the front door still wide open.

Jean calls their attorney, Carl Newquist, and tells him Ron has been arrested. Jean then calls her son Jeff; now in tears, she tells him that Ron has been arrested, and asks him to come with her to get Ron's things and go with her to the jail. Newquist calls the office of the County Attorney, Tom Kelly, but nearly everyone has left for the day. Someone agrees to put a note on Tom Kelly's door, asking him to call Newquist first thing Monday morning.

The Booking

Ron is delivered to the Wright County Jail and has his picture and fingerprints taken. He is then placed into a cell block, with the only available cell located on the second level. Ron cannot manage stairs very well due to his illness and is relocated to a cell on the main floor later that evening. His new cell also had a 120V AC outlet for his C-PAP machine, which Jean had brought to the jail that evening, along with his medications. Ron prepares to spend his first night in jail.

Later that evening, Carl Newquist calls Jean and tells her he won't be able to serve as Ron's attorney as his partner just made judge, and he was now overbooked with work and felt he wouldn't be able to do them justice. "You need to find a new attorney," he says. "I can help. I'll help you try to find a new attorney and if I have to, I'll show up at the first hearing, but no guarantees. I just can't take the case."

Jean hangs up the phone and panic sets in. Her husband is to be arraigned on Monday and he doesn't even have an attorney. She calls her brother and learns that he has a friend that knows an attorney, one of several that are part of a bike group he belongs to. The attorney's name is Jon Hawks. Hawks calls Jean, and she fills him in on Ron's situation. Hawks sends out email to the attorneys in the bike group, asking if anyone is interested in taking the case.

On Saturday morning, Ron is told he has visitors. The visiting area consists of a long rectangular room with a few chairs fastened together in a line in the middle of the room. The chairs face a large wall with seven visiting stations with thick glass panels. There is a chair in front of each panel for visitors, and a telephone used to speak to an inmate on the other side. The inmates are separated from each other by walled compartments, as are the visitors, but all the conversations are monitored, so there is no privacy. To speak with an inmate, you must check in with the officer behind a heavy glass panel, submit identification and request the inmate by name. You are then asked to wait until they bring them up from the cell block. There are several women with small children, sitting and waiting, playing with their kids. Others are at the phones talking with inmates, while their kids play nervously or sit reading books. The atmosphere is truly sad and depressing.

When Ron enters the visiting room area and see's Jean, he breaks down. This is truly a nightmare and it makes no sense to them. They talk and reassure each other that come Monday, this will all be cleared up, the police will realize this was a big mistake and Ron will be released. Jean holds it together until their visit is over, but as she leaves the building, she breaks down.

Attorney Jim Fleming is in front of his computer in his home office. He's reading emails he's printed out from the last few days, preparing his work schedule for the upcoming week. Jim is a lawman turned lawyer. After twenty years in law enforcement positions in Nebraska, he has decided to practice law instead of enforce it. Lured by the challenge more than the money, Jim has set up a practice with a notable partner in Monticello, Minnesota. Work is somewhat slow in coming, but he's a patient man.

Jim is fifty-five years old. Standing five feet nine inches tall, weighing 200 pounds, he's a prominent figure. With his dark brown hair combed straight back, a neatly trimmed short beard, and glasses, he looks commanding and in control; no doubt a carry over from his previous career. He knows he smokes too much, but it helps him think. He favors looking people straight in the eye and speaks in short, direct sentences; those who answer in the same manner seem to please him. He knows he is not as structured inside as he would have people think. He struggles with that.

He hears the tell-tale tones of an incoming email. He looks to the screen and sees a new email from a good friend, Jon Hawks. Hawkeye, as he is known, is an attorney as well. He has a practice in Minneapolis. Hawkeye and Jim belong to a unique organization known as the Street Legal Motorcycle Club. It was started in Minnesota in 1992 for motorcycle-riding individuals working in the legal system. Members include lawyers, judges, law school Deans, law students, bailiffs, paralegals, legal secretaries, private investigators, court reporters and the like. The club and its members raise money for charities, including Legal Aid, Lawyers for Literacy, Multiple Sclerosis, Muscular Dystrophy, and various veterans' events and memorials. Both Jim and Hawkeye have Harleys, and they ride together, as time will allow.

The new email is simple and straightforward, as is customary with Hawkeye.

From: Hawkeye

To: Jim

Subject: Need an attorney for a 1st degree murder defense–Wright County

Call me ASAP or email if you are interested or can make a recommendation or referral.

Defendant–Ronald Michaels

Alleged murder 8–11–79

The family attorney–Carl Newquist - unable to handle–non criminal

Wife Jean Michaels says she can raise 30K. I do not know these people. They are a friend of a friend.

Hawkeye

Jim rereads the email. The date keeps puzzling him. *8–11–79. What is that? Twenty-four, twenty-six years? A twenty-six year old murder? My first murder defense and it's a twenty-six year old murder? $30,000. What is that?* Jim types an email back to Hawkeye asking about the date, and asks him if he would be interested in helping on the case. He ends by including a short rundown on his pheasant hunting trip earlier that weekend. He hits send, and returns to his preparations.

Early Monday morning he confirms the alleged murder date via email with Hawkeye. August 11, 1979. He gives Hawks his current phone number to give to the defendants' wife, and in a closing email, Hawkeye tells Jim he will recommended him over two other names he has to give her.

Monday morning, at 8:00 a.m., Jean gets a call from Carl Newquist saying he cannot go to court with her. He tells her the arraignment is at 9:00 a.m., and that she needs to be there. Jean jumps in her car and begins driving to Buffalo. Her cell phone rings and it's Jon Hawks. He tells her he had three positive responses to his email over the weekend, and gives her a briefing on each of the respondents. He adds that all of the responses, whether positive or not, assured him that they would need an attorney from Wright County, because they are a 'good old boy' county that is rough on city attorneys. Hawks recommends Jim Fleming, an attorney from the neighboring town of Monticello.

At 8:30 a.m., Jean calls Jim Fleming as she's still driving toward Buffalo; he picks up and she explains that Hawks gave her his number. "If you're interested, he's being arraigned at 9:00 a.m. I'm on my way there now," Jean says.

Jim replies, "I'm not dressed for court, but my house is between Monticello and Buffalo. I'll stop and get a suit on and meet you in the courtroom."

When Jim arrives, he and Jean talk briefly, then go into the hearing.

The Arraignment

Officer Mike Erickson brings three men up from the jail in an elevator: Ron Michaels, Dale Todd and Terry Olson. They are directed to a room off to the side of the courtroom, to be transferred into the custody of the Bailiff. They look at each other. No one is talking. Then Terry Olson says to Ron, "Who are you? I don't know you."

Ron replies, "I don't know you and I don't know him either."

Dale Todd says nothing. Terry Olson says, "I know why we are here, but we don't know why you are here." Officer Erickson secures the men together in the court sally and signals to the bailiff. The bailiff opens the port on the opposite side of the sally, and the men are taken to court.

Ron sees Jean in the courtroom and smiles. She is shocked to see him handcuffed and shackled. Jim Fleming walks over to Ron and introduces himself as his new attorney.

The indictments are lengthy, and all of them are read; as each of the three men are charged with the murder of Jeffrey Hammill, twenty six years earlier.

Bail is set at $1,000,000 each for Ron Michaels and Terry Olson. The bail for Dale Todd is set at $500,000. Ron is stunned. *How much will we have to come up with... $100,000? We don't have that kind of money. This is going from bad to worse. Don't they understand that this is a big mistake?*

At the completion of the hearings, the bailiff returns the men to the court sally. The bailiff signals Officer Erickson to return the men to the jail. Dale Todd and Ron are returned to their cells. Olson is being housed in the Sherburne County Jail and has been serving time for a domestic assault. He is returned there.

Later, as Jean and Ron visit through the glass, she tells him that their attorney, Jim, thinks the bail will be reduced to $750,000. "That is still $75,000 cash. We can't afford that, *and* money for a lawyer. If we don't post bail, how long am I going to have to stay in here?" he asks her.

Jean says, "Jim thinks you will be out before Thanksgiving, a couple of weeks."

Ron is numb and sick to his stomach.

The Big Sell

The arrest of three men in the murder of Jeffrey Hammill, a case that went cold some twenty-six years earlier, is very big news.

County attorney Tom Kelly and the Minnesota Bureau of Criminal Apprehension (BCA) agents make quick work of publicizing these arrests statewide. They publicly congratulate each other on solving this twenty-six year old cold case.

Within hours, Wright County Attorney Tom Kelly holds a press conference at a major Minneapolis television station; he parades Jeffrey Hammill's mother, Deputy Sheriff Joe Hagerty and BCA agents Ken McDonald and Dennis Fier in front of the cameras.

On camera, Tom Kelly reports, "In my opinion, I'm very confident that the individuals that are responsible for the savage beating that resulted in the death of Jeff Hammill on August 11, 1979 in Wright County, are now currently in the Wright County Jail."

A national news organization publishes a story in the major papers in the area, claiming that two of the men charged in a decades old murder case in Wright County have given different stories to the police about what happened the night of August 10, 1979.

The article reports that three men are charged in the death of twenty-one year old Jeffrey Hammill of Buffalo. The article continues on, stating that Terry Olson, forty-six, and Ronald Michaels, fifty-one, are charged with first-degree murder. Dale Todd, forty-five, is facing a charge of second-degree murder in the death of Hammill.

The article summarizes the court documents made public the day before, indicating that the four men met twenty-six years ago, on the night of August 10, at the Country West Bar in Rockford. Later, they drove to the home of a relative of one of the defendants, where following a scuffle between Hammill and Olson, Hammill left on foot. The three others soon drove after him in Todd's truck.

The article continues to report that Olson, in the Anoka County jail in September on a domestic assault charge, told a fellow inmate that he and Todd stayed in the vehicle and that Michaels alone killed Hammill. Olson had made the remarks to the inmate after being "distressed" by an interview with homicide investigators. Olson also indicated to the inmate that the three men believed Hammill was homosexual, the criminal complaint said.

County Attorney Tom Kelly reports at a news conference that the three suspects were interviewed immediately after the murder but were never charged. He said inconsistencies recently emerged in their stories. He requests that anyone with information about the case please call the authorities. All three suspects remain in jail.

Minnesota Department of Public Safety News Release - November, 2005

"The diligence of local investigators, with the help of the agents in the cold case unit at the BCA, solved this case," said Wright County Attorney Tom Kelly. "Those investigators never gave up, and today they give Jeff Hammill's family hope for justice in his murder."

On November 8, 2005, KARE 11 TV reports on-site from Ron Michaels' neighborhood. They preface the report with the statement, "On this block, the arrest of a low-profile neighbor is causing a few ripples, but these days nothing really comes as a surprise."

Some of the neighbors are quoted saying, "I couldn't imagine something like that. That would be hard to live with" and "Everybody has secrets. He just had a nastier one".

News articles appear in the Buffalo, Minneapolis and St. Paul newspapers, as well as others around the state, highlighting the arrests and the solving of a twenty-six year old cold case.

On Tuesday morning, Jim Fleming shoots an email to his little brother Rob, a public defender of twenty years, working in Columbia, Mo. He explains what he's about to get involved in, and asks Rob if he would be willing to help out. Rob responds, agreeing to help any way he can. Rob admires his big brother and knows this trial could be a huge boost to his brothers' practice. There is also something else. Jim and Rob's father had always wanted his boys to handle a large, important case together. Jim heads out to meet with the case prosecutor, Ann Mohaupt, and Chief Public Defender Kevin Tierney.

On Wednesday morning November 9, Jim fires off an email to Hawkeye and copies his brother, Rob.

From: Jim Fleming

To: Hawkeye

Hawkeye:

Busy 24 hours. 4 interviews, meetings with case prosecutor, Ann Mohaupt (older experienced woman, no nonsense, but with no agenda and totally unafraid of her boss) and Chief Public Defender Kevin Tierney (they got the other 2 defendants, Todd and Olson).

News conference by County Attorney Kelly oversold the case. BCA revved the case up in 2003, after a call from the victim's daughter, who was searching for information on her biological father. He probably didn't know that a girlfriend was pregnant when he died. BCA puts it up on their website and offers $50,000 for information ....

Some time later, a Vice Lord by the name of Jamari Alexander is in the Olmsted County Jail and claims that Terry Olson "confessed" to him about the killing, placing himself at the scene but, "only in the car". Jamari wants to play let's make a deal. Based upon statements given by all three defendants in 1979, in which they admitted being in the bar with victim, they re-interview all three. Olson and Todd now change their stories. They closed the bar in Rockford, and all went to Debra Segler's home in Montrose for a small "party". Todd says the victim rode there with him in his car. Michaels claims memory impairment and can't even remember being interviewed in 1979.

Todd and Olson are at the bar because they are life long buddies and Olson is Debra Segler's brother. She is at the bar with her later to be boyfriend, later fiancé and husband, Jeff Cardinal on a first date. Michaels is there because he and Jeff Cardinal are best friends (at least Michaels thought so). Victim is there apparently because everybody has to be somewhere.

An argument broke out between victim Hammill and somebody, but not Michaels. A drink got spilled on somebody, there were some words exchanged and some pushing. Hammill leaves the party, walking. Todd and Olson now apparently say they went after him and Michaels went with them. Jeff Cardinal says they left and had been drinking a lot and that Michaels had history of being violent when drunk (everybody else who knew Michaels at the time, says he had no history of being violent and was known only as a mellow guy who never got into fights, instead often apparently breaking them up and talking people down to resolve disputes).

The County attorney has nothing for a motive other than anger, booze and a possible suggestion that the three "thought" that Hammill was gay. However, Hammill apparently had a reputation as a ladies man and for spreading pollen prodigiously.

They have no murder weapon, although the autopsy indicates blunt force trauma caused by instrument or instruments unknown. Other than 2 indicted co-defendants, they have nothing linking Michaels to the arguments, the scene, or the crime. No clear motive but based upon Todd and Olson and some historical stuff from Jeff Cardinal, they believe that Michaels, a guy with no criminal history, no violent behavior, no history of fighting, went with at least two guys he did not even know, tracked Hammill down and while Todd and Olson sat in the car, Michaels beat the victim to death, crushing his skull. They then leave him dead, in a pool of blood, drive back to the party where no one observes any blood on Michaels clothing and then go on with life, never having contact with each other again, and never speaking about the matter until Olson (a white red neck, wife beater) decides to confess his involvement in the case to a black Vice Lord he's never met in his life, while in jail in Olmsted County.

So I look at Ann and said, "You gotta be kidding me. That's all you've got?" She sighs and looks out the window and says, "Yeah, life's a b ... , ya know?"

PD's office is doing the Rule 18[1] motion and will share a copy of the transcript if I toss some coins their way. Ann will not object to the Rule 18 motion, so we can decide if we want to attack the Indictment and will agree to continue the Rule 8[2] hearing, until after we get the banker's boxes full of autopsy reports, investigative dead ends, statements, etc. and can sift our way through what is important what is not.

Right now I got $20 that says it went down this way. At the bar, Hammill is cruising Debra Segler who just met Cardinal a few days before. Hammill is good looking enough, so when

---

1. Rule 18. Place of Prosecution and Trial. Unless a statute or these rules permit otherwise, the government must prosecute an offense in a district where the offense was committed. The court must set the place of trial within the district with due regard for the convenience of the defendant and the witnesses, and the prompt administration of justice.

2. Rule 8. Defendant's Initial Appearance Before the District Court Following the Complaint or Tab Charge in Felony and Gross Misdemeanor Cases. The defendant's initial appearance following the complaint or, for a designated gross misdemeanor shall be held in the district court of the judicial district where the alleged offense was committed.

the bar is closed she invites the group, including Hammill to her place. She talks her brother into bringing Hammill just in case she decides to shine Cardinal on and since Todd is driving for Olson, Hammill ends up in Todd's car. Michaels drives himself. Cardinal is not happy that Hammill is invited, since he knows what Hammill wants to do to his new squeeze. At the party, Hammill continues to promote Debra Segler's booty and eventually Cardinal gets pissed off and braces him. An argument starts, drinks get spilled, the argument escalates and Hammill starts counting friends and ends up with 0, so he books out of there, on foot; he left mad, or he left scared. Michaels is passed out or nearly so. Cardinal still wants to kick Hammill's butt, so he talks Todd and Olson into going with him. They do, leaving Debra Segler at her house with a useless Michaels, telling her they are going on a beer run. They drive around and find Hammill on County 12 about 2 miles north of Montrose headed toward Buffalo. They either hit him with the car, or stop and stomp him, probably hitting him with something taken from the car. Whether he's dead or dying, they leave him there and go back to Debra Segler's.

The case is first reported as a hit and run in the local papers, "Jeez, the dumb ass, he wandered out in to traffic, drunk. I didn't like the jerk, but that's too bad." Michaels doesn't remember Hammill or much of anything from the night before, makes no connection to any argument and goes on with life. Debra Segler (who is by all accounts a couple of tacos short of a fiesta platter) decides on Cardinal as the man of her dreams, too bad about Hammill who got hit by a car, but this one is warm and pays the bills.

Cardinal, Todd and Olson talk often enough to get their stories straight and after giving statements to the cops who aren't terribly excited about investigating a hit and run, much less a possible homicide with no witnesses, no motive, no murder weapon and no evidence, the whole thing kind of dies down, blows over and goes away. Life goes on, kids get born, bills get paid and nobody sees much of anybody anymore, too busy ya know?

And everybody is doin' pretty good until Hammill's daughter, long since born, adopted and now a pretty attractive young woman decides to try to find out something about her natural father. BCA decides to put the case up on the cold case website and Jamari the Vice Lord is sitting in jail with Olson who makes some remark about knowing something about the case and Jamari sees light at the end of the tunnel.

I may raise this bet in time, but that's my gut hunch right now.

On Thursday evening, Rob sends Jim an email.

From: Rob Fleming

To: Jim Fleming

Jim:

Well a couple of thoughts on this one … From the rendition, it sounds like Debra and Cardinal get married and still are? Puts her definitely in the "protect brother and husband" camp … Absent that, however, maybe she has a bone to pick with ex- Mr. Cardinal. One angle. I assume she and brother are still tight; no funny uncle stuff with her kids or other motivation to be seeking his head on a stick … ? That would be too easy, huh … ? Well, you ain't payin' for this, so I will keep rambling …

From there, my attention is turned to possible weapons, sports and cars … I assume in '79 our boys were a lot younger (weren't we all?). If they were jocks or ex-jocks, likely that there would be hockey sticks, baseball bats, your sports weapon of choice, (to name a couple) … Would bear some inquiry about how the boys got their jollies. Some of us still have those old softball bats, etc. sitting in our garage; like we are gonna go out and play next weekend. Hey, you never know … Thinking like a prosecutor here, but sometimes you have to get there before they do … Funny thing about cars, also … you buy 'em, you sell 'em, you drive them in between. But you know what you never get rid of? The ubiquitous tire iron. Every car I have ever owned had one; had it when I bought it, had it when I sold it. No guns involved, and contrary to popular belief, everyone is NOT carrying one. So, what do those chasing down Mr. Hammill use to beat him lifeless? Fists and knuckles get busted up, as one elder brother learned many a year ago ... By the way, I won't take your bet, even if you increase it. But, bats, hockey sticks, etc. may be useful angles or areas of interest. But wood, however wielded (even a 2X4 case I had years ago) leaves a pretty distinctive injury, and one my local M.E. says he can discern from a more dense metal instrument. The skull crush injuries need to be examined by an expert (either archival records or photos if detailed enough; or more likely if not, then by exhumation and examination). Following up on this line, another thing I would find out, if it were me; what cars were all these yahoos driving on the night in question? Our Dept of Revenue (Motor Vehicles) can do a page on any owner, any year. So, back in 1979, what were the players driving? What happened to said cars? Funny how you can check those kinds of things ... And the chariot involved could lead in interesting ways to the "who" in the "whodunit"..., or the what. On the other end of the iron, DNA is really tough stuff... has to be, you see, otherwise we would dry up and blow away. So, should said vehicles and attendant tire irons (or sports implements, etc.) still be on planet Earth, they might deliver up some interesting evidence. Were I the prosecutor, I would be having at least one detective run down this very narrow path. Were I the defense counsel for a poor schmuck as you describe, I would also wonder about these things, and whose car it was they used in the chasing him down, etc.; and falling in line with your scenario, who would have had access to the trunk or under the hood to possibly obtain it. This is dime novel stuff, I know. But my parking lot shoot down case had similar dime novel stuff in it, and when the PA's story got boring, the jury sure enjoyed the detective work ...

Something else on V.L. Alexander - Jamar-eye (pronounced to piss him off at every opportunity) - you want to run this knot-head for every jaywalking ticket on up, and how disposed. Has he made a habit of running to the District Attorney every time he steps in it ... can be a distressing habit, if true, and pointed out to a jury. 'Specially in this day and age of DNA, where guys like this swear they were confessed to by someone, who is later exonerated ... Look for rape cases or the like cleared by the providence of his proximity to the perpetrator ... Alliteration, like other patterns, can be so much fun ...

And ... drum roll ... Cardinal "sin" ... makes a great theme. Fits your scenario. I like it.

Hmmm ... that seems to be the extent of my profound thoughts at this late hour.

On Friday, November 11th, 2005, a WCCO Television report indicates that two of the three men charged in a 1979 murder in Wright County have told different stories about their participation in the beating death of Jeffrey Hammill. They go on to state that two men, Terry Olson, and Ronald Michaels, have been charged with first degree murder; and that Dale Todd has been charged with second degree murder. The report explains that the case had gone cold until 2001, when the biological daughter of the victim had contacted authorities looking for information about the death of her father. In 2003, the BCA posted a $50,000 reward for information about the case. The report claims that Todd, who had worked at a Medina fabrication company, told investigators in 2003 that when they found Hammill, Todd had stayed in the truck while Olson and Michaels assaulted Hammill, Michaels using an unidentifiable weapon. The Wright County Coroner had determined that Hammill's fatal head injuries were caused by a weapon. The report states that Todd claimed that Michaels was laughing when he returned to the truck.

The WCCO report goes on to indicate that according to documents, while in the Anoka County Jail on other charges, Olson told another inmate that he and Todd stayed in the vehicle and that Michaels alone killed Hammill. Olson made the remarks to the inmate after being distressed by an interview with homicide investigators. These documents also reported that the three men believed that Hammill was homosexual.

Today, the report continues, this statement might have led to hate-crime charges, but Wright County Attorney Tom Kelly noted in the report that there were no hate statutes in 1979, so they couldn't be applied in this case.

Jim Fleming, a Monticello attorney representing Michaels, told the reporter he had just received the case and didn't know whether his client had ever given a statement to authorities. The documents did not indicate that Michaels had. Jim told the reporter that Michaels has worked as an accountant for the state of Minnesota and has been on a disability leave.

On Saturday morning, November 12th, 2005, Jim sends an email to his brother Rob.

From: Jim Fleming

To: Rob Fleming

The money went up on the bet after I received the first round of discovery from the Prosecutor on Thursday. Turns out Todd and Olson both knew the victim from work. They didn't know my client, and he didn't know them, nor did he know the victim (Hammill) and had never seen any of them before. He was hanging out with Cardinal who was on a date with Debra Segler at a bar and her brother (Olson) showed up with his buddy Todd. Todd, Olson and Hammill all went to the party together after the bar closed. Cardinal and Segler rode together. Michaels rode by himself. My guy is described as being pretty drunk. Olson admitted in 2003, on re-interview, that he had a confrontation and a scuffle with Hammill at the party before Hammill left on foot. Hammill lived in Buffalo at that time, had no valid D.L and was used to either walking or hitching to get around.

The re-interviews came about because Jamari (who has seen

the light and accepted Jesus Christ as his personal lord and savior) was holding Bible studies in the jail when he was approached by Olson, who was doing time for kicking the crap out of his wife. The cops had just done round one, and had told him some things that Todd had said about the events that night. Olson was freaked out , and babbled telling Jamari that he had to get out to talk with Todd and his sister Debra Segler (Cardinal) because "we all had our stories straight, I don't know what went wrong, Todd shouldn't say that crap, and Debbie, I mean, she should know better." Olson also said that Hammill was beaten up because they thought Hammill, the lady killer, impregnator of other guy's girlfriends and all-around Olympic womanizer, was "gay".

Todd's car was seen at the murder scene by a couple leaving a card party at a friends down the road. On re-interview in 2003, Todd admitted he was there, but claimed that Olson and Michaels murdered Hammill while he waited in the car. Olson, unaware of Todd's new statement, says he and Todd stayed in the car and Michaels killed Hammill by himself with some kind of weapon. Michaels was described by Olson as laughing when he got back to the car.

When asked to re-interview, Cardinal agreed, but his wife demanded that she be present. When the cops refused to allow that, she went ballistic and during the interview, called Cardinal 7 times on his cell phone and tried to get another cop to break up the interview after 30 minutes, yelling that it had gone on too long. Cardinal is described during the interviews as extremely agitated, often shaking, staring in to space, covering his face with his hands and rocking back and forth. He explained this by saying the discussion just brought back some bad memories. Cardinal also spent some time talking about how violent and dangerous Michaels was (this clown was best man at Michaels wedding and spent some time that day trying to talk the bride out of going ahead, so she could marry him.) I have people who have known Michaels all his life who are coming back on their own volition (from Spokane, Portland, Texas, etc.) to testify that Michaels not only was widely known to be non-violent, but was known as a peacemaker, a fight breaker upper, and a guy who was known by many people to have never gotten into a fight in his life.

Hammill had a fracture clear across the base of his skull from ear to ear, a fracture above the right ear and a fracture above the right orbital brow ridge. Whoever hit him, meant to kill him, they fractured his skull with every blow.

And the Prosecutor's case against my client is that he, the non-violent, non-fighting, peacemaker, former high school class-president, went to a party of younger people where he knew only one person (Cardinal), then later left the party at 2:30 a.m. in the company of two guys he had never seen before and didn't even know (without Cardinal) to hunt down a third guy he didn't know, had never seen or heard of before and single-handedly killed him with repeated bone crushing blows to the head while the other two sat in the car. Then returned to the party, never seeing the other two again, or talking with them again and for 26 years of his life, never said a word about this to anybody, not even his parish priest (did I mention that he's also a life-long devout Catholic?)

The cops wanted Cardinal and his wife to take polygraphs but never followed up to have them do that. Both agreed, but only after Todd and Olson both passed polygraphs. Based upon what we know, I wonder who the hell did the graphs on those two; Cheetah, the Chimpanzee? Frank Valentine must be rolling over in his grave. These detectives couldn't detect John Wilkes Booth if they had been sitting in the box with Lincoln. Damn, I hate being right all the time!!

Ron is told he has a visitor, his lawyer Jim Fleming. They meet in a barren white room, with a small table and plastic chairs. Ron smiles as they shake hands and both sit down. This is their second meeting, and this time Jim has prepared a surprise for Ron. He has with him photographs of the body of Jeffrey Hammill, taken at the roadside where he died, in all their gory details. Jim wants to see Ron's reaction to the pictures. He says nothing to

Ron, just looks at him for a few moments; then he passes a file folder containing the graphic photos across the table to Ron. Ron looks at him a moment, then opens the folder. The color instantly drains from his face. His complexion turns pale white as he studies each terrible image, his jaw muscles clenching and unclenching as if he was struggling to swallow. Tears appear in his eyes and flow down his cheeks, dripping from his jaw. He finishes looking through the stack of photographs, looks up at Jim through watery eyes and in a soft, broken voice asks, "They think I did ... *this?*"

As Jim returns home, he is greeted at the door by his wife, Lynne. She asks him how the visit went. He tosses the file folder on the table, points to it and says, "He didn't do that! I don't know what the hell they got goin' here, but he didn't have anything to do with that!"

Jim has worked on two other capital murder cases before, both in Nebraska, a death penalty state; both were on appeals for existing convictions. Of the people he has defended in serious criminal cases, most he feels really were guilty of the charges; guilty of even more than they were charged with, or in some way criminally involved in the case. This case involves three men, not just one. Odds are, he will need to sort out all of their stories to get to the truth. He suddenly felt a strange tinge of fear and uncertainty in his stomach. He realizes that this mans future is dependant upon his ability to build a complete defense, start to finish. No previous trial transcripts or testimony to repudiate or witnesses to discredit. No procedures to question, rights violations to review. This was going to take everything he had, maybe more, and the situation was already stinking from something he found vaguely familiar. And the smell seemed strongest around the County Attorneys' office.

In the weeks and months that follow, Jim's investigation focuses him on the timing of Jeff Hammill's walk home along CR-12 the night of his death. One evening, Jim decides to have his wife Lynne drop him off at the location where Jeffrey Hammill began walking home from the party. Lynne drives out of town and parks alongside the roadway at the site Jeff's body was found. Jim walks the probable route taken by Jeffrey, if he had decided to walk home to Buffalo from the party. It is 2.2 miles from the party house to his wife, parked alongside the road. It takes him approximately thirty minutes to make the trek. He repeats this two more times that evening, walking at different speeds to try to determine an average time for the process. Twenty-five to thirty-five minutes each time. If Jeffrey had left the party around 3:00 a.m. as several witnesses believe, it would have taken him around thirty minutes to reach the site where his body was found. If the Kilgos left the card party at around 3:00 a.m., as indicated in statements from both the Kilgos and the Nowaks, it would be highly unlikely, if not impossible, for Jeffrey Hammill to be in the group of men they heard as they said their goodbyes to the Nowak's. The group of men they later saw, as they slowly drove past the car stopped in the roadway on their way home. This was at the very root of the case, indicating that Todd's vehicle was the vehicle the Kilgo's saw that night.

The vehicle was another interesting facet. How could Todd's vehicle be at the scene when the Kilgo's went by, if the accused had not even left the party to search for Jeff Hammill at that time? The obvious answer is that it wasn't Todd's car. The vehicle description was very detailed. This would need to be looked at. Something about the tail lights, too. Three on each side, flat on the top, round on the bottom.

Jim returns to Montrose some weeks later during the daylight to check out the neighborhood and get the lay of the land. He walks up and down one particular street looking for the house Deb Segler had lived in, back in '79. As he passes one home, he looks into the front bay window to see an elderly woman standing prominently there watching him. He continues walking up and down the street, trying to determine which home was Segler's. The woman is still there in the window, watching him, staring directly at him. Jim stops and looks directly at her. He suddenly feels like he is not alone. He is not sure what is happening here. He feels as if he is being told to go and talk to this woman; he is compelled to do so. He walks up to the house and knocks on the door. The woman answers the door. Jim explains to her that he is an attorney from Monticello, investigating a criminal case involving the death of a young man twenty-six years earlier. The woman says, "I know. You're Ron's attorney."

Jim is floored, and asks her, "You know Ron Michaels?"

"All his life," she answers. "And I know his family, his parents lived right there."

She points to a house just down the block. The woman leaves the house, taking Jim by the hand and walks him around the neighborhood; showing him where Ron grew up, where some of his friends lived; she takes him to the spot where Deb Segler lived back in 1979. The house is gone now and another built in its place. They return to the woman's home, where she invites him in and feeds him homemade cookies with a cold glass of milk. As Jim leaves her house, he realizes that if Ron had been with those other two men that night in August of 1979, and the three had taken off after Jeffrey Hammill, Ron would have had to have ridden directly past his parents, mere feet from them; asleep in their bed, in his boyhood home, on his way to kill Jeffrey. *Something is very wrong here,* Jim thinks.

CHAPTER 3

January, 2003

Courtesy of: "Herald/Journal"

Serving the Minnesota towns of Howard Lake, Lester Prairie, Mayer, Montrose, New Germany, Waverly, & Winsted

The following paragraphs are excerpts directly from the August 27th, 2007 article by Lynda Jensen, Editor

Amanda Thiesse was a baby when her father, Jeffrey Hammill, was found dead along County Road 12 in Marysville Township Aug. 11, 1979.

"I was one year old, and my brother was due to be born in December," she recalled.

The death was reported as a hit and run in the newspaper, even though her father had blunt force trauma to the head, not evidence of an accident, she thought."

Hammill's father, Gene Hammill, 82, of Cokato, remembers that night thinking "What did he do now?" when police officers visited his door about his son.

Jeff was known to get into trouble occasionally, his father said–but he never expected to hear what the cops told him.

The death of Jeffrey effectively dispersed the Hammill family, with both children; Amanda and Mathew, being adopted by loving parents in Brainerd, Amanda said, and their biological mother, Vickey James, relocating out of the area, eventually to die of cancer in Arkansas. Vickey James and Jeffrey Hammill never married.

Amanda said that, although she was raised by wonderful parents, she was curious about her roots, and started asking questions as soon as she was old enough."

In 2001, Amanda began the extensive search for information

regarding her biological parents. Denied information at first, her persistence finally began to pay off. Amanda received a letter from the Wright County Human Services Department that stated her father had died as a result of a 'Hit & Run'. She contacted the Wright County Sheriffs' Department to determine the status of the hit and run investigation. She initially speaks with Captain Miller. Needing verification of whom and what the case was about, she obtains a letter explaining who she is and who her birth parents were, from the Human Services Department. Captain Miller reviews this; then assigns the case to Lt. Hagerty. Lt. Hagerty spends some time going through the files dating back to August, 1979.

Amanda Thiesse and Lt. Hagerty speak on the phone. Amanda relates the statement in the letter she received from Human Services regarding the hit and run. Lt. Hagerty tells her that the letter is not correct; her father had in fact, been murdered.

Medical Examiner Amatuzio changes Death Certificate

Later in 2003, Dr. Janis Amatuzio, the Wright County Coroner since 1995, is contacted by the Wright County Sheriff's Office. They ask her to review the autopsy records of Jeffrey Hammill. This is not a common request, and her services do not come cheap. Dr. Amatuzio has been asked to do this perhaps only two or three times in her twenty-six year career. She knows this will involve gathering all of the information that was available, including police and coroner reports, photographs and autopsy reports, then sitting down and studying this and any new information to see if she can draw any conclusions. This information is submitted to her over a period of several months. The information she is reviewing is being provided to her from an individual employed by the BCA.

Dr. Amatuzio conducts this review and forms an opinion that although the wounds could have been made without a weapon, it is more likely that they were caused by either impacting the pavement in an unsupported fall or being struck by a large, blunt, heavy object. The lack of evidence at the death scene of Jeffrey being struck by a motor vehicle, however, leads her to believe that the death was the result of an assault. She therefore changes the "Manner of Death" on Jeffrey Hammill's death certificate from "undetermined" to "homicide". This meets the requirements in place for the BCA to begin their participation in the investigation of the death of Jeffrey Hammill.

CHAPTER 4

September 23rd, 2003

Dale Todd is now nearly forty-three years old. He is working as a 'remake person' for Dura-Supreme Cabinets in Hutchinson, MN. During his afternoon shift, Dale is called to the office by his boss. Two Minnesota BCA agents are there and they ask him if he will talk to them about the death of Jeffrey Hammill. He agrees to come to the Hutchinson Police Department that day after his shift is over to answer their questions. He is assured he is not being arrested, and that they merely want to interview him. He agrees. At the end of his shift, he gets into his truck and follows the police as they lead him to the police station in Hutchinson.

The 5-Hour Interrogation

Dale enters the small conference room at the police station. There is a small table and three chairs. The table is clear and Dale notices there are no windows. He is anxious. The two agents he had met earlier, Denny Fier and Ken McDonald, join him in the room and close the door. They ask Dale to sit down.

The following are transcribed portions of the 5-hour video-taped interrogation that took place at the Hutchinson Police Department in Hutchinson, MN on September 23rd, 2003. It should be noted here, that Dale Todd had sustained a brain injury as a child, and was reported to have been mentally impaired. His mental development may have been a factor in him not completing his high school education.

BCA AGENTS: Agent Denny Fier and Agent Ken McDonald

DATE OF INTERVIEW 9/23/03

PERSON INTERVIEWED: Dale Todd

D&K: Agent Denny Fier or Agent Ken McDonald

DF: Denny Fier

KM: Ken McDonald

Dale: Dale Todd

Dale: My anxiety is up. Oh, maybe you can refresh my memory, um, and I'll be able to get some details for ya?

D&K: Yup, we'll do that okay. Just like we talked about, ya know, out at the store there, you're not arrested, you don't have to talk to us; in fact, you can leave.

Dale: No, no, I want to help.

D&K: I just wanted to make sure.

Dale: No, I want to make sure that you guys get any information I can give you.

D&K: We have to write a report on everything we do, so I just want to make sure that I have correct information; last name, Todd, first name, Dale, middle name Lawrence?

Dale: Yup.

(They confirm his date of birth, address and phone number)

D&K: What's your wife's name?

Dale: Candace Marie. And we've been married seven years. In fact our anniversary was last weekend.

D&K: Make that seven year thing; they say you're good for, forever.

Dale: Well, I've made it ten years before that, and then it took twelve years to get remarried, so my kids are actually grown up, so.

D&K: Well, Dale, we'll try to bring you up to speed here, and refresh your memory.

Dale: Yeah.

D&K: Currently, we're running what we call a 'Spotlight on Crime' and we have picked cases throughout the state to rework that haven't been solved, and this Jeffrey Hammill case hasn't been solved.

Dale: Okay.

D&K: And you indicated you do know him, correct?

Dale: I knew him from work.

D&K: Okay.

Dale: Um, he had said he got out of the Marine Corp, or I don't even know if he was, cause people that we'd talked to said that he's such a liar that, ya know; the only way I knew him was at work, and that's when I worked at Tamarec Fab.

D&K: And he worked there?

Dale: Yeah. In fact, he only worked there, what was it; maybe a month, month and a half.

D&K: Well, Jeffrey Hammill was found deceased in the early morning hours of August 11, 1979 on County Road 12 in Marysville Township, Wright County.

Dale: Ah-um.

D&K: Hammill was a machinist, and was last seen the evening of August 10, 1979, at the Country West Bar in Rockford.

Dale: He was at the Rockford House.

D&K. Okay.

Dale: Cause there was a bunch of guys, now I remember some, cause there was a bunch of guys.

D&K: Are we up to speed as far as?

Dale: Yeah.

D&K: Okay, I won't read you more of that.

Dale: Well, um, me and a good friend of mine, Terry Olson, which I'm sure you have his name down.

D&K: Ah-um.

Dale: Okay, me and him; we used to be pretty good buddies, ya know, um, we don't associate no more, but, um, me and him went up to the Country West and then we went over to the Rockford House. Well, Jeff come running up to us and said that he needed to get out of here. And I says, 'why'? He says 'they got a 'pool' going, 'cause they want to beat me up'.

D&K: Who's we … … did he point?

Dale: I don't know, he didn't say, he didn't point. While we were at Country West it must have been, it had to have been in between eleven and twelve, maybe; at the time that we went over to the Rockford House, before it burned down.

D&K: All right.

Dale: And that's when he came running up to us, and we just knew him from work.

D&K: Was he alone?

Dale: He was alone. And so, I said, well, where do you got to go? And Terry said, well, why don't we just go home? And then at that time I was living with, … me and Terry were living with his sister in Montrose.

D&K: Is that Deb Segler?

Dale: I think so.

D&K: Okay. So you were living with, Debbie?

Dale: I mean it was only a few days.

D&K: Who else was living there?

Dale: Um, Debbie and her boyfriend, me and Terry. And then when we went over there, there was a bunch a people over there, they were just sitting around watching T.V., having a few drinks, beers, ya know.

D&K: So, when you leave the bar, who's vehicle are you using?

Dale: Mine.

D&K: Okay. And what was it?

Dale: It was a seventy-one, green, Impala. Four door.

D&K: Do you know what time you got to Terry's place, or Deb's place?

Dale: Um, twelve-thirty, one o'clock, maybe. Around in there. Well, what happened was (he pauses for a moment); well I can tell you guys it's been twenty-three years, I mean, if you want to arrest me for stealing a tire, you can. I'm not too worried about the tire now. Um, I had a flat tire, and it used to be a old Mobil Station on the corner of twelve and old twenty-five, okay. And there was a car there, car there that matched mine. So while we were taking the tire, Jeff had left. We didn't know where he went. So, well we figured he went home, cause he said he was just going to walk home, ya know.

D&K: So when you got out to the Mobil Station, who all was with you?

Dale: Well, see, his sister lived on Second Street, or down in that area, okay. So we just snuck up to the gas station and took a tire, me and Terry did, well, we didn't know if Jeff was behind us, or not, ya know. And then we said, well, we'll go get a tire and we'll change it and we'll give you a ride home. And then the next thing, ya know, he was gone and then, that Monday morning, when I went to work, somebody said that he was killed. Or, got hit by a car on County Road, um, what's that road? Old twenty-five and old twelve or something like that ya know.

D&K: Oh, okay, I got a little confused. We'll back up a little bit. You're coming up to Terry's sisters' place, when did you get the flat tire?

Dale: Um, we pulled up and that's when, um, I noticed we had a flat tire. And Jeff wanted a ride home cause he said that these guys were after him and were gonna beat him up, ya know, and Terry said, well don't worry, ya know, you can sit with, ya know, sit with us for a little bit. The last time I seen him, he was in the house. Everybody was having a drink, smoking dope then.

D&K: Okay, so, so Terry and Jeff went inside?

Dale: Well, we all went inside. Then me and Terry decided, well let's go up to the gas station and see if there's a tire that would, ya know. And there was; so me and Terry took that tire out there; and put it on my car and then we were going to give Jeff a ride home and he was gone.

D&K: How'd you get the tire on, did you bring a jack with you, or?

Dale: Ah-um.

D&K: Okay, so you had a jack in your car?

Dale: Ah-um.

D&K: So, okay, you jacked the car up and took the tire off and jacked it back down and took the jack and the tire and left?

Dale: Ah-um. And then by the time we got back, we changed the tire and stuff and then, ah, well, um.

D&K: Is Jeff there when you got back with the tire?

Dale: I don't think he was. To be honest with ya, no, I don't think he was.

D&K: Who was inside drinking beer, or whatever?

Dale: Um, some friends of Debbie's. Couple of them were an asshole.

D&K: Do you have their names?

Dale: No, no, this one guy wanted to fight me.

D&K: You don't remember his name at all?

Dale: Well, I can't remember. I didn't even know who he was. It had something to do with his girlfriend, cause his girlfriend kept eyeing me and Terry. And, me and Terry were just, ya know, we were just sitting there talking to people and getting to know people and stuff, ya know.

D&K: Was Debbie still there then?

Dale: Yeah.

D&K: And her boyfriend?

Dale: Yeah.

D&K: So it'd be Cardinal? Jeff Cardinal?

Dale: Yeah, yeah, well I figured they were just friends of theirs. Neighbors, ya know, neighbors that come over, whatever, ya know, cause, I guess they lived there for a while.

D&K: Would you recognize their names?

Dale: To be honest with you, no, I wouldn't, um, we were kinda in, ya know, I was nineteen then, so it was, smoking dope and had a few beers, I mean but I wasn't stupid, ya know.

D&K: How many people were over at this little social deal?

Dale: Maybe, eight. Maybe eight, or nine.

D&K: You and Terry, maybe Jeff, Deb.

Dale: And then just some neighbors that they knew. And then there was some, couple other guys and a couple, or with their girlfriends from the bar, from the Squire (a local bar in Montrose) and then, um, and that's, then the next thing you know, Monday, went to work and then couple of detectives came in and talked to us, Monday. And then Tuesday was his funeral and we thought, um, since we were the last ones to see him and stuff maybe we should, ya know, like go and pay our respects and. Well, then, the officers come back Wednesday with the place surrounded, with shotguns and everything else and loaded my car up on a hoist and stuff and what's going on. Well, you're being arrested for murder and I said, what? Well, we have an eye witness that they seen you at four-thirty in the morning on that road. And then I says, 'do you believe that, cause I don't, cause I was sleeping in my bed'.

D&K: How long did you stay there? At Terry and Deb's?

Dale: Um, well, we stayed there, cause Jeff already took off, so we just stayed there.

D&K: Stayed the rest of the night?

Dale: We just stayed there the rest of the night and I went back home, I suppose about eight o'clock.

D&K: How well do you know Deb; that would be Terry's sister?

Dale: Yeah.

D&K: And Jeff fairly well, at the time?

Dale: I didn't know them, know them, know them, but I just knew who he was.

D&K: Right. So you knew who he was, and he knew who you were?

Dale: Ah-um.

D&K: How often would you do things together?

Dale: Me and Terry, all the time. Um, with Jeff and Deb it wasn't much at all. It was just run over quick ya know, acquaintances, ya know.

D&K: But you lived there for a period of time like what, how long did you say?

Dale: Probably a week, two weeks, I mean, just a place to crash for right now until like, ya know, but then I just moved back home. So, I don't know how long Terry stayed there.

D&K: Did everybody stay there that night then?

Dale: No.

D&K: Who left?

Dale: Well, that guy that was throwing the drinks on me and Terry and, um, Terry grabbed him and said, 'hey, I think you should leave'. And then they had left. And they were, they were pretty drunk. I don't know where they lived.

D&K: Like a neighbor was doing that, or somebody else?

Dale: I think it was some guy from the bar that they knew. I think they went home. Terry knew some people up at the bar and they all came to their place, ya know, after bar socials.

D&K: So the people who would actually sleep over night were yourself, Jeff Cardinal, Deb Segler, and Terry Olson?

Dale: As far as I can recall.

D&K: What did Terry drive.

Dale: Uh, nothing.

D&K: Okay.

Dale: Well, Terry didn't drive, Terry didn't have car; he rode with me all the time.

D&K: How about Jeff, or Deb?

Dale: Yeah, Jeff had a truck I think at that time.

D&K: Okay. Do you know Ron Michaels?

Dale: Ron Michaels, Ron Michaels. Where's he from?

D&K: I think originally at the time he was from the general area there, uh. Short guy, well built, not thin, five-ten maybe, five-nine, five-ten, fairly well built.

Dale: Is he now?

D&K: Huh?

Dale: Is he now? Fairly well built?

D&K: Fairly well built?

Dale: Yeah, cause that wasn't the guy that wanted to fight me that night.

D&K: Was he a well built guy, strong guy?

Dale: Well at that time he was kinda skinny, but, he wasn't ya know, no slouch and, ya know. Cause at that time too, I was kinda built pretty good.

D&K: What'd he look like?

Dale: I, I, I just remember this guy who was about, well the same height as me, he had black curly type hair and went back sort of like yours, but only it was more of a curl, curly hair. Sorta like curly hair.

D&K: Sounds like him.

Dale: Something like that. But he, he was, he was pretty drunk and he kept, ya know, anytime somebody; ya know, cause his girlfriend, ya know, when she was talking to me, I think he was jealous, or something.

D&K: Do you know his girlfriend's name?

Dale: No, she had, um.

D&K: Sandy sound familiar?

Dale: She had sandy hair, she had sandy hair, she was petit, pretty, um, ya know, I'm thinking she had some freckles, had some freckles. And longer, longer it was middle of her back. Straight like sandy blonde type hair. Maybe it was just a girl-friend, or I don't know if they were married or.

D&K: So, it's fair to say that you and this guy you're describing, um, did you go anywhere that night, or?

Dale: No.

D&K: He's being a pain in the butt to you, ... you're just.

Dale: No, Terry, Terry grabbed him and threw him out. Got into it, just, Terry's a, when we were, when I met Terry he was fighter. He, did some boxing and he don't take crap from nobody, and he won't let no friend of his, take crap either, ya know, so Terry kinda like stuck up for me, ya know. And I told him, Terry, I says I know the guy wants to beat me up, let him beat me up, I says, I'm not, I'm not in shape to, ya know, really care, ya know, and I'm not going to let, ya know, let him sit there pour a bunch of drinks on me, so I ended up throwing one at him, ya know it's 'how does it feel?', ya know. And then, uh, Deb got mad cause the booze was getting all over the carpet and ya know, cause he kept dumping it. I don't know, he just might have had a thing with me that night, I don't know. People drink, they do stupid things and it's been quite a long time since I've drank so. We got a kid now so.

D&K: So when did Hammill leave this social gathering?

Dale: I'd say, it had to have been like one, I'd say one-thirty, two o'clock, even maybe two-thirty.

D&K: Did anyone see him leave?

Dale: I don't know, cause I told you guys, hour in between there, or hour and half in between there, we were ripping off the tire.

D&K: How far is it from the Segler's to this gas station, this Mobil or whatever?

Dale: Two blocks. You know where Red's is in Montrose?

D&K: It was about two blocks that's, that's fine.

Dale: Yeah, something like that. Well, the only reason why it took us a while is because my jack wasn't working right, we broke off a couple lug nuts on the other car, ya know, trying to get the tire and then, um, like I said, we weren't in no shape to even have been out there, ya know, I mean I wasn't totally drunk, blitzed or, whatever; I did that once and I told myself I wasn't going to do it again, so.

D&K: Which tire was it?

Dale: Um, the rear, right tire went flat.

D&K: Who was sitting where in the car? Do you remember that? You were driving?

Dale: I was driving, Terry and Jeff.

D&K: In the back seat?

Dale: Yeah.

D&K: Was it a four door?

Dale: Yeah. So, in fact I think he was, he was sitting in the middle, cause Terry was asking him questions why guys wanted to beat him up and stuff. And he; ... do you know like the middle part between the seats?

D&K: Was he intoxicated?

Dale: I wasn't sure. I knew he was drinking and ah.

D&K: Drinking beer in the car?

Dale: No, uh-uh.

D&K: Not really worried about that either but.

Dale: No, I think we were smoking. Smoking dope. But I haven't smoked since we, that was, twenty three years ago.

D&K: So you get to Terry's, one-thirty, leave, put a tire on, back about two-thirty, Jeff's gone.

Dale: Well, when we got back with the tire we changed it and stuff, ya know, so I'm not, why would I be keeping track of the time, but I'd say around two-thirty, ya know.

D&K: You stayed for the rest of the night?

Dale: Yeah.

D&K: I guess that would make sense cause you were living there, at the time.

Dale: Well, we were in, in fact that was the first weekend that we were, it was just a trial basis, for us, for me, ya know, cause my parents.

D&K: What do you think people would say about you now, that, what were you like back then? Like what would Deb say about you?

Dale: I was a nice person. I wasn't, um, I wasn't a fighter, um, I had quite an anger, temper, but, um, I don't know, sort of I like I am now, I mean. Well actually I'm a lot more mellow, when I'm not, I'm not drinking and I'm not smoking and I mean I smoke cigarettes, but um, other than that I don't, and I've been on anti-depressants pills and stuff like that due to some injuries and stuff. Right now I'm trying to wean myself off, but ah. I was diagnosed with anxiety attacks and stuff, when you get hyped up.

D&K: Are you on meds now?

Dale: I'm suppose to be, but I can't afford them, I ain't got any insurance. But back then, I wasn't.

D&K: How about Jeff Cardinal, how would you describe him?

Dale: I always thought he was kinda mellow. Um, well he was mellow around us, but sometimes Terry went over there and talked to him to and stuff about him and his sister. But I never got involved in any of that.

D&K: What did Jeff look like as far as size?

Dale: Jeff, he was about my height. Five-nine.

D&K: Ah-um.

Dale: And he was, he was five-ten, but he was built pretty good, he was a carpenter?

D&K: Do you know what he's doing now?

Dale: Uh-uh.

D&K: Of all these people, who have you been in contact with lately?

Dale: None. Um, well Terry a couple of times. But that's just, just a falling out between us because he, ya know, he can't get any women himself; he's got to take mine and so. And then he's lost most of his friends because of drugs and stuff. Um, they were all good guys, but they seemed like they wanted to get some distance from him. I never know really. There was only a association to Terry, ya know, some parties some, ya know, at that time and then, um, me and Terry were, we kinda like lost interest, ya know, with each other, cause we're friends and then I got married and then he got married and then he divorced and then I got divorced and, and then I've only seen him probably since that time, maybe four times, five, five times maybe.

D&K: When was the last time you talked to him?

Dale: Two years ago I think it was; two or three years ago, well I just told him, you stay away from me.

D&K: You been married what, … twice?

Dale: Ah-um, this is my second wife.

D&K: Were you guys married at that time?

Dale: No, no. I was … about two years after that.

D&K: Okay.

Dale: I got married when I was twenty-one. And she was eighteen.

D&K: What do you think happened to Jeff?

Dale: Well from what I understand it, um, somebody had ran him over and from the statement and stuff that I got through some, some of his people that, ya know, came up to me and smacked me said I was a murderer and stuff, ya know, and hey, I didn't do anything, I helped the guy out. He was in a situation where they had money, a money pool that they were going to beat him up, or kill him, or whatever. They told me that he was into selling and he was bisexual and this and that and asked me if I was gay and all this crap and that's when I got mad. I said, bullshit, I says, I'm not gay. I said I knew this guy from work and work only. I don't pay attention to somebody else's personal life, or whatever, ya know.

D&K: Where did you hear that he was run over?

Dale: Um, there was some people talking at the bar, or at the funeral about what had happened.

D&K: Ah-um. Did you remember who they were?

Dale: Some lady that knew Jeff good, she had blonde hair, she was kinda fat. Actually, she was fat, um, big mouth. She said that him and his girlfriend had gotten into it that night, or something like that, and I don't know if it was his girlfriend, but, uh, when they came in and arrested us and stuff and took my car and impounded it and all that stuff. They had told me then he was ran over by a car. You could tell when we went to the funeral that his hands were all broken. Then you see his face was just all black and blue, ya know, and then he says well, somebody ran him over. I wouldn't think they'd have an open casket. But, then he said they ran him over or something like that. So, that's all I knew about it. That's all I knew about it.

D&K: Okay.

Dale: And then, then I heard earlier that somebody had beaten him to death. And then backed over him with a car and then threw him in the ditch to lay, or something like that.

D&K: I would imagine you're recollection of the evening twenty some years later; … did you tell the truth of what really did happen that night?

Dale: Yeah, yeah, and I told them everything that was possible. The only thing that we didn't tell them was we went and stole that tire. That was the only thing we didn't say anything about.

D&K: How did you fill that void back then, where were you at, what'd you tell them where you were at when you stole that tire?

Dale: We told them we were at home, at Terry's and Deb's and ya know, we went there and stayed there, ya know, because that's what we did. Like we, ya know cause they were giving us times and this so and we didn't know. We didn't look, I wear a watch now but I still couldn't tell ya, I only look at it when I start, or ready to go home.

D&K: Do you think Hammill was accidently run over, or accidently killed, or out and out murdered?

Dale: Right now?

D&K: Ah-um.

Dale: You mean to be honest with you?

D&K: We're hoping so.

Dale: To be honest with you, I think he was murdered.

D&K: Why do you think that?

Dale: Well for one, the police officers told me. And then I also heard through a, who was it, I can't remember if it was one of the detectives. Hard to say, but I also heard that night at the Rockford House that Jeff had raped a guys' son for money for drugs. Or made him do sexual things for, for money he owed for, for pot, something like that. And that was why one of the guys wanted to beat him up, or something like that, but I'm not sure, don't quote me on it cause I'm not really sure, but I heard something of that sort through a couple of people that were talking about it.

D&K: Was he beat up out on County 12 then, or was he beat somewhere and taken out there?

Dale: I don't, don't know, cause he rode home with us and we didn't touch him, ya know. He was being pushed around in a bar and then he said something about you guys got to get me out of here cause they got a money pool and they're going to beat me up, they're going to kill me. And Terry was asking well, why? And he kept on shrugging it off or making different conversation and then that's when they told us that he was bi-sexual and sold drugs to kids and that, that if he couldn't pay then they'd have to sex acts with him, or something like that.

D&K: Who was telling you this?

Dale: Ah, the detectives when we were being questioned. They asked if we were gay and that's when I stood up and blew a cork. Ya know, I blew a cork when he told me I was gay. Well, did you know he was? I says, no, I says the only time I know this guy is at work. I don't associate; I didn't never associate with him. He was in trouble that night, we thought we'd help out and that was it. And that was it. And then after that we never seen him. And then that's when Monday they talked to us Monday at work.

D&K: Ah-um.

Dale: For a couple hours. And they talked to me and then I went back to work and then they went. Terry went up and talked to them. We did tell the officer where we were, but we didn't, we didn't at that time, we didn't tell them we were up at the Mobil Station stealing the tire.

D&K: Sure.

Dale: Ya know, because, ya know, that's a crime ya know. I don't think now, you could prosecute now can you?

D&K: No, it's a little late for that one.

Dale: Huh?

D&K: Little late for that one. Still got the tire?

Dale: No. I don't even have a car.

D&K: Then you're, okay. What did you do with it?

Dale: What, the car?

D&K: Yeah.

Dale: Um, I sold that for, um, one hundred and fifty bucks.

D&K: Was it in pretty good shape?

Dale: Yeah, well it had a lot of miles left on it, it had two hundred and I suppose almost three hundred thousand miles.

D&K: So you traded it in on something or?

Dale: No, I just sold it out to a friend of mine that lived in Hamel that worked with us.

D&K: Okay.

Dale: His son needed a car and I says well I'll sell you this one for one hundred and fifty bucks. And then he drove it for I think six months, six to eight months and then he blew it up.

D&K: He didn't know how to fix, huh?

Dale: No, well, I think he, I, thought he used it for a demolition derby car, derby car. Instead of junking it I think he used it for a demo, a demolition car. Ya know them demolition derbies?

D&K: You say that the police took your car that one Monday morning, what'd they do with it?

Dale: They didn't take it Monday, they took it Wednesday.

D&K: Oh, Wednesday I'm sorry.

Dale: Yeah, Wednesday they took it, um. Well they, they brang it in to the impound, and the tore the seats out of it, they torn it all apart.

D&K: Did they take anything out of it, do you know? I mean our reports are pretty sketchy from back then.

Dale: Um, no, they, well they got, they took the tire iron, they took the baseball bat and, um, ya know, anything that could be used as a weapon. They analyzed all that they found, um, a bag of pot that was stuffed in the seat where I never knew where that came from. Um.

D&K: Did you get any of that stuff back? Well, you wouldn't get the pot back. Did you get any of the stuff back or?

Dale: Yeah, I got it all back.

D&K: Did ya save the bat, or the tire iron or any?

Dale: Yeah, well there was blood and hair on the bat, but it wasn't mine, nor his.

D&K: Who's was it?

Dale: Well, I borrowed the bat from, from my cousin and when, when we were down at the park playing beer ball. And when I well, ya know, borrowed the bat from him and then I just stuck it in my trunk, ya know, and they, they gave me back my jack, they gave me back the tire iron, they gave me gloves. You might as well say they just stripped the side of the car out.

D&K: Ah-um.

Dale: I mean, they had the front seat out, the back seat out, the whole trunk completely out. They had the tires off, they had the hood up, ya know, they were going through the whole thing. I think they let us out at twelve o'clock at night. Told us to get out of there.

D&K: What's with the bat? Why did you have a bat in your car?

Dale: Cause we played softball.

D&K: Okay.

Dale: We do a lot of things like that. Me and Terry, ya know, into sports, ya know, I'm just kinda of a jock and ya know, we'd, um, play softball, beer ball, ya know, we played football with some of guys who knew the Gophers, on the Gophers Team back then, ya know, down in St. Louis Park, ya know. We got a keg and sat there and played beer football. I had hockey sticks in my trunk too. And they took those cause we played hockey, ya know. There was a pair of skates and they checked them out. And the blood they found on them were mine, ya know.

D&K: So which cousin did you get the bat from? I'm a little curious about the blood and the hair on the bat, I guess.

Dale: Um, Buddy Hughes.

D&K: Buddy Hughes?

Dale: Yeah, he's my first cousin.

D&K: Did you ever ask him how the heck he ever got blood and hair on his bat, or?

Dale: No, I didn't even know about the hair. He just, ya know, he got cut on the hand. And the hair can be just, ya know, unless he hit somebody, but, I don't know, I don't know. He just let me use it, ya know and that was it. And I'm sure they probably checked that out because I told them. Actually it was my, my uncle's; his dad's bat that he had when he was, um, little.

D&K: But there's no way in hell it's Hammill's blood?

Dale: No, they told me it wasn't and they just threw everything inside the car and told me to go.

D&K: I mean, could it be Hammill's?

Dale: No, cause there's, the only way would, no, because the only thing we took out of the trunk was the jack and that was it. And that was there and they would have probably have kept me.

D&K: Well, back then, in fact, let me explain it to you. They swabbed evidence back then, but it was just like AB negative and O positive and things like that.

Dale: I didn't even think Buddy would have that bat.

D&K: But we got a swab. Like they swabbed and tested blood samples on it in the property room.

Dale: Did they?

D&K: But we didn't know exactly where it was from for sure.

Dale: But ya know, unless somebody took it out of there when we were gone getting the tire and stuff .

D&K: It won't be that hard to tell. But, would somebody take it out of there?

Dale: No, cause I'm pretty particular about stuff in my vehicle.

D&K: You probably took the key with you or something.

Dale: I don't know.

D&K: I'm just trying to eliminate all.

Dale: Oh I understand and I'm trying to be cooperative as best I can with the statement I gave back then.

D&K: Ah-um.

Dale: The only difference in my statement back then is that, I'm telling you we had taken the tire at the Mobil Station, but the Mobil Station is not there no more.

D&K: I just want to make sure ya know, you're very clear because it's pretty important.

Dale: No, I understand that.

D&K: If I come back later and you say something different, then something's wrong.

Dale: Right. But it was not me. I, I wasn't that drunk or stoned to where I didn't know what I was doing, okay.

D&K: What I'm saying is.

Dale: Especially when I'm driving a car.

D&K: Right, and I appreciate that, I mean, you know what occurred that evening.

Dale: Not totally. Not totally.

D&K: What part are we missing?

Dale: Well, when we were at the house that's when, ya know, I had a couple more, ya know, I had more to drink, ya know.

D&K: Was that after Jeff left?

Dale: Yeah.

D&K: Okay.

Dale: Cause, ah, I told him I says; well we'll change this tire and stuff and then we'll, we'll get you home. He goes, no, no, I'm just going to go. And that's when he left. Ya know, because he came outside with us cause we were talking about well Terry do you think we could get a him a ride, cause he wanted a ride home. And nobody ever would give him a ride home. And, um, and I says well why don't we sneak up to that station and see if we can find a tire to fit mine, ya know, on my car. And so me and Terry went up there, ya know, and then we were sneaking ya know because the Wright County Police Officers, they always hide behind Red's Café for speeders and.

D&K: Ah-um.

Dale: And they watch the Squire Inn, ya know, for drunk guys, but back then the law was different, but they'd still pull you over.

D&K: Well, do you know if they got any blood on the hockey sticks, or jack, or anything like that?

Dale: No.

D&K: And they just said you're clear to go, okay, that's all they told you? We should check those too.

Dale: They just said you're clear to go and, uh and I said well, I don't have enough gas so I can get home could you, ya know, so.

D&K: So, um, Hammill didn't help you change the tire, so he didn't cut his finger or bleed?

Dale: I don't know.

D&K: Okay.

Dale: I think he was in the house.

D&K: Could he have cut himself or anything like that?

Dale: No because he, I don't even think he was bleeding that night. When we were with him, I mean to be totally honest with you, um.

D&K: I understand, I just want, I'm trying to work clear of this, ya know, sometimes you come back later and we find blood that's his and then we have problems.

Dale: .Yeah, but that's what I can't under, I don't know.

D&K: Okay.

Dale: I, I really don't know because there was, when we were at the Rockford House it was quick, ya know, because like he came running up to us and say hey ya gotta, ya gotta get me out of here, you got to get me out of here. He was crying!

D&K: Okay.

Dale: And then when they asked me if I was gay and I was

involved with the guy I, I kinda like, that's when I got mad, ya know. They ask you them stupid questions on the polygraph, ya know, I think they do it just to get you mad.

D&K: Well this ain't, this ain't positive.

Dale: Well something's are still vague, ya know, cause it was twenty, twenty years ago I think it was. Seventy-nine? And I'm going to be forty three on Thursday and that's twenty-two, twenty-two years ago. Twenty-four years ago. So I'm trying to do the best I can.

D&K: Right, I appreciate that.

Dale: Cause if I was taken that, that medication I probably wouldn't be able to give you as much stuff as I got now. And that's just kinda like going back to where, ya know, like when you're sick, ya know.

D&K: Okay.

Dale: Well and then they gave Terry the polygraph and then they asked Terry a bunch of questions and stuff and his came out good, or something like that and they figured well.

D&K: Yeah, that was a different polygraph then, I mean they've come a long, long, ways.

Dale: Yeah, but, I mean I, didn't even I didn't know what to think, ya know. I was scared. I mean, I was, I was scared out of my life, ya know, cause all we did was try to help the guy out, ya know. And everybody's going to say something behind your back, or this, or that, ya know.

D&K: Well, you pointed it out, with today's science, a lot of advantages now days. We have new science but rewards help us solve a lot of these older cases, I mean. We put money out, like a fifty thousand dollar reward and a few people talk and they give us new information.

Dale: You don't have to give me money.

D&K: But that just, well, ya know.

Dale: I mean, I'll do everything I can to cooperate, I'd even told them, ya know I told the officers that if you want to use me for a sting operation, or something, if you think this guy is a suspect, or whatever I'll help, help. They said, No, we don't need you to do that, just go home and, um, do what you're doing. And I says, how can you go home and do what you're doing. I said you just had me here from six o'clock in the morning till twelve o'clock at night, asking me the same questions over and over and over and over and over and over and over and over.

D&K: Well, like I say, it's easier for us to put people in the picture, or out of the picture. You're very positive none of your blood would be on those items, so if I find that blood on the bat checks, I mean, it either is, or isn't.

Dale: Well then you guys come after me, correct?

D&K: Oh, if it is, yeah.

Dale: Well, yeah, but I never had that bat in my hand. I know.

D&K: It wouldn't have been his?

Dale: No, it couldn't have been his, no, this is a very old bat. It could have been anybodies.

D&K: Did anybody else have that bat?

Dale: No, all we did, well, when we played baseball with it, yeah.

D&K: I understand that, I just wanted to know if it is his blood on there; sometimes you don't seem real positive.

Dale: Well, I can't be positive because, ya know, I was drinking, I was smoking.

D&K: Ah-uh.

Dale: But I knew the bat was in the trunk and I knew the jack was in the trunk, I knew the tire iron was in the trunk, ya know.

D&K: Right, hockey sticks.

Dale: Hockey sticks, skates ya know.

D&K: Is there any possibility someone else got in there and accessed that?

Dale: No. Cause the jack and everything we pulled out of the trunk was with us, me and Terry. I don't even think Jeff was with us, ya know, up there.

D&K: We can see if the hair, if it's Jeff's or not.

Dale: Well, he was in the car.

D&K: But he wasn't in the trunk.

Dale: No.

D&K: Well you still got the bat?

Dale: No. Nah, I mean cause the way you're talking is like maybe you still have that car ya know, or are you just going to go off of what they, they have in the report?

D&K: We're more interested in what they took as evidence, ya know, back then and what they gathered from the items that were in your car.

Dale: No, in fact I don't even know if they gave me that bat back.

D&K: We got the bat.

Dale: You got the bat? So, um, that's. I thought they all, they threw all that back in my trunk. All that means is there's, shouldn't be anything on it, ya know, as far as to Jeff.

D&K: Denny, do you have any questions?

D&K: Yeah. First of all, your story is significantly different today from what you told the original cops.

Dale: But like I said it's twenty-four years ago. I'm trying to remember it like, but I don't know.

D&K: You went with Ron Michaels.

Dale: Who's Ron Michaels?

D&K: The guy we just, we asked you about earlier. The guy that apparently you think was throwing drinks in your face, or on you. At least that's what you told the, the deputies that night, Dale.

Dale: I don't know no Ron Michaels.

D&K: Well, let me read right from the report, ah, if I can find the right spot here.

D&K: Anyhow, while I'm looking for that I have another question for you too and which is also inconsistent in that ah, you told the detective that you picked up Jeff Hammill when he was hitch hiking from Rockford. Does that ring a bell with you?

Dale: No, cause he, we picked him up at the Rockford House. Cause he came out as I was going by and then he ran to the road and we picked him up.

D&K: Let me read to you right from the report here, okay. And we have to go on.

Dale: I know.

D&K: This was a couple, or the day after actually and says, speaker says they been with Jeff on Friday night. They had met in the Country West at about 2330. -"

Dale: Ah, 2330 is?

D&K: Eleven-thirty.

Dale: Eleven-thirty.

D&K: They had left at approximately 0120 hours. That would have been, ah, in the morning, on Saturday morning and picked him up while hitch hiking out of Rockford. This was a report done by Investigator Compton. Dennis Compton, do you know him?

Dale: Let's see. I think you're right, that, that is right. But we did meet him at, at the, ... he wasn't with us the whole night, Jeff wasn't.

D&K: No, you saw him at eleven-thirty.

Dale: Yeah, that's when he told us they were going to beat him up and then he stuck with us, me and Terry, went to the County West, then we went over to the Rockford House. And that's when Jeff said he's got to go. And I says well why don't you give me a few minutes and you can ride back cause we're going to Montrose. And then, that's when I picked him up on the road, hitch hiking; that's when I picked him up.

D&K: In your car?

Dale: In my car. Seventy-one, Chevy Impala, four door, gray-green. It's like a hunter green, darker.

D&K: Darker, is it dark green?

Dale: Pretty dark color.

D&K: What was the scuffle at work between Jeff and Terry? Do you know?

Dale: No I don't. I don't know anything about that. I don't, um, did I say anything on the report?

D&K: Nothing at all it's just an indication that there had been a scuffle between Terry and Jeff in Rockford.

Dale: I think Jeff was just being cocky, I think, maybe, I don't know.

D&K: Okay.

Dale: And like I said, all I knew Jeff from, was work.

D&K: Did you know a girl by the name of Kitty? Jeff's girlfriend?

Dale: No.

D&K: Do you remember Jeff saying anything, that Kitty had some people after him? Kitty had, ya know, asked some people to get him for beating her up? Do you remember that?

Dale: Um, I think he said something like he was in a fight with his girlfriend, I'm not sure.

D&K: Okay.

Dale: I'm not, I'm not really sure, um, but he might have mentioned something about, she, had said something about, I, I don't know, I don't know if I want to say cause you, cause you're, there's stuff off the report all ready and I'm just trying to fill in the blanks. I think, all, all I remember him saying is that his girlfriend had somebody that was going to beat him up. That they were in an argument, or something. But I can't recollect word for word or anything like that. All I know, I remember he'd, he'd had mentioned something at work that he and his girlfriend were having problems. And I says, well, that's between you and her, ya know, during work hours, ya know, and stuff. I never got into his personal life. In fact I don't even think I met her.

D&K: Very possible.

Dale: I don't think I even met her.

D&K: About you: your whereabouts that night, ah, you told the investigators that you went somewhere from Deb's house. You went with Ron Michaels.

Dale: Who?

D&K: Ron Michaels.

Dale: Who's Ron?

D&K: Well.

Dale: I don't remember no Ron.

D&K: It might have been the guy that was throwing the drinks on you, Dale, I don't know. But he was there and he's a friend, Ron is a friend of Deb and Jeff's, okay? And he was at the house. That's what I understand at least; Kenny, you done with you're reading?

KM: Well what it says is Ron Michaels lives south of Montrose, described as a flat house on a hill. Says the guy drives a blue, Hornet. Ron wanted to show Dale his stereo. He wanted Dale to look, listen to his stereo. And I guess other people were interviewed like Deb Segler and Jeff Cardinal and all the individuals there; they also indicated that you left. This was within one, or two days after Hammill died.

Dale: I left where?

KM: You left Segler's place.

Dale: Well, I moved back home.

D&K: No, that night, you left and went with Ron Michaels, or, and perhaps Terry Olson. And left and didn't come back the rest of the night.

Dale: I don't remember that.

DF: Do you remember going and listening to some stereo equipment, or looking at some stereo equipment?

Dale: If I knew who Ron was, I can't remember who Ron is.

D&K: A good friend of Jeff Cardinal's. He was best man at his wedding. Did you go to his wedding?

Dale: No. Well, where was Jeff then?

D&K: Jeff Hammill?

Dale: Yeah.

D&K: Oh, it could be Cardinal too I guess, I'm sorry, which Jeff you talking about?

Dale: Jeff Hammill, where was he?

D&K: Well, that's the fifty thousand dollar question.

Dale: Cause I don't remember him being with us and I don't remember going over to Ron's place, with the stereo, to listen to his stereo. Cause I probably, I probably just stayed there.

D&K: Maybe you were doing drugs; how much did you have to smoke? Or were you doing anything else, other than smoking?

Dale: No, I don't, I never did hard drugs.

D&K: You can see our side here?

Dale: No, I'm just, I understand your side.

D&K: It's really important we get this cleared up because right now we've gotta.

Dale: I'm scared.

D&K: Well.

Dale: You've got me scared.

D&K: Don't be scared because we want you to remember, yeah, we want you to remember and that's why I'm reading you verbatim from the report here. It's high lighted here. Its nothing we're making up. This is what we have to go on after twenty-four years.

Dale: You know I think you're right. I think we did go over to Ron's house.

D&K: Do you remember Ron now?

Dale: I don't. I can't remember Ron.

D&K: Who's we? Who, who.

Dale: Me and Terry were always together, we were best friends.

D&K: Did Jeff go with you?

Dale: Nope, that's what I'm trying to figure out; if he had went with us and took off from there.

D&K: Well, if he did go with you, would that surprise you?

Dale: If he went with us, then he went with us.

D&K: We're just asking you, I mean. Seems like things are coming back to you a little bit more.

Dale: I'm trying.

D&K: If this Ron was the same guy that threw drinks on you, is it logical that you would have left with him?

Dale: No. I wouldn't have left with him then if that was the guy that was throwing drinks on me. I was high. I was trying to be a nice person. I was trying to be, ya know, I didn't want to fight nobody, I, ya know.

D&K: Did Hammill go with you?

Dale: I think he might have. I don't know.

D&K: Okay.

Dale: That's, I'm trying to figure out where, if we drove over in my car, cause I'm trying to picture it, I'm trying to picture who Ron is. Now if I can picture who Ron is, I might be able to figure out if, if Jeff was with us, or not. But, I, I do know that Jeff was pretty scared that night. And, ah.

D&K: Remember what the pool was?

Dale: The pool?

DF: You said they had a pool, money, I believe is what it meant .

Dale: Yeah, Jeff said something about that. Ya know, I just don't want to give you guys a bunch of hot air.

D&K: Oh, I think you're trying. It's a long time, but, ya know Dale, its … it's.

Dale: No, I'm scared. Cause all of a sudden after twenty-four years this has come back to me.

D&K: Well, it's coming back.

Dale: Why, why is it coming back to me, cause I didn't touch the guy, I tried to help the guy and I didn't touch the guy and now, now it's just, it's kinda like.

D&K: Dale, is it possible, I'm just going to throw out this, is it possible that you guys had plenty to drink and plenty to smoke that night, it got late.

Dale: Ah-um.

D&K: Is it possible, that you and Ron.

Dale: No. You mean me and Ron, did something to Jeff? No.

D&K: Not intending to hurt, kill him, not intending to kill him.

Dale: No, no, no, never touched the guy.

D&K: Okay.

Dale: I never touched the guy, I was not that drunk, or I was not that stoned that I would, I would have known if I killed somebody. And no I didn't touch Jeff. No, I did not touch Jeff.

D&K: Let me ask you about this Ron, the guy that was throwing the drinks, let's assume that, that's the guy that was throwing the drinks on you. That apparently Terry threw out of the house, right?

Dale: Yeah, but, see I can't remember if Ron was with us from the bar, and then we went over and looked at his stereo and then came back. When we were at Deb's place, ya know, people started drinking more and stuff and. Cause I know, I after, the bar didn't have another drink.

D&K: No, you said you did at Deb's house.

Dale: At Deb's I had one drink, but then some guy was giving me a hassle and I didn't drink any more after that.

D&K: Well, let me ask you this. What was the plan to get Hammill back home? Where was he living do you know?

Dale: I thought he said he lived in Buffalo.

D&K: And that is correct.

Dale: And, um, but after that I don't know where Jeff went. And I swear to you on a stack of bibles, I did not touch Jeff at all. And I don't know who did. Cause, I think what we did is when we picked up Jeff, this Ron guy said, I cannot remember, we went over to his house cause he said something about a new stereo. And then we went back over to Deb and Jeff's afterwards and I think that's when I had the flat tire. And that was probably around, gees, I don't remember. I'm scared and I'm getting nervous.

D&K: Well don't, then don't get nervous and don't get scared. Ya know you're not under arrest.

Dale: Begins sobbing…

D&K: Dale, you're not going to jail.

Dale: The guys there tried to make it seem like it was me who did it, ya know, I didn't, I, no, I didn't touch this kid.

D&K: Yeah.

Dale: I didn't touch this guy.

D&K: Settle down, you're not, you're not going to jail, okay, you're not under arrest, you're not, okay? All we are trying to do is to resurrect this case.

Dale: (Sobbing)…I'm, I'm, I'm trying to ya know, I'm, I'm…

CHAPTER 5

D&K: On your original statement, it appears that the flat tire was as you were coming into town from Rockford.

Dale: I don't remember who said that in the report.

D&K: I can tell you that you did and that was also verified by Deb, that in fact at about that time around two a.m. is when you showed up with a flat tire.

Dale: But I can't remember if I … .this Ron guy really puzzles me.

D&K: Yeah. Here is a picture of him. That's him.

Dale: I know him, yeah, no this wasn't the guy that was dumping the drinks on me.

D&K: Okay.

Dale: The guy that was dumping drinks on me was skinnier.

D&K: So who's this?

Dale: Him? I don't know, I don't think this is Ron.

D&K: Is this the guy that you went, did you go to his house that night at all?

Dale: I think that this is the guy that we went to his house and he bought a new stereo system. I can't remember if we were at Deb and Jeff's first. But, we had to have been. No, Jeff left, Jeff left before we went over to this guy's house. Jeff had left before we went over to this guy's house and then from that guy's house, we went back to Terry's house, cause I remember waking up in Terry's basement.

D&K: Let me ask you this, Dale, is it possible that you never did go out and listen to the stereo? Is it possible that was a story that you gave to the investigator, huh?

Dale: No, I, I fib and tell little white lies, but, I do not, I was so scared that night, or that day, it's really hard, um.

D&K: Why were you, why were you so scared?

Dale: Cause I didn't do it. And they were asking me if I was gay. They were asking me if I was bisexual or, do I like to screw guys and women and stuff and I have not.

D&K: Well, that's never been brought up, I mean.

Dale: On the lie detector.

D&K: Did they?

Dale: Yeah.

D&K: Oh.

Dale: They asked me if I was gay, and then, I don't know if the detective said something about him being, ya know, I don't know if he was just trying to scare me into something or, ya know, which I was telling the truth. But this guy's got me puzzled, I can't, I've seen him a couple of times.

D&K: Let's just throw …

Dale: But he, he was chunky back then too. I think he was a big guy. Yeah, but, the guy that was throwing drinks on me was about my size. And he had black, long hair down to his shoulders and it was black and curly and I don't remember who this guy was.

D&K: Well was it Jeff, by chance? Could it have been Jeff throwing the drinks on you? Jeff Hammill?

Dale: No, it was not Jeff who was throwing the drinks on me. Cause in fact, I don't even think Jeff was there then. Cause I think when we went up to steal, take the tire, that's when Jeff spilt.

D&K: And, and where'd he go?

Dale: Well, I figured he was going home.

D&K: How?

Dale: Hitch hiking. Hitch hiking, or something, I don't know.

D&K: We're making no bones that Hammill was murdered and we all think that a car doesn't have anything to do with this other than moving people around and we have strong information, that more than one person's involved in this.

Dale: I'm sorry, I'm not involved in this. Yes I seen, was the last person with Jeff, but.

D&K: There are two, three, four people involved, or at least have knowledge of this. You'd think after twenty-four some years that you'd be jostled a little bit? People kinda grew up and went on their separate lives and people have different families and kids. Things are a little bit different than back then. And you're a good example of that. Look at yourself, you got you're act together. You're not out partying, you're not out smoking dope.

Dale: No, like I said, when I got married, I quit.

D&K: Yeah, that's just it, all these other people.

Dale: And that's when me and Terry got distance a little bit, ya know.

D&K: And, and a good point, all these people have grown up and went on their separate ways. When they bring nineteen year old kids in here and they did something they're scared of, or some bad acts that went wrong, ya know, they can still have pretty close ties.

Dale: Well, I'm sorry, but my dad taught me, ya know if you did something wrong you should stand up to the punishment. And sometimes when I did something wrong and my dad spanked me, ya know, I stood up to that punishment. And my values still are like that. Where, ya know if I do, like at work, if I broke something, I'm not going to shove it under the table. I let my boss know that, ya know, I broke this, it wasn't purposely, but I broke this, and what do you want me to do? Do you want me to, ya know, tell the other manager in Millwork that, okay, I broke the window, can you reorder it for this customer.

D&K: Right.

Dale: Ya know and my values haven't changed on that. And I know its in my heart, I did not kill this guy.

D&K: Do you know about it?

Dale: I didn't kill this guy. You know. Only from what I heard after a while that somebody said that he got beat up and ran over by a car on Highway 12, going towards Buffalo.

D&K: So if someone told us that this little group we're talking about here, Michaels, yourself, and Terry Olson had some involvement with that, is that true?

Dale: I don't know. Cause Terry was with me. And I know.

D&K: For example what if Terry Olson, what if we talked to him and he said screw it and can't live this anymore and, and I need to get it off my chest, would that surprise you?

Dale: Yes, it would. That would really surprise me because, I didn't do it and I know I didn't do it and I wasn't around the people that did do it, cause you just told me, he was murdered. And like I said, I just heard through discussions if you know how after a funeral and stuff, ya know, how things develop. I even heard that, at the funeral from some of the people that were there, cause me and Terry we sat right in the back. I even had the obituary in my car, ya know and I circled it cause I didn't know where it was at. And I thought, well, we could represent the company for and we had boughten a card and we had the people sign it at work. And we took it to there. The detectives asked me about why I had the obituaries in the car.

D&K: Can you account for this gentleman.

Dale: No, I cannot account for that guy.

D&K: So you can account only for Terry.

Dale: I only see his face.

D&K: Well, let's just say this is the guy that was the stereo man: Can you account for him? Not being involved in Hammill's death?

Dale: But, if that was the stereo man, I don't think Jeff was with us, I think.

D&K: How do you, how do you explain?

Dale: How do I explain this? I don't, I cannot explain it.

D&K: The detectives, they did mention to you that they saw a car out there on twelve, parked along the road?

Dale: The detective said he had a phone call saying that there dark green car sitting on Highway 12. And there was no dark green car sitting on Highway 12.

D&K: Well, that's one of the things; we interviewed people.

Dale: Right.

D&K: And to day this day they are saying, they are confirming they did.

Dale: Well, it's not true. Cause I was not on that road.

D&K: Well, the problem obviously is that, um, you're recollection is not the same today as it was, the day after when you talked. Now, we got a couple of things that you, number one, you lied to Denny Compton and I think maybe, Brooks Martin, may have talked to you as well, um. Now for whatever reasons you would have, one was the tire, you admitted you did it, you just didn't lie about that, you just never told about that.

Dale: I never said anything about the tire, because we didn't want to get arrested for stealing the tire.

D&K: Could you have had a flat tire out on County Road 12?

Dale: I didn't take that road.

D&K: You know which road we're talking about right?

Dale: Yeah, you're talking about the one, um, that goes through Buffalo.

D&K: Right.

Dale: And it comes out by the lake.

D&K: Yeah, east side.

Dale: I wasn't on that road.

D&K: We're pretty certain, very certain, the person that saw the dark green Chevy, ya know, just sitting there, he picks it out and it's there, sitting on County Road 12, very solid about that information. Good people. Honest people. I mean, we have actually no reason to doubt them, they said it then and they said it again, now. And their minds have not changed a bit and it's a husband and a wife, that seen it. So it isn't just one person, it's a couple that saw it so, we have that to work with.

Dale: I wasn't there.

D&K: If, ah.

Dale: How can somebody see something at four o'clock in the, four-thirty in the morning when it's pitch black out?

D&K: Well, could somebody have taken your car?

Dale: Somebody, somebody could have taken my car.

D&K: It certainly appears to be your car, ya know.

Dale: But, it was not; well, I wouldn't have been driving it.

D&K: Okay, well then let's take a for instance here.

Dale: Terry, could have, well, I let Terry drive my car.

D&K: Terry Olson?

Dale: I always let him drive my car.

D&K: You didn't ever mention to me, of Terry going with you and Ron Michaels, it was you and Ron Michaels that left. Never any mention to me from Deb, or anyone else, that Terry went with you guys. It was just the two of you. All the information that we've read here and we have the likes of Deb and Jeff, they're all saying, well, where's Ron, (grabs the picture of Ron Michaels and puts it in front of Dale) well, that's him, you just looked at his picture. That's Ron Michaels.

Dale: That's Ron.

D&K: And he lived south of Montrose and unless this story is totally cooked up by everyone there and then that makes me real, real, suspicious that, what the hell is going on, what kind of cover up do they have going on here and for who? The information I just read to you, I mean, that's what we had to go on. It was what you said, and what Deb said, and what Jeff said. Ya know, that's all we can go on. But I was trying to figure out how did your car get out on County 12, in the wee hours of the morning, sitting there, with people outside the car? And it's right where, it's right where Jeff was found dead. That is what we're facing.

Dale: I'm sorry, but, I never, I never laid a hand on Jeff. And I'm not covering up for anybody.

D&K: Not saying you did. But you …

Dale: Not saying you did.

D&K: Let me read this, this is what we have. We got your car, we got the bat, we got the blood, we got the hair, we got all those things, we got the hockey sticks, we got all those things, my god, ya know the pieces there all align and then we come here today then they all get, ya know, sorted. Now, granted, it's twenty four years, but we're coming together here on this thing, but we still have the question of, who took your car then? If you didn't do it.

Dale: I swear to you guys, I did not do it. I didn't.

D&K: Well. What are you covering?

Dale: I didn't do it. And I'm not covering for anybody because I don't remember.

D&K: Did Terry do it?

Dale: If Terry did it, I would know. And I don't know. I'm sorry, I don't know.

D&K: Terry and Jeff had a fight at work.

Dale: Yup, and I don't know too much about it. Terry said something that he got cocky with him. And that was all I know.

D&K: You understand that perhaps.

Dale: No I understand, perhaps.

D&K: Let me finish my sentence please. That perhaps down the road, ya don't know now, but, perhaps down the road that some of the evidence gathered then may help us tremendously now.

Dale: No, I understand. And I hope they find the guy who did it, but I didn't.

D&K: What we're generally saying here is, there are more people involved. Because were finding more people are talking more and more.

Dale: Well, I understand that, and I want to help the best way I can, I can't, I can't remember it, um.

D&K: Ya know Dale, I could buy it, if you were if you were really drunk, if you were high on drugs, or both, I can understand this whole thing happened. Cause Jeff Hammill wasn't necessarily a pillar of the community, okay? He could get under your skin; we know that; he wasn't the best guy in the world. He would hit on other peoples girlfriends, other peoples wives, we know that, we know all that, and that I can see …

Dale: I didn't have a girlfriend then.

D&K: I can see where somebody might have wanted to teach him a lesson and hit him harder than they thought. I can see that. But you know the thing is, right now, unless we hear the story, we have to look at this as an intentional murder.

Dale: I understand.

D&K: I know that you had plenty to drink that night. I know

that Terry had plenty to drink that night and I know you guys were good buds back then.

Dale: Yeah, but we're not good buds now and I'm sticking up for him.

D&K: Something went wrong cause.

Dale: Something ended up going wrong, but, I was not involved in it. And I let Terry drive my car, ya know, I was a kid, ya know, I let him drive my car. Ya know, we partied together.

D&K: Do you think, do you think Terry did this? Think logically, just think logically.

Dale: Logically? With Terry's temper and stuff, yes, it could have been. But he, for one, he knows how to box, he knows how to hit a person, ya know.

D&K: So who else? Who was with him?

Dale: Terry knew more of Deb's friends than I did.

D&K: logically, I mean.

Dale: logically? Well, actually I thought it was his girlfriend. That could make sense, cause everybody saying they seen my car, but I don't remember ya know if I passed out, or, or what. I guess maybe what I'm trying to do is cover up myself to where, um, ya know, that I didn't want you guys to think that I was, ya know, a piece crap. And I'm not a piece of crap.

D&K: I don't think that, you're not today.

Dale: And I wasn't then, I wasn't back then either. I was a nice kid. I stayed out of fights, ya know, I was always trying to stay out of trouble.

D&K: So what went wrong?

Dale: Nothing went wrong. It's just that, anytime I was with Terry or something, he'd end up in a bar fight or something, ya know, and then all of sudden it's like, let's get out of here and I says okay, ya know that's all I know.

D&K: It's a pretty traumatic thing that happened.

Dale: Yes, it is.

D&K: It would be hard to give it up, if Terry, if you were there and with Terry, it'd be hard to give it up.

Dale: I'd give it up. I'm sorry. I have a family and stuff and I didn't do it. And if I knew who did it, I would give him up. I would, I would give them up, if I knew who it was, I would give them up. If it was Terry, I'd give him up. If it was that guy (points to picture of Ron Michaels), I'd give him up.

D&K: Even if you were there?

Dale: Even if I was there? I would have probably tried to stop it and then, yes, I would have gave him up. And you guys think, I mean be honest with me, you think I did it, didn't ya? And I didn't.

D&K: I guess to be honest with you, from the information we're getting and other people talking, I'm not saying you did, but I think you know more than you're telling us, to be honest with you.

Dale: I swear to you, I don't. I swear to you, I don't. If I know who did it I would turn him in. I swear to you, I would. Why would I want to go to prison? I don't want to go to prison.

D&K: Nobody does.

Dale: No, I mean it, I don't want to go to prison. I'm scared. I don't want to go to prison. I got a wife, a new wife and we're getting along great and trying to make a new living, ya know. I mean you could put me under hypnosis if you'd like to, if that would help. You can try anything you want. To get any information out of me you, you can. But, ah, I'm scared. Because now you're saying that, that Jeff's blood was on the bat. You're saying his hair was on the bat, ya know, my car was there and this and that and the only person I know that could have taken my car was Terry.

D&K: So it's possible then?

Dale: Yeah.

D&K: You car was out there?

Dale: It's possible, but, not from me. Yes my fingerprints, well it's my car, they'd be all over it, ya know, but.

D&K: Okay.

Dale: Because, I'm, I'm thinking that I'm being trapped into something that I didn't do.

D&K: There are no traps here Dale. There are no traps at all. All we are trying to do is to.

Dale: And ya know.

D&K: I can read the report to you.

Dale: I understand, but I'm confused and I'm scared and, uh, and my chest hurts.

D&K: Just, ya know relax and you'll probably think better.

Dale: I can't relax because I'm trying so hard to remember.

D&K: Dale, let me tell you something and it's something I tell a lot of people is, if you're telling the truth.

Dale: I'm telling the truth.

D&K: Okay, if you're telling the truth, let me finish, you've got nothing to worry about.

Dale: But that doesn't mean I'm not nervous.

D&K: You've got nothing to be nervous about, it's when you lie and you have to cover up those lies.

Dale: You're right.

D&K: Those are the things that gets you in trouble.

Dale: Okay.

D&K: And that's when you get screwed up because you can't remember, do you know, a person can only remember the truth. But you can't remember what lies you told, you know that right? You've probably experienced that, I don't think that's anything new, you've been around a bit.

Dale: Okay.

D&K: So if you don't lie, you don't have anything to worry about.

Dale: Okay.

D&K: And you can relax.

Dale: Okay.

D&K: And tell us the truth.

CHAPTER 6

The investigators continue to press Dale for details, asking him to repeat the events of the evening, comparing the previous version to the one being recounted. When he responds with "I don't remember", they caution him. "Don't get caught in the lies again, Dale. Ya know, settle down; you're telling the truth, okay?"

D&K: Ya know, I think something we need to overcome here, is your, your afraid right now.

Dale: Ah-um. If somebody is saying that I did, I did not hit Jeff.

D&K: Terry?

Dale: I don't think he did.

D&K: I understand, Denny's pointing out that, ya know, and, and it's very true, it's easier to tell the truth cause it's easier to remember and lies are tough to keep clearing your mind and you can see that when you're talking. When you're talking the truth you're nice and fluent and talking, when it gets to the foggy areas then you're bouncing around and having trouble and why is that do you think?

Dale: Cause I don't think I was there.

D&K: Well, another reason is because you're not telling the truth.

Dale: I am telling the truth.

D&K: Okay, I know, Denny has got us up to the point where, ya know, its crystal clear, right up to the point what happened to Hammill ya know, do you know what I mean?

Dale: Yeah.

D&K: And we know that there wasn't one person standing on the roadside. There was more than one person standing out there. These people could see them in their headlights.

Dale: I didn't do it.

D&K: I'm not saying you did it.

Dale: I didn't, I never, I didn't.

D&K: We're saying that now it's time to, you tell us every-thing you know. I think you're close. You're getting close. But, you're scared as hell. You said yourself, ya know, your Dad told you to stand up for the truth, ya know, be a man about it. It's been a living hell for years. Probably very few days go by you don't think about it.

Dale: I'm sorry, I don't remember. And if I did I would tell you.

D&K: So you're blanking out, what is a very important part of the evening, morning whichever. Because this the point in time when, when Jeff ends up dead, okay?

Dale: But I, I didn't touch him.

D&K: You blanked out, number one because it's convenient to do that and not remember. Is it because you're afraid to tell us the truth about what happened?

Dale: I'm not afraid to tell you the truth.

The interrogation continues to focus on who was in the car, who was driving the car and where were they going when they left the party.

Dale Todd cannot recall if he gave his keys to Terry to let him drive, if Ron Michaels was with them and if they went to look for Jeff Hammill or if they went to Ron Michaels home to listen to his new stereo.

The investigators repeatedly grill Dale for any motive for killing Jeff Hammill. They reiterate the way Jeff could agitate people, searching for an event that night that could have trig-gered an attack. Could they have tried to teach him a lesson only to have it go bad? They eventually change the topic to who left the party in Dales' car and when.

D&K: Well, was Jeff driving. Terry?

Dale: I think Terry was driving. And I believe after we had left Deb's house, I think Terry was driving when, I remember going over to somebody's house. We were at somebody else's house and that's all I remember.

(Dale picks up the picture of Ron Michaels and looks at it for a moment) And he does look familiar, but, I don't think his name was Ron.

D&K: What do you think it is?

Dale: I thought it was Steve.

D&K: Ya know Dale, we've, we've bridged a lot of territory here tonight and we've got this thing down to what I feel is the crucial time period here. And you are forgetting a time period in there, that is when Jeff was killed. That's where you are blacked out now, ah, you can't remember. I think you do remember some of it, Dale. I think you, ya know, people don't just black out. Even alcoholics; you remember bits and pieces and there's got to be some remembrance of something that happened then. We've given you the facts as we know them and laid them out to you. Jeff Hammill was with you guys earlier in the evening and then, you gave him a ride to Montrose.

Dale: That's where it's fuzzy, because I can't remember. I remember telling him I'd give him a ride home.

D&K: Yeah.

Dale: And then after that, I didn't even see him. I figured he had left.

D&K: Okay, if you were involved let me . . . .

Dale: I was not involved.

D&K: Yup

Dale: No, I'm not going to say I was involved.

D&K: If you were involved …

Dale: I'm not. There's no ifs. I was not involved, I'm not that type of person.

D&K: Put it this way.

Dale: Even if Jeff agitated me, I would say, Jeff walk home.

D&K: You were talking to Denny about things and you took a deep breathe and went through it again, telling the truth and I was believing you, okay. That's the point where we thought Terry was involved or maybe Terry did something. You kinda looked down, kinda long pause, you were thinking long and hard there.

Dale: Yeah, I'm trying to think of what it was.

D&K: I can tell just by your reaction.

Dale: I was just thinking, ya know, because I always let Terry drive my car. All the time. I was thinking when I was at home with my parents. I always let Terry drive my car. And my parents would get mad at me for it, ya know, letting him drive and drinking and stuff. I mean me and Terry; we were good friends, but not that good of friend to where I would let him kill somebody and me being involved in it.

D&K: If Terry said he was involved; would that make anything easier for you?

Dale: If Terry was involved then, then it's Terry's thing. Because that's the way Terry is cause, I mean, he beat the hell out of this one guy and I stopped him. And then I had to take the guy to the hospital, ya know. And he scared me, Terry scared me. And I was afraid that he was going to beat me up, ya know, if I said something wrong.

D&K: Ah-um.

Dale: Or, if I did something wrong, or if I wouldn't let him do something, ya know.

D&K: This happened back as a nineteen year old kid, Terry

did something and you were scared as hell and you mentioned your heart was just a pounding the next day.

Dale: No, that was Monday. And you said it happened on Saturday.

D&K: All right.

Dale: And I didn't know nothing about it. And then you go and you punch into work and you have two detectives that come in and, and ya know, accuse you. And I have no recollection of any of it.

D&K: Terry gets out of hand. He's hot tempered.

Dale: Yes. Terry makes some statements and drags me in the middle. Rigged me into something. I don't know cause we is drinking and smoking. I remember Terry grabbing something and ah,

D&K: Now your starting to make sense.

Dale: And I don't know if it was Jeff or not, I don't know. I don't know.

The interrogation now focuses on the involvement of the other two suspects, and how they might have killed Jeff. The detectives reassure Dale that they don't think he was involved other than being at the scene. They play back the events of that night as they see them, building the theory that Terry was mad at Jeff and wanted to go find him. They talk in 'possibilities' as in, it is possible that Terry did this and it is possible that Terry wanted to do this and could've done that. Then they tie Ron into the scene as a participant, again with the possibility that he did this or was there. Always playing down the intentional nature of the killing, making it seem accidental. Dale seems to be one question or so behind the detectives with his responses, always trying to remember , but then clear and positive with responses to questions he knows the answers to.

D&K: It makes sense now right? Kind of makes sense to you?

Dale: I don't know. Cause, Terry could be a great guy, and then all of sudden he'll just snap, and a lot of times it, he didn't care if it's a friend or whatever. You know. And I didn't have very many friends, really. I try to be friends with people. I didn't know Jeff, I didn't know him that well. They drag people in this crap and then, you know.

D&K: What do you think Terry would hit him with?

Dale: (whispering voice) I don't know.

D&K: Was it a tire iron? Jack? Hockey stick? Bat with blood on.

Dale: I don't know.

D&K: What do you think, honestly now, from the fact there's blood on the bat. I bet you, Terry ran through your mind.

Dale: What ran through my brain (whispering voice) what's the hell's going on … that's what. What the hell's going on. Yeah, what the hell's going on. I didn't …

D&K: We can understand the bat and the stuff in his trunk. I mean, Denny and I both played baseball and granted you can get cut but the odds are pretty slim on a nice … bat. You're a ball player, you know that. Somehow Terry smacked him with that bat.

Dale: Or something.

D&K: Trying to get him to shut up. You're scared of him right now.

Dale: I don't know.

D&K: I mean it's possible, it could come back to be Hammill's DNA on that bat. Could be his hair. Terry's a hot head, you're with him, you're drunk.

Dale: Depends what his mood is. My heart was racing so fast I was so scared. I'm scared now. But it's very possible Terry could have done it. I've seen him fight. I'm just ... very possible he could.

D&K: It's just very possible he did and he drug you along, to help him. Cause you was two hell raisers.

Dale: Well we've been pretty drunk, doing shit we wish we never, happened, you know. But no matter what you tell us, I keep telling ya, I don't know if he did it or not. That's what, puzzles me. When you get drunk and you do stupid, and I didn't try and I remember ... I can't have gave Terry my keys.

D&K: Did you ever stop in the middle of the road? Do you know?

Dale: Nope.

D&K: It happened when Terry was ... shaking somebody up? Stop on the road and slap him around?

Dale: No.

D&K: Did you go to find Jeff? You and Terry?

Dale: In fact, I think he did say that.

D&K: That's not a surprise.

Dale: That's not a surprise.

D&K: Yeah right. What was he mad about? "

Dale: He wanted a ride home.

D&K: Ah-huh.

Dale: And he was afraid that somebody was gonna beat him up.

D&K: Right. And you and Terry went to look for him. Does this ring a bell, is this coming back now? Cause he was walking on, County Road 12 on his way back to Buffalo. He was mad. Terry was probably mad and you got hooked right in your car, the whole thing.

Dale: ... yeah ...

D&K: No one intends for Jeff to be, dead. No one intended that probably. But, it happened.

Dale: Don't remember.

D&K: Cause this guy's been with you guys. (Detective shows the picture of Ron Michaels to Dale). He's a big guy, he's a strong guy. You have any recollection that way? Dale, we're just trying to bring this stuff back for you, you know.

Dale: I understand.

D&K: You know, if this … if you try …

Dale: Do you trust me?

D&K: yeah.

Dale: Do you trust me?

D&K: I trust the best for you, you, tell us everything you know. Yeah.

Dale: Looks so familiar (looking at Ron Michael's picture). Jeff you know, no matter what, he didn't deserve to die. Believe me.

D&K: Mm-mmm.

Dale: Nobody deserves to die. Not that way.

D&K: Nope. Do you know if it's coming back to you? I know it is. I know you want to tell us, but you don't know how to tell us. I know what happened. Even if it's bits and pieces of it. But you don't know how to tell us. I'm telling you, tonight you're walking out of here, you're going home and you're going over to your, probably beautiful wife, I don't know, but I'm sure she is.

I mean, you talked about her. You know, there's a right way to do things. I don't know what your involvement was. I know that he ends up dead. Okay. You told us everything right up to a point. And you, you just can't get over that … of when this happened. And you're holding back on that part of it. I don't know if you don't know how to tell us.

Dale: I would, but I don't know how to say it.

D&K: You want to ... we want to hear it from you. I don't want to hear it from him (pointing at the picture). I don't want to hear it from Terry.

Dale: But I just don't know how to tell you this.

D&K: we ... we don't want you to get nervous, cause we don't want to scare you. We want the best thing done. This is the time, Dale. This is the time to tell us ...

Dale: ... I understand ...

D&K: to tell your story, and the hell with the others. Don't ... don't let these guys, Terry and ah ... don't let them tell, and then make you the bad guy on this here too. I don't think you are a bad guy. I'll be truthful. I don't think.

Dale: ... No, I'm not.

D&K: I know you're not.

Dale: I couldn't kill anybody, I never hurt any ... never ...

D&K: ... never said you did. But you know, and you were there. And you know. I can tell. Kenny can, you know.

Dale: ... but wouldn't it be (crying) or ... I'm trying so hard.

D&K: Yeah. I know. I think Denny hit it on the head. Yeah. You know, you just don't know how to say it. How about take, more deep breaths again. You seem to do well with that. And just ...

Dale: ... can we go outside?

D&K: Sure.

Dale: Can I have a cigarette?

D&K: By all means. You can have a cigarette in here if you want.

Dale: You're not allowed to smoke in here. I don't have my cigarettes with me, they're in the car. Can you come with me?

D&K: We can sit here for a while. We can open the door for you though.

Dale: Is there anything to drink? Water or anything. Pop or …

D&K: Dale. You ready?

Dale: I don't know …

D&K: Why don't you sit down here, lets talk for five minutes, and then, you can go, we'll all have a break and, tell I us what happened. Okay?

Dale: I don't know, you know. I thought we were good guys. You know.

D&K: We know you're a good guy.

Dale: Terry didn't get in with us. Jeff, that night. And I think Terry did go after him.

D&K: Okay.

Dale: And I think that guy was in the car too.

D&K: And the point is …

Dale: That he was in the car too (pointing to Ron Michaels).

D&K: Okay. What happened? Tell us … step by step just what happened that night.

Dale: I don't know. All I knew is we got into a scuffle.

D&K: Where'd it happen?

Dale: Side of the road.

D&K: What road?

Dale: Hwy 12.

D&K: Who hit him in the scuffle?

Dale: I think Terry got mad at Jeff. And I was trying to fall, to go to sleep. I was trying to go to sleep. And I, and I think, this guy (pointing to Ron Michaels) was in the back seat and I was sitting in the passenger side.

D&K: So. Let me ask you … did you, did you guys go looking for him then?

Dale: I thought we were just gonna go look for him and give him a ride home.

D&K: Okay.

Dale: That's all I remember on that.

D&K: Alright. Was it just you three then? Terry, you and, we'll call him Ron, cause that's who we believe he is. Was it just three of you? Or was someone else with you?

Dale: I don't remember.

D&K: Let's talk about this couple then. What brought that on? (Holds Ron & Jeff's' pictures together)

Dale: Cause I think it was cause Jeff was mad, and he needed a ride home. Right away. Cause I had a flat tire. And then we were in the house, thinking about a way to get the tire fixed so we can give him a ride home. And then I think, that's when Jeff started dumping drinks on me or you know, pretended to dump drinks on me or something like that and, Terry got a little agitated, and that's when, um, Terry hit him. Got in this scuffle and took it outside. And then, broke that up. And then, I think, Jeff started walking home. And that's all I remember. And the scuffle was in front of the house.

D&K: You mentioned earlier along County Road 12.

Dale: We went looking down 12.

D&K: Okay. Did you find him then?

Dale: No. I don't think, no. Cause I can't remember if I was sleeping. All remember is dozing off and then I, put my head back down and I, I had the, you know, on the door part, like a couch.

D&K: Earlier you said, this guy was in the back seat.

Dale: Yeah. I think he was in the back seat.

D&K: You were in the front seat on the passenger side.

Dale: Mm-mm.

D&K: And Terry was driving?

Dale: Mm-mm.

D&K: So the three of you go looking for Jeff Hammill.

Dale: I wasn't looking for anybody.

D&K: No. But you were in the car.

Dale: ... in the car.

D&K: Terry's looking for Jeff Hammill then.

Dale: I figured we could find him on the road and then, give him a ride home. You know, since we got the tire fixed.

D&K: Now, you're thinking that.

Dale: Well, I'm thinking that.

D&K: What was Terry thinking. I mean you got ... Terry thinking, he was already hot. Truthfully now, who was driving?

Dale: Terry.

D&K: Understand you're going north towards Buffalo.

Dale: Yeah, he told us he lived in Buffalo. So, I think Terry was going towards Buffalo.

D&K: I don't want to put words in your mouth, ah. Is that correct?

Dale: I think I'll have a cigarette.

CHAPTER 7

After 4 hours of interrogation, Dale Todd is confused, scared and malleable. The detectives begin constructing the story they need Dale to recount. They help him tell the story. When he bucks them or stumbles on a detail, they bring him back to the sections where he feels comfortable; having him start over from there. When he can't remember a detail or location, they state it for him as 'fact', such as: 'we know this is true', or 'we're pretty sure that this is the case'. Eventually, these points are no longer questioned and become part of the 'truth' of that night. Dale now relents to their pressure. His answers become short and incomplete, mimicking the questions at times. The detectives start to indicate that time is running out and that they have to have Dale finish the story, filling in the blanks with the missing details. Dale starts to create possible scenarios. Maybe they hit a deer with the car; or it might have been Jeff they hit. Dale thinks he remembers puking along side the road between two swampy areas. He believes he saw Jeff Hammill dressed in an Army fatigue jacket. These details don't fit the story and are dismissed by the detectives. They have Dale start re-telling the story from a point where they have established repeatability. However, the motive for the murder is still not clear. The detectives try to convince Dale that it was Jeff Hammill that had spilled the drinks on Terry and him and that Terry was mad about that.

D&K: Why were you fighting so much that it was 'him' (Jeff Hammill) spilling drinks on you?

Dale: This guy had dark, black hair.

D&K: Do you know what Hammill was wearing that night?

Dale: Um. Army jacket, I think? He had an army jacket on? I think.

D&K: Just whatever you remember.

Dale: I think he wore this, this old jacket. It had his, had his name on it, Jeff H. I can't remember. But I know it was, it was like a green army fatigue jacket. And it was kind of cold, that night.

D&K: What was the fight over, between Jeff and Terry? What were they fighting for?

(Silence for approximately 21 seconds)

Dale: Cause I thought maybe it was cause he spilt a drink on his sister or somebody else.

D&K: So who else do you think knows about this?

Dale: I think he does (pointing at Ron Michaels).

D&K: Really? Who else has been told? Ever tell your wife?

Dale: Yeah. I told her about it when we met cause I didn't want to keep anything in the closet.

D&K: And so you told it to her before you were married?

Dale: Yeah, but I didn't.

D&K: What did you tell her?

Dale: I just told her that, this guy here got killed. And that um, I figured that I was a suspect, I guess. I told her that the detectives picked up my car and we sat all day, into the night, answering questions. And then ah, they let us go. Terry took the polygraph. And then they asked a few more questions. And after Terry, they asked me a bunch more questions while Terry was taking the polygraph.

D&K: Did you tell her everything that you told us?

Dale: No.

D&K: Did you tell her, what really happened to Jeff?

Dale: I just told her when we went to the funeral. You know, when we went to the funeral, Terry wasn't even surprised. I was so shocked. I mean, I was so shocked when I looked at him. His hands were bent.

D&K: Why do you think Terry wasn't surprised?

Dale: I don't know.

D&K: What were you logically thinking? You know, if I walked up and looked in the casket, and the guy's all beat to hell and it wouldn't surprise me? Do you think that maybe I knew that he was gonna look that way?

Dale: I think maybe he did, by his face expression. I says, God, I feel like puking. Terry said quit being a puss.

D&K: Which was it; Terry or Ron that got in the argument along the road? Or was it both? (hand on picture)

Dale: I don't remember what they were talking about.

D&K: You were stopping the car, or at least the car was stopping?

Dale: I remember the car stopping, cause I told Terry to stop cause I had to throw up.

D&K: Who all got out of the car?

Dale: I had the door open, and I was puking. Standing on the floor and I was puking over the side. I remember that. But I thought we were going home.

D&K: Is it possible that Jeff Hammill was walking along the road?

Dale: It's possible. Anything's possible.

D&K: You were in the front seat on the passenger side.

Dale: I think I was on the passenger side.

D&K: And Ron Michaels was in the backseat you think?

Dale: I think so.

D&K: Do you remember seeing Jeff?

Dale: Jeff doesn't even come into my head.

D&K: Do you remember seeing Jeff Hammill when you stopped the car?

Dale: No. No I don't. I don't remember Jeff, seeing Jeff.

D&K: What do you remember when the car stopped?

Dale: All I remember is I got out and I puked and then I went back into the car and shut the door.

D&K: Any others get out of the car?

Dale: I don't know. I remember gettin sick. And I remember hanging on to the door.

D&K: O.K. we're gonna get back talking about Terry and the fight with Jeff.

Dale: But I don't know if that was Jeff he was fighting.

D&K: He was fighting with somebody though.

Dale: He was fighting with somebody. It started in the house and then it all of a sudden it all went to ah, outside. And then, everybody was pushing. I think, Jeff and Deb, broke it up.

D&K: Jeff?

Dale: Debbie's boyfriend broke it up.

D&K: I think before the break we were right on the right path of doing all the right things here. I think we'll go back and just focus on that, I mean, you know. Dale, you were within minutes of resolving this whole thing, in your mind.

Dale: I don't know.

D&K: Dale, I think you know. You know what happened. And it's there, and getting back to the point is, you just don't know how to tell us. It's all there, I mean, when you want to tell us something you're sharp as a tack, you know. And, we don't think you're no dummy, and you're not a dummy. When you want to tell us something, it's there. You're no dummy.

Dale: No dummy.

D&K: You may have made a mistake, but you're no dummy.

Dale: I think I made a mistake but I didn't hit him.

D&K: We got to get back to the point where you know that Terry and you know that Ron probably was, and you know what happened. And it gets down to we want to hear it from you. I don't want to hear it from Ron. I don't want to hear it from Terry. Denny and I got only a little bit of a short time here.

Dale: I want to be sure.

D&K: We want to be sure too. We don't want anything but the truth.

Dale: Me too.

D&K: But. We keep going back and forth, I feel very confident you know what happened. You know darn well what happened. And, it's painful, but you know what happened. We're here to listen to it and work with you on it. We walk out of here and you leave very important information out, this looks bad. It looks bad later if, someone beats you to the punch. You know what happened. For God's sake. I know, it's got to be gut-wrenching to tell us. But, over a period of time here you've told us, more and more, you even got into that cloudy spot there, you know, we like to say the blank spot, what really happened to Jeff. You know what happened to him.

Dale: I think them guys beat him up.

D&K: Just tell us how.

Dale: I don't know how. I was scared.

D&K: Understandable. Just tell us what they did to him. Okay. Is it fair to say that at least Terry participated in beating up Hammill the night he was killed?

Dale: I think so. I think so (whispering).

D&K: And was it along County 12?

Dale. I think so (whispering).

D&K: And do you believe that the ...

Dale: I don't know why I was there.

D&K: Probably because it was your car and you were along for the ride. You think? I think you know exactly what happened. It's just too painful to tell us. We're here now though, and its important that you tell us now.

Dale: I want to be sure (whispering).

D&K: Tell us what you think is sure and then we'll work with that. Tell us what you think happened and then we'll work with the details. That sound fair? Sound reasonable to you?

Dale: Very reasonable. I mean the only question I have is, um, I'm just so scared. You know, every time I start getting scared then I start going blank.

D&K: Let's back up to where we were when you needed to take a smoke break. You know, remember where you're at then.

Dale: You're talking about, we were on 12.

D&K: Right. You were, at that point.

Dale: And I remember two swamps on each side of the road.

D&K: Alright. You remember...

Dale: And I remember hanging onto the door, throwing up. And I remember getting back into the car. And, when I looked around there was nobody there.

D&K: In the car. Okay. You were by yourself.

Dale: I was by myself.

D&K: Okay.

Dale: And a few minutes later, them guys got back in the car, and I asked them, I says, "What were you guys doing?" "We were taking a piss."

D&K: Them guys being who?

Dale: I think it was him and Terry (points to Ron Michaels).

D&K: You're saying him, you're referring to this photo of Ron Michaels.

Dale: I'm referring to the photo.

D&K: And this is Ron Michaels.

Dale: O.K. I wanted to be absolutely sure. Cause I remember Terry telling me - uh, this guy here telling me that they were taking a piss while I was losing my lunch and ah, and I was thinking Terry said "Can't hold your liquor, huh?" And I think I said, "No, I can't". So, you know, I asked 'em, I says 'what were you guys doing out there'? I says I thought we were going home or you said something about going to listen to your stereo. And they just said well, we were taking a piss. That's all I remember. And I said O.K. And that's it.

D&K: Dale, now, respectfully here, we've come a long way since we walked into this room. Would you agree with that? We've come a long way. And you've given bits and pieces. That's common. I think Denny and I see that quite a bit because bits and pieces come up, and you're doing that. That's fine, that's fine, hear me out, Dale. But you know we're keeping up that we're on County 12, your with Ron Michaels, you're with Terry, you're driving home, you're in your car, you acknowledge it's your car, your on Hwy 12, you acknowledge that you stopped there, you confirm that your car is out there, it's stopped, people around the car, you're puking. But now we're right down, that window is getting narrower and narrower and narrower. What, you know, getting up to what happened to Jeff, then you're taking a piss in there.

Dale: But the thing is, I didn't see Jeff.

D&K: O.K. Let's say you didn't see Jeff.

Dale: I mean it was really dark out and I didn't see Jeff.

D&K: Let's say you didn't see Jeff. People don't come back into a car after doing what happened to Jeff, and just said they took a piss. I think they would probably be more explicit than that and they talk about it. Every case I can think of, people want to get back and start yappin because they think they're bad asses.

Dale: I would say that was one thing about Terry. He'd never talk about how tough he was or how bad he was.

D&K: You understand we're getting down to the point where, the, the narrow point where Jeff ended up dying. O.K.? We're on 12. People are out of the car. It makes sense with all the witnesses that we have on the scene out there, it all makes sense now. But Jeff Hammill is dead. And he's laying on the road. And it didn't happen because someone pissed on him. (Silence for approximately 19 seconds) It didn't happen because somebody pissed on him. And you know what? It didn't happen because somebody punched him either. Something was used to smack him. And that you don't forget. It's right in the headlights. It's right there in the headlights.

D&K: Dale, did you hit him?

Dale: No.

D&K: Who did?

Dale: I'm not sure (whispering).

D&K: Tell us what you think. Tell us what you're thinking.

Dale: What I think?

D&K: Yep.

Dale: Or what I know?

D&K: What you know. I want to hear, Kenny wants to hear, what you know.

Dale: What's your name?

D&K: I'm Denny.

Dale: Oh.

D&K: We're right there right along the side of the road right now. This happened to you, and, you know. You were drunk, but you still know. Things like that don't, they don't just escape us. You wouldn't show us all the emotion you show us, if you didn't know what happened to Hammill. You want to do the right thing.

Dale: The right thing.

D&K: Yeah. Dale, the right thing, we talked about that earlier this evening. How about this. Tell us what they did to him, what they hit him with. That much we know. (Long pause) Was it a jack? Hockey stick? Bat? Or a combination. I guess the bat would make sense if there's blood on it, huh? You tell us. We can't help you until you talk to us about it. You need to control this. (Long pause) You ready?

Dale: (Dale picks up picture) I think it was him. (Shows picture of Ron Michaels) I think he hit him with a bat.

D&K: Baseball bat?

Dale: It was something; I don't know what. Hit with baseball bat (crying).

D&K: Where'd they get it from?

Dale: There was only one bat in my trunk. And that was a wooden bat. It was an older, wooden bat. Stood roughly about this tall. The bat. I think it was a softball bat. An old wooden softball bat. And I remember when we got over to this guy's house, cranked up the stereo (silence for approximately 22 seconds hand on picture).

D&K: And...

Dale: And I think Terry got mad at him, cause the music was way too loud. He said that stereo was cranked up as loud as you can. And then they, they just sat there and talked, him and Terry talked, about ah...

D&K: Is that before or after he killed Jeff?

Dale: After.

D&K: Could it have been a hockey stick? Or do you think it was the bat?

Dale: I'm not sure if there was a hockey stick in the trunk.

D&K: O.K. I thought you mentioned it earlier, that's the only reason I bring that up.

Dale: And I thought there were some hockey skates, some old CCM hockey skates in the trunk.

D&K: Put it this way, could they get rid of anything they used?

Dale: I don't' know. (whispering)

D&K: How many times did Terry hit him?

Dale: (no response)

D&K: Did -Terry -hit- Jeff?

Dale: I think Terry hit him with his fist.

D&K: Where were you sitting, or standing, where were you at when you saw this?

Dale: Front seat.

D&K: And they were in the front headlights?

Dale: I think they were off to the side.

D&K: Could you see without the lights?

Dale: Not really.

D&K: But you saw Ron hit Jeff with an object?

Dale: I think so. That's, what puzzles me, I, I can't be sure.

D&K: Was there anybody else out there.

Dale: There was a scuffle.

D&K: O.K.

Dale: But I'm not saying they did it, or, I just can't remember. But I don't want them saying I did, because I know I didn't do it. I was incoherent. Most of that night is just a blur. You know, incoherent.

D&K: Dale, was there anybody else besides Ron Michaels and Terry out along side the road on County 12 in front of your car that evening? That, so in other words, it couldn't have been anybody else besides Terry or Ron, that killed Jeff Hammill, is that true?

Dale: (Pause) I'm not even sure, being totally honest, I'm not really sure we were on 12. I remember there was a swamp on each side of the road. And I remember hanging onto the door.

D&K: Do you remember someone hitting Jeff Hammill?

Dale: I'm not sure, it's beginning to, you know, the fight at home. I'm not sure if it was Jeff Hammill or that other guy.

D&K: O.K. Let's forget...

Dale: I'm not sure, I'm not sure if it was, I'm not sure if it was Jeff, cause I thought Jeff was, the last time I seen Jeff he was sittin in the corner.

D&K: Go back to our window there, out along side the road. I think that's what matters. Let's just stay there, along the road, you're in the front seat.

Dale: And I don't want to lie.

D&K: I don't want you to lie and I don't want you to make up anything either.

Dale: I'm trying, I don't want to make nothin up either.

D&K: All we want, Dale, is what you remember, and, these little bits and pieces that are coming out. That is of your own memory, correct?

(Dale nodding)

D&K: O.K., you're saying yes. O.K. You remember this guy, and we'll tell you his name is, Ron Michaels. This guy, you saw him hit Jeff Hammill.

Dale: I think it was him.

D&K: You saw Terry hit Jeff Hammill. (Pause) Now I'm talking along the road. (Pause) Let me go a little further. Do you remember anybody opening the trunk up?

Dale: No.

D&K: How did your trunk open in that car? Did you have to use a key to open it? Or could you open it from inside?

Dale: You had to use a screwdriver.

D&K: Who took that screwdriver to open the trunk? (Pause) Did you?

Dale: No. (Pause)

D&K: Terry.

Dale: Could a been.

D&K: Then I'll ask you again, and I asked you before, do you remember somebody going to open the trunk?

Dale: No. Cause I had a light in my trunk. When you popped it open the light would come on.

D&K: Do you remember seeing that light on?

Dale: I don't remember seeing the light on.

D&K: Were you outside the car?

Dale: I was outside the car when I was throwing up.

D&K: Are you saying that someone got the bat out prior to, then? Like it was planned? Would it work better if, Dale, if we just work backwards from the time you were going over to listen to this guy's stereo music? Would that work better for you to recall? Think of that and where you were just before you went over to his house.

Dale: We were over at his house and they were talking about stereo how cool it was. I think he told me to sit so I wouldn't fall into anything. And I don't think we were there for maybe 20 minutes. Cause I think I wanted to go home.

D&K: O.K. Let's go backwards. You went over to listen to the stereo music after Jeff was killed. Is that correct? Dale?

Dale: (whispering)

D&K: What, what's, what's your biggest fear at this point? What's your biggest fear in life?

Dale: Going to jail for nothing, for something I didn't do.

D&K: That's why you need to work with us. Like, like I told you before, Dale, you get to the point and, you just like, 'I don't want to say shit'.

Dale: My mind goes blank. I can sit here and say, well, you know, I can say what you want me to say and say, you know, it was Terry and him.

D&K: We don't want you to do that. We don't want that.

Dale: You know, and I, and I don't think that's justice. I think it's, I guess you know, I'm not holding, I'm not trying to hold anything back.

D&K: We're just trying to understand.

Dale: And I'm, that's why I'm emotional. I'm, right down to when I'm emotional. I mean I, sometimes I can watch a movie and, and tears are running down my eyes, you know. Or, I can sit there. I think about stupid things. My wife leaving me or, you know, or having an affair with somebody.

D&K: Dale, is the hard part of this just trying to keep yourself distant from this whole thing so you don't go to jail like you said? Is that the hard part here?

Dale: No it's not the hard part. It's one of the parts. It's one of the parts.

D&K: Did you tell your wife that you're going to jail?

Dale: Yeah.

D&K: Why would you go to jail? Why would you tell her that?

Dale: Well, from the first investigation, you know, I was so scared. I mean I told her that this was the scariest thing in my life.

D&K: But we've told you all along tonight that tonight you're not going to jail. Do you trust us on that? I mean, we'd let you walk out to your truck, you could have driven away.

Dale: I want to be cooperative

D&K: Dale, you are.

Dale: And I had a nervous breakdown before and stuff due to the fact of my divorce and stuff.

D&K: Like Denny said before, if you tell the truth, there's no reason to be nervous. Even if you're involved in this, now is the time to let us know, so we can work with you.

Dale: To my knowledge I am.

D&K: O.K. What killed Jeff Hammill? (Silence for approximately 19 seconds) O.K. Dale, we're running out of time. It's time. Who killed Jeff Hammill?

Dale: (Silence for approximately 21 seconds) I want to be right (whispering).

D&K: Who killed Jeff?

Dale: I think it was him (pointing to Ron Michaels).

D&K: You're pointing to Ron Michaels. Who helped kill Jeff Hammill?

Dale: (Silence for approximately 14 seconds) I think it was Terry.

D&K: Terry?

Dale: I think it was him and Terry. I didn't help him.

D&K: Is that what's creating all the pain for you? You regret you didn't do anything? Is that it, Dale?

Dale: Yeah. Cause I think they were beatin him up and I didn't think they were gonna, and I don't think they meant to kill him.

D&K: I don't think that either. Don't beat yourself up cause you didn't do anything.

Dale: I should of did something. I was a puss. I was a puss, I should of did something. That's why I, why I got sick.

D&K: You got sick afterwards, you saw what they did to him.

Dale: I didn't!

D&K: You got sick when you saw him in the coffin. Again, I'm not trying to put words in your mouth. You saw these two beat up Jeff Hammill and you didn't do any thing. And that's what's causing this. Is that correct?

Dale: I think so. I think so.

D&K: Did you look at Jeff' body?

Dale: Yeah.

D&K: Where was it?

Dale: It was in the coffin.

D&K: No, out on the road I'm talking about.

Dale: I can see his coffin.

D&K: How about out on County Road 12. Did you look at him there?

Dale: No.

D&K: Did you see where he was laying?

Dale: No.

D&K: You're there now, Dale. You're right there.

Dale: I don't want to be.

D&K: You're right there. Did they know they killed him?

Dale: No.

D&K: What makes you say that?

Dale: Cause I think Ron was all wound up. You know, how somebody gets wound up?

D&K: What do you mean wound up?

Dale: He was wound up.

D&K: Like, high?

Dale: Yeah. He was wound up and then that's when we were at his house and that's when the stereo got cranked, they cranked the stereo and, stuff.

D&K: Did you talk about it, afterwards?

Dale: I think, I asked em; I'm thinking maybe we should go check and see if, see if he needs help.

D&K: Who said that?

Dale: Me.

D&K: And what did they say?

Dale: They didn't say anything.

D&K: Did you ever go back?

Dale: No.

D&K: Did you drive that road after you left Ron's house?

Dale: No. I don't remember if we did or not. Just little pictures come in my mind and I can't tell what they are.

D&K: When you're, sitting there and you're thinking I should be doing something and watching these two. Did Jeff say anything? How did they approach him? Was he standing up?

Dale: God (whispering).

D&K: Was there some yelling going on?

Dale: There was some yelling going on.

D&K: O.K.

Dale: They were yelling at each other.

D&K: Who was yelling?

Dale: And I think that's when Terry popped him.

D&K: With what?

Dale: His fist.

D&K: Where at?

Dale: I think on the side of the face.

D&K: O.K. Then what?

Dale: Then I just put my head on the dash, and I said. Oh God!

D&K: It would take more than one punch in the face. You been around a few bars.

Dale: This was not a bar fight. I seen Terry hit a guy and split him from one end to the next.

D&K: O.K., but did you see him hit with something else?

Dale: I can't remember. The only person who comes to my head is him (pointing at Ron's picture).

D&K: O.K., how did he hit, Jeff?

Dale: I think he hit him with a baseball bat.

D&K: You still were in the car?

Dale: I was in the car.

D&K: When was this all taking place?

Dale: Off on the side of the road.

D&K: Where was the car parked?

Dale: On the side of the road. The lights were off. All you could see was the dome light.

D&K: And why were they fighting?

Dale: I don't know.

D&K: What did you talk about afterwards?

Dale: (silence)

D&K: And why were they so ticked at him? I mean, you just don't club or thump on somebody for any reason.

Dale: Because he wanted to fight me. And I didn't want to fight anybody.

D&K: So Hammill wanted to fight you early on and Terry was doing the protective thing?

Dale: I think Terry was doing the protective thing.

D&K: And I don't mean to go back and beat a dead horse here, but, that seemed to really bother you early on.

Dale: Yeah, cause some guy was dumping drinks on me.

D&K: Was it Jeff or wasn't it? Yes or no?

Dale: No.

D&K: O.K. Was there a fight outside the house?

Dale: Yes.

D&K: Who was in that fight?

Dale: It was Terry.

D&K: Terry Olson?

Dale: Mmhmm. And one of the guys that was in the house.

D&K: Was it Jeff Hammill?

Dale: I don't think it was Jeff.

D&K: Is it safe to say that Terry was in some kind of an ugly mood this evening? Did he get into a fight out in Rockford too?

Dale: Yeah.

D&K: O.K. He gets in a fight in Rockford. He gets into a fight out in front of the house, down in, in Montrose. And he gets into a fight along County Road 12. That's three we know of.

Dale: Two you knew.

D&K: Huh?

Dale: The two you knew.

D&K: Two we knew. What do you mean?

Dale: I mean you said that you knew Terry was in a fight that night, and you knew Terry was in a fight over at his sister's.

D&K: Well, you told us about that. At his sister's. And then the third one is along County Road 12 when he gets into a fight with Jeff Hammill.

Dale: I think so.

D&K: But, Dale, you gotta know so, you gotta know so.

D&K: Well who else would it have been! (standing arms outstretched)

Dale: That's the problem. I'm trying to remember that guy.

D&K: Which guy? The one at the house?

Dale: The one at the house.

D&K: You know what, don't even worry about that. The point of the matter is, is that Terry got into a fight there. Don't worry about who that was. Now, we're along County Road 12, and you know what? That's really what we're all here about tonight, is what happened there along County Road 12. You know, Dale, it's, when you're talking about a period of time of probably minutes, maybe even less than minutes, we're talking maybe even seconds, when, the very importantist thing that ever probably happened in your life and certainly the most important thing that's ever happened in Jeff Hammill's life, happened. And so it appears that we've got Ron Michaels and Terry Olson and this becoming the most important event in their whole lives, and it's all happening in a matter of a few seconds or minutes. And that's what's so important here tonight, is that we get this right and that we don't try to protect anyone. What you need to do and like you said earlier, is just, 'I want to tell you but I don't know how'. You know what? Now is the time. It's time to tell us the story and it's only a few seconds or a few minutes, to tell, because - you know what? The rest of it, where it's very important, but the very most important part of this whole thing is what happened along County Road 12 when Jeff Hammill ended up dead? Whether it was meant to be, you know, or whether it was drunken … stupidity, which it probably is going to turn out to be. But, if there was a fight and somebody picked up a weapon, whether it be a club, a bat, ah, a ah, a hockey stick, a jack, you know what? The important part is that Jeff is dead. And which one of those instruments, that's the part that we need to know now and that you need to get off your mind before you go entirely crazy with this whole thing.

D&K: Straight up, black and white.

D&K: Yeah. We're not going to jump around anymore. We're going to focus on that, on those few minutes. And once we get that done, then you know what? You're going to feel a ton of relief and we can talk some more. You know what? I think you can do it. Dale. There's a whole bunch of people counting on you right now. Jeff Hammill's mother is one.

Dale: I'm counting on myself.

D&K: And we're counting on you. Let's get this thing ended and let's get the whole story out. If it's about protecting yourself, well you know what? That truth, that incident will come out anyway. It's a matter of let's just hear it straight out and, you know what? If it so happens that somewhere down the line you do get turned to something, if you were involved, and to the extent that you should be charged, well, you know what? It's going to happen anyhow. It's going to happen anyhow. You know what? It's going to be a whole lot better, for you, standing up to, and saying look, this is what happened and this is what my involvement was, I was drunk, and I was stupid. I did a stupid thing. If that's what it does, that you need to tell us. I can't, Kenny can't, because we weren't there. We weren't there. Are you ready?

(Long pause) You know, we've got a lot of bits and pieces, Dale, and, you know there aren't that many pieces left to put together in this whole puzzle, so we can paint the whole picture. Do you understand what I'm saying, Dale?

Dale: I understand what you're saying. I understand what you're saying.

D&K: It's time for you to step up to the plate. You're 43 now, you're not a 19 year old. You know, even your wife. Your wife's counting on you, and supporting you. You know what? She's going to continue to support you if you step up and do the right thing. And she has apparently faith in you to do the right thing. How many wives would do that? Step up and tell them the truth. There's something to be said for that. Let's do it. Let's start. Let's start with what Jeff was doing when you first saw him along the road.

Dale Todd once again repeats the entire story from the beginning as he remembers it, through the trip to Deb's house, the party, spilled drinks, a scuffle in the yard.

Dale: Then um, then Jeff Hammill and Terry got into a little argument about Jeff naggin at him, naggin at us to give him a ride home. And um, I said somethin to Jeff about well, 'Jeff I'm sorry, but you know, I'm kind of drunk and stuff and do you think it would be, you know'? He got mad at me and said well, 'f...you' and that's when Terry grabbed him, and um, and then I think this guy was behind Terry. Ron, Ron you guys keep telling me it was Ron. Then I remember Jeff leavin, said he was going to hitchhike home. Then I remember Ron saying well, let's go over to my house and listen to the stereo. I said well that's kind of cool. You know. And then I'm not sure which direction and stuff we were going, but I remember stopping in the road and throwing up, and I remember hanging onto the door and I remember there was a swamp here and there was a swamp over on this side of the road. And then, I heard some yelling. Looked up. Then Terry got out and then the Ron guy got out. And all I remember is hanging my head, you know, like into a toilet you know, and ah, that's when I start getting all these bits and pieces, just vaguely in my head. The car was sittin here. I think them guys were down a small incline. I think they were down here. And then there was small incline, and there was a swamp there. And then um, that's when I think I, I, I, I see Terry hittin somebody and this guy here (pointing at Ron Michaels' picture) had something in his hand. And I'm not sure if it was the baseball bat or a tire iron or a jack or whatever. And then when he came back into the car, I'm saying well what the hell's going on? And then um, Ron started laughin. I said what's so funny? You know. And he just told me to shut up. And then um, that's, when I turned over and I asked Terry, I said what's going on? Because I'm pretty drunk. I says, what's going on? And um, he didn't say, he didn't say too much either. He just said that he, he beat up, somebody. And I says who? And he just, he started laughin. And I says, who did you beat up? And he said Jeff. And I said why? I says we were supposed to give him a ride home. And he says well, we don't have to. He can walk home now, he said. And then he turned the car around and we left. I'm not sure if it was his mom's house or if it was my house, but then come Monday there was two detectives. And then Wednesday they talked to us and I said what I said there, you know cause I asked Terry, I said what are we gonna do? He said well, just what you remember and I says, well not a whole lot, you know. And he said well, we did this, we did that and say this, say that. And then Tuesday was his funeral, and I told Terry, 'well I think we should go to his funeral', I says. 'We can represent his work.' You know, because we did know him. You know, we did know him. And then Wednesday they had the place surrounded and we were taking lie detectors and stuff you know and then sent home and then I never heard another word about it."

D&K: What did Terry tell you to say when you were asked questions by the police?

Dale: Well, I told Terry, I says, I was too drunk, you know. He said don't worry about it. And he says, well you know you were at the bar right? And I says, ya.

D&K: Did Terry tell you what happened?

Dale: No.

D&K: Did Ron ever get in the picture as far as coming up with an alibi?

Dale: No. There was nothin else said to us. Not until today, from you two.

D&K: What made you decide to tell us the truth?

Dale: I fell in love with a heavenly angel who's scared, really scared. I know, for a fact, I didn't throw one punch, I didn't hit him with nothin, I was too drunk. I couldn't even, I could barely pick myself up. You know. And ah, that's all I recall. And I'm sorry, I can't give you a weapon, I just. This, this guy here comes into my head to where he's swinging something. And that's all I got. And I could be wrong, you know, but, but in my mind, in my heart, I know I had nothin to do with his beating.

D&K: But in your mind, you know who is responsible for Jeff Hammill's death.

Dale: In my mind, I'm thinking Terry and Ron.

D&K: Are there any other possibilities in your mind?

Dale: There is a couple, but that's relative to what, you know you're talking to me about.

D&K: Let me clarify that, please, O.K.? I mean, it's been a long night, but, I guess what I don't understand is, if you see Terry and Ron assaulting Jeff Hammill and Terry comes in and says he beat up Jeff Hammill, and that's where Jeff Hammill is found dead, I guess in my mind, it's Terry and Ron.

Dale: Well I, I think it is Terry and Ron. I'm scared. Because I know, I know what Terry can do. But I don't know this guy very well and I, I don't know what he's capable of. But back then, when I knew Terry, Terry was a good fighter. I mean he took shit from nobody and he, he could make his point clear.

D&K: O.K., is there any doubt as to the location where this happened, this fight?

Dale: There, there, there was a little bit of doubt in my mind, yes.

D&K: Well, we're not trying to get you sidetracked to something else, so what I'm saying is can you be absolutely sure?

Dale: No, I cannot be absolutely sure.

D&K: Your last version there, was that a true, accurate description of what happened that you gave, to the best of your knowledge?

Dale: To, for the state I was, I think so.

D&K: You can't beat yourself up for hind sight, you know.

Dale: Yeah, but I do. I mean, why didn't I stop em? Why didn't they hurt me? Cause I have no involvement with Jeff Hammill's … you might think I do, but I didn't. The only thing I could be guilty of is not helping him. If these two guys did it, then I'm guilty of not helping him and that's just as bad as if I was there, if I did it myself, to me.

D&K: Do you feel bad about not telling the police right away what you?

Dale: Yes. Because it's back in my face. And what comes around goes around, I guess. You know. You lie, like you two were saying, you lie and it's gonna come right back to your face. You know. Like you two were saying. Correct?

D&K: There's some truth to that in there. Well, we appreciate your ah, at the end, honesty here and ah, do you have any more questions, Denny? Well, thanks Dale for your presence here tonight. Do you want to take this with? We put our names on there if you want them.

Dale: Yeah.

D&K: What I was starting to ask you is what you told us tonight, would you be willing to testify?

Dale: To the best of my ability, yeah.

D&K: O.K. That's all we can ever ask. And just based on the last few statements you made, you told us are based on fact not any ah, previous issues …

Dale: Issues.

D&K: Issues, but you're not telling us this just because you're pissed off at Terry, are you?

Dale: No.

D&K: O.K. I wanted to make sure of that. Did we force you?

Dale: Terry is Terry.

D&K: O.K. Did we.

Dale: Like I said, I'm 43 years old and I don't care what he does.

D&K: O.K.

Dale: And ah, if I see him that's what I'm gonna say to him.

D&K: Dale, did we force you in any way to make a statement?

Dale: No. I went all by myself. I don't know whether or not I should ask for a lawyer or anything like that, but, um.

D&K: Did we make any promises?

Dale: Yeah, you did.

D&K: What was that?

Dale: You said I could go home.

D&K: Do you want to go home?

Dale: I want to go home.

D&K: We do too.

Dale: And if I can think of anything, I'll give you a call.

D&K: Sure.

Dale: But I think I better go, I think I better go see a shrink or something.

D&K: That might not be a bad idea.

Dale: Cause I been on these pills for quite a long time. When I'm off them now I can start really feeling the stress.

D&K: Say, Dale, when we asked you earlier, and you said, have you told anybody else, you know, what you told us today? I mean the whole story?

Dale: No.

D&K: Even bits and pieces to anybody?

Dale: The only body I told was my wife.

D&K: Did the Segler's lie? Were they in on this? Were they part of it? Like Deb Segler, and Jeff?

Dale: Deb, Deb is a strong girl.

D&K: Was she in on it or.

Dale: And she'll do anything to protect her brother.

D&K: O.K.

Dale: Put it that way.

D&K: Alright. Jeff Cardinal.

Dale: Jeff, Jeff will go with the ride, because he's in love with Deb.

D&K: Jeff.

Dale: Jeff was a quiet person.

D&K: Do these people know? What do you think, yes or no?

Dale: I think they might.

The agents tell Dale they want to speak with him again the next day. Dale goes home. The next morning, he contacts a lawyer who tells him not to return to the police department and answer anymore questions. Dale calls the police department and tries to talk to either Ken McDonald or Dennis Fier, but neither are available. He leaves them a message that he won't be showing up that day, and why. The agents find him later that day and pull him over. Agent Ken McDonald gets out of his car and walks up to Dale's truck. Dale explains to him what his lawyer told him to do. Ken gets mad and slams his hands down on Dale's truck and shouts "You're going to jail for 25 years!"

CHAPTER 8

False Confessions by Adults

From an article published in the magazine *Justice Denied*
(Authored by Bruce A. Robinson)

Police use of bright lights, rubber hoses and other physical methods to extract confessions was once common in North America. Court decisions since that time have rendered such confessions inadmissible, leading to the abandonment of these techniques. Trial judges have even rejected confessions obtained through threats of long sentences or promises of short sentences. Police now generally use psychological pressures, which may well be more effective.

- Some modern methods include:
- Feigned sympathy and friendship.
- Appeals to God and religion.
- Blaming the victim or an accomplice.
- Placing the suspect in a soundproof, starkly furnished room.
- Approaching the suspect too closely for comfort.
- Overstating or understating the seriousness of the offense and the magnitude of the charges.
- Presenting exaggerated claims about the evidence.
- Falsely claiming that another person has already confessed and implicated the suspect.
- Other forms of trickery and deception.
- Wearing a person down by a very long interview session.

The result is that some individuals confess to crimes they

did not do. Sometimes they even grow to believe that they are guilty.

Some police departments use a 1985 book, "*Criminal Interrogation and Confessions,*" as a reference. It recommends isolating the suspect, and involving the suspect in possible crime scenarios. "*An innocent person will remain steadfast in denying guilt.*"

Saul M. Kassin, professor of Psychology at Williams College, is a leading researcher into false confessions. He divides them into three categories:

Voluntary, involving no external pressure.

"Coerced-compliant" in which the person realizes he is not guilty but confesses to the crime to receive a promised reward or avoid an adverse penalty.

"Coerced-internalized" in which an innocent suspect is induced to believe he or she is guilty.

Police and courts often doubt that the second two cases actually exist.

Lab experiment

Dr. Kassin and his student, Catherine L. Kiechel, designed a lab experiment demonstrating how innocent people can be led to a false confession, to the point that some may even become convinced they are guilty. In the study, college students were asked to type letters on a keyboard as a researcher pronounced them. Some researchers read out the letters quickly (67 per minute), others slowly (47 per minute). The subjects were warned to not touch the ALT key, because a bug in the testing program would cause the computer to crash and lose all the data. One minute into the test, the computer was manually caused to crash. In half the tests, the researchers said they had actually seen the subject depressing the ALT key. At first, the subjects correctly denied hitting the key. The researcher then hand-wrote a confession and asked the subjects to sign it. The penalty would be an angry telephone call to the subject by Dr. Kassin. One hundred per cent of the subjects who had typed the letters quickly, and who were told by the researcher that they had been observed hitting the ALT key, signed the confession; 65% of the subjects believed they were guilty; 35% even confabulated non-existent details to fit their beliefs. Overall, 69% signed the note and 28% believed they were actually guilty.

Suspects who are developmentally handicapped

Richard Ofshe, a sociologist at the University of California, Berkeley has researched the effects of interrogation techniques. He said, "Mentally retarded people get through life by being accommodating whenever there is a disagreement. They've learned that they are often wrong; for them, agreeing is a way of surviving." Obtaining a confession from such people "is like taking candy from a baby." Florida lawyer Delores Norley has trained police in 30 states to handle interviews of developmentally handicapped suspects. She says they often have "an excessive desire to please ... This is especially true with authority figures." She and her colleagues are currently aware of some 100 cases of possibly false confessions by impaired defendants.

Pioneering studies by Gisli Gudjonsson

Gisli Gudjonsson is a professor of forensic psychology at the Institute of Psychiatry in London, England. He and Dr. James MacKeith conducted pioneering research into how people might be induced to make "confessions" to crimes they hadn't committed. According to the Guardian newspaper:

> "He identified a range of important emotional and psychological factors, such as compliance, suggestibility and personality disorders that had been ignored through the entire history of criminal justice. This led him to produce the *Gudjonsson Suggestibility Scales* (GSS), which are now used throughout the world when the issue of false confessions arises."

Gudjonsson said:

"It used to be thought that people only made false confessions if they were mentally defective or suffering from severe
learning disabilities. But that's not the case. Most of the
vulnerabilities have nothing to do with intelligence. In the
cases I looked at, the people were pretty ordinary and their
intellectual functioning wasn't of much relevance. Personality
characteristics are more significant."

The studies have produced major changes in police behavior.
Gudjonsson said:

"There has been a tremendous improvement both in terms of
the interviewing, which is less aggressive and coercive, and
in terms of the quality of information obtained. The Metropolitan Police came to me for advice. They've accepted that
mistakes have been made, and have wanted to learn from
those mistakes. I think that's quite remarkable - you don't see
that in any other country... [Police in] Some countries say,
'We never have a false confession - that's just something that
happens in England.' A police officer in Canada said to me,
'We're 100% sure in (this) confession. We know when people
are telling the truth or not, we can tell by the non-verbal
signs.' In that case, DNA evidence completely exonerated the
man and pointed to someone else."

Some examples of apparently false confessions

Illinois: In 1979, Girvies Davis, aged 20, confessed to 11 crimes,
including the murder of an 89-year-old man in Belleville, IL.
Davis was an alcoholic with a childhood history of brain damage and suicide attempts. During his teen years, he was diagnosed with organic brain dysfunction, which doctors believe was
induced by a bicycle accident when he was 10 years old. They
believe he fell within the "borderline range of intelligence."
There was absolutely no evidence linking him to the murder
other than the confession. Police say he freely gave the confes-

sion; Davis says it was coerced. The State of Illinois executed him on 1995-MAY-18.

Arkansas: The confession of Jessie Misskelley, Jr., convicted of participating in the sex-murders of three boys in West Memphis, AR, in 1993, may well be false. He was 17 years old at the time of the confession, and has an IQ of 72 (vs. a normal value of 100). After the trial was concluded, an independent investigator studied autopsy photographs. He found images of bite marks on the face of one of the murder victims. Their pattern did not match Misskelley's teeth or those of the other two teenagers who were also convicted of the murders. One of the latter is on death row. Although a polygraph test indicated his innocence, Misskelley was interrogated for over 5 hours. He retracted his confession afterwards, claiming that he had caved in under police pressure. He pleaded not guilty at trial. An expert testified at the trial that Jessie was a prime candidate for a false confession because of his young age and low IQ. The Arkansas Supreme Court, in its ruling in this Memphis case, outlined some of its criteria for determining the accuracy of the confession:

The "voluntariness" is judged on the basis of many factors, including: "the age, education and intelligence of the accused, the advice or lack of advice on constitutional rights, the length of detention, the repeated or prolonged nature of questioning, or the use of mental or physical punishment."

Confessions while in custody are assumed to be involuntary, and the burden is on the State to show that the confession was voluntarily made.

"A confession obtained through a false promise of reward or leniency is invalid"

"Youth alone [is] not sufficient to exclude confession."

A "low intelligence quotient alone will not render confession involuntary."

"Between the first time appellant was advised of his rights

and the time he gave his first statement, a period of just over four hours elapsed, which was not undue ..."

"The police may use some psychological tactics in eliciting a custodial statement."

" ...where a person under age eighteen is charged as an adult in circuit court, failure to obtain a parent's signature on a waiver form does not render a confession inadmissible.

The following is courtesy of the Minneapolis Star & Tribune. The Metro article, (written by Bill McAuliffe and dated November 9, 2006) quotes U of M Criminal law Professor Richard Frase regarding 'incentivizing of public officials in their law enforcement decisions'.

Richard Frase, a professor of criminal law at the University of Minnesota, said because cold cases are difficult, they invite incentives and rewards. But he added, "Anytime you have private parties incentivizing public officials in their law enforcement decisions, you have to at least wonder if those decisions are being distorted in some way," Frase said. "That's not to say you shouldn't have cold-case units, but there are warm ones that also could use more resources and are often less problematic."

Spotlight on Crime is a non-profit organization that offers monetary rewards for information in cold cases. An advisory board made up of law enforcement, victim's advocates and the business community use selected criteria to determine whether a reward will be offered in a particular case. According to its Web site, Spotlight on Crime has offered $1 million in rewards in 19 cases.

A simple search of the Internet for "false confessions" will lead to many reports and articles on this subject. This is far more common than people would tend to think. The admission of expert testimony regarding "false or coerced confessions" is debated in courtrooms all over the world.

Ron Michaels is questioned by Police investigators at his home in the summer of 2003

Three detectives show up at the home of Ron and Jean Michaels and announce that they are investigating the death of a young man named Jeffrey Hammill in August of 1979. Ron welcomes them into the house and they all sit at the kitchen table. There is no tape recorder, the detectives are taking notes. The detectives show Ron a picture of a man they call Terry Olson, telling him that he is a bad man who has been in a lot of trouble; this is the guy they think killed Jeffrey Hammill and they are looking for corroborating testimony. They also show him pictures of Jeff Cardinal (his childhood friend), Deb Cardinal and Dale Todd. Ron recognizes Jeff's picture of course, but not Deb Cardinal or Dale Todd. They tell Ron that they think Deb Cardinal knows something about this, but won't talk to them; she is protecting her brother, Terry Olson. They keep showing Ron the picture of Terry Olson, telling him how bad Terry Olson is and asking him if he is being threatened by anyone to keep silent. Ron assures them, several times, that no one is threatening him; that he doesn't know this person or anything about this. Ron tells them he is cooperating fully with them and will tell them anything he can remember to help them. They ask him if he will take a lie detector test, reminding him that he refused to back in 1979 when interviewed shortly after Jeff Hammill was found dead. Ron tells them he doesn't remember being interviewed back in 1979. They show him a note on a file that says Ron had been interviewed, but they have no interview transcript to show him. Ron tells them that he has some medical issues and that these have affected his memory somewhat. The detectives ask Ron if he can validate that with medical records. Ron confirms that he certainly can. The detectives lay out a story of how they think Dale Todd, Terry Olson and Ron left the party at Deb Segler's home the night of August 10th, 1979 for a period of time and then returned. They state that Jeff Cardinal has corroborated this. Ron is told that he, Dale Todd and Terry Olson went to the home Ron was renting, to listen to a new stereo he had recently bought. Then after some time, Dale and Terry left and before returning to the party at Deb Segler's' house, they found Jeff Hammill, and Terry Olson killed him. The detectives continue replaying this story to Ron and Jean, validating events with statements taken from Jeff Cardinal and others until Ron and Jean are convinced that this sequence of events is correct and this Terry Olson guy is bad news. At the end of the interview, the detectives thank them for their time and leave.

In October of 2003, Jean Michaels is at the hospital with her mother who has recently suffered a heart attack. Her cell phone rings. It's Ron and he says he has just received a call from the police detectives who interviewed them a few months before. They asked if they could come over and take a statement from Ron. Jean tells Ron to tell them not to come until she can get home because she wants to be there. Ron tells her they are already on their way. Jean tells Ron not to let them in the house until she gets there and hangs up. She leaves the hospital immediately and begins driving home. The detectives show up a short time later and Ron knows it would be best if he waits until Jean gets home, but he also knows he has nothing to hide, so he lets them in. They sit at the kitchen table once more. This time they set up a tape recorder. About half way through the interview, Ron gets up and places a call to Jean on her cell phone. He is obviously very upset. He tells her that the detectives are there and they say that he killed Jeff Hammill. "Jean," he says, "you need to get home right away." She tells him she is on her way and not to talk to the detectives anymore until she gets home. Ron says "How can I not talk to them, they are already here?"

Jean replies," I don't care! Tell them you have to go to the bathroom, and just stay in there, or kick them out of the house. Just don't talk to them anymore until I get there!"

Jean arrives minutes later. Ron is seated at the kitchen table, obviously shaken. She knows he fatigues easily these days, and in that condition he doesn't think clearly and gets easily confused. The detectives tell Jean that Dale Todd had broken down in his kitchen and confessed to the whole thing and they replay the story that Ron and Terry Olson were there; that Ron and Terry both got out of Dale Todd's car when they found Jeff Hammill and one of them killed Jeff. They thought it was probably Terry Olson because Dale Todd could hear one of them saying "No, no, no" and "Stop, stop, stop". The detectives believe that was probably Ron, and if he will just say that he was there and that he said that, they would go easy on him. Ron says, "I wasn't there. I'm not gonna lie. I'm not gonna tell you things I don't know are true."

Jean shouts at the detectives, "You're putting memories in his head that he doesn't even have! You need to stop right now! Do we need to get an attorney?"

They reply, "Well that's up to you. We're not saying anything one way or the other."

Jean says, "Well, you need to go. We need to get an attorney."

As soon as the detectives hear that, they shut everything down, pack up and leave. They never return to the house.

Over the next week or so, Ron and Jean hire local attorney Carl Newquist. Carl sends a letter to Wright County indicating that he is now representing Ron, and should they need to speak with Ron, they should contact him and he will arrange to bring Ron in for questions. Carl submits multiple letters to Wright County over the next several months, offering to come in to talk to investigators anytime, and also asking for any new information regarding the case. They hear nothing from Wright County for almost 2 years.

In 2005, Ron gets a letter inviting him to testify before a Grand Jury. Ron and Jean contact their attorney, who tells them not to go before the Grand Jury. He advises them that once they go there, the prosecutor can ask them anything. They cannot have their attorney with them. "You have no one helping you. There are no rules. They can attack you," Newquist tells them.

CHAPTER 9

The Grand Jury Convenes

On November 1st, 2005 at approx 10:15 a.m., a Grand Jury is convened at the Wright County Government Center in Buffalo, MN.

The following is the preparation of the grand jurors by Judge Steven Halsey. It is interesting in that it explains the purposes and powers charged to the jurors in the execution of their responsibilities as Grand Jurors.

Judge Halsey addresses the group of twenty jurors selected to sit on the Grand Jury.

"Members of the Grand Jury, by this oath, I will remind you that you have sworn that you will not indict anyone through malice or ill will or because you are angry with any individual or any group of individuals or because you think a person ought to without charge, of all public records in the county."

"In almost all cases, the matters that the Grand Jury will inquire into have already been brought to the attention of law-enforcement authorities in this county. These cases will be presented to you by the county attorney as the prosecuting agent for the state of Minnesota. Generally speaking, it is not necessary or even advisable for you to make any unusual or extraordinary investigation of your own. However, you are not required to confine your inquiry merely to such matters that are brought to your attention by your county attorney. You are the judges of what additional matters, if any, you should investigate. I will, however, emphasize again that your county has a law-enforcement investigative apparatus and a prosecuting authority and nearly all matters will more efficiently come through this apparatus."

"The county attorney of your county is an elected official who is designated to be the prosecuting authority for the state. The county attorney or an assistant county attorney will attend each and every grand jury session. The county attorney is not allowed to be in the Grand Jury room any time the Grand Jury is deliberating or voting. The county attorney is trained in the law and has the duty to present evidence to the Grand Jury, inquire of witnesses before the Grand Jury, and assist the Grand Jury in the proper framing of Indictments. Probably one of the most important functions that the county attorney fulfills with the Grand Jury is that of being its legal adviser. As will be explained in more detail later, an Indictment must be based upon admissible evidence. You should recognize that the county attorney is going to be the only person in the Grand Jury room who is trained in the law and who will be able to assist you in sorting out legally admissible evidence from inadmissible evidence. You should listen closely to this advice and attempt to proceed about your business following their legal advice. If there is any difference of opinion between you and the county attorney that cannot be resolved, the matter should be brought to the attention of the Court. After conclusion of these instructions, you will retire to a private Grand Jury room to meet with the county attorney."

Judge Haley continues to explain the rules that the Grand Jury must abide by, and the protection of secrecy they will enjoy as members of the Grand Jury.

"I do not expect that you are going to remember all of this. The reason I tell you all of this is so you are aware that you will need someone from the county attorney's office in the Grand Jury room to help you with the evidence. There may be reference to some of these rules during the cases that are presented to you. You should be aware that the county attorney is bound to follow these rules and conduct the testimony accordingly. The county attorney's basic obligation in the Grand Jury room is to make sure that inadmissible evidence does not come in front of you. So when a grand juror asks a question of a witness, the county attorney may indicate that the answer will be hearsay or it would not be admissible and the witness will not be allowed to answer. Understand that the purpose of the county attorney stating something like this is to make sure that inadmissible evidence does not come before you and that the indictment is not based upon inadmissible evidence. So rely on their counsel as to the technical rules of evidence and there will not be a problem."

The judge establishes that at least 12 grand jurors need to concur to find each indictment or charge. These charges must be based upon admissible evidence that establishes probable cause to believe an offense was committed and the defendant committed it. He goes on.

"I advise you that the Grand Jury is both a sword and a shield of justice; a sword because it is a terror of criminals; a shield because it is the protection of the innocent against unjust prosecution. These important powers obviously create equally grave responsibilities to see that such powers are in no way perverted or abused. With its extensive power, the Grand Jury might, unless motivated by the highest sense of justice, issue Indictments not supported by the evidence and thus become a source of oppression to our citizens. On the other hand, a Grand Jury might dismiss charges against those who should be prosecuted. The importance of its power is emphasized by the fact that it is a completely independent body, answerable to no one except the Court under unusual circumstances. Your membership on the Grand Jury is a great honor. You are among a very small number of citizens in our community who are chosen to serve as a grand juror. On behalf of your fellow citizens in Wright County, I want to thank you in advance for your service as grand jurors. It is through your efforts that an individual's rights are protected, and popular acceptance of the laws of this state are encouraged among the citizens of our community."

Judge Haley finishes and exits the courtroom.

This Grand Jury is convened to hear the evidence gathered by the County Attorney and the Sheriff's Department, presented through witness testimony and exhibits, and determine whether there is probable cause to issue indictments against three men whom the County Attorney's office believe were responsible for the death of Jeffrey Hammill. Probable cause is defined as a "reasonable ground of suspicion, supported by circumstances sufficiently strong in themselves, to warrant a cautious person for believing the suspect to be guilty". In other words, probable cause is a state of facts that would lead a person of ordinary care and prudence to believe and consciously entertain an honest and strong suspicion that the suspect is guilty of a crime.

The witnesses include officers from the Sheriffs' Department that took part in the investigation by interviewing witnesses and suspects and taking statements; a medical expert that testified to the information presented in the autopsy performed on Jeffrey Hammill and the subsequent Death Certificate and original investigative documents; and several witnesses that either reported being near the location where Jeffrey Hammill was found dead, or who had been with him earlier that evening. Other witnesses include suspect's family members, and even a current inmate of a local county jail who had spoken with one of the targets of the investigation.

Since the transcript of the Grand Jury is considered confidential in the state of Minnesota, and is not permitted to be published, it will not be presented in this novel. There are avenues to access this information by motioning the court for a copy of the transcript and giving reasons as to why permission to review it should be granted. I will leave this up to those who feel that a review of this transcript is in order after they finish reading this novel.

There is a saying among many of those in the law professions that states, "a good lawyer can get a Grand Jury to indict a ham sandwich." I do not intend here to diminish the importance of the Grand Jury's vital oversight of this judicial process of our democracy. I only offer this observation to acknowledge that nothing is perfect and evidence can be presented in various shades and lighting to color the reality of a situation such that desired conclusions can be reached. At the extreme, prosecutorial misconduct and even perjury can find their way into these proceedings.

On November 4th, 2005, the Grand Jury returns multiple

indictments against Ron Michaels, Dale Todd and Terry Olson for the murder of Jeffrey Hammill on August 11th, 1979.

CHAPTER 10

Jim has been trying to get the charges dismissed against Ron due to the fact that he believes that the confession the BCA agents extracted from Dale Todd in 2003 is a "false or involuntary confession", and is the basis for the indictment. He sends the following email to Hawkeye and Rob informing them of his progress.

From: Jim Fleming

To: Jon Hawks, Rob Fleming

Subject: The beat goes on

We did present arguments on the involuntary confession issue, but the Judge has decided that this is a case of first impression in Minnesota and she is not sure whether all the case precedent from other jurisdictions around the country should be followed or what. The prosecutor also managed to piss me off by arguing in court that Todd's car was definitely at the scene that night (but offered no evidence to back this up) and stated that my arguments to the contrary are "ridiculous."

As some of you know, I don't have that good a sense of humor.

Jim sends the following letter brief to Judge Larkin.

Dear Judge Larkin:

During hearing on Defendant's Motion to exclude the September, 2003 statement of co-defendant Dale Todd, you invited counsel for the State and Defendant to provide you with additional briefs if we so desired. Although I initially felt that this was not necessary, after reflecting upon the arguments, I am now of the opinion that such a brief is necessary in order to clarify one of the arguments presented to the court. This relates specifically to the issue of whether or not evidence exists which places Todd's 1971 Chevrolet Impala at the scene where Jeffrey Hammill's body was found on the morning of August 11, 1979.

During the State's argument, the prosecutor emphatically stated to the court that Todd's vehicle was definitely there. During my own argument, I emphasized to the court that no evidence exists establishing this fact, either directly or indirectly. Since the issue goes to the heart of the Defendant's argument on the effect of police deception of Todd, rendering his statement to be more likely involuntary than voluntary, it is necessary to establish the basis for this argument relating to this deception.

The claim that Todd's vehicle was observed at the scene is based upon the statements of witnesses, Bartow Kilgo and his wife, who at the time in question was his fiancé. This is established by law enforcement investigative reports and the fact that both Mr. Kilgo and his wife, testified before the Grand Jury in 2005. However, Mr. Kilgo's earliest statement, given in 1979 within a few days after August 11th, clearly reflects that Mr. Kilgo was quite clear in his recollection that the vehicle in question was a 1967–1969 Chevrolet. Mr. Kilgo specifically described the tail light array on the rear of the vehicle as having three taillights on each side, flat on the top and round on the bottom. A copy of the police report indicating Mr. Kilgo's statement is attached to this letter brief as Exhibit "A".

This statement is significant for several reasons. One of these is that all subsequent questioning of Mr. Kilgo by law enforcement representatives has studiously avoided any reference to this description of the taillights. Mr. Kilgo was interviewed in January, 2003 by an investigator from the Wright County Sheriff's Office. In this statement Mr. Kilgo's memory of the number and location of individuals seen at the spot he and his fiancé drove by changed significantly (he forgot the individual he described sitting behind the steering wheel), as did his ability to remember the clothing worn by one of the individuals he saw (in 1979, he was unable to describe this individual's clothing at all). However, the investigator said nothing to him about the taillight configuration on the vehicle. Mr. Kilgo was, interestingly enough again questioned in September of 2003 by a different Sheriff's Department investigator. For some reason, he was now able to remember to add the individual behind the wheel (he simply added him to the growing list of people at the scene) but again the investigator failed to mention the taillight configuration.

During Mr. Kilgo's testimony before the Grand Jury, his memory of the clothing worn by the individual seen in front of the vehicle has improved even more dramatically. However, again, no one bothered to talk to him about the taillight configuration and the Grand Jury was not allowed to understand the significant differences in his testimony. Why, and why is this significant?

It is significant because his earliest description of the vehicle he and his fiancé saw at approximately 3:00 a.m. on August 11, 1979 does not match Dale Todd's vehicle. The Affidavit attached to this letter brief as Exhibit "B" demonstratively establishes that the taillight configuration described by Mr. Kilgo in 1979 matches only one Chevrolet model year, 1968. This particular taillight shape was only used that year and has not been used before or since. Since the law enforcement investigative records are clear that Dale Todd owned a 1971 Chevrolet Impala, using a significantly different taillight shape and assembly, it is also clear that Mr. Kilgo is not describing Dale Todd's vehicle.

Furthermore, Mr. Kilgo also stated to investigators in 2003 that he was taken by law enforcement personnel to a business located in Plymouth, Minnesota in 1979 (presumably the location where law enforcement personnel were questioning Dale Todd and Terry Olson) and he was unable to recognize any vehicles at that scene. Most importantly, whether Kilgo was shown Todd's vehicle or not, the police investigative records are completely devoid of any reference to Kilgo, or his fiance being able to identify Todd's car (or any other car for that matter) as the one they saw briefly at 3:00 a.m. on August 11, 1979, as they drove by it on the way home to Buffalo.

The crime lab report from the BCA, created in March, 1979, speaks for itself. No blood or hair from Jeffrey Hammill's body was found on the baseball bat confiscated from Dale Todd's car in 1979. Whether Hammill may or may not have been hit with this bat is disingenuous and not the point. The point is that Todd was falsely told by BCA investigators who knew the truth; that the blood and hair on the bat belonged to Hammill. He was specifically told that witnesses placed his car at the scene. None of this was true and it is proven by the police investigative reports themselves.

The impact of this conduct on co-defendant, Dale Todd, is quite easy to discern. During the course of a five hour interview in which Todd repeatedly denies knowing who Ronald Michaels is, he is provided a photograph of Ronald Michaels, told who is in the photograph and told that he was with Ron Michaels that night. He is also told about the witnesses placing his car at the scene, and the blood and hair of Jeffrey Hammill being found on a bat taken from his vehicle's trunk. He is told that he may have been too drunk or to high to be have been involved, but that the investigators are sure that he knows what happened. He is told that if he does not tell them the "story", they will have to consider the matter an "intentional murder".

Given this back ground, the statement provided by Todd is as transparent as glass. He had no choice but to tell them the story that they had telegraphed to him that they wanted to hear, and he did. In their rush to prosecute my client, Ronald Michaels, clear a "cold" case and obtain a conviction, the State has engaged in abusive conduct and deception, not designed to ensure that justice is done, but designed to ensure a conviction. In that regard, close has been good enough and evidence which does not match up with the pre-determined story has been ignored and/or discarded. My client has a constitutional right to a fair trial. If this conduct is allowed to go on, he will be denied that right.

Respectfully submitted,

James B. Fleming

Jim interviews Sandra O'Brien over the phone in late July of 2006, regarding the statements she supposedly made to Deputy Sheriff Joe Hagerty in a phone interview Hagerty conducted with her a couple of weeks earlier. Jim has received and reviewed the report from Hagerty that summarized her statements, and he reads it to her line by line, letting Sandra comment after each statement, as she chooses. He sends her a copy of Hagerty's report following his phone conversation with her, so she can read it as well. A few days later, Sandra asks Jim to draft a statement from her regarding the content of Hagerty's report, so she can sign it and "set the record straight".

Jim receives the statement from Sandra O'Brien and sends a copy via email to Hawkeye.

From: Jim Fleming

To: Jon Hawks

Subject: Now somebody else is really pissed off

My name is Sandra O'Brien, I am married to George O'Brien and I live in Monticello, Minnesota.

On Wednesday, August 2, 2006 at about 7:30 p.m., I received a telephone call at home from Jim Fleming, the attorney for my ex-husband, Ron Michaels. I know Mr. Fleming because I met with him in the Fall of 2005, to talk about the charges that had been brought against Ron and my recollection of various events that occurred around the time of the death of a young man named Jeffrey Hammill in August, 1979.

Mr. Fleming told me that he had received a copy of a report that had been prepared by Deputy Hagerty of the Wright County Sheriff's Office. This report is supposed to be a summary of comments I made to Deputy Hagerty when he called me during the middle of July of this year, 2006. Mr. Fleming asked if he could talk with me about the summary because he wanted to confirm my statements as they were reported by Deputy Hagerty.

I asked Mr. Fleming if he would read the summary to me over the telephone. He agreed to do this, but said that he also wanted to provide me with a copy of the printed summary so that I could be sure that what he was reading was accurate. Mr. Fleming then slowly read the summary to me line by line over the telephone. After each statement, he stopped to give me a chance to comment on what I heard. In some cases, I had him repeat what he read to be sure that I understood what had been written by Deputy Hagerty. After we were finished, Mr. Fleming advised me that he would deliver a copy of the report to me so that I could read it. He did that and now I have not only heard Deputy Hagerty's report, but have read it as well.

I am very angry about what Deputy Hagerty put into this report. He did not accurately report what I said to him. He also left a number of significant comments that I made out of the report. Because of this I asked Mr. Fleming to put my comments down in writing so that I could sign a statement that tells the truth about what I said to Deputy Hagerty. I do not trust him to tell the truth about this matter. I have made this statement in writing and signed it to set the record straight.

I did not tell Deputy Hagerty that it was "possible" that I was with Ron in the Country West or Rockford House on August 10, 1979. I told Deputy Hagerty that I do not believe that I was with Ron, Jeff Cardinal and Deb Segler (Cardinal) in any bars in Rockford on Friday night, August 10th, 1979. I also told him why. I did work until 11:00 p.m. on Friday nights at that time and due to the hour after I got off work if I went anywhere on such evenings after work, it was to Ron's home that he rented south of Montrose on Highway 25. We did this on many occasions and there would often be a number of our friends there just hanging out, listening to music, talking and having drinks.

We sometimes did get together with Jeff Cardinal and Debra Cardinal (Segler) to socialize. We were friends and if our schedules worked out, we enjoyed doing things together. But I am confident that I was not with Ron on that particular evening for several reasons. For one, I know now, that Debra Cardinal's (Segler) brother was there with a friend of his named Dale Todd. I have seen pictures of these men in the papers and I know that I did not, at any time go to a bar with Ron where these two men were also present.

Deputy Hagerty tried to tell me that I was there on that night and that Ron had gotten into a fight in the parking lot of the Rockford House with somebody over a comment made to somebody's sister. I told Deputy Hagerty that did not happen in that way or at that time. I remember very well that Ron tried to break up a fight between two men at the Rockford House and that the two men, who were drunk, and two of their friends then jumped on Ron and were pounding his head against the pavement. I got scared and went inside and got "Tiny", the bartender, to come out to chase them off Ron. Ron thought it was kind of funny because he had gotten into trouble trying to do what he always did, which was trying to get people to stop fighting. Ron hated to see fighting and on more than one occasion during the sixteen years we were together did exactly the same thing, trying to talk other guys out of fighting. I also told Deputy Hagerty that this incident had happened at least a year or two before 1979. I am not "unsure" whether Terry Olson was there, or Debra, his sister. They were not. I know Deb quite well and she was not there on that occasion. I have never met her brother and I know that he was not there with us either. I did not tell Deputy Hagerty that I was unsure of this at all and he has not reported accurately what I told him.

I also did not tell Deputy Hagerty that I was unsure if we went to Deb's house in Montrose for a party afterward. I went to Deb's house with Ron for a party on only one occasion. We had been invited there by Jeff and Deb. When we got there Deb came to the door. She had started feeling ill and said that she would have to cancel the party. We left. I did not attend a party there on any other occasions.

I did not tell Deputy Hagerty it is possible I drove myself to Deb's on August 10, 1979. I did drive to Ron's on many occasions as I have already stated. That night was not one of the times I did this and I most certainly did not drive to Deb's house that night.

It is true I do not recall Ron being in a fight at Debra's because in the entire time that he and I were together, I never saw Ron fight at all. Ron did not get in fights, and everyone who knows him knows this to be true. He had a reputation as a peacemaker and I can say with absolute certainty that I do not know a single person who can say that they have ever seen in him engaged in fighting with anybody.

I told Deputy Hagerty that I do recall someone giving me their phone number. It was at a party at Ron's well before 1979. It was a blond man who played softball with Ron on a team in Waverly. I do not remember his name. I know that he was recently divorced and I know that he had three little blond girls because I saw them at different times. I also told Deputy Hagerty that Ron was never a jealous man and when I showed him the paper with the man's phone number on it, he just laughed and said that the man was probably just lonely because of his divorce. Ron never even brought it up to the man to the best of my knowledge. He just didn't do that sort of thing.

Ron showed off his stereo to many people. It was a nice system and he was proud of it. I know that there was no occasion when Ron came to the house late at night while I was there alone to show another guy the stereo. He respected me and would not come in and make noise to wake me up. Besides, on the occasions when I left work and drove to Ron's, we were together. He would never leave me at the house alone to go out drinking the way they are describing.

Deputy Hagerty also told me that both Terry Olson and Dale Todd have already pleaded guilty. I do not know if this is true. I asked Mr. Fleming about this, but he did not know either at the time of our telephone call. Based upon the way that Deputy Hagerty has misrepresented what I said to him in his report, I do not trust him. I tried very hard to tell him as accurately as I could what I did remember. He has made it sound as though I am admitting that these things might have happened. I want it to be understood clearly that I am saying that they did not.

It appears to me that the Sheriff's Office; and particularly Deputy Hagerty is willing to do anything to make people believe that Ron is guilty of killing Jeffrey Hammill. During one conversation that I had with Deputy Hagerty, he told me that Ron had killed Jeffrey Hammill because he was gay. Now he is trying to say it was because Ron was jealous that

Jeffrey Hammill made a pass at me. Obviously, he will try to make up anything he can and I am not willing to be a part of this. I am frightened for my children and Ron because if this does not work, I don't know what story he will try to come up with next. My children are Ron's children. They have had to suffer a lot while these people have tried very hard to make their father out to be a monster. I know Ron Michaels, as do a large number of other people around this area. We are no longer married, but I know Ron Michaels to be a good man. He is not capable of hurting someone like that, especially a skinny little guy several years younger than he is.

This statement is not what I think. It is what I know and what I intend to testify to during Ron's trial.

Sandra O'Brien

An Email from Jim Fleming to a friend on or about October 27th, 2006:

From: Jim Fleming

Subject: RE: jury selection

We finally picked juror number 15 on Friday at 11:30 a.m. We will start the trial on Monday, the 30th. We have a good jury, which is semi-amazing given the fact that Mohaupt was wasting preemptories on people who were NRA members ("I hate gun people") and people she thought "like you, more than they like me" It took us 59 jurors to get 15, but we did.

We kept one juror (49 YO female) whose brother in law killed her sister and then committed suicide in 1988. Very squared away lady who said, in response to my questions about cops and whether they can be mistaken: "Honey, cops can not only be mistaken, they can lie just like the rest of us."

Mohaupt tried to bounce her for cause but the Judge overruled her and she had no more preemptories; (the NRA is popular out here).

Judge Larkin did ask this lady if there had been any prosecution in the case involving her sister. She just looked at the

Judge for a moment and said, "No, they felt him killing himself was enough." Swear to God. It was a Kodak moment.

Jim Powers, the Chief Deputy at WCSO in 1979, has e-mailed me to let me know they are going to call him on Monday. He is my witness, but he thinks they want to try to pull the stinger by calling him first. They have never interviewed him and have no idea what he is going to say. Mohaput never liked him; he was a "gun guy" and former Marine who is the type that is anathema to her way of looking at the world.

It's a pity. He is very, very pissed at what they are doing here and has every intention of burying them once he gets up on the stand. Turns out that toward the tail end of the investigation in 1979, (which he was supervising) he wrote a supp report for Sheriff Wolff in which he concluded that Hammill had been hit by a vehicle passing by in the dark, due to the lack of any signs of struggle, lack of blood spatter, lack of defensive wounds or facial injuries, the location and the position of the body. Wolff agreed and they scaled back on the investigation. Without a vehicle or anything to work with, it languished and died until Hagerty dusted it off and started thinking about maybe becoming Sheriff himself someday.

Power's report? It has disappeared from the WCSO case file.

Personally, I am just shocked …

Our pathologist, Dan Davis will testify on 11/7 that based upon the forensic evidence available it is impossible to conclusively determine what hit Hammill or why, but that his wounds and the damage to his skull and brain are much more consistent with a vehicle strike than they are with an assault.

Between these two witnesses, lots of fun and games.

Incarceration

Ron Michaels has been kept in the Wright County Jail for nearly a year now. Deadlines and milestones have come and gone, each more disappointing than the previous one. Thanksgiving came and went. Then Christmas, and then the New Year. No news, no release. Ron's lawyer is working on the repudiation of the statement of the co-defendant Dale Todd, as a coerced and involuntary statement extracted by the BCA agents during his five-hour interrogation. This statement and the claim that Todd's car was identified at the scene, even though there is no direct or indirect evidence establishing this, make up the entire case for the prosecution. The Omnibus hearing is held on April 28th, 2006, to determine if there is sufficient evidence to go to trail. The indecision of the judge and the pressure from the prosecution to continue, insisting the Grand Jury testimony would provide more evidence, win out. In early summer at the pre-trial hearing, transcriptions of the Grand Jury testimony are finally available to the defense. After the Omnibus hearing however, Ron has decided not to get his hopes up anymore. He will just take it day by day, trusting in the Lord to see him through it. The routine 'inside' is simple, once you figure it out.

Breakfast is at 7:30 am. Beds are to be made. Everyone is to be dressed in full greens with a T-shirt and wearing shoes and socks. Food carts come to the commons area and everyone stands in line to get their food. You snooze, you lose.

After Breakfast, Hygiene comes around. Toiletries, soap, toothpaste and the like are given out. Razors have to be checked in and out. If you aren't in the commons area when the cart comes, you go without.

Then it's time for Meds. Another line of men; this time waiting for their medicine. One of the CO's says to Ron, 'Hey, you better get used to someone handing out your meds; it's gonna be like this for the rest of your life!' That statement, followed by the laughter of the CO's present, hits Ron like a punch in the face.

You also have to be in the commons for the distribution of 'whites': underwear, socks and T-shirts. Seldom do the disbursements occur on a regular schedule, however. If you are tired, ill or just want to get away from the blaring TV or the people arguing in the commons area of the cell block, and you are in your cell when the carts come, you can easily miss them and they will not return. Ron has difficulty keeping up with the routine as it is very hectic in the morning. Ron eats slowly due to his illness. He struggles to swallow his pills. He tires easily just moving from place to place. Some days he falls behind and misses some of the disbursements.

Ron reads his Bible. There are few magazines or newspapers allowed. The other inmates seldom watch the new channels or anything educational; unless you consider 'The Simpsons' and 'Family Guy' educational. The CO's (correction officers) occasionally bring in videos for the inmates to watch. Many are incredibly violent films. They seem to fit the taste of the CO that brought them in, as they watch them as well. Some bring in new releases of decent films, but this is not the norm. Many of the inmates who have been in prison can't believe the types of movies they show in the County Jail. "We don't even get this kind of stuff in Prison," they exclaim, referring to the violence and sex.

Some of Ron's visitors bring books, magazine articles and some faith based materials in for Ron to read. Most of these are kept from him. Even a simple Christian bookmark his sister brought is denied him.

The CO's 'throw' Ron's cell every now and then. Go in, search through everything looking for weapons or any contraband. One CO liked to look through Ron's papers, mail, even those marked 'For Attorney Only'. This CO went through every piece of paper Ron had. The CO approached Ron and said, 'This isn't for your case,' referring to a piece of paper from his 'Attorney Only' file. Ron, takes the paper, recognizes it as having statements regarding the intrusive behavior of this particular CO. The CO threatens to 'write him up' and lock him down for 24 hours. Ron tears the paper up.

Many nights, lying in bed early in the morning, Ron has this feeling that someone is watching him. He feels a presence, like someone is there. He lays there for a moment, then turns over to see a CO peeking in at him. The CO is just standing there staring at him. Discovered, the CO just walks away. Very creepy. This particular CO always works nights and is well known for doing this.

Ron is 'locked down' on one occasion for having an extra pair of socks. It gets very cold in the cell block during the winter, and many times the men wear their clothes to bed to keep warm. Ron's illness makes it worse for him. Frost would form on the windows and walls of the cells. On one occasion he wears two pair of socks to bed to keep his feet warm. This is discovered and he is locked down for 24 hours.

The Doctor that attends the inmates, doesn't know much about Fibromyalga. Ron explains his condition and diagnosis, but he gets little understanding. It takes a long time for Ron to get an extra blanket.

Many of the inmates are there due to drug arrests. Some are high on meth when they arrive and initially they are okay. However, when they come down from the high, they crash hard and then sleep for a long time. When they wake, they are burnt out, hungry and often mad as hell. This is when they are the most dangerous: paranoid, angry and wanting to fight.

Ron is in no condition to tangle with these people. They could easily knock his head in. In his youth, he would have been able to fend off these attacks. But in his current condition, he knows he will need to outsmart them because he is defenseless. His strategy is to befriend them with gifts of extra food or by ignoring their threats and conversing with them calmly. Most of them are so burnt out, they can't remember what was said two minutes ago and it is relatively easy for Ron to steer the conversation away from whatever it is that is agitating them. Sometimes, it isn't that easy. On one occasion, an inmate comes after Ron. Ron begins praying in his spirit language, that only the Holy Spirit can understand. These strange words confuse and startle the inmate and he backs off. Realizing this, Ron begins walking toward the inmate, praying to the Holy Spirit. The inmate turns, walks away and leaves Ron alone.

On one occasion, while eating in the commons at the community table, an inmate seated across from Ron coughs repeatedly over the table. Ron says to him, "You coughed on your food, could you turn your head, please?" The inmate responds, "No I didn't!" Ron says, "Yes, you did." Another inmate sitting next to Ron is nodding his head in agreement. The inmate, who coughed, now wants to fight Ron. Ron ignores the threat and begins talking to the guy like nothing ever happened. The inmate is so burnt out, he forgets completely about the incident and goes back to eating.

As time goes on, some of the guys start to respect Ron because he has been there the longest and they know that he never starts any trouble. Many inmates know of Ron's prayers and come to him before they go to court, asking Ron to pray for them. It gives Ron a chance to witness to them.

There is only a single shower in the cell block. It is on the main floor level. One person showers at a time. Occasionally during a shower, Ron will look up to see an inmate staring down from the second tier, watching him shower, which they are forbidden to do. It gives him a very creepy and uncomfortable feeling.

Child molesters are not treated well in the Wright County Jail. Other inmates find them regular targets for their anger. However, Ron stands up for these guys. "Hey, we're all sinners! God will forgive him for what he's done; and you need to. No, it's not a good thing that he's done, but there is no reason to put your hands on him and beat the crap out of him. I'm sure you don't like molesters, but who are you to judge him? There is no reason to physically hurt someone."

One instance ends with a molester in Ron's cell, half beaten and trying to escape the two guys pursuing him. They want to come into the cell and finish the job, but Ron prevents them, telling them to stay out!

Inmates play cards often. During one card game, one inmate, a rather large man, looks across the table and suddenly spits a big gob right into the face of his partner, who happens to be a child molester. The molester stands up, picks up his chair, threatening to throw it at his partner, beating it around on the floor and says, 'What did I ever do to you?' Then he backs off a little, because his partner is a pretty big guy. His partner stands up and goes after him. The molester does not fare well. Often fights occur out of the view of the correction officers. These will continue to their natural conclusion.

Mexicans are not popular inmates and often targets of attacks. There is a definite black/white issue as well.

The younger inmates seem to make the most trouble. Anger, arrogance, and disrespect are their trademarks.

Ron quickly learns that you never show weakness. Following a visit by his wife Jean or his kids, Ron is most vulnerable. The emotions flood out during his walk back to the cell block from the visiting area. He sometimes needs to duck into the nurse's office and let it out before returning to his cell. Fortunately, she understands and permits this. He then composes himself and returns to the cell block. When an inmate is distraught following a family visit, others use this to taunt and torture them, claiming their wife is cheating on them and running around. They enjoy messing with their heads.

At one point, two young guys befriend Ron: one young black man who is going to be in prison for quite awhile, and a young white kid. They are like sons to Ron; they stand up for him on several occasions, keeping guys from hurting him. Ron witnesses to these men, neither of whom has any religious training. He teaches them the Lord's Prayer. He shows them where it is in the Bible, along with a few other scriptures, for which they are very grateful. They both come to Ron's cell every night to say goodnight to him.

Medical visits are uncommon. Jean has made several requests to allow Ron to be seen by his own doctor, familiar with his condition. There are disability papers that need to be signed once a year for Ron to maintain his financial support. This requires an examination by Ron's doctor, which means a trip to the doctor's facility. These requests are answered with instructions on what Ron's doctor must say in a letter requesting this visit. Jean gets this letter only to have the jail change their instructions to have the letter say something else. This continues for some time. The visit is finally arranged, all at Ron and Jeans expense of course. When Ron finally sees his doctor, she is given a paper with instructions. She is not allowed to touch Ron. No examination. She is merely to sign the disability papers.

Ron had been receiving Botox injections to treat his condition prior to his incarceration. These are not permitted while in jail, so Ron is forced to use strong narcotics in place of them, which are significantly harder on his system.

Meds are distributed three times a day, no matter what the prescription reads. If you are to take a medicine four times a day, you missed one application. If you cannot afford to replenish your prescription, you go without when it expires.

Dental care is interesting. No preventative maintenance for your teeth. No cavities filled or cleanings or checkups. When your teeth hurt enough, you are brought across the street to their dentist. If they believe you have money or dental insurance, they will take three or four x-rays, then pull the tooth. That costs $400. If you do not have insurance, they just pull the tooth. That costs $100. They will not accept Ron's insurance, so Jean has to pay cash for services. Ron is not allowed to see his own dentist. Jean prepares and submits a list of dentists in the area that are part of their insurance plan, but they are not allowed to use them. "The jail has a contract with this dentist and that's who will attend the inmates," she is told. All inmates pay an 'emergency fee' even though they have scheduled appointments. All told, Ron loses 4 teeth that may never have been pulled had he received any kind of dental care.

The food is not spectacular. Ron eats mostly from the canteen, where you can pay for items through an account set up by the jail and contributed to by your family and friends. The offerings are mostly junk food; nothing healthy. They are distributed twice a week according to what you have ordered. The food served by the jail is barely edible and many inmates choose to rarely eat it, opting instead for the canteen menu, expensive and unhealthy as it is. Much of the fruit is already partly rotten, and you have to remove that part before you can eat it. No fruit can be kept in your cell, as inmates can use it to make 'mash', which they do often. One pair of inmates are very successful at it until they slip up and brag about it; they get their cell 'thrown'. They end up in confinement for some time. Dope smoking in the shower or around the toilet bowl is common; the cell block sometimes smells strongly of the weed. Flushing the bowl often is thought to pull the smoke and smell out effectively. Dope is smuggled in by visitors and some entrepreneuring guards.

Phone calls are expensive, and limited to fifteen minutes. These require either a prepaid phone card, available from the Jail at fifty cents per minute, or a collect call through an agency in concert with the jail. This outside account must carry a prepaid balance to insure payment and it is expensive.

Church on Sundays is limited to an ecumenical service. After weeks of attending this, Ron begins requesting a Catholic priest be allowed to come and give him the sacrament. This is refused time and again. He is told by one CO, "If we let the Catholics in here, then we should get the Satan Worshippers in here too." Ron relays this to Jean during one of her visits. Jean is upset and tells Ron, "They can't do this; we could sue them for keeping a Priest out." All inmate conversations during visits occur over phones and are monitored. A Catholic deacon begins weekly visits shortly thereafter and Ron is able to receive the Sacrament of Communion twice a month, which heretofore is unheard of in the jail. Ron's parish priest is able to visit, but is not allowed to go into the jail.

Many of the inmates are here for DUI violations and

less serious offenses. Some are only there on weekends. Some inmates choose to go out on work detail. Work detail allows inmates to work outside the jail under armed guard supervision. For each three to four days a week you work on this detail, you get two days off of your sentence. No vulgar language or swearing is allowed. One inmate, with substantial time to do, refuses to participate in the detail. Every other word out of his mouth is 'F-this' and 'F-that'. "They don't allow swearing" he says. "I can't. I'm not doing that. I got to swear!"

CHAPTER 11

The Trial Begins

The wind can be brutally cold, blowing into downtown Buffalo off of the lake in late October. A day's bright sunshine does little to counter the chill in the air. On this day, the wind is racing off the water and filling the cobble-stoned downtown streets of the village, with the stinging reminder that the sweltering summer heat has long gone and a Minnesota winter is right around the corner.

Parking at or near the courthouse is difficult at best, and parking restriction signs line the streets for blocks around. The courtrooms are on the second floor, guarded by a security station that rivals that of the Lindberg Terminal at the Minneapolis / St. Paul International Airport. Everyone must pass through a bag screening station and metal detector before they have access to the courtrooms. The world is a changing place. Violence in Americas' courtrooms is a topic for another author, however.

This trial was almost delayed for months due to an incident following the Jury selection. The judge was presenting the Jury and asked the attorneys if they wanted to introduce themselves to the jury and then she did something unheard of and asked Ron to address the Jury. This stunned the attorneys for a few seconds. Ron rose from his seat and said "Hello, my name is Ron Michaels and I swear before God, I am innocent". This put the attorneys in head spins, with long discussions as to whether they should dismiss the jury and start over. The judge decided that because the jury was not sworn in 'voir dire', the trial could commence.

Today, Ron Michaels goes on trial, his freedom hanging in the balance. He has spent a few days short of a full year in the county jail, waiting for the opportunity to present his defense against the charges leveled at him. Charges presented to a Grand Jury by those entrusted with enforcing the laws of our society; those charged with protecting us and serving us, and whose salaries we pay.

Now it is time for a jury of Ron's peers to hear all of the evidence and determine if these charges against him are justifiable and if the evidence indicates his guilt beyond a reasonable doubt. Ron, however, sees things a little bit differently, as you might imagine. For him, the charges are an incredible lie created from thin air, by those trusted to protect and serve his community. He sees these last 12 months of his life as a nightmare he may never escape. He knows his personal freedom and the life he has with his wife and kids and his family and friends has been taken from him; has been handled like it is worthless by his jail keepers, who taunted and took advantage of him. He knows that from the day he was arrested, he has been treated as a convict, without dignity or decency. His past has been subjected to a scrutiny few could sustain without blemish. His children have endured the taunting from their peers, difficult to imagine; and this makes Ron's heart ache like he has never known.

He knows his wife has suffered even more than he from this lie, so callously created by people she doesn't even know. The neighbors look the other way when she comes and goes. The financial hardships are immense and growing each day with the costs of preparing a defense. This lie is destroying them financially. He knows they will have to sell everything they own to pay for his defense.

Ron also wonders who will be held responsible for the time he has had to spend in jail, away from his wife and family. What about the damage done to his reputation, his friendships and his health? Someone must be held accountable. But he also knows it's first things first. He has to go through this trial.

The trial, STATE OF MINNESOTA DISTRICT COURT, COUNTY OF WRIGHT, TENTH JUDICIAL DISTRICT Vs. RONALD JOSEPH MICHAELS, takes place at the Wright County Government Center in the city of Buffalo, County of Wright, State of Minnesota, beginning on October 30th, 2006. The trial is held before the honorable Michelle Larkin. Appearing for the State is Assistant Wright County Attorney Anne Mohaupt. Appearing on behalf of the defendant is James Fleming, Esq. and Jon Hawks, Esq.

Opening Statements

The Prosecution

MS. MOHAUPT: Thank you. Good morning, ladies and gentlemen. I'm Anne Mohaupt. I'm one of the attorneys employed by the Wright County Attorney's Office here in Buffalo. It is the job of the Wright County Attorney's Office to prosecute almost all crimes that occur within the boundary of Wright County. This part of the trial is called 'opening statements'. Now, the purpose of opening statements is to give each attorney, Mr. Fleming and me, the opportunity to give you an overview of what we expect the evidence is going to show. The purpose of opening statements is not to present argument. Argument comes later, after all of the evidence has been provided to you and the attorneys make a final statement. Opening statements are for us, Mr. Fleming and me, to tell you what we expect the evidence is going to show.

Now, I'm going to remind you that you are responsible for judging the facts in this particular case, and that you're judging the facts based upon the evidence that is presented to you through the testimony of the witnesses and the exhibits. Nothing that I say is evidence. Nothing that the defense counsel says is evidence. All of the evidence comes in through the witnesses that are going to sit in that chair and the exhibits that they may tell you about. In this case, the State intends on calling approximately twenty to twenty-five witnesses. We're going to be calling retired and current law enforcement officers, a medical doctor who is the county coroner, also called medical examiner; citizens who are not part of the criminal justice system at all, and several convicted felons. I've tried my best to schedule the testimony so as not to inconvenience the Court, the witnesses or yourselves, but that is often difficult and so we'll have to see how that goes.

As you are all aware, this is what people refer to as a 'cold case'. It involves the murder of a twenty-one-year-old male by the name of Jeffrey Hammill in 1979. This case was investigated badly and basically dropped in 1979. Nothing was done on this case until January of 2003, when a young woman by the name of Amanda Thiesse contacted the Wright County Sheriff's Department. It turns out that Amanda Thiesse was the biological daughter of Jeff Hammill. She had been raised by adoptive parents. As with a lot of adopted people, she wanted to find out about her background. So she contacted the Sheriff's Department in an attempt to find out how her father had died. The sheriff assigned this question to one of the deputies, Joe Hagerty, who, with the help of the BCA Cold Crimes Unit, brought the case back to life sufficiently, so that we are here in this courtroom today. The State expects that the evidence presented to you this week in the form of the witness testimony and the exhibits that you receive, will show you the following:

On August 10 of 1979 Jeffrey Hammill, who was twenty-one years old, was out socializing at a bar called the 'Country West' in Rockford, Minnesota. He got there at about 8:30 and he stayed until closing, 1:00 a.m., on August 11, 1979. A guy by the name of Dale Todd was there. A guy by the name of Terry Olson was there. The Defendant was there. A guy named Jeff Cardinal was there and a girl named Deb Segler was there as were many, many other people. It was quite crowded that night.

Now, the relationship between these people is important and significant to the case. Dale Todd and Terry Olson were good friends. They knew Jeffrey Hammill because they worked together. Dale Todd and Terry Olson have been charged along with this Defendant in this particular case. Dale Todd's case has been resolved. Terry Olson's case is still pending. Deb Segler, the girl who was at the bar with the people, is Terry Olson's sister. Her name at the time was Deb Segler. It is now Deb Cardinal and she is married to a guy named Jeff Cardinal. The Defendant is a very good old friend of Jeff Cardinal.

Now, if not for Jeff Cardinal, the Defendant probably would not have been with this group of people on August 10 of 1979. And if not for Dale Todd and Terry Olson, Jeff Hammill probably would not have been with this group of people on the night that he died. Now, the bar closed at one o'clock. It takes a while for everybody to clear out and get in their cars and get going. After Jeff left the bar, he started hitchhiking or walking on Highway 55 towards Buffalo. Terry Olson and Dale Todd left the bar together. They were going to go to Deb's house, which was in Montrose, to continue partying. They were in Dale Todd's dark colored Chevy driving west on Highway 55. They saw Jeff Hammill and picked him up at about 1:20, 1:30. Jeff Hammill, Terry Olson and Dale Todd rode together in Todd's car to Deb's place in Montrose. They got there about two o'clock a.m. on August 11, 1979. When they got there, they realized that they had a flat tire. Hammill went into the house. Olson and Todd fixed the flat tire and then they went into the house.

Deb was there. Jeff Cardinal, Deb's boyfriend at the time, was there. And the Defendant was there and had driven in a separate car. Now, there may have been some others that were there, too. We think possibly a woman by the name of Sandy Dehn, who was the Defendant's girlfriend at the time, was also there. Olson, Todd and the Defendant were all drunk and they were all loud. Something happened, a fight, an argument, something that caused tension. We think that Jeff Hammill gave his telephone number to the Defendant's girlfriend, Sandy. By now it was about 2:30 in the morning. Jeff Hammill left the party on foot. Shortly after Jeff left, within a half hour or forty-five minutes, Olson, Todd and the Defendant left. They went looking for Jeff. They were angry at Jeff Hammill and they were drunk. They're in Dale Todd's dark green colored or dark colored Chevy. Dale Todd was driving. They find Jeff on the side of the road walking. They stop the car. Olson and this Defendant get out of the car. This Defendant goes into the trunk of the car, gets something. Shortly thereafter, Olson and this Defendant get back into the car. After they get into the car and start to drive away, the Defendant makes the comment, "I guess he doesn't need a ride anymore." Jeff's body was found two-point-two miles from Deb Segler's house.

Now, on this same night, Barto and Jennifer Kilgo, who are married now but weren't married then, were at Robert Nowak's house at a card party. It was just two couples. Nowak's house is less than one-half mile from the location where Jeff's body was found, which was on the east side of County Road 12, two-tenths of a mile north of County Road 107, and two-point-two miles from the Segler residence. Some time between 3:00 and 3:10 a.m., the Kilgos drove by the location where Jeff Hammill's body was subsequently to be found. At this location, they saw a dark colored Chevy with up to four white men, standing outside of the car. At about 3:50 a.m., forty minutes after the Kilgos drove by, Jane Filek drove by the spot where Jeff's body was found on County Road 12. She saw something on the road. She initially thought that it was a piece of wood that would cause an accident so she stopped her vehicle. She got out of her car to investigate. And when she saw a dead young man on the side of the road, she got back into her car as fast as she could and drove to the Sheriff's Department to report what she had seen. It was approximately 4:02 a.m. when Ms. Filek came running into the

Sheriff's Department. Now, driving fast from that location you could make it in about ten minutes. So it appears that Jeff Hammill was killed sometime between 3:10 and 3:50 a.m. on the morning of August 11, which is a forty-minute period of time.

Now, at about 3:45 to 4:15 p.m. Olson, Todd and the Defendant returned to the Segler residence. They were in a much different mood than when they had left. They weren't acting loud and drunk anymore. They were quiet and they wouldn't talk much. They were acting weird. Olson and Michaels were whispering in the corner with Jeff Cardinal and Deb Segler.

Jeff Hammill died from blunt force trauma to the head. He was struck two times with one, maybe two, weapons. Jeff Hammill fell right where he stood. His clothes were not messed up. His slip-on shoes were still on his feet. There was a lot of blood but no splatter. He died immediately from the injury inflicted. He was left to lie in the road until Jane Filek drove by and found him. After Ms. Filek reported finding Jeff's body to the Sheriff's Department, that agency responded to the scene. They took photos of the body and of the scene. They didn't find a weapon. There were no skid marks or tire tracks. There was no broken glass, paint marks or broken metal at the scene, just the body of twenty-one-year-old Jeff Hammill.

The Sheriff's Department investigated the case for a couple of weeks. They interviewed a lot of people and initially they did a pretty good job in that regard, as they were able to identify who was who and where they were, thus narrowing down the range of suspects and documenting events so that they could be used when the case was reopened.

But then, and I hate to say it, the Wright County Sheriff's Department dropped the ball. The investigation, for some unknown reason, was halted and this case lay dormant for over two decades until a young woman inquired about the death of her father.

And here we are twenty-seven years after Jeff was murdered and left by the side of the road. It should not have taken this long but at least we're here now. As I'm sure you're now aware, from our voir dire conversations, there are no eyewitnesses except the people that were there. There's no DNA. There are no fingerprints. This is not a CSI case, but this is a case, I submit, worthy of your consideration.

The State believes that the evidence will convince you beyond a reasonable doubt that this Defendant, Ronald Michaels, is responsible in the death of Jeffrey Hammill on August 11, 1979. And at the close of the evidence we're going to be asking you to return a verdict of guilty to the charges of murder in the indictment. Thank you.

The Defense

MR. FLEMING: Thank you, Your Honor. Good morning, ladies and gentlemen. I've got the podium here. I don't like podiums very much so I'm going to try to see if I can walk around a little bit. Sometimes people get nervous when they're sitting in your chairs but they think that the attorneys are not nervous. We are, in every case of this nature, because it's an extremely important case. So if I grab it from time to time it's because I'm trying to steady myself a little bit as I get warmed up in the presentation. This case that you have been selected to sit as jurors on, sit in judgment of my client, Ronald Michaels, may, without exaggeration, prove to be one of the most important and challenging cases that has ever been tried in Wright County. Time will tell about that. But it is challenging and important for a couple of very interesting reasons. One of which, as Ms. Mohaupt has discussed with you already, is the fact that it involves a focus and an investigation into events that occurred over a quarter of a century ago, over twenty-five years ago. That is compounded by the fact that it also involves two separate law enforcement investigations; one that occurred at the time that Jeffrey Hammill's body was discovered and one that didn't begin until approximately January of 2003; again, separated by a period of nearly a quarter century.

It's challenging because you're going to have to focus your attention on these events that occurred that long ago. You're going to have to be able to focus your attention on the disparities and the differences between the two investigations and what the evidence indicated, in the course of those two investigations. Ms. Mohaupt said that with respect to the initial investigation; that it was closed down for some unknown reason. The evidence will show you that there is not some unknown reason but, in fact, there is a very good reason why that investigation was closed down. But what I'd like to do at this point in time is to just give you a very brief outline of the evidence. Some of it will be repetitive, forgive me for that, but I want to make sure that we're oriented to what we're looking at here. What we're looking at is a situation where in August of 1979, on August 10, in fact, a group of young Minnesota residents from central Minnesota had their lives intersect for a very brief period of time, a matter of a few hours. And this started at a bar, as you know now, located in Rockford, Minnesota called the Country West.

And I want to go back through that list of characters so that you get an understanding, make sure that it's fresh in your mind, and not in any certain order, I will tell you that that group of people included a man by the name of Jeff Cardinal who was in his early twenties. Jeff Cardinal, the evidence will show, was at the bar that evening on a date with his new girlfriend. They had been dating just a very short period of time. Her name was Debbie Segler. And as the prosecutor has advised you, later this couple married and they remain married today as Jeff and Debra Cardinal.

They were joined at that get together at the bar, by my client, Ronald Michaels. The evidence will show that Ron Michaels and Jeff Cardinal had been friends since childhood. And on that particular evening they got together at the bar to spend some time together. Mr. Michaels knew Debra Segler simply because she was now dating his best friend Jeff Cardinal. Coincidentally, the evidence will show that they were joined at the bar by Deb Segler's brother Terry Olson and a very close friend of his by the name of Dale Todd, who had been friends for many, many years. They worked together at a place called Temroc Fabrication, which at that time was located in Plymouth at the intersection of Interstate 494 and Highway 55, somewhere in one of the quadrants of that area.

They worked there for approximately four weeks with Jeffrey Hammill. And that is how they knew Mr. Hammill. Now, the evidence will show that my client, Ron Michaels, did not know Jeffrey Hammill, had never heard of him in his life. The evidence will show that Jeff Cardinal was at least aware of Jeffrey Hammill, having encountered him in some of the bars around that area. You have to remember we're not looking at the present, where these people are in their middle fifties.

We're talking about a group of young people that were twenty-one, twenty-two, twenty-three years old, and like most of us at that point in time, they focused a lot of their socialization on going to bars to drink, listen to music, sit with friends and talk, that sort of thing.

Jeffrey Cardinal did know Jeffrey Hammill, although the evidence will indicate that he did not know him well. Now, sometime during the course of the socialization that took place that evening, Terry Olson and Dale Todd encountered Jeffrey Hammill. There will be evidence that will suggest that this encounter occurred at a nearby bar that was approximately a block away called the Rockford House.

There was some suggestion that Jeffrey Hammill needed a ride. The evidence will suggest to you that at that point in time Jeffrey Hammill did not have a driver's license, but he was quite adept at hitchhiking and hitchhiked great distances from work to home where he lived in Buffalo, Minnesota. And when he wanted to go out and socialize, he would quite often hitchhike.

I can't tell you that I know why he did not have a valid driver's license at that point.

And I don't know that it's terribly important that we even think about that, just as long as you understand, that was his mode of transportation at that time. So, during the discussion it was suggested to him that, "If you're still around at the time that the bars close, look us up and we'll give you a ride." All right. The socialization went on until closing time. At closing time, given a period of fifteen minutes before or after, it's unclear exactly how the suggestion came about of everybody going from Rockford at the Country West to Deb Segler's home that she rented in Montrose, Minnesota.

Now, you will hear testimony from Deb Segler who will tell you, "It's been a long, long time. I don't remember specifically whether I invited everybody to come over to my house that evening or not." But she will also testify that given the usual practice at that time that it was not unusual for her to do so. And so she does not discount the idea that she made the invitation or perhaps she and her boyfriend, Jeff Cardinal, made the invitation to this group of people to come over to the house for an after-bar party.

Now, the evidence will show that because of their date, Jeff Cardinal and Deb Segler drove together from Rockford to Montrose in Mr. Cardinal's vehicle. The evidence will also show that Ron Michaels drove his own vehicle, by himself, from Rockford to Montrose. Terry Olson and Dale Todd were in Dale Todd's 1971 Chevrolet Impala. And as they were driving out of Rockford, they encountered Jeff Hammill hitchhiking by the side of the road. They stopped. The evidence will show that there was some brief discussion, which probably suggested something to the effect, "Well, we're going to a party in Montrose. It's only a few miles south of Buffalo. Why don't you ride with us? We'll go to the party and at some point we'll run you up to Buffalo and drop you off." Now, was that said? I don't know. I can only guess. We don't have any evidence on that point, but logic would tend to suggest something of that nature because the evidence will show Jeffrey Hammill did get into the vehicle with them and go to Montrose. Now, there's some discrepancies in the evidence. You'll hear evidence that will talk about different times that everybody showed up in Montrose over a period of approximately half an hour. Let's say in general terms that the evidence would suggest that they all arrived there approximately two o'clock in the morning. Now, this case focuses heavily on what occurred between two o'clock in the morning when they got there and approximately 3:50 in the morning when, as you've already heard, a woman by the name of Jane Filek was driving from Howard Lake, I believe it was either Howard Lake or Watertown, at two o'clock in the morning with her mother. Why? Because she was a florist and her family owned a floral shop in either Howard Lake or Watertown, I'm nervous and I'm simply forgotten exactly which of those two communities it was, but in any event there was some kind of an event that they had to prepare flowers for that night and they were working late into the night to get all these flowers ready. It might have been a wedding, might have been a funeral. I don't know. But in any event she discovered Jeffrey Hammill's body laying half on and half off of County Road 12 on the east side, as the prosecutor has stated, about two-point-two miles north of Deb Segler's house, which is located, as I've said, in Montrose. She immediately recognized that it was a human being, recognizing that they were either badly injured or perhaps dead; she immediately got into her vehicle and drove as fast as she could to the Sheriff's Department to report this.

So what we're looking at is a brief span of time between whatever time Jeffrey Hammill left this party in Montrose and the time that Jan Filek found his body at 3:50 a.m. up on County Road 12. That's the focus. What happened during that period of time is what this case is all about. The prosecution has suggested to you that my client, Ron Michaels, participated in a violent beating that took Jeffrey Hammill's life and understand, ladies and gentlemen, that there is no question that Jeffrey Hammill did not die of natural causes. The evidence will show you that he suffered massive head trauma. Massive head trauma to the extent that the base of his skull was fractured from one side to the other through the heaviest, thickest part of the bone of the entire skull, and was fractured cleanly. That's not something that occurs as a result of some natural event. There was undoubtedly some sort of violence inflicted on Jeffrey Hammill, but the question is and one of the questions that you're going to have to decide is, whether that violence occurred as a result of somebody taking something and striking Jeffrey Hammill with it or did it happen through some other means. And you will hear evidence that will argue both sides of that issue.

Now, make no mistake, all of you have gone through the jury selection process so you'll understand what I'm about to say. This is not a case that is similar to or reminiscent of the example case of Kathleen Solia. The evidence will show you that Ron Michaels after this August 10, August 11 situation, did not run. The evidence will show you that Ronald Michaels did not hide. It will show you that Ronald Michaels did not change his name. It will show you that Ronald Michaels went on with his life, married, had children, conducted himself in a totally peaceful fashion and did nothing in any way, shape or form to suggest that he had any culpability in this situation, any involvement in this situation.

Now, this is important because you are going to hear evidence that's going to talk about who Ronald Michaels is. And you're going to hear evidence that will tell you from people that have known him since childhood that this is a man who has a unique characteristic. And that unique characteristic is that he has never been involved in a fight in his life. Not once. You are going to hear evidence that will tell you, as you have already heard to some extent, that Ron Michaels did not know Terry Olson. Ron Michaels did not know Dale Todd. This evening in question, when he encountered them by shear coincidence at that bar, the Country West in Rockford, Minnesota, was the first time he had ever seen these individuals in his life. The evidence will show you that Ron Michaels had never heard of Jeffrey Hammill, didn't know who he was, didn't recognize him when he saw him. The evidence will tell you that when he got to the party he was surrounded by people that he had known for a very long time, Jeffrey Cardinal who he worked with, who was a childhood friend, a young man by the name of George Salonek who was, again, a very, very close friend of his that he had known since childhood and Deb Segler who he knew because of her relationship with Jeff Cardinal. And so ultimately the theory of the case for the prosecution is that this man who was surrounded by friends at this party for some reason, for some reason that makes no sense, left all those friends to go out into the night with two men that he did not know to hunt down a third man that he had never seen before in his life and beat him to death, and then as the evidence will show you, that over the next twenty-seven years of his life had no contact with either one of those two individuals ever again. That's their case, ladies and gentlemen. That's the case. Now, what I say now, you know already, is not evidence and you should not be confused by that, but you're going to hear the evidence. And after you've had a chance to hear this evidence, we're going to go back during my closing argument and we're going to review this evidence and we're going to take it apart bit by bit and piece by piece and look at it to see if it fits. And when this is concluded, I'm going to ask you to do one thing. I'm not going to ask you to take pity on this man. I'm not going to ask you to consider what he's done with his life since August of 1979 because it has nothing whatsoever to do with the case. He is not Kathleen Solia. He is not close to Kathleen Solia. But I am going to ask you to use your experience and your good judgment. And one of the things that we asked you about constantly during the course of the selection process, can you maintain an open mind, can you wait to judge until you have heard all the evidence.

Because, ladies and gentlemen of the jury, in this case, when you have heard all the evidence, you will understand that this second investigation, the second law enforcement investigation, has a theme. And that theme is 'close is good enough'. And it will be up to you to decide whether close is good enough. It will be up to you to decide whether justice means close is good enough. And when you have heard this evidence, I'm going to ask you to do one thing. I'm going to ask you to send this man home to his wife and family where he belongs. Thank you.

The Prosecution Begins

Ron Michaels is sitting upright in his chair at the long defense table, almost rigid, his best posture. Underneath his suit coat and shirt & tie, he wears a bulky Taser vest that can be remotely activated. It makes him look much larger than he really is. His family has been told that no one is to approach or touch Ron. His wife hasn't felt the touch of his hand since the day he was taken into custody, almost a year ago now. His mind is busy praying, although his eyes are slowly scanning the room, his fingers rolling a pencil above the blank pad of paper before him. Jon Hawks sits to his left and is organizing notes and documents. Jim Fleming's seat is to Ron's right. Rob Fleming is seated in a chair behind the defense table with cases of documents and note pads. Sitting between his attorneys gives Ron some comfort, and sends a signal of a unified defense to the jury. Ron has prepared himself for this day. He and an army of friends and family have been praying for this trial to begin, after so many disappointments and delays. He looks back at his wife and family seated directly behind him in the gallery. He doesn't smile, but he makes eye contact with each one for a brief second or two. He nods to a few of them.

Jim returns to the council table and takes his seat near Ron. He leans over to Ron and softly says, "Are you ready for this?"

Ron looks at him and nods. Jim thinks to himself, *Well good. That makes one of us.*

Jim, Rob and Hawkeye have spent the last few days together in Jim's kitchen, at his place outside of Monticello, getting organized for this trial. They have been sorting Jim notes and contacting witnesses, making sure they would be available to testify. Over the past few months, Jim has done significant legal research, tracked down and traveled to interview many of the witnesses for the defense in person, and spent countless hours on the phone interviewing others. His brother Rob will be staying in the spare bedroom at Jim's place during the trial, and is setup with an Internet connection and a work space. Hawks will be commuting from his home in the St. Louis Park. Jim hasn't slept well for many weeks. He has been consumed with the preparation for this trial. He knows Ron is in serious trouble and is depending upon him and his team to protect him from this prosecution. He has the list of the prosecution's witnesses, nearly twenty-five of them. None of them, other than co-defendants Dale Todd and Terry Olson, could have been at the scene. Some half dozen on the list are currently incarcerated; jailhouse testimony is not the most credible information. These people would certainly be looking for any way to shorten their own sentences, at anyone's expense. He must be sure these witnesses are not allowed to testify, as they have never met or spoken with Ron Michaels, and their testimony should be inadmissible.

Inmates have been known to use "Spot-Light On Crime", the BCA website program, to become familiar with cases being investigated, so as to fabricate credible information regarding the case. They contact the BCA, sometimes through a family member, to claim they have information regarding the case and are willing to help out in consideration of a shorter sentence, or the reward. These are desperate men with little to lose.

THE COURT: You may call your witness.

MS. MOHAUPT: Thank you. Jane Filek.

THE COURT: You may administer the oath.

A woman in her late 60s or early 70s enters the court-room and approaches the witness stand. She is nicely dressed, but practical for the rural setting. A thin but healthy looking woman, she stops short of the jury box and is sworn in.

Jane Filek, after having been first duly sworn, is examined and testifies as follows:

THE CLERK: Would you please have a seat and state your name for the record, spelling your last name.

THE WITNESS: Jane Filek. F, as in Frank, i-1 -e-k.

THE COURT: The State may proceed.

The Prosecutor rises from her chair and steps out from behind the prosecution's table, to the right of the defense table. She holds a pen in one hand; her other hand hangs at her side. She can sense the support for Ron Michaels represented by the large group behind her. She has never prosecuted such an important case and wants to do the best job she can. It is going to be tough, but she *is* tough and feels up to the task.

Ann Mohaupt tries to put the witness at ease, asking basic questions about her residence and her family; basic small talk. As they begin to get into the questioning, the witness testi-fies that at approximately 3:00 a.m. on the morning of August 11th, she and her elderly mother were returning from her floral shop to their home after working late to prepare an order for a wedding the next day. Just north of Montrose she saw what she believed to be a large piece of wood laying partially in the road-way. She stopped along side it to see if she could move it onto the shoulder where it would be out of the way of traffic. Instead, she found the dead body of Jeff Hammill, and in a panic she raced to the courthouse in Buffalo to report it.

Jim Flemings' cross examination reveals that there was little to no light available for Filek to see any details of the body; she could not recall seeing blood on the body or pooled on the pavement. Filek also states that people had been cutting and hauling wood for some time in that area for use in wood stoves and wood furnaces.

The witness is excused. Jane Filek steps down from the witness stand and exits the courtroom.

THE COURT: The State may call its next witness.

MS. MOHAUPT: Thank you. Janis Amatuzio.

Janis Amatuzio enters the courtroom and approaches the witness stand. She is an attractive woman in her mid 50's, nicely dressed with an air of confidence. She takes the oath.

Dr. Janis Amatuzio, after having been first duly sworn, is examined and testifies as follows:

THE CLERK: Would you have a seat and please state your name for the record, spelling your last name.

THE WITNESS: My name is Janis with an 's', Amatuzio, A-m-a-t-u-z-i-o.

DIRECT EXAMINATION BY MS. MOHAUPT:

Ann: Good Morning.

Dr. Amatuzio: Good morning.

Ann: Could you please advise the jury of your educational background?

Dr. Amatuzio: Yes. I am a medical doctor and a board certified forensic pathologist. I took my training at the University of Minnesota. I graduated from University of Minnesota College of Liberal Arts in 1973 and then went on to medical school there. I graduated in 1977, took an internship at the University of Minnesota Hospitals in Internal Medicine from 1977 to '78, and then transferred into specialty training in pathology. I went to the Hennepin County Medical Center, where I studied for five years. I took two years of subspecialty training in anatomic pathology, two years of training in clinical pathology and an extra year at the Hennepin County Medical Examiner's Office in forensic pathology. When I finished all that training, I had an M.D. I was board certified in anatomic, clinical and forensic pathology as of 1983.

Ann: Could you tell us what anatomic, clinical and forensic pathology is?

Dr. Amatuzio: Yes. Pathology is the study of disease, and it's separated into two broad categories: anatomic and clinical. Anatomic pathology has to do with diagnosing disease by looking at tissues. An example of this might be looking at a tissue biopsy, such as a breast biopsy or prostate biopsy, under the microscope. Another example of this would be performing a postmortem examination or autopsy and, again, looking at the tissues to make a diagnosis. Clinical pathology has to do with diagnosing disease by looking at body fluids such as blood or urine. An example of this might be a blood cholesterol level. Forensic pathology is a subspecialty in pathology and it has to do with studying the patterns of injuries and patterns of disease as they relate to sudden, unexpected and unusual deaths.

Ann: Is it helpful for a person who would be employed as the medical examiner to have all three of those specialties?

Dr. Amatuzio: Yes, it is.

Ann: Could you tell us a little bit about your employment history?

Dr. Amatuzio: Yes. In 1983 I started practice at Regina Hospital in Hastings, and I worked with Dr. John Plunkett. I had worked with him since 1979 as assistant coroner for Scott County and then in 1983 as assistant coroner for Dakota County and in 1986 as assistant coroner in Chisago County. I practiced at Regina as assistant coroner for those three counties until 1989. In 1989 I left that practice and came up to this area and began practicing at Unity and Mercy Hospitals in Coon Rapids and Fridley. And I worked as a consultant for the then Anoka County Medical Examiner, Dr. Joseph Webbington. In 1993 he retired and I became the Anoka County Coroner. In 1995 I became the Wright County Coroner. In 1998 three more counties were added: Mille Lacs, Meeker and Crow Wing. And in 2005 McLeod and Sibley Counties were added. So currently I am the now medical examiner, since the law changed, for seven Minnesota counties, and I direct a system of death investigation.

Ann: Do you publish articles and things on this kind of topic?

Dr. Amatuzio: Yes, I have published articles in the journals, although not so many recently; much more so when I was a little younger. I also am currently an assistant professor at the University of Minnesota School of Medicine in the Department of Mortuary Science and this spring will begin my fifth year of teaching students about pathology and forensic pathology.

Ann: Do you also teach other kinds of training like seminars and things like that?

Dr. Amatuzio: Yes, in my death investigation system I employ death investigators who live and work in each of the counties where I am the medical examiner. As a result, I have to train those individuals, so I have initial and ongoing training for death investigators in each of those counties. I also teach for the Bureau of Criminal Apprehension in their BCA partnership program. And I'm invited to teach in other seminars throughout the state and the four or five state area for death investigation and forensic pathology.

Ann: What does it mean to say that you're a coroner or a medical examiner?

Dr. Amatuzio: Well, a coroner or medical examiner is a designation that is given by the state statute—up until this year the word was coroner—when you are appointed or elected by the county commissioners to serve as the person who's in charge of the death investigation system. In more recent times forensic pathologists are put in charge of death investigation systems, but there simply aren't enough of those to go around, and we find the forensic pathologists serving in that capacity usually in the larger metropolitan areas. But since the state statute was upgraded any system that is directed by a forensic pathologist is now called a medical examiner system.

So since July 1, my name changed from coroner to medical examiner.

Ann: Now, in all seven counties that you listed here, are you the only medical examiner?

Dr. Amatuzio: I am not the only medical examiner. I work with two other full-time physicians and one other part-time physician, all of whom are forensic pathologists.

Ann: Are you the boss?

Dr. Amatuzio: I'm the boss.

Ann: Okay. What are the populations of all these counties added together?

Dr. Amatuzio: Oh, the population comes to about five or 600,000 people.

Ann: Is there a difference between being a medical examiner in more rural areas than more metro areas?

Dr. Amatuzio: The difference is this: in the more rural areas we tend to see slightly different types of deaths. In the more metropolitan areas, for example, we may see more deaths as a result of crimes involving drug use and handguns whereas in the more rural areas, where we tend to have more hunters, we tend to see a slightly different type of pattern of death investigations, usually involving, say, farm implements, tractors, thresh machines, long guns, hunting accidents and things like that.

Ann continues to question Dr. Amatuzio, learning she has performed or supervised directly between 2,500 and 3,000 postmortem examinations or autopsies in her twenty-six-year career. She also testifies at trials from nine to twelve times per year. She explains that her training covered injuries caused by people being struck by motor vehicles and that she has been involved with approximately twenty-five or so of these cases.

Ann: What kinds of things would you normally expect to find if you were dealing with a person who had been struck by a motor vehicle?

Dr. Amatuzio: There's a particular pattern of injury that's seen when an individual is struck by a motor vehicle. There's evidence of contact between the vehicle and the person. This may take the form of transfer of glass, broken glass, plastic, dirt from the vehicle, or black material from the rubber tires. It also involves the transfer of energy if the vehicle was in motion when it struck the person. And as a result we tend to see that the person has … the person's body has moved and many times has contact with the roadway that indicates that the person rolled or tumbled along the roadway. And as a result sometimes we'll pick up the debris that's on the roadway depending on, of course, the season.

Ann: Can you tell us what an autopsy is exactly and why you do them?

Dr. Amatuzio: Yes. An autopsy is part of a death investigation. Sometimes one would think it's the only part of a death investigation, but an investigation involves examination of the death scene, knowledge of the circumstances surrounding the death—both the medical and the social—and then the autopsy when indicated. The purpose of an autopsy is to document injuries or the lack thereof. An autopsy, done by a forensic pathologist, involves a very close look at the external surfaces of the body which will include the clothing, looking for any evidence that's deposited on the clothing; any rips or tears that might be correlated with injuries. It will also include a very close examination of the external surfaces of the body. Examples of this might be fingernail clippings or a sexual assault exam. It might involve x-rays. It always involves photographs. And when the external examination is completed and described, then the internal examination is begun. This is done by making a Y-shaped incision, like I'm showing you on myself, from shoulder to shoulder to the mid-portion of the sternum and then down to approximately the pubic bone. The external tissues are reflected. The ribs are then cut and then all of the organs in the chest cavity and abdomen are examined. During that period of time, blood will be drawn from the heart and from the peripheral blood vessels, urine might be gathered from the bladder, the stomach contents will be checked, a portion of tissue such as liver might be taken or saved. Now, in a forensic autopsy where we might be concerned about any hemorrhage or bleeding or injury to the neck, the neck is saved for last. So when the chest and abdominal organs are completed, we then look at the head. An autopsy on the head involves looking at the scalp surfaces, sometimes shaving the hair and then making an incision on the back of the scalp, like I'm showing you, from the back of the ear to the back of the ear and then reflecting the scalp forward. It's just done by blunt dissection with the fingers reflecting the scalp forward and backward. This exposes the calvarium; that is, skull. Then, using a saw that vibrates, much like what is used to take a cast off with, the bone is cut. In fact, approximately a quarter of the bone of the skull is cut, just the back quarter, and is removed. Then the membranes behind the brain are examined, the brain itself is examined, the brain is removed, weighed, sectioned or cut. And then the membranes that are stuck to the bones, called the dura, are then removed and any fractures that might be present at the base of the skull are examined. Following that examination, then the neck structures are examined. The purpose and the reason for this is so that blood is drained from below from the vessels and from above and that way no artifact can be introduced into the neck organs. And so then the larynx is removed, sometimes the tongue and the cervical spine. The neck spine processes are identified and examined.

Ann: Do you look at the limbs, too?

Dr. Amatuzio: Yes, we look at the limbs both for fracture and for any scrapes or abrasions or injuries. We also look at the surfaces of the hands, feet, between the toes, between the fingers. It's a very intimate examination.

Ann: As a forensic expert, are you occasionally asked to review old autopsy and death records?

Dr. Amatuzio: Yes, I am. If a question still remains in the family's mind or if new evidence has been... has come forward, I might be asked to review findings from the past.

Ann: How unusual is it for you to get such a request?

Dr. Amatuzio: It's not very common. I've had perhaps two or three of these in the twenty-six years I've been practicing.

Ann: Were you asked to review the autopsy records on the death of a young man by the name of Jeffrey Hammill?

Dr. Amatuzio: I was. The Wright County Sheriff's Office asked me to review that in 2003.

Ann: When you did your review, did your observations result in any facts that were different from those noted in the original reports?

Dr. Amatuzio: No. I looked at the autopsy report that Dr. Bozanich from the St. Cloud Hospital had done and my only differences with him would be my terms of description, but I agreed with the photographs that I had seen and his interpretation.

Ann: Did you think the autopsy report was a good report?

Dr. Amatuzio: Yes, I did—for a hospital pathologist. A hospital pathologist is more concerned with diagnosing disease and might not have as much experience looking at injury patterns and interpreting the cause of those patterns. Forensic pathologists are trained to do that. A forensic autopsy performed by a forensic pathologist is now the standard; it's now the state of the art for sudden, unusual and unexpected deaths. In years past it was not the standard because there were not many forensic pathologists present in the state. There are currently between eight and twelve forensic pathologists in the State of Minnesota.

Ann: But if I heard your testimony correctly, it was your opinion that this was, nevertheless, a good autopsy?

Dr. Amatuzio: Yes, it was.

The prosecutor now begins submitting autopsy reports, death certificates, and autopsy photos as evidence, giving each one an exhibit number for future reference. Under direct examination, Dr. Amatuzio states that she disagreed with a term used by the hospital pathologist that performed the original autopsy, in that he referenced a contusion, or bruise, in the back of the lung, which she believes is a normal postmortem finding.

Ann: Under his autopsy Cause of Death, did you agree with his findings?

Dr. Amatuzio: Yes, I do.

Ann: And did the coroner who did the initial investigation make a determination as to the type of death?

Dr. Amatuzio: He listed it as violent.

Ann: Is there a spot on the report of the investigation by the coroner for the individual to indicate whether the death was a result of a motor vehicle accident?

Dr. Amatuzio: Yes.

Ann: Did the coroner indicate that this was a motor vehicle accident?

Dr. Amatuzio: No.

Ann: Thank you. Now, Exhibit Number Four is a new death certificate; is that correct?

Dr. Amatuzio: Yes, that's an amended death certificate.

Ann: And who filed that?

Dr. Amatuzio: I did, because I changed the manner of death from undetermined to homicide.

Ann: So after your review it was your opinion that this was a homicide?

Dr. Amatuzio: Yes.

The prosecutor now presents a series of extremely graphic autopsy photographs of Jeff Hammill. Dr. Amatuzio begins describing what each photograph is showing, beginning with the external injuries, then moving on to the accompanying internal injuries.

Dr. Amatuzio: I'll start with what's been marked as Exhibit Five. This is a photograph of the right side of Jeffrey Hammill's face. His head is laying on a rose-colored head block. What you notice on the right temple area, and I'm indicating that area on myself, is that there is an abrasion or a scrape to the skin. This indicates contact with some object. In addition, there is a tear, a crush type injury to Jeffrey Hammill's right ear, which actually tears up into the cartilage portion of the ear. And behind that, over the bone that I'm indicating on myself, a bone called the mastoid process, there was a bruise and an abrasion as well. Exhibit Number Six is a photograph that's taken of the left side of Jeffrey Hammill's head. It shows a gloved hand holding a ruler near a laceration, or tear, of his scalp. The laceration is gaping open. It's laying a little bit as though it is flopping open. The laceration is approximately, but not quite, four inches in length. Dr. Bozanich also describes a scrape or an abrasion on the skin which immediately is covered by the ruler. You can also see the presence of blood in Mr. Hammill's left ear canal. The injuries that I saw on Exhibits Five and Six are of the external surfaces. I also viewed photographs of the internal surfaces of the head. When the scalp was reflected back, there was bleeding into the soft tissues of the scalp along the entire back of the head in the area I'm showing you on myself. When the front portion of the scalp was reflected forward, there was an irregular, zigzag fracture of the right side of the skull above the right ear that was depressed or pushed into the brain. When the brain itself was removed from the cranial vault, there was a basilar skull fracture which extended and communicated with the depressed skull fracture on the right and extended across in the area I'm indicating to you on myself: the base of the skull through what is called the petrous bones which house the ear organs, the auditory organs. When the fracture extended from the right to the left, it then extended into the back of the skull on the left side. This is the reason that Mr. Hammill had blood exuding from both of his ears at the death scene: because of the basilar skull fracture causing injury to the bones that house the auditory organs and cause bleeding from the ears. The examination of the brain revealed that it was swollen. It weighed more than it normally should weigh. It also showed evidence of injuries and bleeding on the surfaces of the brain as well as bruising; probably bruising on the anterior or inferior surfaces of the brain. The meaning of these injuries is this: looking at both the external findings and the internal findings, it is my opinion that Jeffrey Hammill was struck at least twice, possibly three times, with a blunt instrument. This caused him to fall, and he probably fell backwards, impacting his scalp with a broad, flat surface such as the pavement. Dr. Bozanich did not shave the back of Mr. Hammill's scalp so I could not see if there was any impact injury with the scalp itself. Either the fall or, more likely, the blows both to the left side and to the right side of his skull were sufficient to have caused the fracture at the base of the skull and the associated brain injuries.

Ann: Have you formed an opinion as to what type of an implement or what type of object caused those injuries?

Dr. Amatuzio: Yes. It would be a manufactured item that was blunt but had at least one linear surface and was a heavy instrument.

Ann: You indicated that the basilar skull … did you say it was one of the hardest bones in the body?

Dr. Amatuzio: Yes, the bones at the base of the skull are the hardest bones in the body; that is why they're called petrous.

Ann: So how much force would it take to break them? Dr. Amatuzio: It would take a large amount of force.

Ann: In your opinion, could these wounds have been made without a weapon?

Dr. Amatuzio: It's possible, but more likely that they were caused either by a fall, unsupported fall, impacting the pavement without catching one's self or breaking the fall or by being struck by a large, blunt, heavy object.

Ann: You indicated earlier that you had formed an opinion that Jeffrey Hammill died as a result of a homicide; is that correct?

Dr. Amatuzio: I classified the manner of his death as a homicide.

Ann: Do you have any doubts about that?

Dr. Amatuzio: I don't.

Ann: What about the injuries that you observed convinced you of that?

Dr. Amatuzio: The fact that at the death scene there was no indication that he had been struck by a motor vehicle. The pattern of bleeding was such that he appeared to have been injured where he died and exsanguinated, or bled out, because there was a large amount of blood beneath his head and on the road surfaces adjacent to his body. The autopsy report that I reviewed, along with the photographs of Dr. Bozanich, indicate to me that Mr. Hammill's death was a result of an assault by another person or persons.

Ann: Could he have been hit by an object protruding from a motor vehicle, like a rearview mirror or something like that?

Dr. Amatuzio: Based on the totality of the investigation, my conclusion is no.

Ann: Again, do you have any reservations about your opinion that this was a homicide?

Dr. Amatuzio: I do not.

Ann: We've talked about that the weapon would have been a linear object; what in your opinion are some types of linear objects that you have observed in your twenty-six years to cause these types of injuries?

Dr. Amatuzio: I have observed a metal handrail causing injuries similar to this.

Ann: Would a tire iron cause these kind of injuries?

Dr. Amatuzio: They could.

Ann: Would a bat cause these kinds of injuries?

Dr. Amatuzio: It's possible.

Ann: Would a hockey stick cause these kinds of injuries?

Dr. Amatuzio: Possible, but less likely.

Ann: Thank you. I have no further questions at this time.

CHAPTER 12

THE COURT: Mr. Fleming, you may proceed with your cross-examination.

MR. FLEMING: Thank you, Your Honor.

CROSS-EXAMINATION BY MR. FLEMING:

Jim begins his cross examination, trying to determine when, why and how Dr. Amatuzio was asked to review the autopsy and medical examiner's reports regarding the death of Jeffrey Hammill. Dr. Amatuzio's testimony reveals that she was contacted by the Wright County Sheriff's department in early 2003, given the circumstances of the case and the reason for the investigation. She was told that the daughter of Jeffrey Hammill had come forward and was questioning the circumstances of her fathers' death, and could they shed anymore light on what had happened.

The investigation took some time and involved meetings or conversations with the Minnesota BCA; the review of a summary, prepared by the BCA at Dr Amatuzio's request, of all the case records and photographs, and it wasn't until August of 2005 that Dr. Amatuzio changed the death certificate to 'homicide'.

Jim: You indicated that normally in the course of these investigations and specifically in this one, that you reviewed "old material and new evidence." Do you recall stating that?

Dr. Amatuzio: I probably did say that.

Jim: In the course of making the decision to change the death certificate in this case, did you review any new evidence?

Dr. Amatuzio: I recall reviewing some information that was brought by the Sheriff's Department from 2003 which may have had to do with interviews. In other words, I reviewed a summary of interview material that I believe had come from 1979 so there was no new information.

Jim: Now, you testified that you had only made one change in the original death certificate?

Dr. Amatuzio: Yes.

Jim: Drawing your attention to a little more than halfway down on the right side, box number thirty-two, where it says, "physician viewed the body after death." You marked "Yes"?

Dr. Amatuzio: Yes.

Jim: Okay. I don't see a corresponding box on the original certificate of death?

Dr. Amatuzio: On the original it says, yeah, they don't say yes or no up there. It just says, "Physician viewed the body," and neither box is checked, yes.

Jim: Okay. But you had marked the box "Yes" on the new death certificate.

Dr. Amatuzio: Yes, I did.

Jim: You also indicate in part two, box thirty-four, "Recent ethanol use."

Dr. Amatuzio: Yes.

Jim: And you have ".09."

Dr. Amatuzio: Grams percent.

Jim: Where did you obtain the information as far as the measurement?

Dr. Amatuzio: From the BCA report.

Jim: Okay. So that wasn't part of the original?

Dr. Amatuzio: Dr. Bendix did not list that on the original.

Jim: You testified that you consider the autopsy done by Dr. Bozanich to be good for a hospital pathologist?

Dr. Amatuzio: Yes, I do.

Jim: Okay. Isn't it true that in the grand jury you were asked about your perception of the quality of the autopsy and you said that he had done a very meticulous autopsy?

Dr. Amatuzio: Yes.

Jim: Okay. And you also are now testifying that it was good for a hospital pathologist?

Dr. Amatuzio: That's correct.

Jim: Sounds like there's a gap there to me and what I think—let me just ask it this way, isn't it true that he did as good a job as he could as a hospital or a clinical pathologist, but he did not do the job that a forensic pathologist would do because he didn't have the training?

Dr. Amatuzio: That's correct.

Jim: And as a result of that, you or any doctor that would review this autopsy is in the unfortunate position of being limited by the work that was done by the previous physician who actually was there, viewed the body, took the measurements, made the examinations, all you can do is review what they've done?

Dr. Amatuzio: That's correct.

Jim: You can't go over and redo the whole thing?

Dr. Amatuzio: Unfortunately, not.

Jim: Is it true that there are a variety of different techniques that can be used where information is drawn from the body to help try to determine the time of death based upon some progression of drop in body temperature?

Dr. Amatuzio: Yes.

Jim: Okay. And I understand that one of those is literally putting some type of a medical thermometer into the internal organs and I think it's the liver; is that right?

Dr. Amatuzio: That's a practice that was done when I was in my training in the '70s but I haven't seen it done more recently.

Jim: In 1979 that would have been the standard, would it not?

Dr. Amatuzio: Yes.

Jim: But it wasn't done in this case, was it?

Dr. Amatuzio: Not that I can observe, no.

Jim: You brought up the fact that he had not shaved the back of the head.

Dr. Amatuzio: That's correct.

Jim: Okay. Now, when you are dealing with a basilar skull fracture, wouldn't that be customary?

Dr. Amatuzio: When I'm dealing with a basilar skull fracture and associated head injuries, shaving of the hair from the scalp is customary.

Jim: Okay. The basilar skull fracture, I want to talk about that just for a moment or two, you talked about the … I'm trying to remember … the base of the skull is referred to as petrous bone.

Dr. Amatuzio: That's correct.

Jim: Is it because it's one of the hardest, or is it also the thickness?

Dr. Amatuzio: Both.

Jim: Okay. And you're familiar with the term Turkish saddle?

Dr. Amatuzio: Yes, I am.

Jim: I wasn't, but I want you to tell the jury a little bit about that.

Dr. Amatuzio: At the base of the skull there are actually six fossae or depressions. There's two in the front, two in the middle and two in the back. We call these fossae, cranial fossae, the two anterior, the two middle and the two posterior. At the junction of the two middle and the two anterior, there is a bony formation that looks like a saddle, and I'm showing you that with my hand now, kind of an inverted U-shape, and that is where the pituitary gland sits, at least the upper portion of the pituitary gland. It's also an area which is associated with the optic chias where the optic nerves cross. And frequently when there is a basilar skull fracture, in other words, fracturing on bones on the petrous ridge, and the petrous ridge sits right in that middle cranial fossa, you can actually see where it will go in and fracture through the sella turcica which means saddle Turkish or Turkish saddle.

Jim: Thank you very much. Now, when the base of the skull is fractured in that fashion, isn't it true that there are some arteries running through that petrous bone?

Dr. Amatuzio: Yes, there are.

Jim: Okay. Base of the skull, basilar skull fracture, is the basil or basilar artery one of those arteries?

Dr. Amatuzio: The basilar artery is an artery that's located in that area. It doesn't actually run through the bone. It runs on top of the bone.

Jim: How about the internal carotids?

Dr. Amatuzio: Absolutely.

Jim: And so then that would transverse up through the base of the skull?

Dr. Amatuzio: Yeah. The way it works is the carotid arteries come up the sides, they branch into the internal and external carotid arteries. The internal carotid arteries proceed right on up to the base of the brain. The two vertebral arteries come up right through the transverse processes of the vertebrae in the back. They come up, they form the basilar artery, and they come up and they form something called a circle. In other words, the Circle of Willis, apparently Willis discovered it and described it. And it basically provides for three sources of blood to the brain, one from the right internal carotid, the left internal carotid and one from the basilar artery. So the body is really taking very good care of the blood supply by having three separate blood vessels, which all communicate and which can all supply blood to the brain.

Jim: Thank you. Now, in this particular case isn't it true that as a result of the fracture of the base of the skull that there was a rupturing of that internal carotid artery?

Dr. Amatuzio: There probably was. I don't see that Dr. Bozanich described it, but in all likelihood there was a tearing of those arteries, probably both the right and the left.

Jim: And if that's torn in that fashion, again hypothetical, if that's torn in that fashion and we have an open wound on the side of the head where the scalp is torn away from the skull, that's basically where the blood is coming from, is it not?

Dr. Amatuzio: If that's the only wound you have? Then it would be coming from the basilar skull fracture and the only way for it to get out would be through the ear canal as well as through the scalp wound.

Jim: In the photographs that you examined, did you see significant evidence that would indicate that... you used the term bleeding out.

Dr. Amatuzio: Yes.

Jim: Bleeding to death?

Dr. Amatuzio: Exsanguinating.

Jim: All right. Was there anywhere else that would have provided a route for the escaping blood from the artery other than the wound on the side of the head?

Dr. Amatuzio: The other area where blood could have escaped would have been from the injury to the right ear.

Jim: Did you see any significant evidence of a lot of bleeding from that area?

Dr. Amatuzio: I did not.

Jim: Okay. Basilar skull fractures, you talked about it in terms of something blunt, heavy, with a linear edge.

Dr. Amatuzio: Correct.

Jim: But it's true, is it not, that basilar skull fractures can result from a number of different types of impact dynamics?

Dr. Amatuzio: Absolutely.

Jim: Are you familiar with the race car driver Dale Earnhardt?

Dr. Amatuzio: I am.

Jim: Okay. Do you know why I'm asking the question?

Dr. Amatuzio: Not yet but I know he died and I was very sad.

Jim: Wasn't it in fact the case that the impact that he suffered in the race that took his life resulted in a basilar skull fracture?

Dr. Amatuzio: I'm not sure, but if you told me that was true, I would not be surprised.

Jim: Okay. Isn't it also true that it has been determined by military physicians that in crashes when helicopters lose lift, in other words, if they're shot down or have mechanical failure, that the impact against the side of the Plexiglas even inside the helmet can cause a basilar skull fracture?

Dr. Amatuzio: Yes, it can.

Jim: So, in other words, there are a number of different causes for basilar skull fractures?

Dr. Amatuzio: Yes, there are.

Jim: I was interested in the way that you were describing the injury to the ear because you referred to it as a tearing or crush type injury.

Dr. Amatuzio: Yes.

Jim: Under what circumstances does a crushing type of injury or crushing type of impact, cause something like that to happen?

Dr. Amatuzio: When the force used exceeds the elasticity of the tissue and then the tissue tears.

Jim: You're familiar with a British doctor by the name of W.H. Battle?

Dr. Amatuzio: Yes, I am.

Jim: And you're obviously then familiar with the concept of Battle's sign?

Dr. Amatuzio: I am.

Jim: Could you describe for the jury what Battle's sign is?

Dr. Amatuzio: Battle's sign is a bruise or discoloration of the tissues that occurs; that you can see on the mastoid bone when there's a basilar skull fracture.

Jim: Now, isn't there also another similar type of indicator that would in layman's terms, would be referred to as raccoon eyes?

Dr. Amatuzio: Yes.

Jim: And could you describe that for us?

Dr. Amatuzio: 'Raccoon eyes' refers to discoloration of the soft tissues around the eyes that can occur whenever there is a head injury. It has to do with the infiltration of the soft tissues around the eyes with blood. Blood is red and it causes discoloration. So it can appear as though the individual has been struck in the eye whereas, in fact, it may just be an injury to another spot with the blood traveling to that area.

Jim: Is that common with basilar skull fractures as well?

Dr. Amatuzio: I don't know.

Jim: Is it possible in this situation that what you're seeing in the photograph that you're referring to as a bruise and abrasion to the mastoid could be Battle's signs since we do have a basilar skull fracture?

Dr. Amatuzio: You know, it would help me if I could just refer to Dr. Bozanich's report in his description and I've got it here. Could I just take a quick look? Dr. Bozanich gives us this description and it's about halfway down in the paragraph. Dr. Bozanich describes, "The skin posterior to the laceration," he's referring to the right ear, "presents a small area of semicircular abrasive reddish colored discoloration." So unfortunately we don't have a clear forensic description. He uses the word "abrasive," which gives me an idea that there is an abrasion or scrape to the skin, but he also says, "reddish discoloration," which may indicate bleeding that could be as a result of either a bruise or Battle's sign, or basilar skull fracture.

Jim: May I approach the witness?

The Court: You may.

Jim: Doctor, I'm handing you what's been marked as Exhibit Six and I'm going to ask you a question or two about that. Is it true from your examination of that photograph, that it indicates that immediately… I've got to get my posterior anterior… anterior ?

Dr. Amatuzio: Anterior.

Jim: Immediately in front of, let's put it that way, in front of the area where the tear begins that you've got an area where the scalp has been scraped clean?

Dr. Amatuzio: That's correct.

Jim: Does that indicate to you that whatever struck in that area may have had some type of a mechanical edge?

Dr. Amatuzio: Mechanical or blunt edge as opposed to a sharp edge like a knife.

Jim: But something that could scrape the hair off of the scalp in that area?

Dr. Amatuzio: Yes.

Jim: Are you able to determine from the photograph, if Mr. Hammill were standing upright, at what angle would that tear be moving from front to back?

Dr. Amatuzio: It is moving from front to back and it appears to be moving very slightly upward but predominantly horizontal.

Jim: Okay. Thank you. Does it appear from the photograph that something struck in that area and as it started to move it I'll use the term bit in or caused such a gathering that it began a tear?

Dr. Amatuzio: Yes, it does and that is the classic mechanics of an impact and what we would describe as a laceration where the force exceeds the tissue, the tissue's ability to stretch, and finally it tears. So an impact occurred on the left side causing a scrape. It impacted, scraped. And then the force with which it was delivered was sufficient that the tissue just broke, tore in front of it. And it tore the scalp and it undermined. And in this photograph we can see that the scalp is actually cupping backwards or sagging backwards a bit.

Jim: May I approach, Your Honor?

The Court: You may.

Jim: In the photograph which has been marked as Exhibit Number Seven—

Dr. Amatuzio: Yes.

Jim: You were referring to the injury to the right wrist in any event?

Dr. Amatuzio: Yes.

Jim: And you stated that your opinion was that it could be a defensive wound?

Dr. Amatuzio: Yes.

Jim: Okay. Isn't it true that from just simply looking at that, it's impossible to know definitely whether it is a defensive wound or not?

Dr. Amatuzio: That's correct.

Jim: In fact, I believe in Dr. Bozanich's autopsy he referred to it as a dry wound?

Dr. Amatuzio: As a what?

Jim: As a dry wound?

Dr. Amatuzio: He may have in his autopsy report.

Jim: Okay.

Dr. Amatuzio: The tissues might have appeared to have been dry.

Jim: For a forensic pathologist, what would be the significance of that as a dry wound?

Dr. Amatuzio: The significance of that might mean that the injury had occurred prior to his death; that the injury might have begun to show some areas of healing. However, we won't know that because Dr. Bozanich did not take a section of that skin and look at it under the microscope so we could see if there was any microscopic evidence of healing.

Jim: You talked about the swelling of the brain and the fact that it weighed more than it should have.

Dr. Amatuzio: Yes.

Jim: If a brain is swollen, what would account for the additional weight?

Dr. Amatuzio: Fluid.

Jim: Fluid. Is it blood or–

Dr. Amatuzio: It's usually a component of blood. When the brain is injured, it usually swells. And it swells because the cells are injured. Sometimes the pump that keeps the sodium out and the potassium in, stops working as well. And so water is drawn into the cells from the blood and water is a component of blood. So usually the fluid has to do with water in the cells. And it can also have to do with the presence of blood on the surfaces of the brain or in and around the membranes of the brain.

Jim: Okay. In this case I believe that you said that it appeared as though Mr. Hammill had bled out.

Dr. Amatuzio: That's correct.

Jim: Bleeding would stop when the heart stops; is that correct?

Dr. Amatuzio: Yes.

Jim: So Mr. Hammill bled to death before his brain swelled to the point where that would be a mechanism of death; is that correct?

Dr. Amatuzio: Well you know; the problem with us making statements one way or the other is that dying is a process, and it's going to take a period of minutes to exsanguinate or to bleed out, particularly if one is just bleeding through a scalp laceration. So it certainly is possible for the brain to have begun to swell as part of the injuries that it sustained. And so I think I've lost the point of the question. Perhaps you could restate it.

Jim: Actually, no, I think you answered the question.

Dr. Amatuzio: Okay.

Jim: Just a few more questions. Wouldn't you consider it to be fairly normal in a case where an individual is accosted by one or two assailants and struck multiple times with large, heavy objects with a linear edge that there would be some blood splatter on the clothing, in the area?

Dr. Amatuzio: You know, it would be more common than not to see splatter.

Jim: Okay. I hate to do this to you.

Dr. Amatuzio: Go ahead.

Jim: But do you recognize this book?

Dr. Amatuzio: I do.

Jim: Entitled "Forever Ours"?

Dr. Amatuzio: Yes.

Jim: And I believe that you are the author?

Dr. Amatuzio: I am.

Jim: Okay. The only reason that I bring the book into it is because I saw something as I was reading it that I wanted to talk to you about. And that appears on page sixty where you're talking about, in an explanation of how the process of forensic pathology works, "After a death all the investigator can rely on are clues, telltale signs and observations. The death scene yields an enormous amount of information about the person and his or her habits. The position of the body, the state of the clothing, the postmortem signs of rigor, livor, algor mortis."

Dr. Amatuzio: Yes.

Jim: What is algor mortis?

Dr. Amatuzio: That is the cooling of the body after death. A body cools about a degree and a half per hour.

Jim: Okay.

Dr. Amatuzio: ... after death, Fahrenheit.

Jim: Okay. And also whether the body was moved or the person struggled before dying?

Dr. Amatuzio: Yes.

Jim: In the examination that you conducted on the photographs of Mr. Hammill at the scene, did you see any signs evident in those photographs of any sort of struggle?

Dr. Amatuzio: I did not.

Jim: Okay. Last question, do you recall when you talked with the people from the Bureau of Criminal Apprehension, did they explain to you how they became involved in the case?

Dr. Amatuzio: No.

Jim: You just knew that they were?

Dr. Amatuzio: Yes.

Jim: Was there a point in time where you were advised by representatives of the Sheriff's office that there was a need for you to change the death certificate?

Dr. Amatuzio: Not that there was a need, but they asked me if I was going to change the death certificate.

Jim: Okay. Thank you very much. No further questions, Your Honor.

The Court: Ms. Mohaupt, any redirect?

Ann: Yes, thank you.

REDIRECT EXAMINATION BY MS. MOHAUPT

Ann: I just have a few questions, Doctor. First of all, have any of Mr. Fleming's questions brought anything to mind that has caused you to change your opinion in any way?

Dr. Amatuzio: No.

Ann: Does the fact that the hospital pathologist didn't take the temperature of the internal organs change your opinion?

Dr. Amatuzio: No.

Ann: Does the fact that the hospital pathologist did not shave the back of Mr. Hammill's head change your opinion?

Dr. Amatuzio: No.

Ann: Did your discussion with Mr. Fleming regarding the Turkish saddle and the carotid arteries change your opinion in any way?

Dr. Amatuzio: No.

Ann: Does the lack of raccoon eyes change your opinion in any way?

Dr. Amatuzio: No.

Ann: Does the fact that a basil skull fracture can happen to a race car driver and people in a helicopter during a crash change your opinion in any way?

Dr. Amatuzio: No.

Ann: Did your discussion with Mr. Fleming regarding Battle's sign change your opinion in any way?

Dr. Amatuzio: No.

Ann: You discussed Exhibit Six in depth and talked about how the scalp was scraped by the wound, right?

Dr. Amatuzio: Yes, I did.

Ann: So scraping could have or would have been caused by the instrument that created the wound; is that correct?

Dr. Amatuzio: Yes.

Ann: Again, could a tire iron have made that wound?

Dr. Amatuzio: It could have, a glancing blow.

Ann: Does the fact that the injury was front to back, basically horizontal but slightly up, cause you to change your opinion in any way?

Dr. Amatuzio: No.

Ann: Does the fact that what could have been a defense wound also could have been a dry wound change your opinion in any way?

Dr. Amatuzio: No, it does not.

Ann: Does the fact that the brain was swollen change your opinion in any way?

Dr. Amatuzio: No.

Ann: Does the fact that it's more common to see blood splatter than not change your opinion in any way?

Dr. Amatuzio: No.

Ann: Did your discussion from your book change your opinion in any way?

Dr. Amatuzio: No.

Ann: Is it—is there any significance to the fact that there was no sign of struggle?

Dr. Amatuzio: No.

Ann: How could, or in your opinion, could a vehicle towing something that had something protruding out from it cause the injuries on both sides of Mr. Hammill's head?

Dr. Amatuzio: I don't know how that could have happened.

Ann: No. I guess my question is if there was a vehicle towing something that had something protruding out that struck Mr. Hammill in the head, could that have caused the injuries to both sides of his head?

Dr. Amatuzio: No.

Ann: Nothing further.

The Court: You are excused.

Dr. Amatuzio: Thank you.

(2008) Standing at the spot where Jeffrey Hammill was found, looking south towards the intersection of CR-12 and CR-107.

Photo of site where Jeffrey Hammill's body was found on the morning of August 11th, 1979. Orientation is looking South on CR-12 with CR-107 intersecting from the right about ¼ mile down the road. Victim's blood stains the road and shoulder.

Close up of the body outline on the roadway.
Orientation is facing North on CR-12.

The visiting area at the Wright County Jail. A young child waits, while his mother visits with an inmate. This room is often filled with small children playing on the floor, while their parents visit in the cubicles on the right. A terribly depressing place.

We will probably never know what happened to this young man.
But the family of Jeffrey Hammill should know that
there are many people who have, and will continue to
say prayers for them, to find peace with their loss.

A U.S. Attorney was recently quoted; "Perjury undermines
the fundamental mission of our investigative and judicial
processes - to uncover the truth. Lying under oath to a grand
jury must be vigorously prosecuted, or else this essential
truth-finding mission is significantly undermined."

CHAPTER 13

The trial continues with the prosecution calling several witnesses to recreate the events of the evening of August 10th and the early morning of the 11th through their testimony. The police dispatcher on duty the night that Jane Filek rushed in to the Wright County Courthouse to report the body, testifies that just prior to her arrival, he had received a phone call from an unidentified male caller who had reported a body alongside CR-12, just north of Montrose. The phone calls to the police dispatch were recorded on a tape recorder back in 1979; however the tape was written over with new calls after so many days, so there was no record available for the current investigation.

Testimony by then Deputy Mike Simmons, who, along with Deputy Mike Evens were just south of Buffalo on Highway 25 in a police cruiser when the call came in about the body along side the road, established that they were the first two officers on the scene. Simmons testifies that he and Evens found Jeffrey Hammill lying partially on the roadway and determined immediately that he was dead. Deputy Simmons assisted in the search for evidence at the scene and alongside the roadway, with several other officers that morning, but none of them were able to find anything that indicated what had happened. The prosecutor questions Simmons as to what he thought had happened to Hammill; whether he thought this was a hit and run or an assault scene. Simmons states he saw no evidence of a hit and run, and has since come to believe it was an assault. Under cross examination, Jim Fleming reveals that Simmons had no investigative training at the time and that night he was working under the direct supervision of Chief Deputy Jim Powers, locking down the scene and doing search and survey. Simmons subsequently received extensive training while employed in Minnesota, most of which was sponsored by the Minnesota BCA.

Under Jim's cross-examination, Simmons also confirms the

following: no vomit was found alongside the road. No recollection of swampy areas on either side of the road immediately
adjacent to where the body was found. No evidence of any scuffle in the earth at the side of the road. And no blood-spatter on
any of the victim's clothing.

Simmons had spoken on several occasions with Brooks
Martin and Joe Hagerty, both of whom were involved in the
current investigation of this case, and had recently read the initial report filed by Chief Deputy Jim Powers back in 1979.

Jim Fleming ends his cross, and with no re-direct, the witness is excused.

The prosecution calls its next witness: retired Chief Deputy
Jim Powers.

James Powers, after having been first duly sworn, is examined and testifies as follows:

> The Clerk: Would you have a seat and state your name for the
> record and spell your last name for us, please.

> Mr. Powers: My name is Powers, James Franklin. Last name
> spelled P-o-w-e-r-s.

Mr. Powers gives his date of birth.

> Ann: So that makes you how old?

> Mr. Powers: Seventy-five.

> Ann: And where do you live right now?

> Mr. Powers: I live up in Grand Marais, out of town on a nice
> little lake.

> Ann: How long have you been living there?

> Mr. Powers: We've been up there full time ten years.

> Ann: And are you married?

> Mr. Powers: Yes.

> Ann: How long have you been married?

Mr. Powers: Fifty-four years and four days and about sixteen hours.

Chuckles can be heard coming from the Gallery.

Ann: Are you retired?

Mr. Powers: Yes, I am.

Ann: Did you retire from the Wright County Sheriff's Department?

Mr. Powers: Yes, I did.

Ann: And when was it that you retired from the Sheriff's Department?

Mr. Powers: 1991.

Ann: What is the position that you held at the Sheriff's Department at the time of your retirement?

Mr. Powers: I was chief deputy sheriff.

Ann: When did you first become employed by the Sheriff's Department?

Mr. Powers: 1963.

Ann: Did you work steady for the Sheriff's Department from 1963 until you retired in 1991?

Mr. Powers: I did. I also moonlighted and I worked for Clearwater for twenty-five years; ten, fifteen, twenty hours a week. And then part of the time I ran my own security service and I did quite a bit of work for Northern States Power and General Electric and the Bechtel Corporation.

Ann: Who was the sheriff when you first became employed in 1963?

Mr. Powers: Darrell Wolff.

Ann: So Darrell Wolff was basically your boss for the entire time you were here?

Mr. Powers: He was.

Ann: Okay. How big was the department?

Mr. Powers: When I started, there were eight of us. When I retired there were eighty of us.

Ann: So when there were eight, is it fair to say the department relationships were different than when you retired?

Mr. Powers: Oh, I'm sure it was.

Ann: Were you friends with most of the people you worked with in the old days in the '60s and '70s?

Mr. Powers: Yes, you were.

Ann: When did Darrell Wolff first become sheriff?

Mr. Powers: 1963. Jim Krietlow was sheriff and he had a heart attack, died, and the County Board then appointed Darrell Wolff the sheriff.

Ann: So you were employed by the Sheriff's Department on August 11 of 1979?

Mr. Powers: I was.

Ann Mohaupt continues the questioning of Jim Powers, having him recall his early morning phone call requesting he go to the scene, his activities and those of the other officers present, his trip to the mortuary for further examination of the body and the filing of his reports.

Ann: Now, it's my understanding that this investigation remained open for two or three weeks and then it kind of died; is that right?

Mr. Powers: Well, I guess we ran out of leads for one thing. There wasn't anything to really push it any further and some of that, I'll have to admit, is probably my doing; if I may explain that?

Ann: If you want to, okay.

Mr. Powers: Well, I put together a theory of a vehicular-pedestrian homicide.

Ann: So based upon your experience and your observations, do you have an opinion as to where Jeff Hammill died?

Mr. Powers: Yes.

Ann: And where do you think he died?

Mr. Powers: Where he died? Right there on the spot.

Ann: Right there. And based upon your observations and experience, do you think this kid was hit by a car?

Mr. Powers: I think he was hit by something extended.

Ann: From a car?

Mr. Powers: From a truck or a trailer.

Ann: And what made you think that?

Mr. Powers: Well, okay, the guy—this is like he's two miles from where he had been dropped off at this party or whatever, maybe a little longer. So we have to assume that it's 3 o'clock in the morning, he wants to get to Buffalo. He's hitchhiking, right? There's hardly any traffic out there that time of the night so he is overextending himself. By that I mean he's got his head out here (indicating), he's looking down the road at these headlights and he wants somebody to pick him up, he's desperate.

Ann: Over the course of the investigation, was there any evidence that corroborated that theory in any way?

Mr. Powers: Just the body really.

Ann: Did you find any witnesses or any drivers that said any such a thing?

Mr. Powers: No.

Ann: Now, do you think that his injuries could have also been inflicted by somebody hitting him on the head?

Mr. Powers: No.

Ann: You don't think so?

Mr. Powers: Absolutely not.

Ann: Okay. Do you have any medical training?

Mr. Powers: No, I don't.

Ann: Did you talk to any of the coroners or anybody like that?

Mr. Powers: We did at the time. I don't recall.

Ann: And when is it that you developed that theory?

Mr. Powers: Well, I probably started that morning right after leaving the mortuary.

Ann: Okay. And did you share that theory with any other members of the Sheriff's Department?

Mr. Powers: With the sheriff and I also wrote a report, a follow-up report, should have been in the file.

Ann: But you did share it with the sheriff; is that right?

Mr. Powers: Yes.

Ann: Do you remember the date of the report or anything like that?

Mr. Powers: It would have been within three days.

Ann: Within three days. Okay. And is that part of the reason why the investigation was closed?

Mr. Powers: I think so. I think the Sheriff agreed with me and I think he put it out to the press that way.

Ann: Put it out to the press?

Mr. Powers: To the media, I'm sure.

Ann: Okay. And so that's kind of what closed the case; is that right?

Mr. Powers: Well, it didn't really close it because Compton and Martin kept pounding the pavement talking to a lot of people.

Ann: Well, we'll let other deputies testify about what they did.

Mr. Powers: Sure.

Ann: Okay. I just have a couple more questions. Now, you were subpoenaed to come here by my office, right?

Mr. Powers: Yes.

Ann: And you were also subpoenaed by the defense attorney, Mr. Fleming?

Mr. Powers: Yes.

Ann: Yes. Do you know Mr. Fleming?

Mr. Powers: I've recently met him.

Ann: Okay. Have you met with him in his office?

Mr. Powers: Yes.

Ann: And did you share with him this theory about how Mr. Hammill could have died?

Mr. Powers: Yes, I did.

Ann: Now, how did you connect with Mr. Fleming? Do you have a friend who works in his office?

Mr. Powers: He's a former police officer, he does some investigating. He located me. I was down in Texas at the time.

Ann: So he located you?

Mr. Powers: Yes.

Ann: But you do have a connection with his partner, don't you?

Mr. Powers: He has a partner by the name of Brad Larson and Brad made my will, my wife's will and has done some real estate for us.

Ann: So he's your lawyer?

Mr. Powers: Yes.

Ann: Okay. I have nothing further.

The Court: Mr. Fleming, you may proceed.

Jim: Okay. Thank you, Your Honor.

Jim: Mr. Powers, you had testified that you were the chief deputy at the Sheriff's Department in August of 1979; isn't it also in fact true that you were head of the investigations for the Wright County Sheriff's Office at that time?

Mr. Powers: We didn't really have such a title as far as it being head of this or head of that. It was kind of a joint thing between Darrell Wolff and I. We worked together. We worked with our investigators. I was doing less investigative work at that point in time because we had other investigators. And I was doing more managerial, administrative work.

Jim: Isn't it true that you were supervising the investigators on this case?

Mr. Powers: Yes, I was.

Jim: Do you recall an individual by the name of Weeks?

Mr. Powers: Yes.

Jim: Isn't it true that this was an individual whose death was also being investigated by the sheriff's office at approximately the same time?

Mr. Powers: It was, yes.

Jim: And isn't it true that in that particular case the individual was also believed to have been struck by a moving vehicle?

Mr. Powers: That's true.

Jim: And that body was found on State Highway 12?

Mr. Powers: State Highway 12 just on the western or on the eastern end of Delano.

Jim: Okay. Were you involved in that investigation?

Mr. Powers: Yes, I was asked to go down and take a look at the scene and—by the sheriff. And he wanted to know my feeling on it and I said the guy got hit by something extending from a vehicle, could be a rearview mirror, but it was very obvious that the body was thrown head first down with the head striking the pavement and which killed him, of course.

Jim: Did you see similarities between the Weeks incident and the Hammill incident that gave rise to your thought process about the possibility of this being a vehicle strike?

Mr. Powers: No, not really because I think the Weeks incident was after this one. I don't recall the date but it just seems like it. No, my thought process, and this was after leaving the mortuary and I think all of us as police officers do this, you think how did this happen, what occurred here, you know, all these things are going through your mind, you're trying to figure it out. I remember looking at the wound, it was right here (indicating). It was about as big around as my thumb but it broke the skull and all the bone in there. And it appeared it was a tremendous blow that hit him. So getting back to the scene, I'm thinking two things at the same time. Why are we looking at an assault. How can an assault have been done. Didn't seem right. I'm placing this guy, in my mind, he's out here trying to catch a ride. There's not much traffic, it's dark, he sees headlights come up the road so he's extending himself quite a bit. Not easy to see him, he's all dressed in black; the only thing white is going to be his face. If he does see anything that's extending from this vehicle, it's going to be at the last minute and he won't have a chance to get out of the way and he probably starts turning. That's why he's hit here (indicating) and at the same time something on the top of his head and it drives him right into the ground and into the pavement. It takes a tremendous blow to do that.

Jim: In the immediate area where Mr. Hammill's body was found, did you see any signs off the road in the earth or the soil or whatever, alongside the road, of any kind of a scuffle?

Mr. Powers: Not at all, sir. We looked for any kind of footprint, anything that would indicate that.

Jim: If the individual had been assaulted would you expect to see more physical signs on the clothing or in the immediate area around him that would give you some indication that there was some kind of a struggle of some kind?

Mr. Powers: Yes, sir. I'm thinking if there's an assault you've got one guy with two weapons or you've got to have two guys because you've got one thing that hits him here (indicating) and the machete type whatever it is that hits him on the top of the head. So you're thinking and I'm thinking at the time of this party where he got out of the car couple miles south of there and he's walking up the road because who else is out there, you know, somebody's mad at the guy, they have to have a reason to want to kill him.

If it's this group they're probably drinking heavy. They pull up. They don't even pull over on the shoulder because there's no track out there. You've got to keep him in the headlights because it's dark. Been my experience that in a situation like that you're going to have a lot of hostile, verbal abuse. And I'm thinking the victim is—he's a little guy. He isn't going to stand there and say, "Take your best shot." He's going to be doing something defensive which is off through the brush. And if that would have happened and they were faster than he was, they would have caught him, we would have found the body down in the ditch near the fence line or wherever, not up here (indicating). This here, he had to be standing almost straight up, almost waiting for it, I mean.

Jim: Thank you. No further questions.

The Court: Redirect?

Ann: No, thank you. Nothing further.

The Court: Thank you, Mr. Powers. You are excused.

CHAPTER 14

Day 2

The prosecution's next witness is Robert Nowak, who lived about a quarter mile south of the location where Jeffrey Hammill's body was found on CR-12. The Nowaks were entertaining the Kilgos that evening; playing cards and drinking. Robert can recall hearing noises from up the road early that morning as the Kilgo's departed, but states that he could only hear 'hollering'; and then later when he got into bed, the sound of tires squealing from that area.

The prosecution calls Barto Kilgo to the stand, where he is sworn in.

Ann questions Mr. Kilgo as to what he and his now-wife Jennifer saw that evening as they left the Nowak residence and drove north towards Buffalo, passing a car stopped near the side of the road with its lights on.

Ann: Did you see any people by that car?

Mr. Kilgo: Yes, there was three or four on the right side of the vehicle near the rear door, by the rear quarter back there, and there was one person in front. As far as I could tell, they were all men.

Ann: And were they white men?

Mr. Kilgo: Well, I don't know. The only one I can say for sure would be the one that was in the front. He was in the headlights of the car.

Ann: And was he a white man?

Mr. Kilgo: Yes.

Ann: And did you slow down?

Mr. Kilgo: We slowed down going by, didn't know what was going on there, somebody might step out around the car or into the road, kind of looking to see if there might be some problem that we might be able to help with.

Ann: Do you recall were the lights of the other vehicle on or off?

Mr. Kilgo: The lights were on, yes.

Ann: Were you able to identify what kind of motor vehicle it was?

Mr. Kilgo: No. All I could tell for sure was that it had three taillights on either side.

Ann: Three taillights on either side?

Mr. Kilgo: Yeah.

Ann: Were you able to tell what color it was?

Mr. Kilgo: No. I don't recall the color.

Ann: Were you able to tell whether it was a light color or dark color?

Mr. Kilgo: I would think it seemed to be lighter.

Ann: Did you have any conversation with them?

Mr. Kilgo: No.

Ann: Did you hear any noises or hear them talking at all?

Mr. Kilgo: No.

Ann: Did you have your windows in your car up or down?

Mr. Kilgo: Windows were up.

Ann: Is it fair to say that you would not be able to recognize anybody from that crowd of people?

Mr. Kilgo: Not from the back of the car but I saw the guy in the front clearly and plainly.

Ann: And what did he look like?

Mr. Kilgo: About five foot eight, kind of thin, light colored or blonde hair down to the shoulders, kind of curly, wearing jeans, strap t-shirt and another shirt over it that was unbuttoned, plaid, light brown or tan.

Ann: Could you see anybody in the car?

Mr. Kilgo: No.

Ann: Now, did you know Jeff Hammill?

Mr. Kilgo: I knew him casually. He used to live across the hall from me in Rockford. We chatted a few times. My wife went to school with him.

Ann: Did you ever socialize with him?

Mr. Kilgo: No, no, no going out or anything like that.

Ann: Were you able to recognize him at the scene?

Mr. Kilgo: No, I don't know.

Ann: Okay. And is that because you couldn't recognize anybody?

Mr. Kilgo: With the exception of the one that was in front of the car.

Ann: So if Mr. Hammill could have been there, you just weren't able to tell; is that right?

Mr. Kilgo: No, I wouldn't have been able to tell.

Ann: I have no further questions.

The Court: Okay. Cross-examination?

Jim: Thank you.

Jim: Okay. Thank you. Good morning.

Mr. Kilgo: Yes.

Jim: You stated that you were interviewed the very next day after the evening where you passed by this car, correct?

Mr. Kilgo: Yes.

Jim: Is it possible that you actually over the course of time might forget that you were actually interviewed on August 14, which would have been a couple, three days later?

Mr. Kilgo: No, we went down to the police department the next day. That was when we told them that we were in the area and we had seen this vehicle there. And now that you mention it, the investigators did come later to our house.

Jim: Back in August of 1979 when you were interviewed, do you recall telling the officer that you had a pretty good description of the vehicle?

Mr. Kilgo: No. They asked me about the description of the vehicle. I told them I didn't know what color it was. I didn't have the tag number. All I knew for sure was that it had three taillights on either side.

Jim: Okay. Well, I'm just confused because the officer reported based upon his interviewing you that you described the vehicle as a '67 to '69 Chevrolet; do you recall that?

Mr. Kilgo: Could have been, yeah.

Jim: Okay. Darker green bottom, dark top, probably black?

Mr. Kilgo: I don't recall giving that detail of the description.

Jim: If the officer has it in his report immediately after talking to you, do you have any reason to doubt it?

Mr. Kilgo: I don't doubt that that would be the vehicle. I don't recall saying that.

Jim: All right.

Mr. Kilgo: If it's in the report I must have.

Jim: He reports that you said that you were sure of the car because it had three taillights on each side, all working, with flat tops and round bottoms; do you recall that?

Mr. Kilgo: I don't recall saying it but I don't see why they would put it in the report if I didn't.

Jim: Do you recall when you looked at the car as you were driving by it and you said that all the taillights were working?

Mr. Kilgo: Um-hmm.

Jim: Okay. So all the taillights were showing red?

Mr. Kilgo: Right.

Jim: Now, at that time you told the officer that there was one person sitting in the driver's seat and one male person standing near the right front; do you recall that?

Mr. Kilgo: There was a person in the right front. I don't recall the person sitting by the driver's seat.

Jim: Okay. But, again, do you have any reason to doubt that the officer would misstate this purposely in his report?

Mr. Kilgo: No, I don't.

Jim: So that would make two people, wouldn't it?

Mr. Kilgo: Well, that's two so far, one in front of the car and apparently one sitting in the driver's seat, but there were two, three or four on the other side of the vehicle near the back.

Jim: Okay. Well, we'll get to that, but at that time you told them that there was one person in the driver's seat and one person out in front of the car and that was it; isn't that true?

Mr. Kilgo: No, no, I told them that there were people on the outside of the car.

Jim: Okay. Since that's not included in the officer's report, how do you account for that?

Mr. Kilgo: Well, I have no idea.

Jim: The officer also reports, "Barto could not remember his clothing," talking about the individual in front of the car.

Mr. Kilgo: Well, with a lot of things that people when they go to describe them, they go with the generalities to start with and then they remember the details later on.

Jim: Twenty-seven years later on?

Mr. Kilgo: Well, in this case it sure looks that way.

Jim: Do you recall being interviewed on January 16 of 2003 by a detective from the Wright County Sheriff's Department by the name of Gary Reiten?

Mr. Kilgo: I don't remember the date. I was interviewed again, yes.

Jim: Okay. And at that time do you recall telling Detective Reiten that around sometime after 2:30 while you were still at the Nowak residence that you heard tires squealing and kids racing around?

Mr. Kilgo: We did hear noises like that, yes.

Jim: Okay. And when you talked with Detective Reiten, you said that you noticed a dark colored Chevrolet with its lights on parked on the right side of the road.

Mr. Kilgo: That's when we were driving home, yes.

Jim: Okay. Well, now I've got two different reports, separated by a period of over twenty years. In both cases you've said it was a Chevrolet; wouldn't it be safe to assume that you saw a Chevrolet?

Mr. Kilgo: Could have been a Chevrolet.

Jim: Because you would have no reason to tell the officer it was a Chevrolet in 1979 and then tell the officer in 2003 that it's a Chevrolet if that wasn't true, would you?

Mr. Kilgo: From what I remember body styles and all of that back at that time, it seemed to be in that area.

Jim: Okay. And you also told Detective Reiten that you could describe the clothing on the individual in front of the car as a plaid shirt open at the collar with a t-shirt underneath and believed to be blue jeans; do you recall saying that to Detective Reiten?

Mr. Kilgo: Yeah.

Jim: You described the male as medium to small in size with blonde, curly, light-colored hair?

Mr. Kilgo: Yes.

Jim: Okay. You also told Detective Reiten that two or three guys were standing at the rear of the car near the passenger side.

Mr. Kilgo: Right.

Jim: Okay. You told Detective Reiten that you know cars and that you were certain it was a Chevrolet.

Mr. Kilgo: That was the body style of a Chevrolet, yes.

Jim: Okay. So you're pretty sure it was a Chevrolet?

Mr. Kilgo: I'm pretty sure it was a Chevrolet, yes.

Jim: Okay. But Detective Reiten never questioned you about the first report that you had given in 1979, did he?

Mr. Kilgo: No, I don't remember any of that coming up, no.

Jim: He did not bring up the fact that you had said in 1979 that this vehicle had three taillights on each side that were flat on the top and round on the bottom, he didn't talk about that, did he?

Mr. Kilgo: No, I don't think so, no.

Jim: Do you recall telling him that there were two or three guys standing at the rear of the car near the passenger side?

Mr. Kilgo: The rear passenger side, yes.

Jim: Okay. Do you recall telling him that you didn't recognize any of the people by the car?

Mr. Kilgo: I never said that I recognized any of them, no, to anybody.

Jim: All right. Now, do you recall being interviewed again in 2003, in September of 2003, by Detective Reiten in which situation he drew a diagram and had you establish for him on the diagram, where these people were located that you saw around the car?

Mr. Kilgo: I believe he did do that, yes.

Jim: Okay. And isn't it true that during the course of that

statement in September of 2003 you suddenly remembered that you forgot to talk about the guy that was in the driver's seat. And so now all of a sudden instead of two or three behind the car, we've got one out in front of the car, one in the driver's seat and two or three behind the car.

Mr. Kilgo: You know, I really don't recall saying that there was one in the driver's seat. Maybe it's my memory, maybe it's not.

Jim: Okay. Well, I guess that's what we're after, sir, here is what your memory is.

Mr. Kilgo: The thing I'll tell you right now that I am certain of there was two to four guys on the right side rear and one in the headlights.

Jim: Now you're certain of that?

Mr. Kilgo: Oh, I've always been certain of that.

Jim: But you didn't say that to the officers in 1979, did you?

Mr. Kilgo: We went down to tell them that we were there. Okay.

Jim: Sir, please answer my question.

Mr. Kilgo: What?

Jim: My question is you did not tell them in 1979 that there were two to three guys standing behind the car, did you?

Mr. Kilgo: It should be in the police report. I've told them the same thing all along.

Jim: Well, that's the problem now, isn't it, then, because it's not in the police report. You said just a moment ago that if the officer described your statement in 1979 then that must have been what you said; do you recall saying that?

Mr. Kilgo: I remember seeing people by the car and, like I said, I remember the generalities right away and picked up on more of the details later on.

Jim: It certainly sounds that way. May I have a moment, Your Honor?

The Court: You may. Can everyone see the easel from their vantage point, including Ms. Mohaupt?

Ann: Yes, thank you.

Jim: Okay. I'm not an artist but I'll try to draw a car and I'm going to ask you to accept my representation that this is the car that you passed on August 11, 1979 approximately three o'clock in the morning, okay?

Mr. Kilgo: All right.

Jim: I'd like to have you take a look at that officer's report from August 14 of 1979.

Mr. Kilgo: Okay.

Mr. Kilgo takes three to four minutes to read the report.

Jim: You've had a chance to review it?

Mr. Kilgo: Yes.

Jim: Now, you would agree with me then that the officer taking a statement from you indicates in the report that you put one individual behind the steering wheel of the car, and where would you say the other individual was?

Mr. Kilgo: By the right front headlight.

Jim: Up in this area or over to the side?

Mr. Kilgo: He was in front of the vehicle clearly illuminated by the light.

Jim: Now, at that point in 1979 you gave a description of the hair color and length and so forth and the style, longer, curly, blondish hair, but you testified or you didn't testify but you gave a statement that you could not describe that individual's clothing, didn't you?

Mr. Kilgo: Not at that time, no.

Jim: Not at that time. Okay. So then we move to January

16 of 2003. Now, in January of 2003 when you were questioned again by Detective Reiten, you placed an individual up here in the same spot. And you said there were two or three behind the vehicle.

Mr. Kilgo: On the right side, not behind it, on the right side near the rear.

Jim: Nobody behind the wheel?

Mr. Kilgo: I didn't recall anybody behind the wheel, no.

Jim: And whereas in 1979 you had described the taillights on the car as being three on each side, flat on the top and round on the bottom, didn't you?

Mr. Kilgo: I believe so, yes.

Jim: All three red lights were on?

Mr. Kilgo: Yes.

Jim: But in 2003 in January despite the fact that you had made that statement about this '67 to '69 Chevrolet in 1979, Detective Reiten never talked to you about these taillights, did he?

Mr. Kilgo: I don't recall if he asked me about them or not.

Jim: Okay. Never brought that up. Your description of this individual up here all of a sudden now whereas in 1979 you could not describe the clothing, now you're describing the clothing, aren't you, in 2003?

Mr. Kilgo: Yes.

Jim: Now, we'll call that one of 2003 and now we'll move to September of 2003.

Now, in September of 2003 you're questioned again, aren't you?

Mr. Kilgo: Yes.

Jim: Did they tell you why?

Mr. Kilgo: Something about something new in the case. They were asking me about the same thing over and over again.

Jim: Over and over again. Isn't it true that the something new in the case they were referring to is the fact that you forgot the driver and so when you describe it for them in September 2003, they wanted you to put that driver back behind the wheel of that car so that it would be consistent with the statement that you gave in 1979?

Mr. Kilgo: I still don't recall that, no, I don't recall that there was a driver, somebody sitting in the driver's seat.

Jim: Okay. But yet twice during police questioning you've put somebody behind the wheel of that car, haven't you?

Mr. Kilgo: Could be from my wife said that she saw somebody beside the wheel of the car, but I didn't.

Jim: Okay. Let me ask you the question again, sir. Twice you've read the reports, twice you have stated to police officers that there was a driver sitting in the driver's seat behind the wheel, haven't you?

Mr. Kilgo: That's what the report says, yes.

Jim: Sure is. During September of 2003, they never talked to you again about the taillights, did they?

Mr. Kilgo: No.

Jim: Never brought that up, did they?

Mr. Kilgo: No.

Jim: Okay. In January of 2003 you described the t-shirt that the individual was wearing underneath the plaid shirt as a t-shirt; do you recall that?

Mr. Kilgo: I've always called it a strap t-shirt.

Jim: I'm sorry?

Mr. Kilgo: I believe I've always referred to it as a strap t-shirt.

Jim: Would you like to take a look at the reports again?

Mr. Kilgo: No.

Jim: Okay. All right. You read them just a moment ago. Isn't it in fact true that you referred to it as a t-shirt in January of 2003 and a strapped t-shirt in September of 2003?

Mr. Kilgo: That sounds right.

Jim: Okay. Now, in 1979 at one point you were taken by law enforcement officers down to a business in Plymouth, Minnesota, weren't you?

Mr. Kilgo: Yes.

Jim: Okay. And they showed you a car there, didn't they?

Mr. Kilgo: They didn't show me a car. They drove me through the parking lot to see if I recognized any of the cars.

Jim: Okay. And you didn't recognize any of the cars?

Mr. Kilgo: No, I didn't. I didn't.

Jim: Isn't it true that Jeff Hammill dated one of your wife Jennifer's relatives at one point in time?

Mr. Kilgo: I don't know.

Jim: You don't know. But you knew Jeff?

Mr. Kilgo: I knew Jeff, yes, casually; I didn't know him real well.

Jim: Sure. And when you went by in 1979, you didn't see Jeff Hammill, did you?

Mr. Kilgo: I didn't see him, no, not that I could recognize him. He could have been one of the ones that was standing in the dark.

Jim: Sure, but I could have been one of the ones that was standing beside the car, couldn't I have?

Mr. Kilgo: Yes, you could have.

Jim: Okay. You didn't see Jeff Hammill, did you?

Mr. Kilgo: I didn't see him, no.

Jim: Just one last question; in the course of talking with the law enforcement officers, you were never asked to identify any individuals, were you?

Mr. Kilgo: No.

Jim: You were never shown any pictures of anybody?

Mr. Kilgo: No.

Jim: You were never taken to a lineup where you sat behind the one-way glass and people walked up and stood, you know, with the lights on them and all that stuff?

Mr. Kilgo: No.

Jim: No further questions of the witness, Your Honor.

The Court: Thank you. Redirect?

Ann: Thank you.

Ann: I just have a few more questions, Mr. Kilgo. Do you have any idea over the course of the years how many different police officers you've spoken to?

Mr. Kilgo: No, I don't recall, no.

Ann: Was it at least two?

Mr. Kilgo: There was, yeah, there was two or three, yeah.

Ann: Two or three. And did any of those two or three police officers ever tell you what to say?

Mr. Kilgo: No.

Ann: And after you spoke to those police officers, did any of them ever bring their reports and let you look at them so that you could guarantee what was in there was what you wanted to say?

Mr. Kilgo: No, they just came and talked to me and then they were gone.

Ann: Okay. So they never brought you your reports to correct or verify or anything?

Mr. Kilgo: No, no, I never saw any of that.

Ann: Okay. And isn't it always true that any time anybody ever asked about the car you always said there were three lights on either side?

Mr. Kilgo: That's correct.

Ann: Thank you, sir. Nothing further.

Jim: Nothing further, Your Honor.

The Court: Thank you. Mr. Kilgo, you are excused. Thank you.

Mr. Kilgo: Thank you.

The next witness called is Jennifer Kilgo, who reiterates most of what her husband testified to, except she states that as they drove past, "I could hear a bunch of hollering, you know, like they were … it wasn't mean hollering. It was like having fun hollering type of thing, having a good time".

When asked by Ann, "Could you hear what they were hollering, what words?" she replies "No".

DIRECT EXAMINATION BY MS. MOHAUPT

Ann: Would you know for sure whether anybody was behind the wheel or you just didn't see it?

Mrs. Kilgo: No, I just didn't see anybody. I couldn't tell if there was or wasn't.

Ann: Did you know any of the people?

Mrs. Kilgo: No.

Ann: Now, you knew Jeff Hammill, right?

Mrs. Kilgo: Yes, I did.

Ann: And how did you know him?

Mrs. Kilgo: I went to school with him and he used to live across the hail from Bart for a little while in Rockford.

Ann: Okay. If he had been standing there would you have been able to identify him as being there?

Mrs. Kilgo: Only if he was facing me, not from behind.

Ann: Okay. And so you weren't able to see?

Mrs. Kilgo: No.

Ann: Nothing further.

The Court: Cross-examination?

Jim: Thank you, Your Honor.

Jim: Good morning.

Mrs. Kilgo: Good morning.

Jim: You recall giving testimony before the grand jury in this case, don't you?

Mrs. Kilgo: Correct.

Jim: Okay. I just want to go over a couple things there. In that testimony you described the car that you passed as an old Impala; do you remember that?

Mrs. Kilgo: That's what it basically kind of looked like, yeah. I'm not really an expert in cars, but my parents used to have an Impala. That's why I kind of remembered it looking like that.

Jim: Okay. Do you recall what year Impala your parents had?

Mrs. Kilgo: I think it was a '63, '65, I'm not sure.

Jim: All right. But it looked kind of like that?

Mrs. Kilgo: Kind of, yeah.

Jim: All right. No further questions for the witness, Your Honor.

The Court: Redirect.

Ann: No, thank you. Thank you, ma'am.

The Court: Mrs. Kilgo, you are excused. Thank you.

Mrs. Kilgo: Thank you.

The Court: State may call its next witness.

Ann: Call Jeff Cardinal.

The Court: Good morning. Please come forward. Stop there to take the oath. Then you may be seated in the witness stand.

The Clerk: Take a seat, please, and state your name for the record, spelling your last name, please.

Mr. Cardinal: My name is Jeffrey John Cardinal, C-a-r-d-i-n-a-1.

Ann begins her direct examination of Jeff Cardinal, exploring the relationships between Jeff and his wife Debra and her brother Terry Olson. Jeff is not real fond of Terry, as he seems to constantly get himself into trouble. His sister Debra has had it with Terry, as well and seldom answers his phone calls.

Jeff testifies that he and Ron Michaels have been friends for many years, starting back in grade school when they both lived in Montrose. In fact, Jeff was Ron's best man at Ron's wedding to his first wife Sandy. He considers Ron one of the best friends he has ever had, even though they haven't seen all that much of each other in the last few years.

Ann's questions move to the night of August 10, 1979.

Jeff recalls meeting Jeff Hammill once or twice at the Rockford House or the Country West bars, when he was there with others. He considered Jeff merely an acquaintance. He recalls being at the Country West on a date with Debra Segler that evening. He remembers several others being there as well, including Debra's brother Terry and Terry's friend, Dale Todd, among them. He recalls many of them leaving the bar after it closed and heading to Deb's house to continue the party. He recalls other people being there as well but can't remember how many or who exactly showed up.

Ann: Did you see Jeff Hammill leave the party at Deb's on August 11 of '79?

Mr. Cardinal: Well, it was in my '79 phone statement and that's what I have to go by because it was so long ago. And I said in there that I seen him walking east on the street right in front of Deb's.

Ann: Okay. And do you recall what time it was that you saw Jeff outside of Deb's house?

Mr. Cardinal: I don't recall now but whatever I said in that '79 statement would be more accurate than I can remember now.

Ann: Okay. If you testified at the grand jury that it was sometime between 2:30, around 2:30, 3 o'clock, would that be right?

Mr. Cardinal: If that's what is in that '79 phone statement, I think that's what it was approximately.

Ann: Okay. Did he leave by himself?

Mr. Cardinal: I believe he did.

Ann: And do you know why he left?

Mr. Cardinal: I think it was because he wanted a ride to Buffalo or something. There was some kind of commotion outside.

Ann: Okay. Was anybody giving him a ride?

Mr. Cardinal: Not that I know of.

Ann: Okay. When you say there was some kind of commotion, what do you mean some kind of commotion?

Mr. Cardinal: That he wanted a ride. He was friends of Terry's and Dale Todd, I think, or they worked together.

Ann: But what does that have to do with a commotion?

Mr. Cardinal: Well, I guess I didn't mean a commotion. They were ... he just wanted a ride or something. I was in the house.

Ann: Okay. So he wanted a ride and you saw him walking away?

Mr. Cardinal: Yeah.

Ann: Nobody gave him a ride?

Mr. Cardinal: I don't think so.

Ann: Was there any sort of fight or argument or anything like that that you remember that caused—

Mr. Cardinal: I don't recall any fight.

Ann: Could there have been a fight or an argument or something that caused it?

Mr. Cardinal: It could have been but it wouldn't have been abnormal. Some people have little disagreements but it's no big deal.

Ann: At some point after Jeff Hammill left Deb's and started walking away, did Terry Olson, Dale Todd and this Defendant also leave?

Mr. Cardinal: I don't know. People were coming and going.

Ann: Okay. Now, have you been interviewed in the past about the events of August 10 and August 11?

Mr. Cardinal: I've been interrogated, yes.

Ann: Your Honor, could I ask that the witness simply answer my questions yes or no?

The Court: I believe the witness has.

Ann: Do you recall talking on the phone with a police officer on August 15, 1979?

Mr. Cardinal: Vaguely, yeah, I think, we didn't have any cell phones back then or anything like that. I think I was called to a construction trailer and talked to somebody over the phone, yes.

Ann: Is it fair to say that on August 15, 1979 the events of August 11, 1979 would be fresher in your mind than they are today?

Mr. Cardinal: For sure, yes.

Ann: Now, when you spoke to the officer on the phone on August 15 of 1979, you knew that Jeff Hammill was dead, did you not?

Mr. Cardinal: Yes.

Ann: And if the report says that you told that officer that the Defendant Ron Michaels and Dale Todd left Deb's at 4:30 or so on August 11, on August 11 of '79, would that be right?

Mr. Cardinal: I never said that in that report in '79.

Ann: So if the report says that, that would be wrong?

Mr. Cardinal: Yes.

Ann questions Jeff about the flat tire on Dale Todd's car, and about Jeff Hammill leaving the party on foot because he couldn't get a ride from anyone. He can't recall the exact time that Jeff or anyone else left the party, saying, "I do not remember. It was a long time ago. It was just another regular night out."

Ann: Have you spoken with the Defendant's attorney about this case?

Mr. Cardinal: Yeah, he called and was wondering if we could talk. And we said it would be okay and he came over for a while.

Ann: How many times did you talk about the case?

Mr. Cardinal: I think I might have talked to him twice.

Ann: Did you talk about your testimony? Just yes or no.

Mr. Cardinal: Yes.

Ann: Okay. Did you talk with your wife about this case?

Mr. Cardinal: Yes.

Ann: How often?

Mr. Cardinal: Well, it's on our mind just about every day.

Ann: Have you spoken to your brother-in-law about the case, Terry?

Mr. Cardinal: No, I haven't.

Ann: But your wife has?

Mr. Cardinal: She talks to him about once a week maybe.

Ann: I don't think I have anything further.

The Court: Thank you. Cross-examination?

Jim: Thank you.

Jim: Mr. Cardinal, do you recall during the evening at the party after arriving there in Montrose, do you ever recall Jeff Hammill coming into the house?

Mr. Cardinal: I don't think he ever came in.

Jim: Okay. Do you recall seeing him outside the house?

Mr. Cardinal: Yes.

Jim: Are you familiar with a young woman by the name of Sandy or Sandra Dehn?

Mr. Cardinal: That was Ron's wife, I believe.

Jim: Okay. Did you know her before they got married?

Mr. Cardinal: Yes.

Jim: Okay. And her name at that time would have been Sandra Dehn; is that correct?

Mr. Cardinal: I believe that was her maiden name.

Jim: Okay. And you stood up in their wedding?

Mr. Cardinal: Yes.

Jim: Okay. Now, think about this just for a minute because of what you just said, did you stand up in their wedding after this party or before this party occurred?

Mr. Cardinal: I think it was after. I can't remember exactly what year Ron got married.

Jim: Okay. So it would be more likely that they were not married at the time of the party?

Mr. Cardinal: I don't think so.

Jim: Okay. Now, do you have any recollection of seeing Sandra Dehn at the party?

Mr. Cardinal: I don't remember seeing her there. I'm not quite—I'm not sure if she was there or not.

Jim: Okay. Do you have any recollection of seeing her and talking with her at the bar, at the Country West Bar, earlier that evening?

Mr. Cardinal: I don't recall seeing her at the bar. I don't know if she was there or not.

Jim: Thank you, sir. No further questions, Your Honor.

The Court: Any redirect?

Ann: Yes, thank you.

Ann: Mr. Cardinal, when you were answering questions for Mr. Fleming, you indicated that you did not recall Jeff coming in the house. You're not saying he didn't come in, are you?

Mr. Cardinal: I'm saying I don't recall him being in the house.

Ann: So he could have come in the house?

Mr. Cardinal: He could have been. I don't recall him being in the house.

Ann: Thank you. Nothing further.

Jim: Nothing further, Your Honor.

The Court: Thank you. Mr. Cardinal, you are excused.

Mr. Cardinal: Thank you.

CHAPTER 15

The Court: Is the State prepared with its next witness?

Ann: Yes. Dale Todd.

The Court: Thank you.

The Clerk: Would you take a seat and please state your name for the record, spelling your first and your last name, please?

Mr. Todd: Dale, d-a-1 -e, Todd, t-o-d-d.

DIRECT EXAMINATION BY MS. MOHAUPT

Ann: Good afternoon. How are you?

Mr. Todd: Okay.

Ann: How old are you?

Mr. Todd: Forty-six.

Ann: I can tell by what you're wearing that you're not living at home right now, are you?

Mr. Todd: Correct.

Ann: Where are you residing?

Mr. Todd: Wright County Jail.

Ann: How long have you been there?

Mr. Todd: 358 days.

Ann: Did you graduate from high school?

Mr. Todd: No.

Ann: Did you quit?

Mr. Todd: Yes.

Ann: What grade were you in when you quit?

Mr. Todd: Twelve.

Ann: Have you ever been married?

Mr. Todd: Twice.

Ann: Do you have any kids?

Mr. Todd: Yes. Two.

Ann: How old are they?

Mr. Todd: twenty-five and twenty-two.

Ann: Mr. Todd, what kind of work have you done in your life?

Mr. Todd: I did stucco for sixteen years.

Ann: What company?

Mr. Todd: Zimmerman Stucco.

Ann: And how old were you when you left?

Mr. Todd: It was 2000. I didn't leave. I was injured.

Ann: Oh, you had an injury. What happened?

Mr. Todd: I went over the roof.

Ann: Oh, fell off the roof?

Mr. Todd: I got two scars on my elbows.

Ann: Okay. What kind of work did you do after that?

Mr. Todd: I worked for Menards in the yard after my injuries healed.

Ann: And did you have any other jobs after that?

Mr. Todd: I quit Menards and I started for Dura Supreme Cabinet.

Ann: Can you read and write?

Mr. Todd: Not very well but yes, I can read and write.

Ann: Sometimes do you have trouble understanding things?

Mr. Todd: Yes, I do.

Ann: And if I ask you something that you don't understand, will you let me know?

Mr. Todd: Yes, I will.

Ann: Are you one of three people that were indicted by the grand jury involving the death of Jeff Hammill?

Mr. Todd: Yes, I was.

Ann: And did the grand jury indict you for one count of Murder in the Second Degree and two counts of Murder in the Third Degree?

Mr. Todd: Yes.

Ann: Were you allowed to plead guilty to a lessor offense that's called Aiding an Offender?

Mr. Todd: Yes.

Ann: And did you do that on July 21 of this year?

Mr. Todd: Yes.

Ann: Are you scheduled to be sentenced at the completion of the case against this Defendant and the case against Mr. Olson?

Mr. Todd: November 7.

Ann: Okay. Were you allowed to plead guilty to the amended charge of Aiding an Offender partly in exchange for your testimony in the cases against this Defendant and Mr. Olson?

Mr. Todd: Yes.

Ann: Did you give a statement to law enforcement on July 19, just a couple of days before you pled guilty?

Mr. Todd: July 21. That was that morning and then I came up to court.

Ann: So you gave the statement before you pled guilty; is that right?

Mr. Todd: Yes.

Ann: And were you truthful in the statement that you made to the Court when you pled guilty to the charge you pled guilty to?

Mr. Todd: Yes.

Ann: And are you going to be truthful here today?

Mr. Todd: Yes.

Ann: Do you remember the evening of August 10, 1979?

Mr. Todd: Yes.

Ann begins a line of questioning that has Mr. Todd recalling the events of that evening: who he met with at the Rockford House, when Jeff Hammill joined them and why, and when they left the bar after closing. He recalls that several people decided to go over to Terry' sister Debra's house to continue the party; among them, Ron Michaels and his wife, whose name he can't recall.

Ann: Now, the person that you're referring to as Ron Michaels as one of the people that you left the bar with, is he in the courtroom today?

Mr. Todd: Yes.

Ann: Can you point him out?

Mr. Todd: Sitting on my right.

Ann: May the record reflect the witness has identified the Defendant?

The Court: Any objection?

Jim: No objection, Your Honor.

The Court: The record so shall reflect.

Ann resumes the questions, with Dale recalling picking up Jeff Hammill hitchhiking and bringing him along to the party, intending to give him a ride home afterwards. He tells of the flat tire on his car, stealing one up the street and putting it on his car and then going into the house. He states that this was the first time he had met Ron Michaels and his girlfriend, that he thought they were friends of Jeff and Debra, and that Ron's girlfriend, whose name he believed to be Sandy or Pam, had left the party after about an hour; but he wasn't really sure who she talked to or whether she was there at all. Ann questions Dale regarding contact between Ron's girlfriend and Jeff Hammill. She asks him if he saw Jeff Hammill pass a note to Ron's girlfriend. He responds "no", but that he was told this. When asked who told him about the note passing, he begins to retell the story about someone spilling drinks on him in the house, then a fight breaking out between Terry Olson and someone named George, whom he recalled from the paperwork he had been shown.

> Ann: But now I don't want you to talk about anything from the paperwork. I want you to just remember from your own mind.

> Mr. Todd: I'm not sure of his name.

> Ann: But that didn't have anything to do with the Defendant's girlfriend, did it?

> Mr. Todd: No. I don't know. It was just said.

> Ann: Okay. Now, this fight, was that inside or outside?

> Mr. Todd: Well, it kind of started a little bit inside and went to the outside.

> Ann: How long did that fight last?

> Mr. Todd: Probably ten minutes or so.

> Ann: Okay. Did something happen at the party where you saw that the Defendant Ron Michaels was mad at Jeff Hammill?

> Mr. Todd: No, not at that time.

> Ann: Did you ever see something where you saw that Ron Michaels was mad at Jeff Hammill?

Mr. Todd: No.

Ann: Okay. So there was nothing that happened that caused this Defendant to get mad at Jeff Hammill ever?

Mr. Todd: Not at that time.

Ann: Okay. But did it happen later?

Mr. Todd: Later.

Ann: What happened that caused him to get mad at Jeff Hammill?

Mr. Todd: I'm not really sure.

Ann: Okay. I'm going to go back a little bit. Did you notice Jeff Hammill giving a piece of paper to anybody?

Mr. Todd: No, I did not.

Ann: Do you remember when you pled guilty?

Mr. Todd: Yes.

Ann: And you remember you were in court and you were sitting … might even have been there and the woman was taking things down?

Mr. Todd: Yes.

Ann: Okay. And when I read what happened at that hearing, it says that you said that you saw Jeff give the Defendant's girlfriend a piece of paper; do you remember saying that?

Mr. Todd: No, I don't.

Ann: Okay. And you can't remember that today?

Mr. Todd: Not at this time.

Ann asks more questions about who left the party, in whose car and why they left. "I wasn't really sure; maybe I thought we were just going to give him a ride home," Todd says.

Ann: Okay. At that point in time when you were in the car and going out looking for Jeff, was there any indication that anybody was mad at him?

Mr. Todd: No.

Ann: Okay. Not that you could recall?

Mr. Todd: No, not that I can recall.

Ann: You were driving?

Mr. Todd: Yeah.

Ann: Where was Terry Olson sitting?

Mr. Todd: Passenger seat.

Ann: And where was Ron Michaels sitting?

Mr. Todd: On the back.

Ann: Behind Terry?

Mr. Todd: Yes.

Ann: Did you pull up when you saw Jeff?

Mr. Todd: Pulled up around him.

Ann: What do you mean? Could you be more specific?

Mr. Todd: Pulled up in front of him.

Ann: Okay. And after you stopped the car, what happened?

Mr. Todd: Terry and Ron got out.

Ann: Okay. And was any conversation had?

Mr. Todd: Jeff was coming up to the car and then when he seen Terry they were arguing.

Ann: Jeff and Terry were arguing?

Mr. Todd: Yes.

Ann: Do you know what they were arguing about?

Mr. Todd: Because he was mad because I didn't give him a ride home at first, so Terry had pushed him to the back of the car.

Ann: Okay. And then what happened?

Mr. Todd: Terry went up to the front and then they were—Ron and him were in the back.

Ann: Ron and who were in the back?

Mr. Todd: Jeff.

Ann: So Ron had gotten out of the car, too?

Mr. Todd: Yes.

Ann: Okay. Did they go into the trunk?

Mr. Todd: Yeah, the trunk was open. I don't know if they went into it. It just was open.

Ann: Was there something weird about your trunk?

Mr. Todd: Yeah, you had to have a screwdriver to open it. The lock was punched out.

Ann: Okay. And where was the screwdriver kept?

Mr. Todd: I had a few of them. They were in the back seat, the floor, then I kept one by the door.

Ann: Okay. And so after you pulled up, was the trunk open?

Mr. Todd: : Yes.

Ann: Well, had it been open when you left the party?

Mr. Todd: It could have been, I mean, maybe because we fixed the tire and I don't know, it could have been just shut down, you know. And then when we stopped, it could have just popped up, too.

Ann: And then when you say that the trunk was open, do you mean that it was open wide?

Mr. Todd: Yeah, when we pulled in and stuff and that's when the hassle started. Terry went to the front and I figured he was just going to the bathroom or, you know, just relieving himself. Then he got back in the front seat.

Ann: Okay.

Mr. Todd: And then he said, "We ain't going to give him a ride home."

Ann: That was Terry that said that?

Mr. Todd: Yeah, and then Terry sat in the front seat and Ron was in the back. And then when I looked in the rearview mirror, there was a car coming southbound and we were northbound.

Ann: Okay.

Mr. Todd: And that's when after the car went by then I turned on my lights and stuff and that's when I just seen movement and then got in the car about—

Ann: I got to slow you down.

Mr. Todd:—couple minutes after that Ron got in the car and then he just said, "He won't need a ride."

Ann: Okay.

Mr. Todd: And then we just turned around and went back to the party.

Ann: Okay. We need to slow down just a little bit. Okay. You found Jeff and you pulled up, right?

Mr. Todd: Right.

Ann: Okay. And did you see Jeff?

Mr. Todd: No.

Ann: You saw him when you pulled up?

Mr. Todd: Right.

Ann: But then you pulled up in front of him and you didn't look back?

Mr. Todd: No. He was on the side of the car when Terry and Ron were out. Then they got in a scuffle, Terry got mad and pushed him back towards the end of the car. Then he went up to the front of the car.

Ann: So when there was a scuffle, who all was out of the car?

Mr. Todd: Terry and Ron.

Ann: Okay. And the trunk was open?

Mr. Todd: That's what I seen in my rearview mirror.

Ann: Did you hear any yelling?

Mr. Todd: No.

Ann: Did you hear what anybody—

Mr. Todd: The radio was up pretty loud.

Ann: Okay.

Mr. Todd: The radio was on.

Ann: Okay. How long were they out of the car?

Mr. Todd: Ten, twelve minutes. Terry was maybe six, seven minutes.

Ann: Okay. So Terry got back in the car first?

Mr. Todd: Yes.

Ann: And did Terry say or do anything when he got back in the car?

Mr. Todd: Just lit a cigarette. And said, "That guy pissed me off."

Ann: Okay. And didn't you just say he said you weren't going to give him a ride?

Mr. Todd: And said we weren't going to give him a ride.

Ann: Okay. And then how long did you and Terry sit in the car before the Defendant Ron Michaels came back?

Mr. Todd: Probably about five minutes.

Ann: Okay.

Mr. Todd: Five, six minutes.

Ann: Did you hear anything or see anything?

Mr. Todd: No, just when Terry said, "Let's go." I looked in the mirror and all I seen was movement and then Ron came into the door.

Ann: Okay. So I want to make sure I have this right, okay, Terry and Ron got out of the car?

Mr. Todd: Yes.

Ann: Terry was out of the car for about six minutes, and Ron was out of the car about five minutes longer?

Mr. Todd: I'd say so, about that.

Ann: Okay. When Terry came in, he said that the guy had pissed him off?

Mr. Todd: Yes.

Ann: And he lit a cigarette?

Mr. Todd: Well, he said—yeah, he lit a cigarette then he said something about not giving him a ride home and pissed off.

Ann: Okay. Okay. Then what then, did he say anything else?

Mr. Todd: No.

Ann: Terry? I thought you just said he said, "Let's go."

Mr. Todd: Well, yeah, he said, "Let's go," or probably, you know, couple minutes after that after lighting the cigarette and stuff and waiting for Ron to come back in.

Ann: Did he say, "Let's go" before Ron Michaels got back in the car?

Mr. Todd: Yes, that's when the car was running. I turned on the lights after the car had passed us.

Ann: Okay. A car came by you?

Mr. Todd: Yes.

Ann: And did you see anybody in the car?

Mr. Todd: No.

Ann: Did you see what kind of a car?

Mr. Todd: No.

Ann: Did it go by slow?

Mr. Todd: Probably about forty miles an hour, I suppose. I don't know.

Ann: Did it seem like it kind of slowed down to go by you?

Mr. Todd: I didn't pay attention to it.

Ann: Okay.

Mr. Todd: But I think the car was like white.

Ann: So then after Terry said, "Let's go," what happened?

Mr. Todd: About five minutes later that's when Ron got in the car and then we just … he said, "He won't need a ride home," and then we turned around, just did a U-ee right in the road.

Ann: So Ron said, "He won't need a ride home"?

Mr. Todd: Yeah.

Ann: And then you—

Mr. Todd: Just whipped a U-ee and went back to Deb's house.

Ann: And did either one of those two say anything else?

Mr. Todd: No.

Ann: Did you see Jeff Hammill when you whipped the U-ee?

Mr. Todd: No, no.

Ann: You didn't see him standing there by the side of the road?

Mr. Todd: No.

Ann: Where did you think he was?

Mr. Todd: I don't know, maybe I just figured maybe they just punched him or something and threw him in the ditch or something.

Ann: What made you think that?

Mr. Todd: Because I didn't see anybody.

Ann: Did you ever see Jeff Hammill alive again after Terry Olson and Ron Michaels left the car?

Mr. Todd: No. I assumed he was still alive, you know.

Ann: Did you find out different?

Mr. Todd: Yeah.

The questioning continues with Dale describing the return to Debra's house and Dale thinking he might have called 911, "just to have them check it out, you know, to see if he was OK."

Ann: Why would you have called them?

Mr. Todd: Well, it was kind of chilly out and if he was hurt or something, you know, then, you know, I didn't want to feel bad.

Ann: Were you worried about him?

Mr. Todd: In a way, yeah.

Ann: Were you kind of freaked out?

Mr. Todd: No, I wasn't really, really paying attention a lot. I just came in, thought I'd, you know … it's kind of vague. And then I just went in and sat on the couch.

Dale says he brought Ron Michaels home somewhere between 4 a.m. and 5 a.m. because Ron's car had a flat tire. He recalls it was about a ten minute drive. He says Ron showed him his new stereo system and they listened to it until Ron's girlfriend came down and talked to Ron. Ron and Dale never talked about Jeff Hammill. Then Dale drove back to Debra's house and when he entered, Terry woke up off of the couch and Dale told Terry he had given Ron a ride home. Then Dale says he lay down on the floor and slept for a few hours.

Ann: Now, it's my understanding that you and Terry went to the funeral of Jeff Hammill?

Mr. Todd: Yes.

Ann: And why did you decide you were going to go to the funeral?

Mr. Todd: Being nosy.

Ann: Nosy?

Mr. Todd: You know, because the officers had come Monday to talk to us about Jeff and they told us he had been killed.

Ann: Is that the first you heard he was dead?

Mr. Todd: Yes.

Ann: Okay. What were you nosy about? Why did you—

Mr. Todd: Well, because I wanted to know why he was dead.

Ann: Okay. And did going to the funeral help you figure that out?

Mr. Todd: Yes.

Ann: And what did you figure out?

Mr. Todd: Well, he was hurt.

Ann: Okay.

Mr. Todd: I seen there was a gash in his right side of his head, like a crack, like a crack and then … in his head, when you went up to the body, when you went up to the body—

Ann: You could see it?

Mr. Todd: Yes.

Ann: Did you and Terry talk about it?

Mr. Todd: I looked at him and I says, "I think we're in trouble."

Ann: What did he say?

Mr. Todd: He says, "Don't worry about it. We didn't do nothing wrong."

Ann: That wasn't really true, was it?

Mr. Todd: Apparently not because the next day they came and arrested us, well, not arrested us but brang us in for questioning.

Ann: But you and Terry had come up with a story, right?

Mr. Todd: Yeah.

Ann: What was your story?

Mr. Todd: Just to go with the basics of that evening.

Ann: Okay. What do you mean?

Mr. Todd: Just with the basics of what we went through that night.

Ann: Can you tell me what you mean by the basics?

Mr. Todd: Well, where we were, and, you know, from what questions the police officers asked us and stuff.

Ann: And did you stick with this story for a pretty long time?

Mr. Todd: Yes. Actually over the years I had forgotten mostly about it at all until 2003.

Ann: How could you forget about somebody dying?

Mr. Todd: Because I didn't think we did it.

Ann: Then why did you say, "I think we're in trouble"?

Mr. Todd: Because he was the last one to be seen with us.

Ann: Are you sorry about any of this?

Mr. Todd: Deeply, deeply sorry.

Ann: Thank you. How come it took you so long to tell about this?

Mr. Todd: Mainly I put it out of my mind.

Ann: Were you afraid?

Mr. Todd: Yes.

Ann: Do you think that this has affected your life?

Mr. Todd: Yes.

Ann: How?

Mr. Todd: Well, I lost everything I own. And I've been incarcerated so, you know, my wife filed for a divorce. I've been depressed and stuff from being in jail for a long time, which I've never been in jail. Well, I'll rephrase that. I was in jail three days one time. That was like fourteen years ago.

Ann: Did you personally do anything to Jeff Hammill?

Mr. Todd: No.

Ann: Did you see Terry Olson or the defendant Ron Michaels do anything to Jeff Hammill?

Mr. Todd: The only thing I saw was Terry pushing him, pushing him towards the back of the car.

Ann: Otherwise you didn't see who hit him?

Mr. Todd: No.

Ann: Have you told the truth here today?

Mr. Todd: Yes.

Ann: Complete truth?

Mr. Todd: Yes.

Ann: You're not falsely accusing this man in order to get a deal on your case, are you?

Mr. Todd: No.

Ann: Is there anything else you want to say about this?

Mr. Todd: No.

Ann: I have nothing further.

The Court: The defense may proceed.

Jim: Okay. Thank you.

Jim: Mr. Todd, good afternoon.

Mr. Todd: Afternoon.

Jim begins his line of questioning, reviewing with Dale Todd the number of times he has been questioned by authorities regarding this case. After five different sessions, the first one alone lasting five hours, he establishes that the police had continually told Dale they had the bat with Jeffrey Hammill's blood and hair on it, and they had witnesses that saw his car out on Country Road 12 at the spot where Jeff's body was found. No one has ever told Dale Todd that both of those statements are false; that the blood and hair found on the bat does not belong to Jeff Hammill, and there are no witnesses that saw his car on CR-12. And to this day, Dale still believes these claims to be true. Dale confirms that he does.

> Jim: Okay. You testified on direct examination that at some point that you and Terry sat down and talked about the events of that night so that you could put together a story, correct?
>
> Mr. Todd: We didn't really ... it was at the funeral and he just says, "Just keep your mouth shut and just, you know, just tell them you were at the party and that's that".
>
> Jim: Well, I think you testified on direct examination that the two of you talked about it and you talked about what you were going to say in case you were questioned; do you recall that? Do you recall that testimony?
>
> Jim: I'm sorry, she can't take down the nodding of the head so you have to either say yes or no.
>
> Mr. Todd: You got to explain what you want me to, you know, to say.

Jim: Well, sir, I don't want you … I don't want you to say anything.

Mr. Todd: I said Terry had said—

Jim: Do you recall testifying when you were being questioned by the prosecutor that you and Terry discussed what you were going to say in case you were questioned?

Mr. Todd: Yes.

Jim: Okay. So you did do that?

Mr. Todd: In a way, yes, I think so, yes.

Jim: All right. And it's true that Ron Michaels was not involved in those discussions, was he?

Mr. Todd: No.

Jim begins a series of questions, focusing on the inconsistencies in Todd's 2003 and 2006 statements. In many instances, his responses to questions in the 2003 statement contained less detail than his responses to those same questions asked in the 2006 record, and a lot of "There's a little bit of doubt in my mind, yes," and "I'm not even sure we were there". In 2003 Dale stated, "No, I don't remember a car, I remember it was pitch black". Yet in testimony today, he stated a car passed them at about forty miles per hour and he thought it was white. What Jim begins to show the jury is that Dale is being asked a series of questions that tell a specific story: questions that, for the most part, only require a yes or no answer.

Jim believes Dale is coughing up the story that has been fed to him time and time again, by the BCA; first back in 2003 and then again by those who took the 2006 statement. However, this time the story has more details; a car that passed them while they were at the scene (the Kilgos); his car's trunk lid up. Yet in 2003 he states the trunk lid wasn't up, because when you popped the trunk, the trunk light would come on and he didn't see the light on.

Jim: Do you recall telling them, "I'm getting kind of confused"?

Mr. Todd: Yes.

Jim: Now, in that statement, do you recall how many times you told them that you were scared?

Mr. Todd: About fifty.

Jim: And you were scared, weren't you?

Mr. Todd: Yes, I was. I still am.

Jim: Because they sat you down in that room and for five hours they talked with you about this situation and they told you about the blood and the hair on the baseball bat. They told you about witnesses that saw your car at the scene, and you told them repeatedly, "I'm not sure that any of this ever happened", didn't you?

Mr. Todd: Yes.

Jim: Now, I want to focus these next questions exclusively on that interview back in 2003. So we're not going to talk about right now July of 2006 at all, okay? When you were interviewed, they asked you numerous times if you remembered Ron Michaels, didn't they?

Mr. Todd: Yes.

Jim: Okay. And, in fact, they asked you for at least an hour and forty-five minutes of that five hours if you remembered Ron Michaels, didn't they?

Mr. Todd: I think so.

Jim: And repeatedly during that hour and forty-five minutes you told them, "I don't know who Ron Michaels is", didn't you?

Mr. Todd: Yes.

Jim: But after an hour and forty-five minutes they produced a picture and they set it down in front of you and they told you,

"This is Ron Michaels. This is the guy that you were with", didn't they?

Mr. Todd: Yes.

Jim: And up until that point you didn't know who Ron Michaels was, did you?

Mr. Todd: Not until that point.

Jim: And until they put their finger on the picture and said, "That's him. That's Ron Michaels. That's the guy you were with", you didn't know that, did you?

Mr. Todd: No.

Jim: Okay. But at the same time, at the same time they had told you about this baseball bat and they had told you about the witnesses that saw your car; hadn't they?

Mr. Todd: Yes.

Jim: And you believed at that point in time that that was true, didn't you?

Mr. Todd: Yes.

Jim: And you were scared, weren't you?

Mr. Todd: Yes.

Jim: And you're still scared?

Mr. Todd: Yes.

Jim: And no one has ever come to you and said, "Dale, that baseball bat didn't have any blood and hair on it"?

Mr. Todd: No.

Jim: Nobody's ever come to you and said, "Dale, there are no witnesses that saw your car out on the scene", have they?

Mr. Todd: No.

CHAPTER 16

Day 3

Jim: Mr. Todd, before I get started with the balance of the cross-examination, I want to ask you something. You had mentioned that you have been dealing with some issues of depression, that sort of thing, down in the jail; is that correct?

Mr. Todd: Correct.

Jim: Are you on medication at the present time?

Mr. Todd: Just take Lipitor, that's for my cholesterol and stuff.

Jim: Okay. So nothing for the depression, no pain medication of any kind?

Mr. Todd: No.

Jim: Okay. Good. Thank you. I appreciate that. I'd like to start out by going through a little bit of the testimony that you gave yesterday on direct examination. You testified yesterday that you knew that Mr. Michaels' girlfriend Sandy Dehn was at the party, correct?

Mr. Todd: Yes.

Jim: Do you recall the statement that you gave to your attorney, Mr. Benson, and to an investigator from the Wright County Sheriff's Office, I believe by the name of Lieutenant Joe Hagerty on July 19, 2006?

Mr. Todd: Correct.

Jim: And at that point in time you were asked, weren't you, if you knew Ron Michaels' girlfriend's name and you answered the question by saying, "No, I didn't know her name." Isn't that correct?

Mr. Todd: Right.

Jim: And, in fact, they asked you again about that and you said, "And I can't remember if, um, Ron, I don't know, I can't remember Ron's girl's name, but I think she was there for a little bit and then had gone home and I think she had left right after that fight." Do you recall stating that? This would have been just prior to your plea hearing.

Mr. Todd: I think so.

Jim: Okay. Now, you also testified yesterday that you didn't see any contact between Mr. Michaels' girlfriend and Jeff Hammill at the party, didn't you?

Mr. Todd: Correct, as far as I can remember.

Jim: And you also said that you didn't see any evidence of Mr. Michaels becoming angry at Jeffrey Hammill, did you?

Mr. Todd: No.

Jim: In fact, I believe that you also stated that you don't remember anybody specifically being mad at Jeffrey Hammill that night, do you, with the possible exception of whomever he was talking about at the bar when he said that there were people looking for him?

Mr. Todd: Correct.

Jim: And they wanted to beat him up, didn't they?

Mr. Todd: Correct, that's what he had told us.

Jim: Now, when you are leaving the party to go out and look for Jeff, you said, "I'm not sure why we went looking for Jeff."

Mr. Todd: Correct.

Jim: Okay. But it was your conclusion that somebody was mad at Jeff; is that correct?

Mr. Todd: I would assume so.

Jim: Okay. Now, yesterday you testified that when you pulled up on County Road 12 to where Jeff Hammill was, that Terry Olson got out and pushed him to the rear of the car.

Mr. Todd: Well, there was some words said. And then he pushed him.

Jim: To the rear of the car?

Mr. Todd: To the rear of the car.

Jim: That's all right. Now, during the course of that questioning in July of this year, you were asked, "Okay. Now, do you remember an earlier statement, Dale, that you had mentioned to us that you had seen Olson hit with his fist, hit Jeff Hammill?" And you said, "No, I don't recall.

Mr. Todd: Yes.

Jim: The fact of the matter is you never saw Terry Olson hit Jeff Hammill at all, did you?

Mr. Todd: No.

Jim: And you didn't see Ron Michaels hit Jeff Hammill, did you?

Mr. Todd: No.

Jim: In 1979 you were nineteen years old, correct?

Mr. Todd: Yes, I would have been nineteen in about a month or so prior to it. I was eighteen at the time.

Jim: And up to that point you had never been in any trouble, had you?

Mr. Todd: No.

Jim: You had no criminal record? Hadn't been arrested?

Mr. Todd: No. I think I was mainly just a couple of tickets and then I got one for we were in the park and we were drinking beer and stuff, and then the sheriff showed up and I got a ticket for some marijuana I had in my car and beer cans I had in the trunk.

Jim: Okay. But nothing very serious at that point in time, correct?

Mr. Todd: No, the charges was ... I think the charges were dismissed.

Jim: Okay. Now, all of a sudden you go to a party, have some fun, do some things, and a couple of days later the sheriff's office shows up at your place of work and starts questioning you, didn't they?

Mr. Todd: Correct.

Jim: And they weren't questioning you about marijuana in the park, they were questioning you about a death; is that correct?

Mr. Todd: Correct.

Jim: And I believe that you told them in 2003 that at the time that this happened you were scared out of your mind, weren't you?

Mr. Todd: Correct.

Jim: Okay. And you were scared because this is a serious situation, correct?

Mr. Todd: Correct.

Jim: And you told them as much as you could about the matter at that time, didn't you? And you don't hear anything more from them for quite a long period of time, do you?

Mr. Todd: Correct.

Jim: And you got married and you went on with life?

Mr. Todd: Yes.

Jim: All right. And now, all of a sudden, you're being questioned again, about the thing that they questioned you about back ... clear back in 1979, correct?

Mr. Todd: Correct.

Jim: And so they called you in and you didn't have an attorney with you, did you?

Mr. Todd: No. I asked for one and they said I didn't need one.

Jim: You didn't need one?

Mr. Todd: Yes.

Jim: And they didn't read you any rights or anything, did they?

Mr. Todd: No.

Jim: They didn't tell you that you had the right to remain silent?

Mr. Todd: No.

Jim: They didn't tell you that anything you said could be used against you in a court of law?

Mr. Todd: No.

Jim: Okay. They didn't tell you that you had the right to have an attorney, to have that attorney present during questioning, did they?

Mr. Todd: No.

Ann: Objection.

The Court: Basis?

Ann: Relevance.

The Court: Overruled.

Jim: All right. And so then they sit down in a small room, wasn't like this, was it?

Mr. Todd: No.

Jim: And in the course of talking with you, they asked you the following questions: "Okay. Do you know Ron Michaels?" And you answered, "Ron Michaels? Where's he from", didn't you?

Mr. Todd: Correct.

Jim: And they told you, "You went with Ron Michaels". And you said, "Who's Ron Michaels," didn't you?

Mr. Todd: Correct.

Jim: And they said, "About your whereabouts that night, you told the investigators that you went somewhere from Deb's house, you went with Ron Michaels". And you said, "Who? Ron Michaels. Who's Ron? Don't remember no Ron". And then they told you, "Well, it says Ron Michaels lives south of Montrose, described as a flat house on a hill. Says the guy drives a blue Hornet. Ron wanted to show Dale his stereo. He wanted Ron to look, listen to his stereo. And then you left with Ron Michaels and didn't come back the rest of the night". And you answered, "I don't remember that", didn't you?

Mr. Todd: Yeah.

Jim: And that went on—

Mr. Todd: That went on for quite a while.

Jim: And you told them, "You've got me scared", didn't you?

Mr. Todd: Yes.

Jim: And they said to you at one point, "Well, here's what we've got: We've got the car. We've got the bat. We've got the hair. We've got the blood", didn't they?

Mr. Todd: Yes.

Jim: And you said again to them, "I'm scared because now you're telling me that somebody saw my car out there and that Jeff's hair and blood is on this baseball bat and we didn't have anything to do with that", didn't you?

Mr. Todd: Yes.

Jim: But there was no question in your mind at that point in time that they were telling you that they had a witness that saw your car at the scene and that Jeff's blood and Jeff's hair were on that baseball bat taken from the trunk of your car back in 1979?

Mr. Todd: Correct.

Jim: And you believed them, didn't you?

Mr. Todd: Yes, that's what … that's why I was really scared.

Jim: And isn't it true, Mr. Todd, that the reason that you were scared is because they were asking you questions that you didn't have any answers to?

Mr. Todd: Correct.

Jim: But when they'd ask you a question and you didn't know the answer to it, they gave you the answer, didn't they?

Mr. Todd: In a lot of the questions, yes.

Jim: They asked you, "Well, what do you think he hit him with? Was it a baseball bat? Was it a tire iron? Was it a hockey stick?" And you said, "It could have been a baseball bat or it could have been a tire iron or it could have been a hockey stick,", didn't you?

Mr. Todd: Yes.

Jim: Because you didn't know?

Mr. Todd: Correct.

Jim: But there's one thing that you did know and that that was that they were telling you that a witness saw your car there and that Jeff's blood and hair were on that baseball bat, correct?

Mr. Todd: They told me they found hair, his hair in my car, and that there was blood and hair on the baseball bat, yes.

Jim: And you were scared at that time and you gave them that statement because that's what they wanted, wasn't it?

Mr. Todd: Yes.

Jim: And you told them, "I can say anything you want me to say, I can tell you it was them", didn't you?

Mr. Todd: Yes.

Jim: And then you also said to them, "But I don't know if that's true. All I know is I wasn't involved", didn't you?

Mr. Todd: Yes.

Jim: Because the truth of the matter is you didn't know that they were involved either. And when I say they, I mean Terry Olson and Ron Michaels, this man sitting right here. You didn't know that, but you were told that, weren't you?

Mr. Todd: Yes.

Jim: And that's why we're here right now, isn't it?

Mr. Todd: Yes.

Jim: Because the truth of the matter is that night you were a nineteen-year-old kid, and you're with friends and you'd never been in any trouble and you weren't an aggressive kid and all you wanted to do was meet some people and have some fun, didn't you?

Mr. Todd: Yes.

Jim: Now, yesterday I showed you an exhibit, and I'll ask you if you remember it, if you don't I'll get up and show it to you, that you identified as being a fair representation of the tail-lights on your 1971 Chevrolet Impala.

Mr. Todd: Correct.

Jim: Okay. And you said, "Yeah, that's what the taillights looked like on my car", didn't you?

Mr. Todd: Yes.

Jim: Okay. The taillights on your car were not flat on the top and round on the bottom, were they?

Mr. Todd: No.

Jim: And all three of the taillights on each side were not red, were they?

Mr. Todd: No.

Jim: Do you understand what I'm asking you? There was one in the middle—

Mr. Todd: No, the left one was red, the right one was red and the middle one was red with a white square in it.

Jim: And what do they call that?

Mr. Todd: Backup lights.

Jim: And the only time that goes on—

Mr. Todd: Is when you're backing up.

Jim: And then it wouldn't show red, would it?

Mr. Todd: No, it would show white.

Jim: So if the only witness that the law enforcement officers have talked to described a car with three red lights, taillights on each side, all of them red that were flat on the top and round on the bottom, they would not be describing your car, would they?

Mr. Todd: No.

Jim: If that same witness told the officers in 1979 that he thought it was a '67 to '69 Chevrolet Impala or at least a '67 to '69 Chevrolet, he would not be describing your car, would he?

Mr. Todd: No, he would not.

Jim: Because you drove a 1971 Chevrolet, didn't you?

Mr. Todd: Correct.

Jim: And it had rectangular taillights?

Mr. Todd: Correct.

Jim: Now, if you had known that in 2003 when you were questioned, would you have been as scared?

Mr. Todd: If I would have known that, I would have told them that.

Jim: But, I mean, they told you that they had a witness that saw your car there.

Mr. Todd: Correct.

Jim: Does it sound to you now as though they have a witness that saw your car there?

Mr. Todd: No.

Jim: Would you have been as scared in 2003 had you known that?

Mr. Todd: Yes.

Jim: You would have been just as scared?

Mr. Todd: Yes.

Jim: Okay. All right.

Mr. Todd: Only because of the whole situation.

Jim: All right. If they had told you that there was no trace of Jeff Hammill's blood or hair on that baseball bat, would you have been as scared at that point?

Mr. Todd: Yeah.

Jim: You think you would still have been just as scared?

Mr. Todd: Yeah, I would have been pretty nervous.

Jim: And that's because you were being asked to tell them a story.

Mr. Todd: Correct.

Jim: And they said that to you, "Tell us the story", didn't they?

Mr. Todd: Correct.

Jim: "Because if you don't tell us the story, we're going to have to look at this as a first degree murder", didn't they say that?

Mr. Todd: They said that after the interview the next day. I seeked legal counsel and then I was supposed to return back there, but I didn't ... when I got legal counsel, he told me not to go there, so I called them up and said I wasn't coming back. And then they said, well, they didn't get the message. So they pulled me over on the side of the road and I told them that. And then Ken, he got mad and hit my truck with his hand and said, "You're going to jail for twenty-five years". And then I was still pretty ... you know, I was still scared.

Jim: But now they've come to you and said, "Well, you know what, there's a way out of this. Give us a statement and we'll let you plead guilty to a much lessor offense", haven't they?

Mr. Todd: Yes.

Jim: But the fact of the matter is, Mr. Todd, at this point in time, not through your fault, but you don't know whether that statement's accurate or not, do you?

Mr. Todd: Correct.

Jim: Because you don't know what happened that night, do you?

Mr. Todd: Correct.

Jim: Because you were at a party, you were at the bars, and you were having fun with friends, and you got drunk. And you were smoking a little pot. And you were having a good time.

Mr. Todd: Correct.

Jim: And the next thing you know this young man that you worked with was dead.

Mr. Todd: Correct.

Jim: And they told you that you were involved.

Mr. Todd: Correct.

Jim: And they said, "We want to hear the story from you". And you had to tell them something.

Mr. Todd: Correct.

Jim: And so isn't that why in this entire five-hour statement that the best that you could do is tell them, "I think I remember, I think I saw this, I think I remember that"?

Mr. Todd: Yes.

Jim: Because you don't know?

Mr. Todd: Right.

Jim: Thank you. No further questions, Your Honor.

The Court: Redirect?

Ann: Thank you, yes.

Ann: Good morning. I have a few more questions that I need to ask you this morning. Now, I want to talk a little bit about when you spoke with the police on September 23 of '03. You remember that day, right?

Mr. Todd: That's when they came to my work.

Ann: Right. Now, the interview, as I understand it, took place at the Hutchinson Police Department; is that correct?

Mr. Todd: Correct.

Ann: Well, how did it come to pass that you were at the Hutchinson Police Department? Did they call you up?

Mr. Todd: They came to my work.

Ann: They came to your work. And did they ask you whether you would be willing to talk to them?

Mr. Todd: Yes, I think so.

Ann: Okay. And did you set up a day and time that you were going to go and talk to them?

Mr. Todd: They wanted to see me that day, that evening.

Ann: Okay. That evening?

Mr. Todd: After I got off work.

Ann: Okay. So what time did you get off work?

Mr. Todd: I think it was 3:30.

Ann: Okay. So how did you get to the Hutchinson Police Department?

Mr. Todd: They followed me. They told me to follow them.

Ann: Okay. So you drove in your own car?

Mr. Todd: Yes.

Ann: And you were going to this interview voluntarily, right?

Mr. Todd: Yeah.

Ann: And they told you, you could leave any time you wanted, didn't they?

Mr. Todd: Yes.

Ann: Okay. And, as a matter of fact, during the course of this interview, there were several breaks, weren't there?

Mr. Todd: There was a couple.

Ann: Did you go outside and have cigarettes during those breaks?

Mr. Todd: One time.

Ann: Did you go to have a cigarette in your truck?

Mr. Todd: Yeah, that was the first time.

Ann: Okay. And did you make any phone calls?

Mr. Todd: I had called my wife.

Ann: Okay. And so they weren't making you stay there, were they?

Mr. Todd: No, the door was locked. So I had to wait for them and I had to go to the bathroom one time and they had to unlock the door.

Ann: And they let you go, right?

Mr. Todd: To the bathroom, yes.

Ann: You weren't under arrest, were you?

Mr. Todd: They kept on telling me no.

Ann: They kept telling you no, you weren't under arrest. And when you were done talking to them, did they let you go home?

Mr. Todd: Yes. They said they would let me go home.

Ann: And you were never picked up by them until after the grand jury, right?

Mr. Todd: The next day.

Ann: Well, they didn't bring you into custody and arrest you, did they?

Mr. Todd: No, they just pulled me over on the side of the road when I had left work.

Ann: Okay. Now, when you heard from these law enforcement officers in September of '03, it had been a long time since you had heard from anybody about this, hadn't it?

Mr. Todd: Yes.

Ann: How long had it been?

Mr. Todd: I'd say roughly about twenty-six years.

Ann: Were you surprised to hear from them?

Mr. Todd: Yes. I was actually scared.

Ann: You were surprised—were you surprised that they were looking at this case again?

Mr. Todd: Yes.

Ann: And were you scared because you didn't want to get in trouble?

Mr. Todd: Yes.

Ann: And were you scared that you were going to get in trouble because you were involved in it?

Mr. Todd: Well, I was the last one, you know, I picked up Jeff and that's why I thought I was going to be in trouble.

Ann: You wanted to stick to your story that you and Terry had figured out, didn't you?

Mr. Todd: Yes.

Ann: And did you try—

Mr. Todd: There wasn't really "figured out". It was just stuff that we had left out from the interview on Monday at work from the first police officers in '79.

Ann: Uh-huh.

Mr. Todd: Then me and Terry, we were wondering what was really going on and stuff. And the next day was his funeral so we asked for the day off to go.

Ann: Okay.

Mr. Todd: So I looked through the newspaper and found where they were having it. And Terry knew the area a little bit so we drove out there.

Ann: Okay.

Mr. Todd: And then Wednesday they said they had—

Ann: I got to stop you a little bit here, okay? You indicated "There wasn't really a story. It was just what we left out". So there were things that you left out when you talked to the police in 1979; is that correct?

Mr. Todd: The first interview, correct.

Ann: Okay. Did you leave out the part about you and the Defendant and Mr. Olson leaving Deb Segler's party?

Mr. Todd: Yes.

Ann: And did you leave out the part about going to find Jeff Hammill?

Mr. Todd: Yes.

Ann: Okay. Did you leave out the part about finding him at the side of the road?

Mr. Todd: Yes.

Ann: And did you leave out the part of Terry Olson and Ron Michaels getting out of the car?

Mr. Todd: Yes.

Ann: And did you leave out the part about them getting back into the car—

Mr. Todd: Yes.

Ann: And saying, "I guess he won't need a ride home"?

Mr. Todd: Yes.

Ann: And did you leave that out because you didn't want them to know about it?

Mr. Todd: No.

Ann: Why did you leave it out?

Mr. Todd: I don't know.

Ann: So you just left that out for some unknown reason; is that right?

Mr. Todd: Correct.

Ann: Okay. Now, is it true that you were trying to stick to that version of events when the police came and talked to you in 2003?

Mr. Todd: I was trying to remember, yes.

Ann: Remember what you had told them in 1979?

Mr. Todd: They went through some of the transcripts of '79, to try to refresh my memory.

Ann: Okay. But what I'm asking you is, were you trying to remember to stick to the story that you and Terry Olson had come up with?

Mr. Todd: I'm not sure.

Ann: Okay.

Mr. Todd: I would think so.

Ann: Okay. You can't remember exactly what you said in five hours in September of 2003, can you?

Mr. Todd: To be honest, no.

Ann: And you can't remember exactly what you said this last July of 2006, can you?

Mr. Todd: Some of it, yes.

Ann: But you can't remember exactly everything, can you?

Mr. Todd: Correct.

Ann: And you can't remember exactly what you said yesterday, can you?

Mr. Todd: Correct.

Ann: Now, when you were indicted for this case and when you were charged, you got a lawyer, didn't you?

Mr. Todd: Correct.

Ann: Was his name Dan Benson?

Mr. Todd: Kevin Tierney.

Ann: Okay. Then did Dan Benson represent you after a while?

Mr. Todd: About six months.

Ann: Okay. And when Mr. Benson represented you, did he have someone from his staff come and see you and read all of the police reports and evidence to you?

Mr. Todd: Correct.

Ann: And how long did it take to read all of that?

Mr. Todd: Four days.

Ann: Four days. And how many hours was the person there reading to you?

Mr. Todd: It would be like a couple hours a day.

Ann: Okay. So it took at least eight hours to read every piece of paper to you; is that right?

Mr. Todd: Maybe a little more.

Ann: Maybe a little more. Could it be more like ten or twelve hours?

Mr. Todd: Could be, yes.

Ann: It was a lot of paper, right?

Mr. Todd: Correct.

Ann: And they read you all the police reports; is that right?

Mr. Todd: The only ones they had yellow tagged.

Ann: Okay. But as far as you knew they read you everything there was; is that right?

Mr. Todd: No.

Ann: Okay.

Mr. Todd: Just the ones that they tagged.

Ann: Okay. They had them tagged before they came, right?

Mr. Todd: I think so.

Ann: Okay.

Mr. Todd: I think Dan had some stuff that he wanted me to go through.

Ann: Okay. Did they talk to you about all the evidence that the State had?

Mr. Todd: No.

Ann: They didn't?

Mr. Todd: Not that I remember.

Ann: Okay. Well, did they … didn't Mr. Benson talk to you about your case?

Mr. Todd: Yes.

Ann: Okay. And didn't his associate talk to you about your case?

Mr. Todd: His associates just went through the transcripts with me so I could understand them better.

Ann: Okay. And did they talk to you about any tests on any items?

Mr. Todd: No.

Ann: Did they talk to you about the baseball bat?

Mr. Todd: I'm not sure.

Ann: Okay. That baseball bat that you were referring to, that was from your trunk, wasn't it?

Mr. Todd: Yes.

Ann: Okay. And didn't Mr. Benson tell you that that had been examined and there was no usable evidence on it?

Mr. Todd: He might have had said something to me about it.

Ann: Okay.

Mr. Todd: I'm not sure, you know.

Ann: Okay. Now you testified yesterday that August 10 of 1979 was the first time you ever met Ron Michaels; is that right?

Mr. Todd: Right.

Ann: And you never saw him again for years and years and years?

Mr. Todd: Correct.

Ann: And so when the police were asking you if you knew Ron Michaels in 2003, you didn't know his name; is that right?

Mr. Todd: Correct. I didn't know who ... I didn't know who the name went to.

Ann: And you needed to see a picture in order to know who they were talking about?

Mr. Todd: Correct.

Ann: Okay. And so when they showed you the picture, is that when you knew who they were talking about?

Mr. Todd: Right.

Ann: And when they showed you the picture, is that when you identified him as being with you on July... on August 11, 1979?

Mr. Todd: Yes.

Ann: Okay. So you weren't able to say the name till you heard the name; is that right?

Mr. Todd: Correct.

Ann: But you knew his face when you saw it; is that right?

Mr. Todd: Correct. When they pointed it to me, correct.

Ann: Okay. You said that back in 1979 was the first time you had ever met Ron Michaels' girlfriend; is that right?

Mr. Todd: Right.

Ann: And you never saw her again after that night?

Mr. Todd: Correct.

Ann: Have you ever seen her again?

Mr. Todd: Correct.

Ann: And are you sure of what her name is?

Mr. Todd: No.

Ann: Okay. So yesterday you said Sandy or Pam but you're not really positive what her name is, are you?

Mr. Todd: Correct.

Ann: Now, today and yesterday you said you saw Terry Olson pushing Jeff Hammill; is that correct?

Mr. Todd: Correct.

Ann: And did you see that?

Mr. Todd: Correct.

Ann: And would you show us what you meant by pushing?

Mr. Todd: Just push.

Ann: Pushing him hard?

Mr. Todd: Just push.

Ann: Okay.

Mr. Todd: Pushing him away.

Ann: Could that have been what you meant back in 2003 when you said you saw Terry Olson hitting Jeff Hammill?

Mr. Todd: Yes.

Ann: Yesterday when I was asking you questions here, Mr. Todd, did you tell the truth to the questions that I asked you?

Mr. Todd: Yes.

Ann: Were you at this party on August 11, 1979?

Mr. Todd: Yes.

Ann: And did you leave that party with the Defendant Ron Michaels and your friend Terry Olson?

Mr. Todd: No.

Ann: You did not?

Mr. Todd: No.

Ann: You did not?

Mr. Todd: No.

Ann: Are you here now, today, saying that you lied yesterday when you said that Ron Michaels had something to do with the death of Jeffrey Hammill?

Mr. Todd: Correct.

Ann: Why?

Mr. Todd: Because I'm … I was scared.

Ann: Why?

Mr. Todd: Because I didn't do this, we didn't do this.

Ann: Why did you tell the police you did it?

Mr. Todd: Because I was … I didn't want to go to jail for something I didn't do.

Ann: So you're now saying that your statement to the police in September of '03 was a lie?

Mr. Todd: Some of it was … most of the statement in '03 was the first part and I had told my attorney that I had lied on the last part of the statement.

Ann: Are you saying that your statement to the police in July of—

Mr. Todd: You wanted me to be honest. I'm being honest.

Ann: Yes.

Mr. Todd: Yes, I did.

Ann: Okay.

Mr. Todd: Okay. What I am saying is that nobody wanted to believe me!

Ann: Okay.

Mr. Todd: They kept hounding me and hounding me and what they wanted me to say!

Ann: Okay. So—

Mr. Todd: And I just … nobody would believe me.

Ann: So did you leave the party or not?

Mr. Todd: No, we did not leave the party. The only time I had left the party was to give Ron a ride home and he was telling me about his stereo. So I stayed over at his house for a little bit. His wife came down or his girlfriend, wife, girlfriend in her bathrobe, her night gown, bathrobe on, and said, "Ron, the lights. .the sun is coming up, you need to go to sleep." And then we said, "Yeah." And then he told me how to get home. He told me how to get home. He said, "Just go down the road. Take a left. Come to the tar. Take a right and that will bring you back into Montrose." I'm not sure where the house was or whatever.

Ann: Okay.

Mr. Todd: But I can't do this no more. I just can't. I mean, I've already...you know, one person is already gone out of this whole thing. And now three more. And if it's taking me, I guess it's taking me. I can't do it no more.

Ann: Okay. Thank you, Mr. Todd. We want you to tell the truth.

Mr. Todd: No, I can't do this no more...

Ann: Thank you. We want you to tell the truth.

Mr. Todd: The first part of it—

The Court: Mr. Todd, please, there is no question before you.

Ann: Thank you. I have no further questions.

The Court: Any cross-examination?

Jim: No.

The Court: Thank you. The witness may be excused.

Ron Michaels and Dale Todd are looking at each other intently. Michaels, expressionless for most of the trial, now shows a slight smile, to which Todd, with teary eyes, returns a knowing nod of the head. Ron makes the sign of the cross in Dale's direction. For Ron, a miracle has just occurred. He and Jean and many of their family and friends, have been praying for a miracle. Praying for the judge, the jury, their attorneys and mostly for Dale Todd; praying for Dale to tell the truth. They have gotten their miracle. Dale is led from the courtroom, still in cuffs and shackles.

> The Court: We will take our midmorning break at this point and resume at 10:45.

> Ann: If I could have even a little longer than that.

> The Court: We will resume at 11 o'clock.

> Ann: Thank you.

> The Court: The jury is excused. You may be seated. We are in recess.

The jury exits the courtroom.

CHAPTER 17

The gallery is on their feet, trying to absorb what just happened. They are looking at each other, stunned, wondering if they really just heard what they thought they did. The primary witness for the prosecution has just recanted everything he has said regarding the involvement of Ron Michaels, Terry Olson and himself in the death of Jeffrey Hammill. He has stated that he was afraid of going to jail for something he didn't do, so he lied to get a shorter sentence. The BCA agents and Chief Deputy Joe Hagerty had hounded him and hounded him, regarding what they wanted him to say. Nobody wanted to believe him, so he relented. But now, he could not continue to lie, he didn't want innocent men to have to pay for something they didn't do. He was resigning himself to the fact that he may face more severe punishment, but he was not going to lie anymore.

As Ann walks back to her table, she stops, looks at Jim and the defense team and says, "Now that's a Perry Mason moment." She takes her seat.

Dale Todd's mother has been sitting front row center, watching her son testify. Their eyes have been locked on each other for most of his testimony, tears appearing in hers at times; Dale had looked at the floor on occasion, then at Ron Michaels, then at his mother.

Jean rushes over to Dale's mother at the other end of the front row of seats, leans down and hugs her, speaking softly in her ear, comforting her, both of them in tears.

As the courtroom empties, there are smiles and laughing from Ron's supporters in the gallery. Not everyone is thrilled however. The parents of Jeffrey Hammill, along with other family members, have just watched Dale Todd slam the door on any likelihood of a conviction here, and closure for their decades old heartache. They have been assured by the County, by Tom Kelly, by law enforcement, and by the BCA that there was ample evidence that these three men were guilty of Jeffrey's murder. Now, it appears the Michaels trial will be over shortly with the dropping of the charges against him due to lack of evidence.

Today, lunch at J's Family Restaurant is a joyous event. Jean starts the lunch by thanking the Lord for answering their prayers. Plans are being made for a party when Ron gets home. No one has ever heard of such a remarkable confession at a trial. Jim informs Jean that Ann Mohaupt would be meeting with her boss, County Attorney Tom Kelly, during the lunch break to request that the charges against Ron be dropped. She feels there is no further need to continue, as their primary witness has recanted. His testimony is crucial to her case.

Following lunch, as everyone files back into the courtroom, there seems to be a concerned look on the faces of Jim, Rob and Hawk. They are talking among themselves at the defense table. The judge enters the courtroom and summons Jim and Ann to the bench. There is a discussion at the bench for five minutes. Something is frustrating Jim. The judge is not smiling. The attorneys return to their tables.

The Court: Could we bring in the jury, please?

The jury enters courtroom.

The Court: Please be seated. We are ready to resume testimony. Does the State have a witness available?

Ann: Yes, Your Honor. Brooks Martin.

There is total silence in the courtroom. People are looking at each other in disbelief. The jurors look angry and confused. Did the judge just tell them to resume the trial? How could this trial continue? The prosecution's primary witness has recanted his testimony and stated that Ron Michaels was driven home and dropped off. All of the evidence against him was a fabrication. Can't someone explain what's going on here? Everyone is looking at each other and at the defense team, hoping someone will explain why this trial is continuing.

The Clerk: Would you have a seat, please, and state your name for the record, spelling both your first and your last name.

Mr. Martin: Okay. My name is Brooks J. Martin. B-r-o-o-k-s. M-a-r-t-i-n.

The Court: Thank you. You may proceed, Ms. Mohaupt.

Ann questions former detective Martin about the investigation into the death of Jeffrey Hammill. She begins by covering his twenty-six-year employment history with the Wright County Sheriff's Office, then his investigation work with fellow detective Denny Compton on the Hammill case. He recalls interviewing approximately seventy-five witnesses in the course of the investigation. He states that as far as he was concerned, they were investigating a homicide, not a hit-and-run.

Ann: Now, how long did this investigation go on?

Mr. Martin: Actually several months. We had hit it quite hard the first few months and, you know, it's one of those that never really ended but you got involved in other cases at a point down the road.

Ann: So was it ever officially stopped?

Mr. Martin: As far as I know, it's always been open.

Ann: Were you ever told not to investigate it again?

Mr. Martin: No, I did not get much assistance. Our polygraph operator was going to re-run someone. And he didn't. And the sheriff, at one point, it wasn't talked about.

Ann: Is it fair to say that there was kind of a lack of interest on the part of management at the Sheriff's Department?

Mr. Martin: After a couple months went by, yes.

Ann: And how did that make you feel?

Mr. Martin: Well, I wasn't happy with it, but we did have a lot of other cases and you just kind of go on with it.

Ann: Okay. As part of your investigation did you talk with this defendant, Ronald Michaels?

Mr. Martin: Yes, I did.

Ann: And what date did you talk to him?

Mr. Martin: I think that was the fourteenth of August. On the fourteenth of August I stopped at his residence and talked to him.

Ann: That was in 1979?

Mr. Martin: Yup.

Ann: And what did the Defendant tell you about his activities on the evening of August 10 and the morning of August 11?

Mr. Martin: Okay. When I had talked to him about that, he said that he had gone to the Country West with, yeah, Debbie Segler and Jeff Cardinal and there was a couple other subjects there, he said Dale Todd. And he had mentioned three people and then one person extra was there, and that's when I showed him a picture of Jeff.

Ann: What did he say about Jeff?

Mr. Martin: He stated that he did not recognize him, didn't know him.

Ann: Okay. Did he talk to you at all about leaving the party at Ms. Segler's and going someplace else?

Mr. Martin: Oh, yes, he stated that him and Dale Todd went to his residence and listened to a new stereo he had.

Ann: And does your report indicate what time the Defendant told you that he and Dale Todd left the residence?

Mr. Martin: Yes, he had said that I think it was right around, yeah, 2:30 and 3:00 in the morning, and he wasn't sure on the time he came back. He indicated he had been drinking a little.

Ann: Okay. Thank you. Nothing further.

The Court: Cross-examination?

Jim: Yes, thank you.

Jim: Good afternoon.

Mr. Martin: Afternoon.

Jim: Now, during the course of the investigation, who was your immediate supervisor?

Mr. Martin: Well, probably Powers and the Sheriff themselves as far as this investigation.

Jim: Okay. And you said that you believed that during the course of the time that you were questioning people that you probably interviewed seventy-five people?

Mr. Martin: That would be the joint investigation between several of us.

Jim: Okay. I'm going to ask a question, I don't want you mad at me.

Mr. Martin: Okay.

Jim: Do you think you dropped the ball on this investigation?

Mr. Martin: I think it was a combination that the ball was dropped. Like I say, after a couple months time, we had so much going on, we went into another investigation, so yeah.

Jim: Okay. But you wouldn't have done that, you would have stayed on this case and would have continued to apply resources to this case if you had had leads to go on, wouldn't you?

Mr. Martin: Yes, we followed up on leads.

Jim: Okay. Isn't it true that you just simply ran out of leads?

Mr. Martin: I guess you could word it that way, yeah.

Jim: Okay. Isn't it true that it is police practice, that with an open investigation that it's never closed, but it's just simply not worked because of a lack of resources?

Mr. Martin: Yes, that's the case much of the time.

Jim: All right. Did you ever have an opportunity to talk with Chief Deputy Powers about his perception of the case and the conclusions that he'd drawn during the course of the investigation?

Mr. Martin: Yes, I did.

Jim: Okay. During the course of that, did he give you any indication that he believed that the matter was a motor vehicle pedestrian collision?

Mr. Martin: No.

Jim: Okay. You're sure of that?

Mr. Martin: Yes, I'm sure of that.

Jim: Okay. Isn't it true, though, that Chief Deputy Powers was spending his time during the course of this investigation driving around to different farms, looking at farm equipment?

Mr. Martin: That I'm not sure about.

Jim: No further questions, Your Honor.

The Court: Any redirect?

Ann: Thank you. No. Thank you.

The Court: Mr. Martin, you are excused. Thank you, sir.

The Court: State may call its next witness.

Ann: Call Brent Krause.

The Court: Please come forward.

The Clerk: Would you take a seat and please state your name for the record, spelling both your first and your last name.

Mr. Krause: Brent Krause. B-r-e-n-t, K-r-a-u-s-e.

Ann begins her questions of Mr. Krause by exploring his relationship with Dale Todd. They were co-workers for some time at Zimmerman Stucco. They became friends and Dale would stop by occasionally at Brent's home on Saturdays to share some coffee and shoot the bull. On one particular Saturday in the summer of 2005, Dale stopped by to visit. At one point he begins telling Brent about being questioned by the FBI.

Mr. Krause: Well, I guess it all started out that he just got done talking with his parents or something about the FBI being there. And I had questioned him, "FBI? For what?" And he had said something about being involved in a murder. And I kind of chuckled at him at first because he's been known to be a story teller in the past. So there again it was just another story as far as I was concerned. So he had mentioned about being involved in this murder and I kind of chuckled and I looked at him and I says, "What are you talking about?" He said, yeah, that the FBI was just at his parents' house questioning him about this homicide that had happened years prior. And I asked him, well, if he did it, if he didn't, "why aren't you talking to these people if you're innocent? You know, why don't you go and talk to them? Why are you running?" And he just claimed that he had no proof he was innocent, he was scared, didn't know what to do, and at that time it was just pretty much left at that. There again, I thought it was one of his typical stories. I didn't really believe it. And never even believed it until last November when everything finally came through and he was actually convicted.

Ann: Did he tell you about being at a party in Montrose?

Mr. Krause: Not that I recall. There again, typical story, I didn't ask, I didn't question, I didn't really care, you know, I guess I wasn't too involved.

Ann: You gave a statement to the police; is that right?

Mr. Krause: One of the private investigators, yes.

Ann: Okay. And was the statement given on about March 13 of '06, would that be right?

Mr. Krause: That sounds about right, yes.

Ann: Could you please tell us more specifically what Mr. Todd told you about this crime?

Mr. Krause: Well, there again, I guess it wasn't til I asked him whether he actually did it or not that he had mentioned that they were partying, they had left the bar in Rockford, were going to a party somewhere in Montrose, I believe it was, and that couple of them had gotten into a fight. Mr. Hammill, I believe his name was, had left because of the fight. Dale and his two buddies went looking for him, I guess, and they came across him walking home and that's when Dale said they stopped and the two got out, I have no clue what happened, came back in, and as far as I know they drove away.

Ann: Did he tell you whether he got out of the car or just—

Mr. Krause: Just the other two. He was driving.

Ann: Okay. He said he was driving. Did he talk about a weapon?

Mr. Krause: There again, he said that the cops had found some kind of a bat in his car, aluminum bat. And there again, that was one of the reasons why he didn't want to come forward and say anything. He was scared he had no proof of being innocent. He didn't know what to do.

Ann: Did you speak with the authorities about it?

Mr. Krause: No, I didn't. There again, I didn't believe him. I still didn't believe him until as of last November when it came over the news and everything, but, no, I never did.

Ann: Nothing further. Thank you.

The Court: Cross-examination?

Jim: Yes, Your Honor.

CROSS-EXAMINATION BY MR. FLEMING

Jim confirms that Dale Todd told Mr. Krause that the police had taken an aluminum bat from his trunk and that "he was scared because he had no proof that he was innocent". Then during Mr. Krause's interview with authorities in March of 2006, when asked whether Dale mentioned that the other two with him actually killed this fellow, Brent's response was "No.

I don't even believe he actually knew that what they had done, went to that extreme either. I don't think he would have put himself in that position".

Ann asks a few clarifying questions under re-direct. Jim follows with a few under re-cross.

Jim: Just very quickly. When you had this conversation with Mr. Todd back last summer, did he mention anything to you at that point about already having been questioned by any law enforcement agencies?

Mr. Krause: No.

Jim: Okay. Thank you. Nothing further.

The Court: The witness is excused. State may call its next witness.

Ann: Call Mike Erickson.

The Clerk: Would you please have a seat? State your name for the record, spelling both your first and your last name, please.

Mr. Erickson: Michael Douglas Erickson. M-i-c-h-a-e-l. Erickson is E-r-i-c-k-s-o-n

Ann establishes that Mike Erickson is one of the COs (correctional officers) working in the Wright County Jail. He was on duty on November 8 of 2005 when Ron Michaels, Dale Todd and Terry Olson were arraigned. Erickson escorted all three defendants up to the court sally to hand them over to the bailiffs to be taken to court.

Ann: Okay. Mr. Erickson, I just want you to answer yes or no to the next couple of questions. Did you hear Mr. Olson say something to the other two codefendants in the elevator?

Mr. Erickson: Yes.

Ann: Did you hear Mr. Todd say something to the other two codefendants in the elevator?

Mr. Erickson: Yes.

Ann: Did you hear Mr. Michaels say something to the other codefendants in the elevator?

Mr. Erickson: Yes.

Ann: What did you hear the Defendant Mr. Michaels say?

Mr. Erickson: He said, "I don't know you either."

Ann: Thank you. Nothing further.

The Court: Cross-examination?

Jim: No cross.

The Court: Thank you, Mr. Erickson. You are excused.

CHAPTER 18

Day 4

The Court: Thank you. Please be seated. We are ready to resume testimony in this matter. The State may call its next witness.

Ann: Thank you. State calls Dennis Fier.

The Clerk: Would you please have a seat and state your name for the record, spelling both your first and your last name.

Mr. Fier: Okay. My name is Dennis Fier. First name spelled D-e-n-n-i-s. Last name is spelled F-i-e-r.

The Court: You may proceed.

Ann: Thank you. Would you please advise us of your educational background relative to law enforcement?

Mr. Fier: Yeah, I have a bachelor's degree in criminal justice. I have attended numerous schools. Suburban Police Academy was my basic course when I went into police work in 1963. I have attended the FBI National Academy. I've attended the Southern Police Institute Homicide School. I've attended the forensic pathology course put on by the Ramsey County Medical Examiner and numerous schools and training courses.

Ann: And you are a licensed police officer in the State of Minnesota?

Mr. Fier: Yes. Forty-three plus years. I worked for the City of St. Louis Park for just short of eight years. I worked for the DNR as a conservation officer about three months. The rest of the time was spent at the BCA as a special agent.

Ann: Can you explain what the BCA is and what its purpose is?

Mr. Fier: The BCA, it's the Bureau of Criminal Apprehension. It's a State of Minnesota agency. It's a part of the Department of Public Safety. It's an investigative unit. We assist, generally speaking, assist local law enforcement when they request our assistance. I work in the homicide unit. We also have a drug unit. We have sex offender registration units. We have the forensic laboratory. We also have different record keeping for criminal histories and that sort of stuff. That's pretty general.

Ann: Could you tell the jurors a little bit about what the cold case unit is?

Mr. Fier: Yes, the cold case unit was started in the BCA about 1989. What we look at are unsolved cases, most all are homicide cases. And we have a process that we go through in looking at these cases and reviewing them. Generally, we're looking at them for the possibility of solvability and what evidence might exist, what today's new technology might lend to solving these cases, but generally reviewing, reorganizing these cases and looking at them. And it's always at the request of local law enforcement and in cooperation with them.

Ann: How long have you been with the cold case unit, Mr. Fier?

Mr. Fier: About three and a half years.

Ann: Does the BCA have a forensics department?

Mr. Fier: Yes, they are a part of the BCA forensic laboratory.

Ann: Is the use of forensics relatively new to law enforcement?

Mr. Fier: No I don't think so. I mean, it's been around forever.

Ann: What about DNA?

Mr. Fier: Well DNA came into existence in basically the very late '80s and into the early '90s.

Ann: So you were a police officer with the BCA prior to the use of DNA and cases got solved back then?

Mr. Fier: Did they get solved? Oh, yes.

Ann: Who were the individuals that worked on it besides yourself?

Mr. Fier: Special Agent Ken McDonald, Special Agent Jen May, Sergeant Richard Eddinger from Minneapolis Police Department.

Ann: And did the BCA put together a file that contains the results of its investigation? Mr. Fier: Yes, it has.

Ann: Okay. And how many pages of reports have been created as a result of your investigation? Do you have any idea?

Mr. Fier: I think there's approximately a thousand pages of reports and statements.

The witness continues testifying, stating that that there were two formal statements taken from Dale Todd, one in September of 2003 and the other in July of 2006.

Ann: Did he ever say whether Ron Michaels' girlfriend was there?

Mr. Fier: Yes, he said she was there.

Ann: Did he tell you why they were looking for Jeff Hammill?

Mr. Fier: I can't be certain exactly. They were going to look for him. It was not to give him a ride home.

Ann: Okay. Did he tell you whether people were angry at Mr. Hammill?

Mr. Fier: They were upset, and it was basically concerning the fact that he wanted a ride home and was pretty adamant about getting a ride home.

Ann: At some point towards the end of the interview did Dale Todd give you kind of a summary of what had happened?

Mr. Fier: He said that Terry Olson had hit Jeffrey Hammill with his fist, that he observed Ron Michaels swing something at Jeff Hammill.

Ann: How did you and Special Agent Ken McDonald get Mr. Todd to tell you about this event?

Mr. Fier: Basically, we kept talking to him and asking him questions, confronting him with his ... the inconsistencies. It just took a long time.

Ann: Did you tell Dale Todd when you were interviewing him that there were people who placed his car at the scene?

Mr. Fier: I believe we did.

Ann: Okay. And did you also tell Mr. Todd that you had a baseball bat with what you thought was blood or hair on it?

Mr. Fier: Yes.

Ann: And did the BCA subsequently, after talking to Dale Todd, have that bat analyzed? Mr. Fier: Yes.

Ann: Was any usable evidence obtained?

Mr. Fier: No.

Ann: When you told Dale Todd that you had that bat, did you tell him that you thought there was evidence on it?

Mr. Fier: I think we may have; it was not Jeff Hammill's hair.

Ann: Were they even able to determine if it was human?

Mr. Fier: It was human hair.

Ann: Were you involved with the interview of Dale Todd on July 19 of '06?

Mr. Fier: Yes. It took place here at the Wright County Sheriff's Office.

Ann: And who all was there?

Mr. Fier: Lieutenant Joe Hagerty from the Wright County Sheriff's Office and Dan Benson, attorney representing Dale Todd.

Ann: Did he tell you whether there was any sort of altercation or anything on the way to the bar?

Mr. Fier: I don't recall anything on the way to the bar. There was something at the bar. It was between Terry Olson and an unknown male, and it resulted because of somebody pinching Deb Segler on her buttocks.

Ann: Did he tell you whether there was an altercation involving the Defendant, Mr. Michaels?

Mr. Fier: Yes, and there was a fight. It was Ron Michaels and someone else.

Ann: Did he tell you anything in 2006 about any contact between Mr. Hammill and a female at the party?

Mr. Fier: He had talked about Ron Michaels' girlfriend. I'm not certain that he knew her name, but he did indicate that Jeff Hammill was flirting and there may have been a note or a piece of paper passed between them.

Ann: Did he tell you what happened after Mr. Hammill left?

Mr. Fier: They basically went to look for him. At one point he indicated that Ron Michaels was angry because Jeff Hammill had made what he referred to as a pass at Ron's girlfriend at the party.

Ann: Did he tell you whether he heard or saw anything?

Mr. Fier: He did hear somebody holler, he was not able to say exactly who, after they had gotten out of the car.

Ann: Did he tell you whether any other vehicle passed by while they were there?

Mr. Fier: He said a vehicle had passed.

Ann: What did he say happened?

Mr. Fier: That first Terry Olson got back into the car and said, "Let's get out of here," something to that effect. And as he started moving, the trunk slammed shut and Ron Michaels jumped into the back seat of the car.

Ann: Did he tell you whether Mr. Michaels said anything when he got back into the car?

Mr. Fier: He said, "Let's get going. He won't need a ride. He won't need a ride anymore," something to that effect.

Ann: Did he tell you where they went?

Mr. Fier: They went back to Montrose to Deb Segler's house.

Ann: Did he observe any conversation between Mr. Olson and Mr. Michaels that he told you about?

Mr. Fier: They had conversation away from him in an area away from … like in a corner sort of. I'm having a hard time finding it here but my recollection is it was in an area of the house away from where the little conference between Terry Olson, Deb Segler and Ron Michaels was taking place. I believe it may have been in the kitchen area. I'm not absolutely sure of that.

Ann: Okay. So what was this phone call that Mr. Todd told you he might have made? Mr. Fier: It would have been a call to the Wright County Sheriff's Office reporting a body on the road.

Ann: Was there anything about the two statements that was so different that caused you to feel you had to go on another path or focus on something else?

Mr. Fier: No.

Ann: Based upon your review of the evidence in this particular case, do you have an opinion as to how Jeff Hammill was killed?

Mr. Fier: He was struck at least twice and possibly more times by an object. There was blunt force trauma to the head and what appeared to be a defensive wound possibly on his hands.

Ann: Thank you. Nothing further.

CHAPTER 19

CROSS-EXAMINATION BY MR. FLEMING:

Jim: Let's talk just for a moment, so that we can kind of set the stage with the BCA cold case unit. I believe that you testified that the majority of the cases that the cold case unit investigates are homicide cases.

Mr. Fier: Yes

Jim: There was an article that appeared in the Minneapolis Star & Tribune back on February 15 of this year, indicating that the Target Corporation had given the Bureau of Criminal Apprehension a grant, if I'm not mistaken, or some type of a donation. $160,000?

Mr. Fier: That's correct.

Jim: And that $160,000 was to pay salaries for two cold case investigators, correct?

Mr. Fier: That's correct, yes.

Jim: You're quoted in here talking about this; you sometimes will borrow law enforcement officers from other departments, correct? In fact, I think Sergeant Eddinger is a member of the Minneapolis Police Department homicide unit, isn't he?

Mr. Fier: Right, and he was assigned to the BCA cold case unit. We picked up his salary for that year that he was with us.

Jim: So, in other words, under those circumstances, the State is paying that salary?

Mr. Fier: That's correct, yes.

Jim: And the $160,000 grant was on top of one that had been given the year before of $150,000 by Target, correct?

Mr. Fier: No, I don't believe so.

Jim: Okay. It says here, "Target last year gave the BCA $150,000 to fund the positions. They have agreed to donate $160,000 for this year".

Mr. Fier: I stand corrected. That is true. We have the same two investigators working with us. They were funded for a second year. That's my mistake, yes.

Jim: And one of the reasons that the Target Corporation gave these grants was because of two cases that the cold case unit had solved, correct?

Mr. Fier: I don't believe that would necessarily be true, no.

Jim: Okay. Well, it says here that, "The Dakota and Wright County cases, both involving fatal beatings from the late 1970's, were among the oldest on file at the BCA." So I'm assuming that this case would be one of those?

Mr. Fier: This was the Wright County case that they were referring to, yes.

Jim: Okay. So the grants were provided for the fact that the cases were solved, correct? Mr. Fier: If that's what the article said, yes.

Jim: And, of course, having been a law enforcement officer for a long period of time, forty-three years if I'm not mistaken, generally speaking, wouldn't you say that it's true that a case isn't solved until you get a conviction?

Mr. Fier: No, I don't believe that's necessarily true. I think cases are often solved and never go to court.

Jim: Okay. But this one did?

Mr. Fier: This one went to court.

Jim: May I approach, Your Honor?

The Court: You may.

Jim: May I approach the witness?

The Court: You may.

Jim: Okay.

Jim: Mr. Fier—excuse me, I'm sorry, is it Mr. Fier?

Mr. Fier: Agent Fier is fine.

Jim: Okay. Agent, you've earned it, would you take a look at Exhibit Number Twenty-two and tell me if you recognize that?

Mr. Fier: I recognize it as a report generated by our forensic science laboratory.

Jim: And does it not indicate on that report that it is the Hammill case?

Mr. Fier: Yes.

Jim: And isn't it true that on that report that it indicates that a baseball bat, that was taken from the trunk of Dale Todd's car, had been tested?

Mr. Fier: Yes.

Jim: It indicates on the report that they did not find any human DNA on the bat, did they?

Mr. Fier: That's correct.

Jim: And that report is dated June of 2003?

Mr. Fier: Yes.

Jim: So that report that you reviewed when you first got involved in the case was issued three months before you questioned Dale Todd in September of 2003, wasn't it?

Mr. Fier: Yes, it would have been.

Jim: In any event, you had received a report back from your lab before you questioned Dale Todd indicating that there was no human DNA found on the bat, correct?

Mr. Fier: That's correct.

Jim: You testified on direct that it was human hair, but in truth you don't know whether it was human hair or not, do you?

Mr. Fier: I was told it was by our laboratory.

Jim: On that report?

Mr. Fier: I'm not sure if it's in a report or not. I did have knowledge that it was human hair.

Jim: Okay. So to that extent, if they tested the bat for hair and blood and they found no human DNA, that presupposes that the blood on the bat was not human, correct?

Mr. Fier: That would be correct.

Jim: And under those circumstances it most certainly wouldn't have been Jeff Hammill's blood on the bat, correct?

Mr. Fier: It was not Jeff Hammill's blood on the bat.

Jim: Okay. But you testified on direct examination that in the course of your 2003 statement of Dale Todd you told him, or gave him reason to believe that it was, correct? Mr. Fier: Either myself or Agent McDonald did.

Jim: When you questioned Dale Todd in 2003, you also gave him reason to believe that there were witnesses that saw his car at the scene where Jeff Hammill's body had been found later, correct?

Mr. Fier: That's correct.

Jim: May I approach the witness?

THE COURT: You may.

Jim asks Agent Fier if he ever recalled seeing a report subsequent to the August 15th, 1979 report, where Mr. Kilgo described the taillights any differently than he did in his initial report. All of the follow-up reports seem to only mention that the car was a dark colored Chevrolet, or a dark green Chevrolet, with no reference to the configuration of the taillights.

Jim: You also testified on direct that when they left the house looking for Jeff, and I wrote the statement down, "It was not to give him a ride home". Do you recall saying that?

Mr. Fier: Yes, I do recall saying that.

Jim: Okay. But, in fact, isn't it true that what Dale Todd said in 2003 was, "I thought that's where we were going, I thought we were going to find him to give him a ride home"?

Mr. Fier: That was, I believe, now my recollection that he might have said that, yes.

Jim: All right. So at least it's clear then, isn't it, that based upon what Dale Todd said in that statement, "It was not to give him a ride home," that's not accurate?

Mr. Fier: That would not be accurate, that's correct.

Jim: Now, what I'd like to do is take just a moment to contrast the two statements, 2003 and 2006, on some very specific points. So if you'll bear with me, in 2006 you recall during your interview that Dale Todd said that he saw Jeff Hammill talking with Sandy Dehn and possibly giving her a note, correct?

Mr. Fier: That's correct.

Jim: But he hadn't said anything about that in 2003, did he?

Mr. Fier: I don't think so. I don't recall that.

Jim: And in 2006 Dale Todd also said that there had been a fight at the bar between Ron Michaels and somebody else, I think at the Country West, correct?

Mr. Fier: Yes, that's correct.

Jim: But in 2003 he didn't say anything about that, did he?

Mr. Fier: No, I don't believe he did.

Jim: Okay. So when you testified on direct examination with respect to the phone call, you said, "It would have been a call to the Wright County Sheriff's Office to report a body on the road,", didn't you?

Mr. Fier: Yes.

Jim: Okay. The fact of the matter is you don't have any evidence that suggests that he actually did make a telephone call, do you?

Mr. Fier: We have a phone call that was placed to the sheriff's office that we have no accountability for who made that call. That's why the question was asked.

Jim: Well, certainly. But you just testified it would have been a call to the Wright County Sheriff's Office to report a body on road. And the fact of the matter is, you don't know whether he called or not and there's no way that you can tell the jury that it was a call to the Wright County Sheriff's Office to report a body on the road, can you?

Mr. Fier: No, only that we asked the question.

Jim: In any event, there are a number of differences between these two renditions of this incident from him between 2003 and 2006, correct?

Mr. Fier: There are some differences, of course, yes.

Jim: If you didn't question him between 2003 and 2006, did you ever stop to wonder where is this stuff coming from?

Mr. Fier: No, I really didn't.

Jim: If, as you have opined here, this was a situation involving an assault, where somebody struck him with something, wouldn't you expect to find some signs of a scuffle, some signs of struggle?

Mr. Fier: I think we did find those.

Jim: If he was standing off at the side of the road in the soil, wouldn't you expect to see some signs of a scuffle, footprints or kicked up dirt or disturbed soil or something?

Mr. Fier: Well, if there is a scuffle as such, a fight, then you would expect to find that, I believe.

Jim: Agent Fier, now, you know from the autopsy report that Jeff Hammill was a young man that was approximately five feet seven inches tall. And you know from the autopsy report that the wound to the left side of the head was a laceration, a tearing of the scalp over on the left side of the head?

Mr. Fier: Yes.

Jim: And Dr. Amatuzio confirmed that it was from the front to the rear at an upward angle, right?

Mr. Fier: I believe that's correct.

Jim: Okay. If that were true, would you find it unusual for a situation where a taller assailant would strike an individual in the head in such a way that it would cause an upward tear rather than a downward tear?

Mr. Fier: No, not unusual at all. If I may explain?

Jim: Please, please.

Mr. Fier: If you are swinging an instrument from, say, waist or chest high even and coming across, I think that instrument would, when it hits its blow, contact is made that it is moving in an angle such as that.

Jim: All right. Thank you very much. No further questions, Your Honor.

The Court: Redirect?

Ann: Oh, just a little bit.

Ann: Do you get any of that $160,000 grant money?

Mr. Fier: Do I personally get, oh, no, that's used for wages for the two investigators, one from St. Paul homicide division and another one from Hennepin County Sheriff's Office investigator.

Ann: And do you have anything to do with the budget of the BCA?

Mr. Fier: No, I do not.

Ann: Dale Todd told you that his vehicle was at the scene, didn't he?

Mr. Fier: Yes, he did.

Ann: Nothing further.

Jim: Nothing, Your Honor.

The Court: Thank you, sir. You are excused.

DAY 5

The Court: Is the State prepared to call its next witness?

Ann: Yes.

The Court: And that is?

Ann: Ken McDonald.

The Court: Thank you.

The Clerk: Would you have a seat and state your name for the record, spelling both your first and your last name, please.

The Witness: Kenneth McDonald. K-e-n-n-e-t-h. McDonald, M-c-D-o-n-a-1-d.

Ann MoHaupt establishes that Ken McDonald worked for the BCA during 2003 and assisted Dennis Fier in the interview with Dale Todd in September of 2003 at the Hutchinson Police Department. She produces two VHS tapes and asks Ken McDonald if these are the tapes of that September interview. He verifies that they are.

The Jury and the gallery are now shown a video of the five-hour interrogation of Dale Todd conducted by Dennis Fier and Ken McDonald at the Hutchinson Police Station on September 23, 2003.

CHAPTER 20

Day 6

The Court: Thank you. Is the State ready to call its next witness?

Ann: Call Joseph Hagerty.

The Court: Please have a seat in the witness stand. Would you state your full name for the record, spelling your first and last names, please.

Lt. Hagerty: Sure. It's Joe Hagerty. H-a-g-e-r-t-y. Joseph is actually the first name,

J-o-s-e-p-h.

The Court: You may proceed.

Ann's initial questions establish that Lt. Joe Hagerty has been a police officer since 1985, and is currently a Deputy Sheriff with the Wright County Sheriffs Department. Ann determines that sometime in 2001, the biological daughter of Jeffrey Hammill contacted the Wright County Human Services office inquiring as to who her birth parents were. She was forwarded a letter from Human Services, explaining who her birth parents were and what had happened to them. Seeing that the case was unsolved, she contacted the Sheriff's Department and Captain Miller. Captain Miller asked Hagerty if he would look over the case file, which he did. Seeing that it wasn't pushed in '79, Hagerty became interested in the case and started working it.

Ann: Did you call the BCA for assistance?

Lt. Hagerty: I called the BCA on, I believe, January 18 of '03, talked to cold case person in charge Randy Stricker, and Randy was immediately interested in it. Unfortunately, during the investigation, he suffered some heart trouble and had to retire.

Ann: And then the other BCA agents took over. Is that right?

Lt. Hagerty: Correct, probably mid-summer of '03.

Ann: Have you reviewed all the old Wright County Sheriff's Department records, all the new records and all of the BCA records that are available in this file?

Lt. Hagerty: Yes, several times.

Ann: Nothing further.

The Court: Cross-examination?

Jim: Okay. Thank you, Your Honor.

Jim: Good morning.

Lt. Hagerty: Morning.

Jim: Now, you indicated that you have reviewed all of the records that were historical records from the investigation in 1979 and also the records that were created during the new investigation starting in … I believe you said January 3 of 2003.

Lt. Hagerty: Correct, regarding the historical ones, the ones that we had, the ones that we found.

Jim: Sure. I understand. Okay. You don't know at this point whether there were additional records that had been part of that file, that were no longer part of the file when you started your examination?

Lt. Hagerty: That I don't know.

Jim: Was there any kind of a master index of all these different kinds of reports kept so that when something came in after an interview or whatever that they would log it on index saying, "Okay, here's a new report with this date by this investigator, here's a new report by this investigator on this date", or anything of that nature?

Lt. Hagerty: Yeah, in 2003 the BCA did do that for us.

Jim: But there wasn't one in 1979?

Lt. Hagerty: There was not.

Jim: Okay. And I just wanted to clear up one thing: it was probably just a mistake, but at one point you testified that the location where the body was found was two miles north of 107 and then you came back and said it was two-tenths of a mile north of 107.

Lt. Hagerty: Yeah, two-tenths, correct.

Jim: When Amanda Thiesse came to talk with you in 2003 ... that was in January?

Lt. Hagerty: Yeah, she never came to see me. I've never met her. She called our office and spoke with Captain Miller.

Jim: Okay. So you never talked with her directly?

Lt. Hagerty: I spoke to her one time in January of '03 by phone briefly.

Jim: You said that she had received a letter from Wright County Human Services or Wright County Social Services?

Lt. Hagerty: Correct

Jim: Okay. And isn't it true that in that letter that she was advised that her father had died as a result of hit-and-run?

Lt. Hagerty: That's correct.

Jim: But you corrected that, didn't you?

Lt. Hagerty: I believe so.

Jim: Yes, and you told her that her father had been murdered?

Lt. Hagerty: That I don't know. I don't know if we ever talked about that specifically.

Jim: But if you testified before the Grand Jury in this case and told them that you had informed Amanda Thiesse that her father had been murdered during that telephone conversation, you wouldn't have any reason to doubt that, would you?

Lt. Hagerty: I don't know if I said that. I don't recall.

Jim: Okay. You recall testifying before the Grand Jury in which you were describing this telephone call with her and you said that that information that she had received from Wright County Social Services was not right; do you recall testifying to that?

Lt. Hagerty: Possibly.

Jim: Okay. Do you know when the investigation was initiated in 1979? You had talked a little bit about whether or not there was a tape recording of the telephone call and the fact that they cycle the tapes and would erase them every thirty days?

Lt. Hagerty: Correct.

Jim: Do you know whether there was any effort ever made to have Gerald Mitlyng, the dispatcher, hear the voices of the three suspects in the case?

Lt. Hagerty: I don't believe so.

Jim: But yet you testified before the Grand Jury and you told them in response to this issue of the telephone call to Mitlyng, a voice match with one of the three suspects would have been very probable; do you recall testifying to that?

Lt. Hagerty: I don't.

Jim: Okay. You testified before the Grand Jury, "We would have probably tried something down at the BCA and seeing if we could match it up with one of our three suspects", referring to the voice. And you were asked, 'It would have been very probable, wouldn't it?'" And you said, "Oh, yes". Do you recall testifying to that?

Lt. Hagerty: I don't.

Jim: Okay. Well, in the absence of any tape recording that would allow an examination of a voice match, I'm just curious, how is it that you could testify before the Grand Jury that a voice match would be very probable?

Lt. Hagerty: I don't know if it would be probable.

Jim: Okay. But that's not what you told the Grand Jury, is it?

Lt. Hagerty: I don't recall.

Jim: Okay. You were talking to the Grand Jury, you were testifying under oath before the Grand Jury about the issue of vehicles with the taillight array with three on each side?

Lt. Hagerty: I remember the three-light configuration.

Jim gives the witness a document marked as Exhibit Number Twenty-Three. Hagerty examines it for a minute.

Jim: Okay. That's a report that was prepared in 1979, was it not?

Lt. Hagerty: Correct.

Jim: Okay. And down at the right corner where the officer is to initial we have the initials BO. And that was Jack Bodine?

Lt. Hagerty: That's our belief, yes.

Jim: Isn't it true that in Sergeant Bodine's report he indicates that Kilgo was very specific about the description of the vehicle, wasn't he?

Lt. Hagerty: He didn't say he was specific but he did give the three-light configuration on either side.

Jim: He also said it was a '67 to '69 Chevrolet, didn't he?

Lt. Hagerty: That's what the report says.

Jim: Okay. And he also described the taillights as being flat on the top and round on the bottom, didn't he?

Lt. Hagerty: Flat tops and round bottoms, correct.

Jim: Okay. Now, you contacted the BCA cold case unit about the case?

Lt. Hagerty: I did.

Jim: Isn't it true that before the BCA could invest their resources from the cold case unit into this investigation that they needed to be sure that they were looking at a possible homicide?

Lt. Hagerty: That's correct.

Jim: And in the original death certificate that had been prepared by Dr. Bendix, it was not listed as a homicide, was it?

Lt. Hagerty: That's correct.

Jim: Okay. And in order to then get the BCA interested and convince their superiors that they would commit the resources, that death certificate needed to be changed, didn't it?

Lt. Hagerty: They were interested in it immediately and part of our process was getting that death certificate changed.

Jim: Okay. And so when you testified before the grand jury and said, "When we reopened the case, we needed the death certificate changed to homicide and we accomplished that", that's what you were referring to, correct?

Lt. Hagerty: I may have said that. I testified for hours and I've never seen a transcript of it.

Jim: But you know what you said, don't you?

Lt. Hagerty: If I said that, yes.

Jim: Lieutenant, I'm showing you what's been marked as Exhibit Number Twenty-two by the court. Would you take a look at that and see if you recognize it?

Lt. Hagerty: I'm looking at a report of examination of physical evidence dated 6–13–03 from the Minnesota Department of Public Safety, talking about DNA from a sample that was submitted.

Jim: Okay. And that report does indicate, does it not, that the crime lab had done some DNA testing on a baseball bat that had been taken from Dale Todd's car?

Lt. Hagerty: That's correct.

Jim: Okay. And it indicates on there, does it not, that there was no human DNA found on the baseball bat, does it not?

Lt. Hagerty: That's correct.

Jim: Do you recall testifying before the Grand Jury and being asked as to whether there had been any forensic testing done on the baseball bat?

Lt. Hagerty: Again, I don't know.

Jim: Okay. Do you recall testifying before the grand jury that there had been no DNA testing done on the baseball bat?

Lt. Hagerty: I don't recall.

Jim: No further questions, Your Honor.

The Court: Thank you. Any redirect?

Ann: Yes, thank you. Just a few more questions.

Ann: What did the original death certificate list as the cause of death?

Lt. Hagerty: I believe it was undetermined.

Ann: Were there other reports in the old Wright County Sheriff's Department file that discussed the identity of the vehicle that the Kilgos identified as a Chevy without identifying the year?

Lt. Hagerty: I believe so.

Ann: Okay. Your grand jury testimony was how long ago?

Lt. Hagerty: Early November of '05.

Ann: So a year ago?

Lt. Hagerty: Right.

Ann: And have you ever seen the transcript of your testimony?

Lt. Hagerty: I have not.

Ann: Thank you. Nothing further.

The Court: You are excused.

The Court: Does the State have additional evidence to present in this matter?

Ann: Not at this time.

The Court: Does the State then rest?

Ann: Yes.

The Court: Thank you. Please be seated. The defense at this time may begin its case in chief, if it intends to call any witnesses or offer any exhibits.

CHAPTER 21

Jim is prepared to begin the presentation of the witnesses for the defense. His list is not long, but their testimony should prove strong and convincing. People who know Ron, went to high school with him, or grew up with him, have offered to travel across the United States to testify as to his character. This is it. Jim must connect with this jury. He has identified one or two of the jurors who are veterans of the armed forces. He has seen their reactions to Ann MoHaupt's presentations, and knows they are not happy that this trial is continuing after the recantation of testimony by Dale Todd. Jim is more relaxed now. He knows what is coming; he has planned this defense in great detail, and gone over and over it in his head, night after night, preparing. No surprises. At least, that's what he is hoping for.

Jim: Yes, Your Honor. At this time we would call George Salonek to the stand.

The Clerk: Would you please have a seat and state your name for the record, spelling both your first and your last name.

Mr. Salonek: George Salonek. S as in Sam, a-1 -o-n-e-k.

The Court: Thank you. Mr. Fleming, you may proceed.

Jim: Thank you. Mr. Salonek, are you acquainted with Ron Michaels?

Mr. Salonek: Yes, sir.

Jim: Would you point out Ron Michaels?

George points at Ron seated next to Hawks.

Jim: Could you tell the jury how long have you known Ron Michaels?

Mr. Salonek : Since I was in the seventh grade; probably about '66, '67.

Jim: Did you go to school together?

Mr. Salonek: Yes, sir. In Buffalo. It would have been starting with the seventh grade on, in Buffalo School District.

Jim: Now, where did your family live at that point?

Mr. Salonek: Two and a half miles south of Montrose.

Jim: And do you know where Ronald Michaels' family lived?

Mr. Salonek: In Montrose. I don't know the street addresses, but across the street from what was called Yager's Grocery Store. Second house in from the intersection of County Road 12 and I don't know what the street was.

Jim: Thank you. So the two of you went to junior high school together. When you got to high school, did you attend high school together?

Mr. Salonek: Yes, sir.

Jim: Did you participate in activities together?

Mr. Salonek: Yes.

Jim: Could you describe for the jury those types of activities?

Mr. Salonek: Right. Wrestling. I went out for football one year it seems to me, but mostly wrestling.

Jim: So you were on the wrestling team at Buffalo High School with Mr. Michaels?

Mr. Salonek: Yeah, we were co-captains in wrestling by our senior year. We were the same weight and, you know, a lot of times the coach would jockey our positions around to use us more.

Jim: Okay. So lose weight, gain weight?

Mr. Salonek: Right, right, whatever strategy would work so the Bison could win.

Jim: Okay. Good enough. What year did you graduate from high school?

Mr. Salonek: 1972.

Jim: All right. And, obviously, then, you graduated with Mr. Michaels?

Mr. Salonek: Yup, he was the class king.

Jim: I'm sorry?

Mr. Salonek: He was the class king. The king and queen … you know, of the class … in our senior year.

Jim: I'm not familiar with that. I'm sorry.

Mr. Salonek: The … I don't know what they … it's class *king*. Like you have a senior … I mean they're picked out of the senior class. *King* and *queen*, people that people have a lot of respect for and et cetera, and then you vote on who's the king and queen.

Jim: I got it. Thank you.

Jim explores the relationship between the two men further, determining that they had worked together at Ray Wormoth Construction for a couple of years as carpenters, framing residential housing. He also learns that George had worked with Jeff Cardinal and another mutual friend, Dave Emon, both of whom he knew from Montrose and from Buffalo High School.

Jim continues his questioning, revealing to the jury that in 1979, George had known Deb Segler as the wife of Bob Segler, a painter from Montrose. They had divorced, and Deb had just recently begun dating Jeff Cardinal. George Salonek had married his high school sweetheart, Kathy Endreson, and the two of them lived half a block away from Deb Segler. George also confirms that he knew Sandy Dehn, Ron Michaels' girlfriend, and had met her many times and could easily recognize her.

Jim establishes that George and his wife Kathy had been to the Rockford House on the night of August 10, 1979. They met up with Jeff Cardinal, Deb Segler and Ron Michaels in the parking lot outside the Rockford House shortly after closing.

Jim: Now, are you familiar with a bar that was located in Rockford at that time, called the Country West?

Mr. Salonek: Yes, it was a very short walking distance away from the Rockford House. There was a parking lot in between them. They were maybe, I don't know, perhaps 300 feet apart or something like that.

Jim: Okay. On either end of a big parking lot?

Mr. Salonek: Yes, sir.

Jim: What time did you leave the Rockford House that evening?

Mr. Salonek: It was probably minutes after closing. I'm guessing, if my memory serves me, that we would have recognized each other in the parking lot and decided to spend some time together.

Jim: When you met them in the parking lot, was Sandy Dehn with Ronald Michaels?

Mr. Salonek: No.

Jim: And as a result of this running into each other like that, what happened?

Mr. Salonek: Well, I worked with the Montrose guys, Ron and his brother Ray and Dave Emon and Jeff Cardinal and myself. We were all from Montrose and grew up together and stuff so, we might have had a beer or something at a bar after work, but never with our women, or never on a weekend and so, you know, Jeff had his girlfriend, I had my wife All of us at that time, were living around or in Montrose and so, you know, let's visit together and, you know, so let's all go over to Debbie's house, or Debbie volunteered, I can't remember, and we went to her house.

Jim: So your testimony is that you were invited to go to Debbie Segler's house that evening?

Mr. Salonek: Yes, sir.

Jim: All right. When you arrived in Montrose, did you go to Debbie Segler's house? Did you just drive there and park?

Mr. Salonek: No, we went home and parked and then walked over.

Jim: Okay. And when you got to Debbie Segler's, who was there?

Mr. Salonek: I don't know what time anybody got there. My intent was to get there as soon as possible because she had an extremely small house and so we'd have a place to sit down. There was only going to be room for a couple people and to go ahead and get there. And so Jeff and Debbie were there at some time and Kathy and I went in there. You know, that's all I remember; going in there or being in there for sometime. The TV was on and it was kind of dark in the living room and whether people came in and out to use the bathroom or to say "Hi" or something, but that's all I remember.

Jim: Now, just so that we're clear, once you're inside the house did you see Jeff Cardinal and Debbie Segler inside the house?

Mr. Salonek: Yes.

Jim: Did you see Ron Michaels inside the house?

Mr. Salonek: I don't remember him sitting down but he might have came in, you know, to say "Hi" and visit once and a while, but I don't recall him sitting in there as much as Jeff or Debbie or Kathy or I, but I wouldn't doubt that people did come in and out or sit down or whatever.

Jim: Okay. At any time after you arrived at the Segler residence, did you ever see Sandy Dehn at the residence?

Mr. Salonek: No.

Jim: Okay. Were you outside at any point in time while you were still participating in the party?

Mr. Salonek: Yes.

Jim: Did you ever see Sandy Dehn outside the house?

Mr. Salonek: No.

Jim: Did you talk with Mr. Michaels and ask him about, you know, where is Sandy?

Mr. Salonek: Oh, sure to say in a respectful, greeting way, "How's Sandy doing?", something like that. I knew where she was.

Jim: You knew where she was?

Mr. Salonek: Yes. Working at Federal Cartridge in Elk River where she had been working for years on the night shift.

Jim: Okay. So, in other words, you didn't expect to see her at the party?

Mr. Salonek: No, I'd have been surprised if I did see her.

Jim: Now, during the time that you were at the house, did you ever see Ron Michaels engage in any kind of an argument or a fight with anybody?

Mr. Salonek: No.

Jim: Did you yourself, at any point during that evening while you were at the Segler residence, end up in any kind of an argument or a dispute with anybody?

Mr. Salonek: I think from prompting during interrogations I got, I might have recalled … I mean, I recall facing off with, I think, Terry Olson and he was upset about something and—

Jim: Excuse me, let me interrupt you. Was that inside the house or outside the house?

Mr. Salonek: No, outside the house.

Jim: Were there any words between the two of you while you were inside the house?

Mr. Salonek: I don't recollect any words—

Jim: Did you spill any drinks on either Mr. Olson or Dale Todd?

Mr. Salonek: Not that I can recall. I can't say that I didn't, but not that I can recall.

Jim: Okay. When I mention these two individuals, do you know who Terry Olson is?

Mr. Salonek: Not real well. I might have met him at a party or somebody might have said that's Debbie Segler's brother, but I didn't know him on a "Hi, how you doing" first name basis or anything.

Jim: Okay. And did you know who Dale Todd was?

Mr. Salonek: In the same familiarity; I knew who they were.

Jim: So you were outside and there's some kind of a dispute between yourself and Terry Olson; do you remember what it was about?

Mr. Salonek: No.

Jim: Did that dispute rise to the level of any kind of physical confrontation?

Mr. Salonek: No.

Jim: At any point in time did Terry Olson strike you?

Mr. Salonek: No.

Jim: And did you strike Terry Olson?

Mr. Salonek: No.

Jim: But there was a facing off of some kind or another?

Mr. Salonek: Yes, you know, there was tension and I remember that he was upset about something and before anything got anywhere, you know, I can remember, after the police interviewed me, I then kind of remembered that something like that happened, we're talking twenty-five or more years ago. And so we're looking at each other and then Ron coming in between us and that was it. And Kathy and I got the heck out of there, you know.

Jim: So are you saying that whatever dispute there was before it went any further, before it escalated any further, that Mr. Michaels intervened?

Mr. Salonek: Yes.

Jim: Okay. Did he intervene in an angry way?

Mr. Salonek: No.

Jim: Did he grab either of the two of you and push you aside or push between you or anything of that nature?

Mr. Salonek: No, he stepped in with a reluctant, "Come on you guys, knock it off", kind of deal.

Jim: Okay. During the course of your relationship with Ronald Michaels going back to the seventh grade, had you seen him do that sort of thing before?

Mr. Salonek: Yes.

Jim: Okay. On more than one occasion?

Mr. Salonek: Yes.

Jim: From the time that you knew him in the seventh grade until today, has Ronald Michaels ever had a reputation as a fighter?

Mr. Salonek: No.

Jim: Have you ever, in the course of the time that you've known Ronald Michaels, seen him engage in a fight of any kind?

Mr. Salonek: No.

Jim: Have you ever had Ronald Michaels come to you and tell you that he was involved in any kind of a fight?

Mr. Salonek: No.

Jim: Did Ronald Michaels have a reputation as it related to getting in between people and breaking up fights?

Mr. Salonek: My only experience was of him mellowing people out, not being in a fight. No, you know, no.

Jim: Okay. Isn't it in fact true, that Ronald Michaels hated fighting?

Mr. Salonek: Well, he sure … you would think that if he liked it … he was physically gifted. People liked being around him. He was a successful athlete and he was humble and he, you know, he wouldn't mind competing on the mat or at a football game, but going by the rules, he wasn't a, you know, out of the sand box kind of guy. You know, he carried himself admirably all the time. He wasn't a fighter or he didn't need … he didn't have a huge ego that he needed to show somebody that he could kick their butt.

Jim: Now, after Mr. Michaels intervened in the situation between yourself and Terry Olson, was there any kind of conversation between Mr. Michaels and Terry Olson about that issue?

Mr. Salonek: I don't know. If there was, it probably would have been along the lines of 'Let him go", because I was getting out of there. That was my out.

Jim: Okay. At that point what did you do?

Mr. Salonek: I got out of there. I left with my wife Kathy.

Jim: Okay. And you went home?

Mr. Salonek: Right.

Jim: And you didn't return to the party?

Mr. Salonek: No.

Jim: Do you know what time it was when you got home?

Mr. Salonek: No.

Jim: You did have occasion to see Ron Michaels together with Sandy Dehn at different times, didn't you?

Mr. Salonek: Yes.

Jim: Which of the two of them was taller?

Mr. Salonek: Sandy.

Jim: Okay. So she would not, in reference to Mr. Michaels, would not be referred to as a short blonde?

Mr. Salonek: No. She was a tall, slim blonde.

Jim: All right. Thank you. No further questions, Your Honor.

The Court: Okay. Cross-examination?

Ann: I just have a few questions for this witness.

CROSS-EXAMINATION BY MS. MOHAUPT

Ann cross-examines the witness, asking him details about what Sandy Dehn looked like: her hair style, the length of her hair, and how tall she was. She asks George how it is that he can remember these things from a night twenty-seven years ago. George tells her the police interrogations, newspaper accounts about the case and subsequent interviews with police and council have helped him remember. Ann asks George if he can remember how many people showed up at the party. He indicates he knew that Debbie and Jeff, Kathy and him and Ron Michaels, then Terry Olson and someone that was with him.

Ann: You also testified that Jeff Hammill could have been there, too?

Mr. Salonek: There could have been twenty more people there, but that's all I remember. But Jeff Hammill…I can't say that he was there or wasn't there.

Ann: Okay. So you don't know how many were there?

Mr. Salonek: Correct.

Ann: All right. And you don't know anything about the death of Jeff Hammill, do you? Mr. Salonek: No

Ann: Thank you. Nothing further.

The Court: Redirect?

Jim: No, Your Honor.

The Court: Thank you. You are excused.

The Court: Is the defense ready to call its next witness?

Jim: We are, Your Honor.

The Court: You may do so.

Jim: We would call Sandy O'Brien.

The Court: Please come forward. You may stop here in the center and face the clerk to take the oath.

The Clerk: Would you have a seat and please state your name for the record, spelling your last name.

Ms. O'Brien: Okay. My name is Sandra Marie O'Brien, O-b-r-i-e-n.

Jim: Thank you, Your Honor.

Jim: Good afternoon.

Mrs. O'Brien: Hi.

Jim: Would you please tell the jury what your maiden name was?

Mrs. O'Brien: My maiden name was Sandra Marie Dehn.

Jim: Okay. And you are now married and your married name is O'Brien; is that correct?

Mrs. O'Brien: Right.

Jim: Have you been married previously?

Mrs. O'Brien: Yes.

Jim: And what was your married name at that point?

Mrs. O'Brien: It was Sandra Marie Michaels.

Jim: Okay. And you are acquainted with Ronald Michaels?

Mrs. O'Brien: Yes. He's my ex-husband.

Jim: And do you recall when you and Mr. Michaels first started dating?

Mrs. O'Brien: Yes, yes, I do. I believe I was twenty.

Jim: So that's thirty years ago. So if we do the math, that would be 1976?

Mrs. O'Brien: Right.

Jim: At that time where did you live?

Mrs. O'Brien: I believe I lived with my parents in Elk River.

Jim: And do you recall when you and Mr. Michaels were married?

Mrs. O'Brien: May 3, 1980.

Jim: Okay. Now, I'd like to draw your attention to the period focusing specifically in August of 1979. Were you dating Mr. Michaels at that time?

Mrs. O'Brien: Yes, I was engaged to him at that time.

Jim: Okay. And were you employed at that time?

Mrs. O'Brien: Yes, Federal Cartridge in Anoka. I worked third shift.

Jim: And what were the hours of third shift?

Mrs. O'Brien: I believe it was from 11:30 to 7:00 in the morning.

Jim: Okay. Was that something where you would rotate, like maybe you'd work for six months on the late night shift and then you'd rotate one direction or the other to a different shift?

Mrs. O'Brien: No, I strictly worked third shift, Monday through Friday.

Jim: So you had Saturdays and Sundays off?

Mrs. O'Brien: Right.

Jim: Now, I'd like to draw your attention specifically to the evening of August 10 into the morning hours of August 11, 1979. Do you recall whether you were working at Federal Cartridge on that evening on August 10?

Mrs. O'Brien: I would have been.

Jim: And that was a Friday?

Mrs. O'Brien: Right.

Jim: There have been some representations made in the course of this case, in this trial, that you were on a date with Mr. Michaels on that evening and the two of you went to the Country West Bar in Rockford, Minnesota. Are you familiar with the Country West Bar?

Mrs. O'Brien: Yes, I am.

Jim: And you have been there on more than one occasion?

Mrs. O'Brien: Yes, usually Saturday night.

Jim: Were you at the Country West Bar on Friday, August 10, 1979 in the company of Ronald Michaels?

Mrs. O'Brien: It's very doubtful.

Jim: Do you have a specific recollection?

Mrs. O'Brien: I cannot recall being there.

Jim: All right. Was it common for you to take time off during those days to go on a date or that type of thing?

Mrs. O'Brien: The most I would have taken off would have been a half a day because I was trying to save my vacation for our honeymoon.

Jim: Okay. It's also been represented that you were at a party in the early morning hours of August 11, 1979 at the home of Debbie Segler in Montrose. Now, here's what I want to ask you about that: do you know Debbie Segler?

Mrs. O'Brien: Yes, I do.

Jim: And were you also acquainted with her boyfriend Jeff Cardinal?

Mrs. O'Brien: Yes.

Jim: And did you from time to time socialize informally while in the company of Mr. Michaels with Jeff Cardinal and Deb Segler?

Mrs. O'Brien: Yes.

Jim: Did you attend a party on the early morning hours of August 11, 1979 with Rob Michaels at Deb Segler's house?

Mrs. O'Brien: I have never attended a party at Deb Segler's house.

Jim: Okay. Do you recall any instance where you had been invited to go to a party at Deb Segler's house along with Mr. Michaels?

Mrs. O'Brien: Yes, I do. We went over there and Deb came to the door in her nightgown and robe and said she wasn't feeling well. So we didn't have a party.

Jim: Now, do you recall—I'm going to describe an event for you and I want you to listen to me carefully—do you recall an incident where you were in the company of Mr. Michaels at a bar and a fight broke out in a parking lot and Mr. Michaels went to intervene to try to break up the fight? Does that sound familiar to you?

Mrs. O'Brien: That would have been the first year we went out. 1976 or 1977.

Jim: Okay. Thank you. In that incident did you rush into the bar to fetch one of the employees in the bar to break up what was going on?

Mrs. O'Brien: Yes, I did.

Jim: And the individual that you went into the bar to get, was that an individual by the nickname of Slimmy?

Mrs. O'Brien: I don't remember his nickname. He was a really tall, big guy.

Jim: Okay. But this incident did not take place on the evening of August 10, 1979 at the Country West Bar, did it?

Mrs. O'Brien: No, it did not.

Jim: With respect to the investigation that has resulted in this trial, do you recall having an interview with a Lieutenant Hagerty from the Wright County Sheriff's Office?

Mrs. O'Brien: Quite a few times.

Jim: Okay. Do you recall telling Lieutenant Hagerty about that incident?

Mrs. O'Brien: Yes.

Jim: Okay. Have you ever told anyone else about that incident?

Mrs. O'Brien: I'm not sure. I may have told my husband after this all came about.

Jim: Now, in that incident was Mr. Michaels one of the participants in the fight?

Mrs. O'Brien: No, he was trying to break it up.

Jim: Was that something that you had seen him do on other occasions?

Mrs. O'Brien: One other time.

Jim: Okay. Did he have a reputation for attempting to try to break up fights between other individuals?

Mrs. O'Brien: He was a good mediator. Even if people were arguing, he would try to calm things down.

Jim: Okay. Now, I'd like to describe another incident for you and, again, I need to have you listen carefully. Do you recall an incident at a party where you were in attendance with Mr. Michaels and someone came up and gave you a piece of paper with a telephone number on it?

Mrs. O'Brien: Yes, I do.

Jim: Did that occur on August 10 or August 11 of 1979?

Mrs. O'Brien: No, it did not.

Jim: Do you recall the name of the individual who gave you the piece of paper?

Mrs. O'Brien: He was on Ron's fast pitch, or whatever you call it, baseball team or softball team.

Jim: Okay. Do you recall approximately when that happened?

Mrs. O'Brien: Probably '77.

Jim: And when that occurred, did you take the note or the slip of paper with the telephone number on it, and bring it to Mr. Michaels' attention?

Mrs. O'Brien: Yes, I showed it to Ron.

Jim: Okay. What was his reaction to that?

Mrs. O'Brien: He laughed.

Jim: Did he say anything to you about what you should do with the note?

Mrs. O'Brien: No, I just threw it away.

Jim: Okay. During that period of time, was Ron Michaels a jealous person?

Mrs. O'Brien: No.

Jim: During your interviews with Lieutenant Hagerty, did you ever relate that incident to Lieutenant Hagerty?

Mrs. O'Brien: I believe I did.

Jim: Okay. And was that an incident that you talked with other people about?

Mrs. O'Brien: Probably after all this came about, yeah, maybe.

Jim: Are you acquainted with an individual by the name of Terry Olson?

Mrs. O'Brien: Is that Deb's brother? I'm not sure if I am or not. If it is Deb's brother, I met him once.

Jim: Are you acquainted or familiar with an individual by the name of Dale Todd?

Mrs. O'Brien: No, no, I mean, if that's Deb's brother I met him once, whichever one that is.

Jim: You do not recall having any conversation with an individual by the name of Dale Todd where you had told Dale Todd about the incident involving the fight that Ron tried to break up in 1976 or '77?

Mrs. O'Brien: No, I don't even know who for sure that is.

Jim: Okay. Do you recall ever having an opportunity to talk with a Dale Todd or an individual introduced to you as Dale Todd about the incident where the note was passed to you with the gentleman's phone number on it?

Mrs. O'Brien: No.

Jim: You recall back at that point in time, that Mr. Michaels had a stereo system at his home?

Mrs. O'Brien: Yes.

Jim: Where did he live at that point?

Mrs. O'Brien: In a basement house.

Jim: So when you say a basement house, was he renting the basement of a house, is that what you mean?

Mrs. O'Brien: No, it was just a basement of a house. That's all there was, was the basement.

Jim: So there was no upper level?

Mrs. O'Brien: No sir.

Jim: Do you recall at any time being over at Mr. Michaels' home at that point spending the night where he invited anyone over after you were already in bed to listen to his stereo?

Mrs. O'Brien: No.

Jim: How many times were you interviewed by Lieutenant Hagerty?

Mrs. O'Brien: Oh, boy, at least five times.

Jim: During those interviews, did Lieutenant Hagerty attempt to convince you that your memories concerning this incident were inaccurate?

Mrs. O'Brien: Yes, yes, he did.

Jim: Could you describe for the jury how he did that?

Mrs. O'Brien: He came up with different scenarios or whatever and kept, I mean, asking me if I remembered this or remembered that or he had like two totally different stories of how things could have happened.

Jim: Did any of his suggestions in any way, shape or form square with your recollections of what happened and what you were doing on that night?

Mrs. O'Brien: No.

Jim: How far was it from your home where you were living with your parents to Federal Cartridge in Anoka?

Mrs. O'Brien: I'm not really sure. I think probably forty minutes at the minimum.

Jim: Okay. Let's say it's a Friday night and you worked Friday night into Saturday morning getting off at what time: 7:30?

Mrs. O'Brien: I believe it was 7:00.

Jim: Okay. What was your common practice at that point when you got off work; what would you do?

Mrs. O'Brien: I would go out to Ron's.

Jim: So when you did that, how long would it take you to go from Federal Cartridge to Ron Michaels' home?

Mrs. O'Brien: A long time, over an hour, I would guess.

Jim: No further questions, Your Honor.

The Court: Cross-examination?

Ann: Thank you.

CROSS–EXAMINATION BY MS. MOHAUPT

Ann begins her cross-examination. She establishes that Sandy and Ron's marriage was the first for both of them; she was twenty-four, he was twenty-six. They usually dated every Saturday night, with many of those dates at the clubs in Rockford. Occasionally, they went to parties after the bars closed. "Maybe six or seven times a year," Sandy recalls.

Ann: Is it fair to say that it's hard to remember things from that long ago?

Mrs. O'Brien: The little things, non-events, it's hard to remember. Stuff that's eventful in my life, it's not hard to remember.

Ann: Now, during your marriage, how many children did you and the Defendant have? Mrs. O'Brien: We have three.

Ann: And what are their ages now?

Mrs. O'Brien: Sixteen, eighteen and twenty-four.

Ann: And are they close with their father?

Mrs. O'Brien: Yes, they are. They usually went to see him every other weekend. He taught them basketball and he would come to their sports.

Ann: How long did your marriage to the Defendant last?

Mrs. O'Brien: Legally, I believe, thirteen years. We didn't live together for the last two years.

Ann: Why did your marriage break up?

Jim objects, and following a discussion at the bench, his objection is sustained.

Ann continues, asking Sandy if her employer at the time could have verified if she had been working on the evening of August 10th, 1979. Sandy tells her she had not and that she was sure she had been working. "At the very least I would have been there at least a half a shift. I would have never taken a whole shift off. Like I said, I was saving for our honeymoon."

Following Ann's line of questioning, Sandy reveals that the police had questioned her several times regarding the incident. She had spoken with several different officers, although she couldn't recall all their names. She recalls several interviews with Joe Hagerty of the Sheriff's Department, and that there were others with him at times. The prosecution's documentation indicates that Sandy had been interviewed by Joe Hagerty and BCA agent Jan May on September 24, 2003; by Deputy Greg Howell and Detective David Fundingsland on October 8, 2003; and also by Sergeant Eddinger from the BCA, on an unspecified date. Subsequent interviews took place on October 8, 2003 and July 20, 2006. Sandy acknowledges that she probably did speak to all of these people. She can't recall all of them; she remembers being very stressed out because they kept coming to her place of work.

> Ann: Why is it that you never told any of these police officers that interviewed you on these different occasions that you were at work on August 10, 1979?

Jim objects, and following a discussion at the bench, the court responds.

> The Court: Objection sustained. Please ask a different question.

> Ann: Certainly. Ms. O'Brien, when you spoke with Deputy Hagerty and BCA Agent May on September 24 of '03, did you tell them that you were at work on August 10, 1979?

> Mrs. O'Brien: They didn't tell me it was a Friday so I didn't know, you know, that it was a Friday. If they had told me it was a Friday I would have told them I was at work.

> Ann: Okay. So you didn't tell them that?

> Mrs. O'Brien: I asked them what day of the week it was and they never told me what day of the week it was.

> Ann: When you spoke with BCA Agent May and Deputy Hagerty on September 24 of '03, did you tell them that you would be afraid to testify against your husband Ron?

Mrs. O'Brien: I don't believe I said afraid. I believe what I meant by that is because I have three sons with him and I don't want... I would not want my boys to be affected.

Ann: So you didn't give them any other reason than that?

Mrs. O'Brien: Any other reason than what?

Ann: For being afraid to testify against him?

Mrs. O'Brien: No.

Ann: So if the report indicates there was some other reason that you gave them, that would be incorrect?

Mrs. O'Brien: Yes.

Ann: Do you recall telling the police in September of '03 that your boyfriend Ron didn't have a motor vehicle in 1979?

Mrs. O'Brien: No, I remember telling them he didn't have a motor vehicle when I met him. He had an Omni in 1979.

Ann: Do you recall an individual other than this person who was on the Defendant's softball team giving you a piece of paper with his phone number on it?

Mrs. O'Brien: No, I do not.

Ann: So when you were interviewed on September 24 of '03, the individual that you were referring to was the person who was on this softball team?

Mrs. O'Brien: That's correct.

Ann: And why is it you didn't tell them that?

Mrs. O'Brien: I tried to tell them. It's just like they just boom, boom, boom, they're asking so many questions and stuff, you know.

Ann: So when you say that, you're referring to Joe Hagerty?

Mrs. O'Brien: Yes.

Ann: And you're also referring to BCA Agent May?

Mrs. O'Brien: Mostly Joe Hagerty.

Ann: What about Greg Howell and Dave Fundingsland?

Mrs. O'Brien: I don't remember them being quite this bad about that.

Ann: Do you remember telling them that the Defendant would fight easily when drinking?

Mrs. O'Brien: No.

Ann: So if that's written here in this report, that's wrong?

Mrs. O'Brien: That's incorrect. I remember him talking, you know, rather silly but no fighting.

Ann: So that would be incorrect in this report?

Mrs. O'Brien: That's true.

Ann: Do you remember telling them that the Defendant would like to get in people's faces to provoke an altercation?

Mrs. O'Brien: I think the first year we went out, he did that to this one really big guy once; he mouthed off to him, and then he bought the guy a drink.

Ann: Now, you indicated earlier that you talked about the Defendant breaking up a fight with some guys outside of the Rockford House; is that right?

Mrs. O'Brien: Yes.

Ann: And you went inside the bar to get the … somebody named Slim?

Mrs. O'Brien: I'm not sure what his name was. He was the bartender.

Ann: Okay. And you testified that you had told that incident to Deputy Hagerty; is that correct?

Mrs. O'Brien: Yes.

Ann: Isn't it true that it was Deputy Howell and Deputy Fundingsland that you told that story to?

Mrs. O'Brien: I believe I told it to both.

Ann: Do you recall telling him on that date that it is possible that you and Ron were with a group of people at the Rockford House and Country West on the eve that Jeff Hammill died?

Mrs. O'Brien: That's before I knew it was a Friday.

Ann: So the report, then, would be correct that you told him that, you just didn't know it was a Friday; is that right?

Mrs. O'Brien: Yes.

Ann: And if the report says that you said that you and Ron had been to Deb Cardinal's for parties but is unsure about being present at a particular party, that would be wrong?

Mrs. O'Brien: That's also wrong.

Ann: You don't know anything about the death of Jeffrey Hammill, do you?

Mrs. O'Brien: No, I don't.

Ann: Thank you. I have nothing further.

The Court: Redirect?

Jim: No further questions.

The Court: Recross?

Ann: Thank you, no.

The Court: Would the defense like to call its next witness?

Jim: We would call Dave Emon to the stand, Your Honor.

The Court: Would you please remain standing for a moment to take the oath. Then you may be seated.

The Clerk: Would you have a seat and spell your name for the record, please.

Mr. Emon: My name is Dave Emon.

The Court: How do you spell your last name?

Mr. Emon: David, D-a-v-i-d. E-m-o-n.

Jim: Thank you, Your Honor.

Jim: Good afternoon. Mr. Emon, where did you grow up?

Mr. Emon: In Montrose.

Jim: Are you acquainted with Ronald Michaels?

Mr. Emon: Yes.

Jim: How long have you known Mr. Michaels?

Mr. Emon: About forty-five years.

Jim: Now, you graduated in 1973. Were you a year behind Mr. Michaels in school?

Mr. Emon: Yes, I was.

Jim: Did you engage in social activities with Mr. Michaels?

Mr. Emon: Yes, I did.

Jim: Did you work with Mr. Michaels?

Mr. Emon: Yes, I did, at Wormoth Construction.

Jim: Now, would you say that based upon the continued, long-term contact that you've had with Mr. Michaels over the years, that you have knowledge of his general reputation with respect to whether or not he was the type of person that would engage in fights and arguments and things of that nature?

Mr. Emon: Yes.

Jim: Okay. Is that a reputation that you are aware of because you have heard other people speak of it and what you know and have observed of him?

Mr. Emon: Yes

Jim: Have you ever in the entire time that you've known Mr. Michaels, ever seen Mr. Michaels engage in a fight?

Mr. Emon: No, I have not.

Jim: Okay. Have you seen him engage in activities where he attempted to break up fights?

Mr. Emon: Yes, I have.

Jim: Did Mr. Michaels, during the course of your relationship with him, have a reputation as a peace maker?

Mr. Emon: Yes.

Jim: Do you recall being interviewed by a deputy from the Wright County Sheriff's Department by the name of David Fundingsland?

Mr. Emon: I don't know his name, but I was interviewed.

Jim: Okay. During the course of that interview … I guess I should say after the interview, Deputy Fundingsland prepared a synopsis of your statement to him, in which he reports that you said to him, "Ron Michaels had a reputation as a tough guy back then. You didn't mess with Ron". Did you ever say that to Deputy Fundingsland?

Mr. Emon: No, I don't believe I ever did.

Jim: Your Honor, may I approach?

The Court: You may.

Jim: I'd like to have you read over that transcript. No. I'm sorry. You don't have to read it out loud. Just read it to yourself.

Jim: Did that refresh your recollection as to the substance of the interview that you had with Detective Fundingsland?

Mr. Emon: Yes, it does.

Jim: Okay. Based upon the review of that transcript, when Deputy Fundingsland indicated in his synopsis that you made the statement that, "Ron Michaels had a reputation as a tough guy back then. You didn't mess with Ron". Did you ever say that to Detective Fundingsland?

Mr. Emon: No, I did not.

Jim: No further questions, Your Honor.

The Court: Cross-examination?

Ann: Thank you. I'll be brief. Is it Mr. Emon?

Mr. Emon: Yes, Emon.

Ann: Emon. Okay. So the transcript that you just read was pretty accurate with respect to your conversation with the deputy?

Mr. Emon: From what I can remember of it; it was three years ago.

Ann: Right, it was a long time ago. You indicated when you first talked to Mr. Fleming that you weren't aware that a tape recorder was on; is that right?

Mr. Emon: Right, according to this, it was. I didn't remember it at the time.

Ann: So you don't recall having any other conversations about him before you went in the room or after you left the room?

Mr. Emon: No, I don't.

Ann: Thank you. Nothing further.

Jim: No redirect.

The Court: Thank you. You are excused.

The Court: The defense may call its next witness.

Jim: Thank you, Your Honor. We would call Jordan Dickinson to the stand, please.

The Clerk: Would you have a seat, please, and state your name for the record, spelling your last and your first name, please?

Mr. Dickinson: Sure. My name is Jordan Dickinson. J-o-r-d-a-n. D-i-c-k-i-n-s-o-n.

The Court: Thank you. You may proceed.

Jim's memory flashes to an event several weeks earlier. It is the middle of the night; he's lying in bed next to Lynne. He wakes up with a start. Lynne awakens also and asks, "What's wrong?" Jim is experiencing that same 'feeling of presence', the urgency to comply, to follow along, that he felt the afternoon he was walking the street in Montrose and saw the Michaels' family friend in the bay window of her home.

Jim tells her, "Nothing, I'm fine, go back to sleep." He gets out of bed and goes to the computer in his home office and sits down. He begins an Internet search for "1971 Chevy Tail Lights". Almost instantly, he finds pictures of the rear tail light assembly for a 1971 Chevy Impala. They are not flat on the top and round on the bottom. He looks at other models of 1971 Chevrolet sedans. All that he finds have three long, rectangular lights on either side of the license plate mounting; none of which have any round features what-so-ever. He begins looking at late 1960's model Impalas and finds the flat on top, round on the bottom taillights recalled by a witness on a 1968 model. He sits back in his chair, not really sure if this means what he thinks it does. He prints off the images and saves the files, then returns to his bed. He decides he will take these pictures to a local car customizing shop in town in the morning and see what he can learn. His flash of memory ends.

Jim returns to the moment, focuses himself on the task at hand and looks around the court room, then at his witness.

DIRECT EXAMINATION BY MR. FLEMING

Jim: Okay. Mr. Dickinson, excuse me, would you please tell us how old you are?

Mr. Dickinson: Twenty-three.

Jim: And are you employed?

Mr. Dickinson: Yes. I own a shop in Monticello called Old School Customs.

Jim: And what does Old School Customs do?

Mr. Dickinson: We are a custom shop for classic cars. We work on street rods, hot rods, anything kind of older. We do electronics, upholstery, sheet metal fabrication, chassis fabrication, that kind of stuff.

Jim: So if I have a 1965 Plymouth that I want to have restored—needs body work, needs electrical work, more work, things of that nature—are those the types of things that you do?

Mr. Dickinson: Yes.

Jim: Now, are you the only owner of the business?

Mr. Dickinson: No, there's one other owner: my brother Josh Dickinson.

Jim: In connection with the work that you do, have you had any formal training?

Mr. Dickinson: Yes. I went out to college in Wyoming: Wyotech. Basically, it is college for body work, street rod building, chassis fabrication, engine building, all that type of stuff. Primarily classic cars. And then also, prior to that, I had schooling up in St. Cloud Technical College for body work, collision finishing, all that.

Jim: Now, in the course of your work have you spent time working on older, what you would call "classic", Chevrolets from, say, maybe 1960 to 1970?

Mr. Dickinson: Yes.

Jim: Your Honor, may I approach the witness?

The Court: You may

Jim: Mr. Dickinson, I'm going to show you a photograph and I want you to take a good look and examine that photograph for me.
Mr. Dickinson: Okay.

Jim: Can you tell the jury what you're looking at there in that photograph?

Mr. Dickinson: Looks to be a '68 ... 1968 Chevy convertible.

Jim: How do you know it's a 1968 Chevrolet?

Mr. Dickinson: Well, the '68s were kind of particular because they'd have the taillight shape flat on the top and round on the bottom, and the taillights were also recessed into the bumper. Those taillights were specific to that year; it was the only year that they had produced that.

Jim: Okay. So that I'm clear on this, when you say that's the only year that they produced that ... let me ask it to you this way: did Chevrolet at any time prior to 1968 use that taillight shape and formation?

Mr. Dickinson: No, not this specific taillight.

Jim: So there is no question in your mind, then, that what you're looking at could only be a 1968 Chevrolet?

Mr. Dickinson: Yup.

Jim: May I approach the witness, Your Honor?

The Court: You may.

Jim: I'm going to show you another photograph. Can you tell the jury what you're looking at in that photograph?

Mr. Dickinson: This is a 1971 Chevy, looks to be either a Caprice or an Impala, I would assume.

Jim: Can you describe on each side the organization of the three taillights that are appearing on each side of the license plate?

Mr. Dickinson: Well, there's three on each side. One on the very far left is just red and then there's a ... in the center there's a reverse indicator, which is just a clear light, and the very far right there's just a red also.

Jim: Okay. Now, if an individual were describing a vehicle that they saw parked alongside a road and they described the taillights as three lights on each side, flat on the top and round on the bottom, would there be any way possible that they would be describing a 1971 Chevrolet?

Mr. Dickinson: No, because they're square. I mean, I wouldn't imagine that you could because, for one, they aren't in the bumper and, for two, they're a square light.

Jim: Okay. Thank you.

Mr. Dickinson: Yup.

Jim: Your Honor, I intend to use the photographs that the witness has testified about only as demonstrative exhibits. May I publish them to the jury?

The Court: Any objection?

Ann: No objection.

The Court: You may publish.

Jim: Your Honor, I have no further questions.

The Court: Thank you. Cross-examination?

Ann: Just a moment.

Ann: Mr. Dickinson, you don't have any information or any knowledge about the death of a young man named Jeffrey Hammill in 1979, do you?

Mr. Dickinson: No.

Ann: Nothing further.

Jim: Nothing further, Your Honor.

The Court: Very well. You are excused.

CHAPTER 22

Day 7

The Court: Thank you. Is the defense ready with its next witness?

Jim: We are, Your Honor.

The Court: The defense may call its witness.

Jim: We would call Dr. Daniel Davis to the stand.

The Clerk: Would you have a seat and please state your name for the record, and spell both your first and your last name, please.

Mr. Davis: My name is Daniel Wade Davis. D-a-n-i-e-1. Middle name Wade, W-a-d-e. Last name Davis, D-a-v-i-s.

The Court: You may proceed.

Jim: Thank you, Your Honor.

Jim: Good morning, sir.

Dr. Davis: Good morning.

Jim: Dr. Davis, could you please tell us what sort of doctor you are?

Dr. Davis: I'm a forensic pathologist.

Jim: Okay. Where do you live?

Dr. Davis: Now I live in Phoenix, Arizona.

Jim: How long have you lived in Phoenix?

Dr. Davis: Five months.

Jim: Where did you move from?

Dr. Davis: Here; Minneapolis.

Jim: Could you tell us who you work for?

Dr. Davis: I work for Maricopa County, M-a-r-i-c-o-p-a, as the deputy chief medical examiner for the office of the medical examiner there.

Jim: Maricopa County, is that Phoenix?

Dr. Davis: It is.

Jim: And prior to that time, did you work somewhere else as a forensic pathologist?

Dr. Davis: Yes, I was an assistant medical examiner with the Hennepin County Medical Examiner's Office for fifteen years.

Jim: Have you worked in any other field of pathology?

Dr. Davis: Yes. Well, after I did my four years of specialty training to become a pathologist, I performed that in El Paso, Texas at the William Beaumont Army Regional Medical Center. I practiced as a hospital-based pathologist for approximately two years at the Landstuhl Army Regional Medical Center in the town of the same name, in what's now just Germany. Back then there was still an East and a West Germany. It was during that time that the buildup for the first war called Desert Shield started. I was asked if I wanted to participate as a forensic guy, as an associate regional medical examiner, with another pathologist that already had subspecialty trained in forensic pathology, in handling the suspicious deaths that occurred in Germany and all of the fallen soldiers that died during the Desert Shield Operation. And we did those death investigations and autopsies at Landstuhl for that last year I was there.

Jim: Can you tell the jury where did you receive your M.D. degree, your medical degree?

Dr. Davis: From the University of Minnesota, in 1984.

Jim establishes the Doctors credentials to include Board Certified Forensic Pathologist.

Jim: What does a forensic pathologist do?

Dr. Davis: Well, the forensic pathologist, broadly speaking, does two things. And that is to determine cause and manner of death. Cause of death is what kills people. Could be blunt force injuries, gunshot wounds, arteriosclerotic heart disease. They're a legion, they go on forever. But manner of death is generally confined to just a few categories, and it varies a little bit state by state, but generally it's the decision to call the case a natural, accident, homicide, suicide and occasionally undetermined.

Jim: Okay.

Dr. Davis: In order to determine those two things, the pathologist does a variety of ... makes a variety of efforts to investigate any particular case that comes under the jurisdiction of that forensic pathologist in order to determine cause and manner of death. And part of that armamentarium that he or she has at their disposal is the autopsy, but that's just one test among many. The pathologist also has the investigation available to them so that they can see, you know, what happened, who said what, who investigated what and found out what. We have the ability to go to scenes many times so we can appreciate what happened at the scene and use those details in our understanding of what happened to the person. We can do laboratory tests, toxicology cultures, on and on and on, prior to ultimately deciding those two important things, the cause and manner of death.

Jim: Okay. Fine. This is probably the question that all doctors hate to respond to, but do you have some kind of an estimate for us how many times you have conducted autopsies in the course of your career?

Dr. Davis: I get asked that all the time. And I don't have an exact number but at the point that I left Hennepin County I'm fairly confident I performed perhaps 2,000 autopsies myself. I'm fairly confident I supervised another couple thousand autopsies where we had doctors in training to become forensic pathologists. And in Phoenix I'm working at a rate of about 500 autopsies a year, so it's a pretty busy place, but quite a few autopsies.

Jim: All right. Now, in the course of that number of autopsies, have you had the opportunity to be involved in a significant number of autopsies involving situations where individuals were beaten to death?

Dr. Davis: Yes, many times.

Jim: Okay. And have you also had opportunities in a significant number of instances to be involved in autopsies where people were the victims of some type of motor vehicle, pedestrian collision?

Dr. Davis: Yes, many times.

Jim then establishes that the doctor has many times reviewed the work of other pathologists and has rendered opinions; most of these at the request of attorneys, either prosecutors or defense attorneys.

Dr. Davis: Most of the time where I'm reviewing other people's results is when I am examining cases privately. When I'm at work, either in Minneapolis with the Hennepin County Medical Examiner's Office in the past or in Phoenix with the Maricopa Medical Examiner's Office, my attention is focused on the cases where they're going to determine cause and manner of death for legal reasons. But I also have a private consulting practice that I've had going for about ten years, where typically attorneys will send me cases for a second look, if you will. So I probably examined fifty of those cases a year and have been doing that for about ten years; so whatever that calculates out to, 500, maybe, cases.

Jim determines that the doctor has a particular interest in understanding brain injury as he does research into child abuse cases. Jim establishes that it was he that contacted Dr. Davis to review the Jeff Hammill case. Dr. Davis points out the importance of having all of the investigative material when reviewing the work of other pathologists. Autopsy reports alone won't shed as much light on the case as reviewing all of the interviews and other evidence gathered during the investigation will. Dr. Davis states that although he might have conducted it that way, he wasn't certain that Dr. Bozanich didn't demonstrate some experience and competence in his autopsy of Jeff Hammill. He reviewed the reflecting forward of the scalp and the cleaning of the field prior to photographs as some things he would have done better, but went on to say "All in all it's not the worst report I've ever read."

Jim questions Dr. Davis regarding the various photos in the autopsy report and from the scene on the side of the road, getting much the same information that was learned from the prosecution's questioning of Dr. Amatuzio: basilar skull fracture; no blood splatter or transfer or blood stain anywhere around the body, in the dirt or on the roadway; tear of the right ear, clean scrape on the head and a small trail of blood from the nose and mouth adding to the large pool under the head.

> Jim: With respect to the pictures that you looked at earlier from the scene where the individual was found, and the amount of blood, do you have any kind of an estimate based on your experience as to how long it would take for that volume of blood to be pushed out of the body?
>
> Dr. Davis: A matter of seconds; possibly ten or fifteen seconds.
>
> Jim: In that kind of a situation, are you likely to see evidence of Battle's sign?
>
> Dr. Davis: I don't think I could be definitive on that. I don't know why it couldn't pour into that area and look blue later on. What it really requires is a communication between the fracture line and this bony stuff here, but it may just be a bruise of the skin overlying. I can't tell from the photograph. For me it is inconclusive.
>
> Jim: Did you see anything in that photograph that provided any information to you in terms of your analysis of either the manner of death or the cause?
>
> Dr. Davis: Well, clearly we're looking at the left side of this individual at the time of autopsy and there is a large tear or laceration in the scalp skin approximately where I'm depicting, that shows a margin running along here that clearly is

the result of something that's either semi-sharp or semi-blunt that has impacted the skin, and then forced the skin back this way until it's ripped, and then made a flap such that the flap is like this on the skin. So the direction of force is going front to back from some edged object or surface that has impacted with this poor man's scalp on this side.

Jim: Okay. On the front side of this laceration, do you see anything that gives you any kind of an indication of scraping or anything of that nature?

Dr. Davis: Yes, there's the part that helps me to understand the nature of the instrument or surface, is that there's a very discreet straight line here and that is followed by an area of scraping that tells me this is the edge of some object or surface.

Jim: Okay. When you're talking about blunt force, edged device, things of that nature, could that wound be caused by a baseball bat?

Dr. Davis: I would not expect this type of wound to be the result of a baseball bat.

Jim: Is there any indication from looking at that photograph of that wound as to the direction of force that was applied to the side of the head?

Dr. Davis: Yes, the direction of force is going this way, scraping tangentially against the head in this direction.

Jim: Okay. Is there any upward or downward angle, or is it just straight back?

Dr. Davis: Very slightly upward, I think, and it just really depends; but relative to the body it's very slightly upwards on the head.

Jim: So if an individual … if this individual were approximately five feet seven inches tall and he was attacked by an assailant that was five feet ten inches tall, would you say that the direction of that injury would be consistent with some type of a strike from a weapon?

Dr. Davis: I don't think we have enough information to be able to answer that. I mean, are we striking down? Are we striking this way? Are we striking with something in the right hand, the left hand? There just isn't enough information. Anybody can create an injury on somebody else if they're facing each other, no matter what their heights are, the weights, anything like that.

Jim: But the fact of the matter is you don't know?

Dr. Davis: I don't know.

Jim: And you can't know?

Dr. Davis: Not with the information we have in this case, it's not possible.

As Jim and Dr. Davis go through the various photographs of the autopsy, Dr. Davis relates the various conditions, bruises, and scenes visible in the photos, again indicating that if the fields had been rinsed, more information might have been available to those reviewing them. He reviews the fracture line that travels through the central part of the skull, through the "Turkish Saddle", and the subsequent tearing of the carotid arteries.

Jim: Now, if a man my size—you obviously can see how tall I am or whatnot—if I were to get a really, really good grip on a baseball bat and swing it with all my might against the side of somebody's head, are the injuries that may result from that going to be consistent with what you see in the photographs?

Dr. Davis: It's possible, it's possible.

Jim: Are you going to see the type of laceration where you've got the scraping on the side of the head in that kind of a situation?

Dr. Davis: No, I don't favor that particular skin injury on the left side of the head as consistent with a baseball bat type injury. That ... to me, that's the edge of an object, not something round. I would expect a baseball bat to create a huge bruise or possibly a star shaped—sometimes refer to those as stellate shaped—crush of the skin because it's a round surface impacting the skin and just squishing it out of the way rather than a clean, tangential type of a edge injury that we see here. But the fracture pattern is … it's potentially consistent with being impacted with a very heavy object, although I'd have to say that that's not been my experience with impacting instruments to most people's heads to see this kind of fracture pattern. I mean, it's consistent with it but it's just not usual.

Jim: Okay. Is it possible to create these types of wounds if an individual is standing alongside the road and is struck by something that's protruding from a passing vehicle or maybe a piece of towed farm equipment?

Dr. Davis: Yes, that could fit.

Jim: Is it common to see someone suffer such an extensive basilar skull fracture as a result of an impact with something like a tire iron or a baseball bat?

Dr. Davis: In my experience, no. In my experience, this type of a fracture is typically seen in people who have left their motorcycle and, you know, crashed into something; bodily plowed into a wall or they've been in a car where they've left the car, the car is rolling and they fall out the windows and the car rolls over them and crushes their head. Or in certain type of industrial accidents where they fall a significant distance onto their head. But I'd have to say this would be very unusual to see this kind of fracture where somebody is clonked on the head with an object. You would expect to see a fracture … an impact and a fracture immediately underneath the point of impact but not a fracture that runs through the base of the skull. That would be distinctly unusual in my experience.

Jim: All right. In the course of asking you for an opinion, I'm going to tell that you Jeffrey Hammill was discovered approximately 3:50 a.m., laying in the position that's depicted in those photographs on a dark roadway dressed entirely in black. And the testimony from witnesses indicates that there was no sign of any scuffle or struggle, that his clothing was clean, that there was no blood splatter, that there was no dust on his shoes or any type of debris around the body. And I'm going to ask you based upon what you have done in terms of your investigation and that information, do you have an opinion as to a reasonable degree of medical certainty as to whether Jeffrey Hammill may have been the victim of some type of homicidal act by another person or other persons? Dr. Davis: I don't have an opinion to a reasonable degree of medical certainty. I don't think there's enough information here to distinguish whether or not he died as a result of some type of a vehicle accident with him or an assault or even potentially even a combination; I mean, there just isn't enough information. If he were found out in the field 200 yards and had lacerations to his lips from being punched in the mouth and injuries to his knuckles and injuries like this to his head, I'd have to seriously consider that he was beaten to death. I mean, that would be the conclusion that I would draw. Considering he's still on the roadway and he has a fracture pattern to his head and injuries that I have seen multiple times in motor vehicle type collisions with people, I would be very reluctant to say this is obviously a homicide based on just the scene photos and his autopsy. I don't think there is enough information.

Jim: All right. Well, let's do it the other way. Based on the information that you've received and based on the information I provided to you, do you have an opinion based upon a reasonable degree of medical certainty that he was the victim of some type of tragic accident?

Dr. Davis: I don't have enough information. There just isn't enough to sort that out.

Jim: So basically what you're telling us is it's not something that we're capable of knowing based upon the available information?

Dr. Davis: In my opinion, this is not a case that I would myself sign out as a homicide or an accident based on the materials we have here. There just is not enough information.

Jim: No further questions.

The Court: Cross-examination?

Ann cross examines Dr. Davis, determining that he is to receive approximately $5,000 for his review and testimony in this case from the defense of Ron Michaels. She also re-establishes the fact that he conducts these reviews for clients all over the United States.

Ann: What kinds of attorneys are usually your clients?

Dr. Davis: I would say that seventy-five to eighty percent of my client attorneys are involved in criminal trials. Half of them are probably prosecutors, half defense attorneys and the other twenty-five percent are civil attorneys; they're typically injury type attorneys.

Ann: You've been both a deputy and the assistant medical examiner in Hennepin County, right?

Dr. Davis: Yes.

Ann: You haven't ever been the medical examiner for Hennepin County, though, have you?

Dr. Davis: No.

Ann: Have you been the coroner or the medical examiner for any Minnesota county?

Dr. Davis: No.

Ann: Okay. It's my understanding from looking at your resume, too, that your area of special expertise is child abuse and computer graphics; is that correct?

Dr. Davis: The areas that I claim an interest in, correct.

Ann: Okay. And it's my understanding that you are certified in anatomic pathology; is that right?

Dr. Davis: And forensic pathology.

Ann: But you're not certified in clinical pathology?

Dr. Davis: I'm not.

Ann: Now, in your report you indicate, and I'm going to quote here, that you reserve the right to modify any or all of the above opinions should new evidence become available to you that offers different or contradicting information; do you still feel that way?

Dr. Davis: Yes.

Ann: And you were not here during the presentation of any of the evidence in this court trial and in this jury trial, were you?

Dr. Davis: No.

Ann: And so you didn't hear the testimony of any of the witnesses?

Dr. Davis: Correct.

Ann: And it's possible had you been here and heard the testimony of the witnesses that that could be something that would have caused you to change your opinion?

Dr. Davis: That's possible.

Ann: Thank you. Nothing further.

The Court: Thank you. You are excused.

CHAPTER 23

The Court: Is the State ready for closing argument?

Ann: Yes.

The Court: The State may proceed.

Ann addresses the jury. She thanks them for their time and attention and for their service. She expresses the appreciation of prosecution and the defense and all of those involved in doing the judicial work of the county and state. She emphasizes the importance of the participation of the jurors in the success of our democratic government and the criminal justice system. She reminds them that as jurors, they are the absolute sole judges of the facts in this case. Secondly, that Judge Larkin is the sole authority and judge on the law. Any statements by the defense or prosecution that conflicts with the evidence given by the witnesses, or the rule of law given by Judge Larkin, are to be ignored. She tells them that these upcoming closing statements are the opportunity for the prosecution and the defense to give argument as to what each thinks the evidence shows.

Ann summarizes her concerns at this point in the proceedings. She expresses her concern that she will forget to mention important points that need mentioning. She apologizes for her handful of notes written last night to help her remember her talking points. She reminds them of their initial instructions regarding the presumption of innocence and that the State must prove them guilty beyond a reasonable doubt. In the United States, as opposed to some other nations, a person is presumed to be innocent. She has heard it described as a "cloak" or "coat" of innocence that wraps a person; sometimes as a "shield" of innocence that stands between the defendant and the State and protects the defendant from police and prosecutors. But she also reminds them that this shield or cloak is not impervious. When reason and common sense come up against the presumption of innocence and if the evidence is sufficient, this presumption will crumble and fall away revealing the truth behind it. Mr. Michaels has been protected by this presumption from the time of his arrest until this moment in the trial. They, the jury, are the only ones who can remove this presumption that continues to protect him. The tools the jury has to remove this presumption of innocence are the facts as testified to by the witnesses.

"I submit," she says, "that you have more than enough facts to remove the presumption and see clearly what happened twenty-seven years ago on a dark night on the side of the road near Montrose, Minnesota. The judge has instructed you on proof beyond a reasonable doubt. She has told you that it is not beyond all doubt because, of course, that's impossible. She has told you that it's not to a mathematical certainty. There are absolutely no numbers or percentages attached to it. It's not a theoretical concept that we ask you to figure out. It's not an abstract principle. It's not something only judges and lawyers can understand. It's not something that should frighten you or paralyze you so that you cannot do what is right. It is reason and common sense. Something we all use in our daily lives. The judge has said it's the kind of doubt you'd exercise in making the most important decisions in your own lives. 'Beyond a reasonable doubt'. It's a concept that has been thought up by human beings of normal intelligence, to explain the standard by which we judge the criminal behavior of members of our society. I don't think it was divinely inspired although it might have been. It's not in the Bible. As a matter of fact, it is part of England's common law that the people of this country decided to use after the Revolutionary War. It's an important concept. It should be treated with respect. It should not be taken lightly. But it's a concept that the average American can understand and apply. The State asks that you keep things in perspective and stand firm against any attempt to take what is a standard of common sense and make it into something other than a standard of common sense. Now, if at the close of this case you have a doubt that is based upon reason and common sense, it is your duty to find the defendant not guilty. However, if you have no such reasonable doubt, it's your duty to find him guilty. It may be difficult for you to judge. You may for some reason have sympathy for the defendant, but sympathy can play no part. You must follow your oath, judge the facts, apply the law, and render a decision. There's only one person in this room who has any legal authority to show sympathy for the defendant and that's Judge Larkin."

Ann goes on to review the differences between direct and circumstantial evidence, the later being inferred from other more direct evidence. "You go to bed at night; there's no snow on the ground. You get up in the morning; there is snow on the ground. You can reasonably infer that it snowed during the night. Remember, too, ladies and gentlemen, the judge has told you that the law does not prefer one form of evidence over the other. Neither one is better than the other. So from now on when you hear somebody on one of those cop or lawyer shows start saying things derogatory about circumstantial evidence, you will know that they are wrong."

Ann reviews the meaning of 'premeditation' and reminds the jury that it can be inferred from the surrounding circumstances, and no minimum length of time must pass, it can occur in seconds. Ann goes on, "The Judge has instructed you on accomplice testimony. You can't convict somebody based only on the testimony of an accomplice. There must be evidence to corroborate what the accomplice said. Now, what are some examples of evidence in this case that corroborate Dale Todd's testimony? The State submits that there are dozens and dozens of examples and I'm only going to give you a few of them.

The stipulation of the parties at the very beginning that I read into the record corroborates what Dale Todd says because it indicates who all was at the bar, who went to the party and how they got there. The testimony of Robert Nowak regarding the time and the hollering. The testimony of the Kilgos regarding the time, the location, the motor vehicle, three or four white guys, and hollering. The testimony of Brooks Martin regarding the defendant's statements in 1979 that he left Deb Segler's house with Dale Todd at 2:30 to three o'clock in the morning. The testimony of Jeff Cardinal regarding who was at the party and that the defendant, Todd and Olson certainly could have left. The testimony of Dr. Amatuzio regarding the types of weapons that could cause the injury and the testimony of possible weapons in Mr. Todd's trunk: bats, tire irons, hockey sticks and ice skates. The testimony regarding the defendant's stereo and the basement house. The testimony regarding the altercation between George Salonek and Terry Olson."

Ann goes over the details of each of the charges against Ron Michaels, including all of the elements of each. She then summarizes the testimony of each and every witness called by the prosecution in this trial. When she gets to the testimony from Dale Tood, she says, "Now, you heard from Dale Todd. Mr. Todd's participation in this trial resulted in a more TV like atmosphere than is usual. His recantation on cross-examination was certainly a surprise to the State. It's my guess that the defense will want you to disregard everything that Mr. Todd has said on the witness stand and everything else he's ever said because he obviously lied under oath right here in front of you. Well, as the Judge has said, is entirely up to you. It's up to you to decide all the issues with regard to witness credibility and you can decide to believe nothing he has ever said, or you can decide to believe portions of what he has said. Now, it's the State's position that Mr. Todd was truthful in his direct examination when questioned by me. Now why do I say this? Because it's consistent with what he said when he was interviewed in 2003. It's consistent with his interview in July of '06. And it's consistent with his plea hearing in July of '06. And it's consistent with all of the other corroborating evidence. It's the State's position that Dale Todd's recantation was the lie. But why would he do that? Why would he recant everything he had said since 2003? When I asked him why he had supposedly lied on direct examination, remember what he said? He said they had just pressured him too much. Who had pressured Dale Todd too much? Law enforcement talked to Dale Todd in 2003 and then didn't interview him again until three years later in July of '06. Do you think that that's the pressure that he was talking about? The State submits that you know why Dale Todd lied. Why? Because Dale Todd is one scared guy. What is he scared of? Is it the police officers who interviewed him in 2003? It's three years later. Why would he be afraid of them? You saw the tape. They didn't do anything to Dale Todd. They weren't intimidating to him in the least. It couldn't be the interview in July of '06 or the plea hearing that scared him so much. He had a lawyer representing him who was there all the time and he worked out a fair deal for himself. The State submits that we all know who Dale Todd is afraid of. He told us that at the end of the 2003 interview that you saw on tape. He said, 'I'm scared because I know, I know what Terry can do.' Dale Todd has been scared out of his mind since Jeff Hammill was murdered. He knows what Terry Olson and the Defendant are capable of doing and he is scared half to death. And I would submit to you that Dale Todd's fear is another example of the circumstantial and corroborating evidence pointing to this defendant's guilt."

Ann reviews the testimony of the BCA agents and the Todd interview in 2003. She remarks as to how gentle they were with Dale and didn't pressure him into making his statement. Ann goes on to review the testimony of the witnesses for the Defense. She claims the testimony of several of the defense witnesses corroborates that of Dale Todd in many cases: being at the Rockford House, then at Deb Seglers' house, the flat tire, an altercation in the yard or house, people leaving the party. Ann also compares the testimony of the two doctors and notes their close similarity, claiming that Dr. Davis' testimony validates that of Dr. Amatuzio, who has more experience in forensics.

Ann says, "Now, ladies and gentlemen, the Defendant wants you to believe that Jeff Hammill died as a result of a motor vehicle accident. The State submits that the evidence has shown beyond a doubt that it was not. It was a homicide. It was murder. And further, if you don't believe it was a hit and run and you believe it was murder, then the Defendant wants you to believe that Jeff Hammill was killed by someone other than himself and Terry Olson. Maybe you will believe that it was the people that Jeff was afraid were going to beat him up earlier at the bar. However, it doesn't appear that Jeff Hammill was afraid of being beat up by anyone that night. If he was why did he leave the bar at 1:30 a.m. and start hitchhiking home? If he was so scared why did he leave Deb Segler's on foot alone to hitchhike home in the black of night? It does not appear, ladies and gentlemen, that Jeff Hammill was afraid of being beat up on the night that he died but he certainly should have been. Ladies and gentlemen, the State submits that the Defendant wants you to believe in this giant, weird coincidence. The Defendant wants you to believe that on a summer night in 1979 on a dark, deserted, county road outside of the little town of Montrose, Minnesota, that there were three other white guys in a dark colored Chevy Impala with three taillights on each side of the vehicle who had not been with Jeff Hammill but were angry enough at him to strike him with a hard, blunt, linear object and drive away leaving him at the side of the road and somehow, somehow imprinting this grizzly scene on the mind of Dale Todd who wasn't even there.

The State hopes, ladies and gentlemen, that this is just too much for you to believe.

Ladies and gentlemen, something happened at Deb Segler's on August 11, 1979 that caused this defendant and Terry Olson to be mad at Jeff Hammill. Dale Todd, Terry Olson and this defendant left Segler's in Dale Todd's 1971 Chevy Impala to go looking for Jeff. They searched for him along the roadway and when they found him, they went into the trunk for weapons. This is premeditation. They took the weapon or weapons and struck Jeff Hammill with such force that they killed him. This is intent. Ladies and gentlemen, the State submits that the evidence in this case points only in one direction. We submit that the evidence has shown you what happened to Jeff Hammill on the night of August 11, 1979 and we ask that you find the Defendant guilty of Murder in the First Degree. Thank you."

The Court: Ladies and gentlemen of the jury, we are going to take a brief recess before we continue with final argument. We will be in recess until quarter of four.

CHAPTER 24

The Court: Would you bring in the jury, please. Thank you. Please be seated. We are ready to continue with closing arguments. The defense may present any closing argument it would like at this time.

Jim begins his closing statements. "Thank you. Good afternoon. Reasonable doubt. You've had it described to you twice now. And you know that before very long, you're going to have to go into the jury room and begin your deliberations as to whether there is reasonable doubt in this case. When I talked to you during my opening statement, I told you that this case is about a claim, that my client Ron Michaels, who the witnesses that know him best, people that have known him all his life, testified they've never seen him involved in a fight before in his life, went out on an evening back on August 11, 1979, leaving a party where there were friends that he had known for a very, very long time and drove off into the night with two men that he had just met that evening for a few brief hours to hunt down another young man that he'd never seen before in his life and did not know, for the purpose of beating him to death. That's their case. But there's no 'why?'

You heard a lot about, well, could have, probably, may be, consistent with. I submit to you that there is no evidence to suggest that my client was involved in these activities at all. Now, every law student, every attorney that goes into the practice of law at some point in time, in the middle of the night, in the back of their minds, they have those little fantasies about being involved in a First Degree Murder case and making the arguments and making the objections, standing up in front of the jury and waving their arms in the air and delivering these compelling opening statements and these telling closing arguments. And they always wonder, what's that like, you know, can I do that? The reality of it is far different than the fantasy because the reality is about fear. And so during the entire course of it, there's that gut-wrenching fear, did I get the job done that I was supposed to do? That I needed to do. Fear. Dale Todd knows all about fear. Dale Todd testified on the stand that he was afraid, that he had been afraid for years. Now, Ernie Pyle, probably the most famous of all the war correspondents during World War II, had this to say about that issue. He was writing home to the people whose sons were over there fighting, dying and he said, 'There's a difference between a fearless man and a courageous man because a fearless man goes into combat and he knows no fear, he knows no risk, he does not appreciate the danger, but a courageous man understands very well the danger. He understands the fear and he masters the fear.' I submit to you that in the final analysis when this is all said and done, that what you saw on the witness stand from Dale Todd was finally the emergence of a courageous man; because he mastered the fear. He faced it. He appreciated the danger. And he did the right thing."

Jim continues. "Now, we can argue about whether what Dale Todd said on the stand when he said to you, 'I lied. I lied. I was afraid. They told me that if I didn't tell that story I would go to prison for twenty-five years, but I can't do it anymore. I can't live with myself anymore.' We can argue about whether that was the real Dale Todd, or whether there was another Dale Todd that was somehow much more believable in the course of the five-hour video that you saw. The five-hour video where the officers were gentle, where the officers were encouraging, where the officers were quiet. The officers lied to Dale Todd but they did it in a gentle way. They did it in a quiet way. They did it in an encouraging way but they still lied to Dale Todd because they told Dale Todd, 'We have witnesses that saw your car at the scene', and they did not. They told Dale Todd, 'We have a baseball bat with Jeff Hammill's blood and hair on it', and they did not. And they put Dale Todd in a position where he had nowhere to go. And then they said, 'But we want to hear the story from you, because if we don't we're going to have to look at this'-now this is very interesting, listen to this language- 'if we don't, we're going to have to look at this as a First Degree Murder', but he was free to go at any time. I think you have to ask yourselves at this point, would you have felt free to go? Did Dale Todd feel free to go?"

Jim continues his argument. "Dale Todd testified on the stand that he was a young guy and that he had been at a party and all of a sudden here, he's got this situation. He's confronted with, 'They've got my car at the scene and they've got this baseball bat that was taken from my trunk that has the victim's hair and blood on it and now they want to hear a story from me'. And I submit to you that what Dale Todd did was tell them a story. He told them the only story that he could think of because Dale Todd was like a car. Dale Todd is the car driving down the road and the car runs out of gas and it will stop moving unless somebody puts gas in the tank. And that's what they did; over and over and over again, every time that Dale Todd didn't have the information that they wanted, they suggested it to him, but they were gentle and they were encouraging and they were quiet. And during a five-hour interview for the first hour and forty-seven minutes, Dale Todd tells them over and over again, 'Ron Michaels. Who is Ron Michaels? I don't know Ron Michaels.' Until finally they pull out a picture of Ron Michaels and they say to him, 'There, that's Ron Michaels.' And Dale Todd says, 'I recognize him.' He wasn't asked, 'Do you recognize him because you saw him after that event?' That was good enough, because in this case, as I told you before, close has always been good enough. And you know when 'close is good enough' stops? Right here, right now, because of what you do. I can talk to you about the evidence, but you already know I'm his guy. Win, lose or draw, I'm here for him because nobody else is, unless you decide that you are here for him. Unless you decide that you're going to say to them, 'This is enough. This has gone on long enough. There have been enough lies.' There has been enough cooked up testimony and suggestions of testimony, to the point where they've got police reports saying, 'Well, she said she could have done this. She possibly did that'. What do they have here that suggests that anybody can definitely say, I saw this happen? If you forget what Dale Todd said on the stand when he broke down and said, 'I can't do this anymore; I can't lie anymore'; what else did he say? Do you remember? He said, 'The first part of what I told them was true'. And it was true, because he could remember that, but they suddenly confront him with 'Your car is out there and the baseball bat'. And he doesn't know the answers to that because he wasn't there. But in this case, close is good enough. We've got law enforcement officers that are involved in this second investigation; that broke a rule. And the rule is, 'you let the evidence lead you to the suspects'. And what they did was they used the suspects to lead them to the evidence and that's not the way it's supposed to work, but that's what they did. What did Barto Kilgo tell them in 1979? 'We drove by. I saw the car. It had three taillights on each side. This was a '67 to '69 Impala. The taillights were flat on the top and round on the bottom.' Now, you've seen the pictures of the taillights and you've heard the testimony from Jordan Dickinson. And when Barto Kilgo described that car to them, they didn't know it, but there's only one model Chevrolet that has ever been manufactured since the company came into existence that had that specific taillight configuration and that was in 1968. And Dale Todd was not driving a 1968 Chevrolet. So let's fast forward to January of 2003. Now the investigator goes and sits and talks with Bartow Kilgo again. Does the investigator take that prior report and say, 'What about this? What about the fact that you were taken for a ride to look at cars down in Plymouth, Minnesota and you didn't recognize any cars while you were down there? What about that?' Did they do that? No. Why? Because in order to make Dale Todd's 1971 Chevrolet the same as the car that Barto Kilgo told them he had seen, when interviewed two days after the event, they had to get rid of those taillights. And they did and they were never brought up again."

Jim continues to review the testimony of Mr. Kilgo, reminding the jury of the contradicting testimony of Jennifer Kilgo, who states she believed the car was a late 60s Chevrolet, and that the man standing in the headlights of the car that night was facing the ditch and she couldn't see his face, much less his "blue plaid shirt with a strap T-shirt underneath". Jim tells the jury that Mr. Kilgo's description of this individual's clothing and his testimony regarding other details gets better and better over the course of time. He says, "This should suggest something to you." He compares the tactics of the investigators to those of a golfer, improving the lie of his ball when no one is watching.

Jim goes over the testimony of Chief Deputy Jim Powers, recalling how detailed his investigation of the scene was, directing the officers to scour the immediate area around the body on both sides of the road; finding nothing that would validate the testimony given by Dale Todd regarding vomit along the roadside where they would have stopped, or swampy areas on either side of the road. And then the filing of Powers' report with the Sheriff as to his thoughts on the possibility of a strike to the victim by a passing truck or trailer carrying wood or a farm implement, that Powers states he reviewed with the Sheriff. However, Brooks Martin claims no one had ever seen that report, and maybe Martin had not, but the jury didn't hear testimony from anyone who was in the department at that time in 1979 other than Jim Powers.

Jim reminds the jury of the statements of several police investigators that claim that their professional opinion is that this was a homicide. However, Dr. Dan Davis, a forensic pathologist for sixteen years, now Chief Deputy Medical Examiner for Maricopa County, Arizona, testifies that on the basis of all the case statements, reports, witness statements, pictures, everything he read and reviewed, "You can't tell. I can't tell you what happened. I can't give you an opinion that it was a homicide or a hit and run." Dr. Davis testified that after sixteen years and over 4,000 autopsies, many of them beating deaths and many involved people hit by motor vehicles, the evidence in this case was not conclusive.

Jim continues, "Now, when you're looking at these charges that have been brought against my client, the first element or the second element of every one of them is that he caused the death. And you've got a professional, Dr. Davis, and yes I paid him, because he doesn't do that kind of thing out of the goodness of his heart. Is that any kind of a surprise to anybody here? If it is, hold up your hand. He got paid for doing what he does.

When he does it in Maricopa County, he gets a check every two weeks. When he does it for other people, he gets a check when he's done. Does that mean that because he's getting paid for his expertise that somehow he's not credible? Does that mean that when you go out and do your job and you get paid for it somehow you're not credible? No. All he was here to do was to show you that it is impossible to tell whether Jeff Hammill died as a result of an assault by other parties or whether he died as a result of getting hit by something that was sticking out of the back of a truck being hauled behind a truck. We'll never know. Jeff Hammill's family would like to know. I'm sure they would very much like to know, but the plain and simple truth of this situation is based on what has been done in this investigation, they're not going to know because the law enforcement officers that worked this case the second time were more interested in getting a conviction than they were in finding out the truth. And I make no bones about that."

Jim goes on to say, "Now in 2003 when Dale Todd is interviewed and they've got him sitting there for five hours and they've already laid this impossible scenario out for him and now all of a sudden they want a story from him. And they're feeding him stuff when he runs out of gas; to make sure that they get the story right. Did he say anything about Sandy Dehn? No. Did he say anything about the issue of this note passing by this mysterious gentleman? No. Did he say anything about the fight at the Rockford House? No. Did in 2006. And it's interesting because the only people that Sandy Dehn had told about the note passing and the fight that Ron had tried to break up where she had to run back into the bar to get the bartender to come out and pull these guys off Ron, okay, the only people she told about that were law enforcement officers when they questioned her four times. *Four times.* Was there a reason why once wasn't good enough? Sure. You go back, you maybe talk to other people. You find out a couple of things, you go back. You try to nail it down. Okay, because you're looking for the truth, but not in this case. They go back four times because they're not getting the story from her that they want and when they can't get the story from her that they want; the next thing you know, poor old Dale Todd shows up in 2006, and now he's telling the story. You have to decide in your own minds based upon your own experience what do you think happened between 2003 and 2006 so that Dale Todd suddenly starts talking about this fight outside the bar and starts talking about this note passing incident. Now we're back to reasonable doubt. Dave Emon. Dave Emon didn't really have a lot to say except something really, really important. He said that he's known Ron Michaels for over forty-five years and that during that period of time he has never once seen Ron Michaels involved in a fight. He did not have a reputation for getting involved in fights. He was a peace maker. Now, I don't know many people like that. The people I grew up around weren't like that but when you have witness after witness talking about that man right there and they all say the same thing, you kind of get the impression that's the kind of guy this is. But then somehow magically Dave Emon is quoted as saying, 'He had a reputation as a tough guy. You didn't mess with Ron.' And so I had Dave Emon sit there and painfully go through and read line by line, his entire statement. And when he was done, I asked him about that again and what did he tell you? 'I never said that.' Somebody did. Why?"

Jim pauses for a few moments, catching his breath. "BCA gets, what, $150,000 one year, $160,000 the next year for what? Salaries. For who? For their cold case investigative unit. Why did they get it? For solving this case. For solving this case. What do you think? Is a case solved until there's a conviction? You have to decide that. But does that provide a certain amount of incentive to make sure that the case stays solved by getting the conviction? You bet. You heard an argument that it was amazing; amazing that after all these years Dale Todd could remember all this. When you go back into that jury room to start your deliberations, I want each one of you to ask yourself based on what you've seen and based on what you've heard, do you think it's amazing now? 'That's him. That's Ron Michaels. That's the guy you were with. Witnesses saw your car at the scene. Jeff Hammill's hair and blood was found on a baseball bat taken from your trunk.' Do you think it's amazing now? You have received instructions on the issue of corroboration of the evidence. You know from the instructions that even if you accept this tortured tale that Dale Todd told over the course of time, 'I think, I have visions in my head, I think I remember but I'm not really sure we were even ever out there, you know, but if they did it, why didn't I stop them?' Not 'They did it and I should have stopped them.' If you accept that story and you ignore what the man did on the stand where he finally stood up and said, 'I can't do it anymore, I can't lie anymore,' if you want to accept that statement, then you have to find corroboration. And corroboration has to be corroboration of my client's involvement in the death of Jeff Hammill, not corroboration that he was at the party, not corroboration that he was with George Salonek, not corroboration that he sat and had drinks at the Rockford House with Jeff Cardinal and Deb Segler earlier in the evening. You have to find corroboration of the fact that he stood out there on that road and beat that boy to death. I submit to you that what you have been told is corroboration, is not corroboration at all, because it doesn't corroborate that single thing."

Jim pauses, then goes on. "One of the things that I'm scared about in this situation is that I don't want the jury to go back and deliberate and say, 'Well, you know, we don't want to find him guilty of first degree murder but, geez, you know, this has gone on for such a long time, there's been so much trouble and everything else, we should probably find him guilty of something.' It's called a compromised verdict. We don't find the evidence of the big one that's going to send him to prison for the rest of his life but maybe we can find a little one, we'll just kind of throw that in there. This is a case where the evidence shows that my client was not there because Dale Todd said, and I remind you again, 'I didn't lie about the first part of it.' And there was no reason why he should, because he knew about the first part of it. Dr. Amatuzio testified that she had no doubt that Jeff Hammill was the victim of a homicide and that was based upon the information that she had. But Dr. Amatuzio was not here when Dale Todd said, 'I lied. It's not true. I can't do this anymore.' Would that have changed her opinion? We'll never know. But you can look at her testimony where she said, 'No, I looked at this and I looked at that and I examined this and I've got this experience,' and she does. I'm not attacking her credentials. She is a forensic pathologist. She is the Wright County Coroner. But what you have to think about is why would that individual get up on the stand and say to you, 'There is absolutely no doubt that this was a homicide,' when another doctor with at least equal credentials that has been doing it at least as long as she has comes in and doesn't do the easy thing, gets up on the stand and say, 'Oh, no, this was clearly a hit and run.' He told you, 'We can't tell. There was not enough evidence to be sure one way or the other.' So when you're thinking about how this all fits together, you need to think about that. Folks, you're the ones, you're the ones now that make the decision. You're the ones that are going to say either my client is guilty beyond a reasonable doubt of one of these crimes that he's been charged with or you're going to say, 'There is not enough evidence to convict this man on any of these charges. I have reasonable doubt. I have reasonable doubt that this boy was even murdered.' As tragic as his death was and make no mistake, it was a tragic death, can you determine beyond a reasonable doubt, that that death resulted from a murder; and then can you determine beyond a reasonable doubt that that man sitting right there, looking at you, was somebody that was responsible for that murder?"

Jim comes to the conclusion of his closing statement. "I submit to you on the evidence that you have here, on common sense, on your own judgment and your life experience, that when you think about it, you roll this around in your heart, that you're going to recognize, yes, there is reasonable doubt. And instead of going back through what all of the witnesses have said, all the little bits and pieces of contradictory evidence, I've said everything that I want to say, except one thing: can he go home now?"

CHAPTER 25

The jury has been dismissed to begin deliberations. Jim, Hawkeye and Rob exit the courtroom, followed by Jean and Ron's other family members and friends. Jim and Rob meet with Jean and the family, answering their questions as they have done throughout the trial, during recesses, and at the end of each day. Rob has been an immense help to Jim by preparing and organizing Jim's notes, reminding him of important points and making suggestions. His legal expertise and intuition has helped Jim stay ahead of the trial and anticipate the prosecution's maneuvers. Hawkeye has stood alongside Jim at the defense table keeping Ron Michaels calm and collected, explaining points of law and court procedures to him and discussing notes Ron has made, and then briefing Jim to their pertinence. Everyone knows that now it's up to the jury to decide Ron's fate. They are all confident that the jury will see Ron as a victim of the system, and will return a verdict of "not guilty".

Jim, however, is not so sure. Inside, he feels like one of those onion appetizers: sliced into many pieces, all pulled apart, barely hanging together in the center, hoping to pull everything back into a whole with a favorable verdict from the jury. He hasn't slept well for weeks. He has been consumed by the preparation. His mind is racing. Did he say anything wrong? Did he dress properly? Was his demeanor irritating to any of the jurors? Did his expert witnesses connect with the jury? Had *he* connected with them? Did the jury understand the medical testimony, indicating the death of Jeffrey Hammill could not possibly have occurred as the prosecution claimed? So many details! Did the jury weigh them all correctly? He believes Ron is innocent. If he loses this case, an innocent man will be convicted. He is not sure how he can live with this. Is this really how he wants to make a living? Was he prepared enough? Smart enough? Jim is in his own little world; reviewing every moment of the trial and looking for something he missed, if only to justify a bad verdict. Jim has put it all on the line, shot his wad, done the best job he could. He knows Ron could forgive him if he lost; that's the kind of man Ron is. But Jim knows he could never forgive himself.

Jim will need to stay close to the courthouse with his cell phone on to be sure he's available when the jury is ready to return a verdict. Jim, Rob and Hawkeye walk downstairs to the front of the courthouse and step outside to have a smoke. The jury has several charges to consider; this could take awhile. Days, maybe.

The three men look at each other, knowing the other's thoughts. Don't need to say too much. No joking around. They know what they've been up against. Small town. Big case. Not many murder trials in Wright County. Lots of pre-trial publicity. These folks trust the authorities. This is middle America, not New York or Los Angeles. Things operate like they are supposed to around here, for the most part. The justice system charges criminals, not innocent citizens. Coerced confessions? Convictions more important than the truth?

The defense team has no idea what happened to Jeffrey Hammill. No one may ever find out for sure. Jeffrey's family has been present for much of the trial. Their suffering is so apparent; reconstituted and raw as it was in August 1979 as they listened to the testimony. They hope for justice for Jeffrey and closure for themselves. Jim knows they will find neither, if justice is served here today. But Jim's concern now is more for Ron and his future. Ron and Jean have trusted him to put forth an adequate defense. He knows that Ron and Jean believe God has helped him present their case. He is not sure, but he wishes he knew that were true; the results would then be a given. All Jim is sure of is that this trial has tested him like nothing ever has. So much is at stake. How strong are the freedoms our country enjoys, yet how fragile the freedom of its individual citizens. Jim knows this injustice occurs across the country on a much too frequent basis. And many defendants claim this who do not deserve to. But not this time. Not with this man.

Jim's cell phone rings. He answers it and learns that the jury has reached a verdict. It has been only fifteen minutes since he left the courtroom! Jim relays the news to Rob and Hawkeye. They are stunned as they hurry back into the courthouse.

The judge asks the bailiff to hand the verdict forms to the court reporter, so they can be read to the court. The defense is seated at their table, as is the prosecution. The court reporter begins to read aloud the verdict forms, one at a time.

Jim and Rob are standing underneath a big maple tree across the street from the Wright County Jail, having a smoke. It has been several hours since the jury returned its verdict. They are both exhausted and emotionally spent. Hawkeye has left for home, having done all he can. Jim's eyes begin to tear as his little brother puts his arm around his shoulder. They all can be proud for having done their best.

The doors to the Wright County Jail open wide and out walks Ron and Jean Michaels. They are followed by a small group of Ron's family and friends, some carrying Ron's few possessions from his jail cell. They are all happy, hugging and crying and anxious to get home to celebrate. "You should be over there with them," Rob tells Jim.

Jim looks at the group and says, "This is their time. I don't belong there now. Let's go home, I'm spent."

That evening, in an email to friends and family, Jim Fleming writes:

From: Jim Fleming

Subject: Its over

The jury was sent into deliberation today at 4:45 p.m. Twenty-nine minutes later they advised the Baliff they had reached a verdict and came in and acquitted my client on all six counts. Ron Michaels is home with his wife and family tonight where he belongs. My brother Rob is making a ten hour drive to Missouri so he can be in court tomorrow with his own case load. If it had not been for his help, Jon Hawks standing beside me every step of the way through trial, my wife Lynne coordinating communications with witnesses, producing enlarged photos for exhibits, and providing transportation for witnesses, Dan Wickman flying to the airport to pick up our expert and my sister-in-law Jodi taking time from work to provide his transportation back to Minneapolis, and my brother Chris providing help for me to understand medical terminology and Jim Powers driving all the way from Grand Marais (MN) to testify on Ron's behalf, this would not have happened.

It's been a long year. I don't have to try to go to sleep, afraid anymore.

I'm tired and I'm going to bed. I'll see you all in a few days when I wake up again.

To my family, thank you. To Jim Powers, who is pretty close to family, Semper Fi; this tour is over.

After one year and three days of incarceration, the Bison King is home.

EPILOGUE

Ron Michaels was released on November 7, 2005, from the Wright County Jail. He spent one year and three days incarcerated there, separated from his wife, family and friends. His health had deteriorated, his spirit weakened, but throughout his ordeal, his faith remained strong. He took several opportunities to witness to his fellow inmates, teaching some of them the Lord's Prayer and teaching others how to use their faith to deal with their situations.

Ron has been home for nearly two and a half years now. He regularly suffers from nightmares and his health is little improved, although now he finds temporary relief from his fibromyalgia with regular doctor visits and treatment. He is thankful for each day with his wife and family. Health permitting, he attends family functions and church services.

Dale Todd was not as fortunate as Ron. His deal with the State was voided when he failed to tell the story the prosecution expected from him at Ron's trial. He was not released on November 7 as he expected to be. He had pled to a lesser charge and that plea bargain was no longer valid. He faced many years in jail as a result of his honesty and courage, standing up for what he believed was right. He knew that his recantation of his statement would have dire consequences. And it did. But all was not lost. He was given the option of testifying at the trial of Terry Olson, telling the story the prosecution wanted him to tell at the Michaels trial. The sheriffs' department brought Dale's parents and brother to visit him at the Wright County Jail the evening before Terry Olson's trial began. Only those present there know what was discussed.

Dale Todd was called as a witness for the prosecution, along with several inmates that had been incarcerated with Terry Olson at some time or another. Dale did not recant his statement as he had at Ron's trial. Todd was released shortly after the completion of Olson's trial. Terry Olson was subsequently convicted and sentenced to forty years in prison. He sits in the Stillwater Prison today, wondering what in the world happened.

AFTERWORD

As the author of *The Bison King,* I want it known that I am a long-time-friend of Ron Michaels. Having gone to high school with Ron, and after spending endless hours hunting and fishing with him then, and over the many years since, I believe him to be everything that his other friends and family claim him to be. I can't ever recall him cursing, I have never seen him angry and I can't ever remember a time spent with him that wasn't filled with laughter and good feelings.

I was not near Montrose in the early morning hours of August 11, 1979. I was not at the Country West that night or at the party at Deb Segler's house. But I do know many of the people who were there that evening to be good and honest folk, of good character and disposition. I have not met Dale Todd or Terry Olson and have only seen them once, when they appeared in handcuffs and shackles at the Michaels trial. I cannot vouch for their character, but what I do know is that good people don't usually make friends and hang out with bad people. We all tend to seek out those with similar beliefs and habits as our own, especially as young adults trying to figure things out and fit in. It makes us comfortable to be around them and it reinforces our preferred behavior and attitudes.

Could Dale Todd and Terry Olson have gone searching for, found and killed Jeffrey Hammill that night? As Dale Todd said over and over during his five-hour interrogation, "anything is possible". Did Wright County and the State of Minnesota provide any credible evidence that any of these three men were involved in any way with the death of Jeffrey Hammill? I don't believe so. Neither did the Michaels' jury, at least as far as Ron was concerned.

What remains are questions. Lots of questions. What did happen to Jeffrey Hammill? Was his death accidental or a murder? What motivated the BCA and Wright County to try these three men so aggressively based upon what certainly appears to be a false confession? Who would benefit from prosecuting this twenty-six year-old cold case without sufficient, credible evidence?

I can tell you who did not benefit: Ron Michaels, Dale Todd and Terry Olson. And what of Jeffrey Hammill's family and loved ones? They had to endure the resurrection of all of the details of this tragedy, while being reassured by the authorities that they had found those responsible. And what about the citizens of Wright County and of Minnesota who had to pay for this event, and who continue to be served by some who would take away a person's freedom so callously?

We can remember when Mike Nifong and the Duke University lacrosse case were in the news. Nifong manipulated an investigation to boost his chances of winning his first election for Durham County district attorney. In doing so, he committed "a clear case of intentional prosecutorial misconduct" that involved "dishonesty, fraud, deceit and misrepresentation".

I cannot say that the prosecution of these three men is another case of prosecutorial misconduct, but I believe there are similarities that are worthy of investigation.

"Perjury undermines the fundamental mission of our investigative and judicial processes: to uncover the truth," U.S. Attorney Kevin Ryan said in a statement about a witness who had lied to the grand jury. "Lying under oath to a grand jury must be vigorously prosecuted, or else this essential truth-finding mission is significantly undermined."

As long as we live within the rules governing our society, we all deserve to be free. As Americans, we believe this to be true. As Americans, we should fight against those who unjustly take away the freedom of others, especially when it is done to further personal agendas. There was nothing American about the way these three men were prosecuted. Their indictments should have never been brought.

I wrote this novel to give the reader the opportunity to understand the events that took place and make their own judgment as to who is telling the truth. It was written without bias, until the story was complete. I found it a long and sometimes difficult task, but rewarding beyond my hopes. I know the Holy Spirit touched some of those in this story and I believe he had a hand in guiding me as I worked on this novel. I hope the message you get from this work, causes you to reflect on *your* freedom: what it means to you, and how easily it can be taken from you. We must not allow those with so little regard for freedom to abuse the authority we give them.

Now, there is the matter of Terry Olson...

LIVE

listen|imagine|view|experience

AUDIO BOOK DOWNLOAD INCLUDED WITH THIS BOOK!

In your hands you hold a complete digital entertainment package. Besides purchasing the paper version of this book, this book includes a free download of the audio version of this book. Simply use the code listed below when visiting our website. Once downloaded to your computer, you can listen to the book through your computer's speakers, burn it to an audio CD or save the file to your portable music device (such as Apple's popular iPod) and listen on the go!

How to get your free audio book digital download:

1. Visit www.tatepublishing.com and click on the e|LIVE logo on the home page.
2. Enter the following coupon code:
   c7e3-5550-ab68-e95c-4a1d-3f62-b96a-01d5
3. Download the audio book from your e|LIVE digital locker and begin enjoying your new digital entertainment package today!